The Judgment Of Christ

James Joseph Cook

Dear Bria,
This book is about life, love, and everything we share as common concern. I hope you find something worthwhile in the attempt, if not the execution.
Love & peace,
Jim

PublishAmerica

Baltimore

© 2003 by James Joseph Cook.
All rights reserved. No part of this book may be reproduced, stored in a retrieval system, or transmitted in any form or by any means without the prior written permission of the publishers, except by a reviewer who may quote brief passages in a review to be printed in a newspaper, magazine, or journal.

First printing

ISBN: 1-4137-0663-0
PUBLISHED BY PUBLISHAMERICA, LLLP
www.publishamerica.com
Baltimore

Printed in the United States of America

To My Beloved Yuko,
    who reminds me every day of why I love life.

Acknowledgments

The cover art is by my daughter, Kelila Rose.
The cover photo is by my wife, Yuko Takatori.
The cover layout is by my son, Elisha Fitch-Cook.

My deepest gratitude to you all.

PART I: HEAVEN

Chapter 1

His heart burst open and light streamed forth in pain and ecstasy. Out of his light he made them, and onto their darkness they yoked him. He took that yoke upon himself and dragged them, kicking and screaming, into life. So the world was born. So it all began.

* * *

"They have nothing!"
They have everything.
"They have nothing."
Silence.
"They're weak, naked, pathetic creatures, and you'd send them out alone."
What would you have me do?
"Go with them."
Silence.
"If you won't go, then send me with them."
What would you do for them?
"Help them. Guide them."
Rule them?
"Yes, if need be. And why not? How else will they survive?"
They don't need ruling.
"What do they need?"
Love.
"Ha! What is love if not giving them what they need?"
Silence.
"I'm going no matter what you say or don't say!"

Silence.

"I'd prefer to have your blessing."

Silence.

"I'm going." Lucifer floated in meditation with his will fixed upon his goal. All was peace, and then he felt himself torn apart. Half of him floated with the lightness of spirit, and half sank with the weight of his will. If he gave up, he realized, he would rise back up, whole and unburdened, to the airy empyrean. But it was not in him to give up. He fought to keep will and spirit together, and the pain of the struggle drove his mind into a dream world filled with images of battle. He seemed to be fighting all the hosts of heaven, all the beings of "light" who feared their own shadows, who refused the risk. A few of his brothers fought by his side. Their swords flashed with the lightning of freedom and crashed like thunder against the shields of tyranny, but the enemy were too many. Besides, they had *him* on their side. They hacked Lucifer and his fellows apart, and then he sank into a dreamless sleep. When he awoke, it was to the sound of his own heartbeat. He had become flesh.

Through countless eons he carried on the struggle to bring light into darkness and order out of chaos, and slowly gained an army of followers who bowed to him as their lord. "The Dark Lord," they called him, doubtless because his brilliance bewildered their feeble minds. No matter. Now that the time for action had come, they would be unwitting tools of their own salvation. Both sides were of a match, the tension between the opposites had reached the breaking point, and the universe must go one way or the other. The final battle would soon be joined, and at stake was being itself.

* * *

A pang, as of fierce heartburn, a spasmodic sigh that drowned out the ticking of the grandfather clock still drumming cadence to the strategic retreat from public affairs that had been the last years of his life, one final strained glimpse of sunlight mocking the heavy horsehide furniture with which he and Fanny had been accustomed to surround themselves, and Wendell belched out the last of his breath, closed his eyes, and fell into what he believed would be endless oblivion.

The perfection of this oblivion, however, was marred by dream-like memories of his boyhood in Cambridge and his service during the war. One image in particular kept recurring, that of Little Abbot swinging his sword like a cane, marching nonchalantly into the enemy fusillade at Fredericksburg. Strange, though Wendell had told the story many times, he had never seen it in his mind's eye, not like this, as if it were really happening, because he had not been at Fredericksburg!

A vague feeling of shame—everything in this penumbral realm was vague—took hold of him. If he could he would have rolled over to shake it off, but he had no body to roll. He was all feeling. *To a man who had used action all his life to avoid feeling*, Wendell startled himself with a flash of ruthless self-honesty, *this could be hell*.

Then his eyes opened, and then Wendell knew that he still had eyes. Were they those same keen, steel-blue shields that in life had turned proudly to the world to ward off its slings and arrows? Or were they the soft, iris-hued pools that, in unguarded moments, drank in the majesty of a mountain peak or the fragile beauty of a blossoming dogwood? Both perhaps, or perhaps neither. It was hard to say. Everything was hard to say. Nothing was certain. He did not feel in his usual command. He did not feel in control of himself at all.

* * *

Rachel gave birth to twins, one boy and one girl. The girl came out of the womb a walking, talking, normal-size toddler; but the boy was tiny, so tiny he looked like a pink worm. She gave suck to both of them, but soon took the breast away from the boy because he looked as if he would burst. Shadows played upon the walls and the room loomed dark and musty, like a school or prison. Instead of crying and clinging to her, he turned away in disgust. Singing like a bird, he crawled to the stairs. At the bottom of the stairs lay the cellar, its dirt floor alive with mice and maggots. She knew that if he got among those creatures, he'd be lost to her forever. She ran after and caught up with him on the stairs. But as she poised her hand to pick him up without doing him harm, the girl appeared at her side and jostled her arm. He escaped down into the vermin and their chirping swallowed him up. She was about to scream when she awoke.

She lay in bed, listening to the birds outside her window and wondering what the Lord was saying to her through the dream. Already the sun shone upon the early summer morning like his blessing upon the day. She smelled the sausage her mother was frying and a mild, sweet nausea assailed her. She knew now that indeed she carried new life in her. She smiled to herself, but then she remembered. Today they were coming to take Rachel and her family away.

* * *

Lucifer eyed Azazael with more than his usual intensity as the latter made his way into the golden, hemispherical, and disquietingly spacious Hall of Communion. It was what passed for day in the pleroma, a soft, sourceless light obscuring the stars of the empyrean. Nevertheless, the windowless hall was dark save for its very center, where a globe of self-contained light promised revelation to those who knew how to unlock its secrets.

"My Lord," saluted Azazael with irrepressible glee, "it's come!"

A smile dawned slowly, reluctantly on Lucifer's face. "Show me," he commanded.

Azazael faced the sphere and made the sign of vivification, and the scene began to play itself out before them in multidimensional splendor.

It was clearly one of the Nazi death camps that had become so infamous since their discovery at the close of earth's second world conflict. Azazael sensed Lucifer wince inside, but the Dark Lord betrayed nothing to the outside observer, and all save his coterie of a dozen lieutenants were outside observers. Needful though force might be at times to teach a salutary lesson, Lucifer disliked blood and pain. He also resented the blame monsters like Hitler drew to his name. He was not the one responsible for a world gone mad.

The SS guards and the camp inmates were a study in contrast. The soldiers strode like giants—tall, fair-haired, clean-shaven and uniformed in immaculate black. The sallow, sunken-cheeked, bare-boned prisoners flopped about like grimy dishrags. Most notable were the shoes. The guards sported glistening, sable-leather boots that clung to their calves. Their skeletal charges limped along in the remnants of urban footwear, and here and there shuffled feet wrapped with desperate efficiency in cardboard and rags. Even though it appeared to be a bright and sunny day, mud spattered the inmates from head to toe. The guards swaggered above the muck as if they were gods.

At first it was not clear what was happening. A young woman with dark hair and jaundiced skin, who might perhaps have been beautiful before the camp's ravaging, knelt in the midst of the crowd. With a savagery all the more brutal because it was instinctive, habitual and unpremeditated, the soldiers struck randomly at the inmates with their batons, fists and rifle-butts to maintain a semblance of order. Then they noticed the girl. She was praying in the ancient language of Hebrew. Lucifer mused upon the irony that none of the guards present understood her prayer, whereas any denizen of the pleroma, where language was no barrier to communication, could have done so. And of all prayers, this one deserved to be heard. It was not like any ever uttered, not through all the ages.

"O Holy One of Israel!" she cried out in a voice that cracked like thunder, charged no doubt by torment, shame, hardship and despair. "Cursed be thee for all the works of thy hands! Cursed be thee for the murder of my mother and father, the rape and butchering of my sister, the disappearance of my little brother into the showers, the crucifixion of Rabbi Abramson, the suicides on the wire of Miriam and Elena Goldstein, the drowning in the latrines of Anna and Muriel and Sarah and Helena..."

It was a litany of outrage. Lucifer listened, entranced. The girl went on and on without once repeating herself, as if she had committed to memory every one of the millions of atrocities whose sum total made up what Yeshua had called, in bad taste as far as Lucifer was concerned, the "Holocaust." The SS guards were hypnotized as well. Five long minutes seemed to pass before their commander, a dueling-scarred, bemonocled Hauptmann, realizing he had to take the matter into his own hands, unholstered his elegant Luger and delicately, almost tenderly, put a bullet through the girl's temple. Under the circumstances it was perhaps a merciful resolution. Nevertheless, it sickened Lucifer more than the most sadistic torture.

The camp vanished into the globe's light. Azazael caught his master's eye and said with mocking, fawning zeal, "What do you think, My Lord?"

"It may be," Lucifer replied darkly.

"It's perfect, is it not, My Lord?" Azazael insisted. He knew better than to leave his master in one of his sullen moods, no matter how laudable the emotion that gave it rise. "I'm no expert in such matters, but I've no mean eye. For purity of intent and strength of purpose, I've never seen her match. I don't think this is a prayer *he* can ignore." Lucifer remained silent, brooding. "Her soul is passing from sleep, My Lord." Lucifer stared at some imaginary point on some imaginary horizon as if he had not heard. "My Lord, our chance has come! Shall I approach her?"

Lucifer roused himself. "No, she's not for the likes of you!" The Light-Bearer smiled. He always enjoyed putting Azazael in his place. Though this henchman was a useful and even necessary tool, with talents many and diverse as well as clever tricks and amusing ways, he was at bottom worthy only of contempt, and Lucifer always gave each creature its due. "I've other work for you."

"But My Lord, it was I who found her!"

Azazael's eagerness to deflower the pure of heart was all too pathetic. "There's no surer way to drive this saint into the enemy's arms than to entrust her handling to you." The slight but unmistakable edge to Lucifer's voice brooked no contradiction. Azazael knelt in submission. "Besides," the Light-Bearer smiled generously as he waved to his minion to rise, "I've other work for you, more suited to your genius and, I think, more to your liking."

* * *

Uriel flew high, higher than she had ever flown before. There was no real up or down in the heavenly realm, only that imagined by the earth souls to guard themselves from the insanity of the infinite. Angels were not prone to this insanity. Still, if she ventured too far into the empyrean, there was danger she would not find her way back for many an age. She wondered what the Lord would do without her for so long, and then she wondered if he would even notice she was gone.

She and her fellow angels had been with him through the ages, witnessing the creation and destruction of worlds, yet it seemed as if she understood him less than ever. No, that was not true. She understood him all too well, and it broke her heart.

Uriel loved the anonymity, the impersonality of the energy patterns of the empyrean. However intricate the interplay of light and darkness, fire and ice, attraction and repulsion, there were no humans, with their capricious and insolent free will, to spoil its order. However random it might appear to the thoughtless eye, the cosmic extravaganza was thoroughly predictable. The Lord was in absolute control.

Uriel enjoyed projecting the course of the divine creativity by analyzing the spectra of the stars and planets as she passed through their auras, and by noting their motion relative to the cosmic vortices out of which every heavenly body arose and into which all eventually disappeared. She sometimes found it hard to master her curiosity concerning these gentian holes in the creative tapestry. She wondered where they led and what would happen to her should she try to find out. The Lord, however, had warned of the dire consequences of such exploration, and angels, unlike humans, did not regard divine taboo as challenge to adventure.

Space was beautiful, it was true, and refreshing, but she had to admit that it was not enough. As inertia continued to speed her through the galaxies, sightseeing, she realized, did not meet her deeper need for personal communion. Unfortunately, neither did her fellowship with other angels or, for that matter, with the Lord himself! Something was lacking in all of it, and had been as far back as she cared to remember. She had tried expressing her feelings to Mikael. Though the most exalted of their kind, he was also the one with whom she sensed the deepest affinity. He had only nodded sagely and said nothing, intimating that she had given voice to a universal dilemma about which it was useless to worry because nothing could be done. She had not dared take it up with Yeshua. After all the millennia of human selfishness, infidelity, cruelty, greed and lust, she wished never to seem ungrateful for the life he had given her. Perhaps the Buddhists were right. Perhaps the heart of all being was emptiness, and the only way to peace was to accept that fulfillment was impossible, to release all desire.

The thought of the Lord, however, only filled her with pain. Mortals in the present age pictured the empyrean as empty, an occasional rock or ball of fire floating through a sea of darkness. As usual, they had everything upside down and inside out. The real void was within.

* * *

Yeshua sat on the edge of the precipice, peering down into the misty green and blue valley that was earth. Only he and his angels could make out anything but varying shades of darkness when looking over this heavenly cliff, perhaps because the earthly souls wanted to forget whence they came. Life in the spirit realm was free of earth's trials, pains and heartaches. Now that they had entered into their heavenly rest, why dwell upon the unpleasant past? "They don't know," he mused in a lowering blend of pity and sorrow, bitterness and contempt, "but they will come to know."

"Know what?" Mara asked softly, embracing him from behind. "Why are you still brooding, My Lord?"

Yeshua had tried to rid Mara of the habit of addressing him as "Lord", but to no avail. At first he thought she did so out of humility, but lately he wondered if it were not pride. By reminding all that he was king, she also made them remember she was their queen.

A heaviness settled over Yeshua's heart. A chasm had opened between Mara and him, one that, with the brightest of wills, he was unable to bridge. In response, the most he could manage was to clasp his hand over hers. The gesture felt mechanical, at best a sign of his desire to reach her rather than an act of genuine communion. He hoped she did not notice.

"Why, you're crying, My Lord!" He had tried to stifle his tears, but Mara felt the salty moisture splash upon her arm. "No one weeps in heaven!" she insisted gaily, turning him about and smiling into his sorrowful eyes. "What's there to cry about? Here we have all the joy and beauty of the earth, but none of its pain and ugliness."

Her long, slightly curled auburn tresses framed a countenance that had once been the most beautiful to him in all the universe. Like him, she was a Galilean, and so lighter haired and fairer skinned than their Judean brethren. Her eyes betrayed Greek or Persian ancestry, for they were the color of the Sea of Galilee. He had once found them enthralling, but now he realized he had never really looked into them. From the beginning their eyes had met only in conversation. Too long a silence and she always turned hers away. Now he could not help turning his away. He revolved in her arms and resumed his watch over the earth.

"I know you cry for the earthbound souls suffering below, but one day they'll come here and all misery will be at an end."

Her words were tender and meant to comfort. He turned back and embraced her. No, she did not understand, but how could she? He was just beginning to understand himself. No, that was not it. Her lack of understanding was not what threw up this wall between them. When the awesome and unthinkable possibility he felt coming finally broke into the world, he would find it wonderful, the most wonderful possibility of all. Unless Mara changed direction soon—and real change, he knew, was the rarest miracle—she would find it terrifying.

The atmosphere of the pleroma grew darker now. Since there was no sun or clouds, everyone assumed such changes reflected Yeshua's mood. Yeshua himself knew this was but one of the determinants. The universe was so much more alive and responsive to spirit than even the most imaginative mystics realized, and at bottom all beings were spirit. Though he had tried to enlighten her on this point, Mara shared in the common fallacy and stiffened in his arms. She took the lowering light as an insult, and he was powerless to convince her otherwise. Besides, even if the sky were not a real indication, his humor, already gloomy, had darkened since her coming. She broke away without another word and glided swiftly off toward the Heavenly City, down from the craggy and joyless wilderness where Yeshua kept his lonely vigil. He knew she wanted him to come after her, but he felt powerless to move. Held in his Father's grip or the paralysis of despair? He did not know. Sometimes he felt they were the same thing. Seating himself upon the stony ground, he returned to his contemplation of the earth.

"She was angry, Lord."

Despite his grim mood, Yeshua smiled, but he did not turn around. Uriel insisted upon addressing him with a formality precisely equivalent to that of Mara. Uriel did not like Mara. "Have you studied the earth lately?" he asked.

"No, My Lord, I've been investigating the stars. At least they change, grow, undergo transformation. Everything on earth always stays the same."

"That's not true, Uriel," he demurred lightly. "Things on earth are getting worse." He smiled briefly at his own joke, but the smile only highlighted his gloom.

"The war has come to an end," Uriel whispered as she embraced him from behind, exactly as Mara had done, except with her aura rather than her arms. Yeshua felt a pang of guilt and grief as he realized that Uriel's embrace was now more comforting than Mara's. The sky continued to darken, but that did not seem to bother Uriel. He felt as if they were two children lost in a world overcome with adult madness. He wanted to pour his heart out to her, to speak of all his dreams and forebodings. He would have, if only he could have named them.

"Has it?" he finally said, turning to confront her. She too had blue eyes, like Mara's, only hers were like the sky. A cold fire now leapt from them to complement the passion in his soul. Nevertheless, she curbed her tongue and let him speak his piece. "Has it ended, or is it just beginning? What does it mean, that the world would follow a man like Hitler?"

"Not all followed him!" Uriel protested. She well knew Yeshua's penchant for hyperbole. "Many gave their lives to stop him."

"Did they?" He spat out the words, and Uriel shrank within a contracted aura. More overwhelming than the despair in his voice was its sheer intensity. Something new was happening here. Never in the spirit realm had she witnessed Yeshua overcome by such hopelessness, only when he was incarnate on earth. "Did they?" he repeated. "What was Hitler's greatest crime?"

"The Holocaust," she murmured, overcome with memories of the horrors she had witnessed as she and the other angels strived to bring solace and strength to millions of maimed and traumatized souls.

"If Hitler hadn't attacked the other nations, if he'd just quietly gone about exterminating the Jews and Gypsies and other sundry misfits he could get his hands on without resorting to war, would the rest of the world have lifted a finger to stop him?"

Uriel should have rejoiced. Yeshua was giving voice to feelings she herself knew well. Coming from his lips, however, the words were unbearable. "Who can say?" she protested, but without conviction.

Again he smiled, though this time out of compassion for her. "Yes, my angelic friend, who can say?" Unaccountably, his heaviness departed. He hoped he had not unloaded it onto this, not always his most obedient, but certainly most zealous servant. "She was angry, wasn't she?" he smiled. "As you well know, that's perfectly understandable when dealing with me."

Slowly Uriel returned his smile. "Why did you summon me, Lord?"

"The time has almost come," he answered, drawing himself a little apart as if to emphasize the importance of what he was telling her. "The time of testing is upon us, and no one, myself included, will escape the fire."

Uriel was startled, not so much by what he said as by the forced conviction in his voice, as if he were referring to something so unthinkable that he had to persuade himself of its truth. "What form will it take?" she asked softly.

"That's in my Father's hands," he whispered in turn, more to himself than to her. "I only know that it's coming." Once again the sorrow fell upon him. They both stood sentinel, gazing upon the earth, while the lowering twilight slowly, caressingly deepened into night.

* * *

When Wendell did open his eyes, at first he saw only a face. It was round but not fleshy, and the long white beard that hung down from it seemed less an outgrowth than an accidental appendage. Likewise, the snowy hair and eyebrows seemed to have obtained their unflattering hue not from any natural process of aging, but by a trick of light and shadow, as in a photograph. In other words, the visage before him, while having all the features belonging to the winter of human discontent, did not look elderly at all. Rather, Wendell thought, it seemed a living icon of eternal youth. The eyes were a soft and twinkling hazel, the lips warm and sensual, and the chin, which in older men tended either to jut out in caricatured defiance or retreat into defeated insignificance, was strong without being overbearing. Wendell knew this face. The nose! The nose was the giveaway! Only one individual in all the cosmos could have that weather vane nose, so denominated not because of its size or shape, neither of which was unusual, but because it changed complexion with every shift in its owner's emotional climate. Wendell closed his eyes again to assure himself that he was not still dreaming.

"Yes, it's me," said a manly but gentle voice that was not one whit less familiar for Wendell's not having heard it for many a decade. Again he opened his eyes, and this time sat up in astonishment, only then aware that he had been reclining.

"Will James!" He would have shouted had he not grown so unused to speech during his internal sojourn. As it was, the exclamation came in a hoarse, croaking whisper. "But you're dead! I'm dead!" These last words were almost clarion. Wendell was regaining the ability to speak with marvelous rapidity.

James smiled. "You never did believe in the spirit realm."

Wendell looked around and saw a room not much different from the one he had recently, or perhaps not so recently, left: feather bed, mahogany night table, horsehide furniture, grandfather clock, New England landscapes, casement windows fringed with ornate French curtains—not a detail seemed out of place. He smiled. "This spirit realm of yours could be mistaken by lesser mortals for Washington, D.C."

James' smile turned into a frown, as if he were the only one permitted levity under the circumstances. "That's for continuity," he offered as what Wendell supposed was explanation. Then he brightened. "Would you like some tea?" He rang a bell and a young man appeared, looking for all the world like one of the law students on whom Wendell had relied as personal aides, meaning all-purpose servants, after Fanny had passed. Indeed, the lad was so generic in aspect that Wendell wondered if he were not some supernatural composite. "If this is the afterlife," he said after taking a few tentative sips, "where's Fanny?"

James' expression remained composed and helpful, but something about him darkened. "I don't know."

Wendell snorted. "Isn't that what you said when none of your mediums or séances ever panned out?"

"Not everyone is here," he replied seriously, ignoring Wendell's sarcasm. "Nobody knows why."

Wendell hesitated before stating the obvious. "Wouldn't they be in the other place?"

"You mean hell?" queried James.

Wendell laughed. "Of course not, you fool! And you always accused me of having too high an opinion of myself. If this is the afterlife, do you think the likes of you and me would be in paradise while Fanny languished in the inferno?"

"It doesn't seem to be like that," said James, resuming his serious monotone. "The Lord is here, but so is Lucifer. They call this place the pleroma. It's an ancient Gnostic term referring to the realm of the pure spirit beings."

Wendell suddenly had an inspiration. He leaned over the side of the bed so he could examine the shelf on the lower tier of the night table. Sure enough, it was there! He seized the stiff cardboard red-and-white box as if it were a trophy of war, fished out a cigar, cut the end with the familiar instrument adjacent to the box, fired up with the newfangled lighter presented to him by his colleagues at his retirement dinner in lieu of the traditional pocket watch, and took a deep drag. He was pleased to find these heavenly stogies tasted as good as the finest Havanas. "No doubt about it," he sighed contentedly while attempting to remaster the art of the smoke ring. "Pure spirit!"

James slowly smiled, evidently pleased at last to discover his erstwhile friend had not lost his mischievous sense of humor. "As I said, it's for continuity. You must ease into the spirit-world gently, lest you leave part of your soul behind."

Wendell detected a faint lack of conviction. "But?" he asked.

James squirmed evasively, but Wendell knew him too well for him to be able to hide his misgivings. "At least, that's how I think it works," he finally replied. "But recently there's been a marked increase in what I can only call the 'physicality' of this place. Everything seems to be getting heavier and more sharply defined. Plus the old rules no longer seem to hold, at least not consistently."

"Such as?" Wendell was all genuine interest.

"Why did you take so long to get here?" James' question was directed as much to himself as to Wendell. "Every soul undergoes a period of transition, a 'dream time,' one might say, but yours lasted over a decade. Since your passing, madmen brought the earth into a second 'war to end all wars' in which over fifty million perished!"

"Hitler?" was all Wendell could manage to murmur.

James solemnly nodded.

Wendell could not easily digest this information so, as was his habit with the unthinkable, he filed it away for future consideration. "Perhaps," he said, sticking to the problem immediately before them, "it took me that long because I didn't believe. In fact, I'm not sure I believe now!"

"Perhaps," James echoed dubiously, "but I've known more obstinate skeptics than you. Until now, as far as I know, the longest dream time has been a few earth months. No, it's as if your arrival were timed for a purpose."

"There you go!" laughed Wendell uneasily. "I'm not here more than ten minutes, and already we're back into our old debate of efficient versus final causality!"

James regarded Wendell intently. "Why do you think I'm here?"

Wendell decided to get up and try out his legs. They seemed serviceable. "That's a stupid question, Professor James," he blustered. "If this is the afterlife, you're here because you're dead."

"No, why do you think I'm *here*?" James persisted, sitting motionless but following Wendell's pacing with his eyes. "Here, with you?"

Wendell thought of several repartees, but none that would dispel the air of ominous mystery James' question evoked.

"I was sent here," James declared.

"By whom?" Wendell asked, stupidly since he felt he already knew the answer, even if he could not think or say it.

"By *him*."

"Why?" asked Wendell, a strange feeling of dread, almost panic, rising up from the pit of his stomach.

"Ultimately, I don't know," James replied anticlimactically. "For the moment, to be your guide."

Wendell's anxiety abated, but left him uneasy. "Awfully considerate of him, old chap, though I would have much preferred an escort of the gentler sex."

"It's not unusual that you'd be assigned a guide," James went on with that way he had of ignoring everything that did not fit his own agenda. "Nor is it noteworthy that I should be the guide, since we knew each other, and even liked each other, at one time." James so skillfully reeled in Wendell's attention with his conversational feints and ploys that the latter found himself hanging upon the psychology professor's every word before he realized what James had done. "The mystery here," James concluded with what to Wendell was perverse relish, "is why delay your arrival and then give me only three days to acquaint you with this place!"

Wendell got the point, but he'd be damned if he'd give James the satisfaction of seeing how much he shared in his concern. "You keep talking about days and years." On impulse, he flung back a curtain and peered up into the sky. "Just as I suspected!" he cried triumphantly, though he had no idea whence this suspicion came. "No sun! How do you mark the passage of time?"

"Yes, the light is revealingly diffuse," chuckled James. "Nevertheless, we do have day and night. The sky brightens and darkens at roughly what the average spirit perceives to be twelve-hour intervals. All other atmospheric changes, such as rain and thunder, appear to occur at random."

"You have rain?"

"Occasionally, yes. Some souls call it 'the tears of God.'" Evidently tempted by the aroma of Wendell's cigar, James took one for himself. "But there's an anomaly in all this of which you should be apprized. Time here doesn't run at he same rate as earth time."

"How so?" Wendell asked with something more than idle curiosity.

"Like just about anything else you could ask," James replied, "that question can receive only a tentative and highly speculative answer. Time is elastic here, at least when measured against the objective standard of the motion of the stars and planets. Sometimes a week in the pleroma is a day on earth, and sometimes vice-versa. There appears to be no fixed rule of conversion. Nonetheless, it all seems to even out periodically, so we more or less keep pace with the earth."

"Sounds dizzying," commented Wendell with some distaste.

"Doubtless it would be," said James sardonically, "if anybody ever noticed."

"What do you mean?" asked Wendell.

"That," smiled James teasingly, "is best shown rather than told."

* * *

As she recited the benediction for the dead, Rachel closed her eyes. The hunger, the cold, the filth, the humiliation, the sheer wretchedness of it all fueled her rage, and at the same time receded as she went on and on, making it seem as if this solitary commemoration of all the horrors she had witnessed were an escape route to a sanctuary beyond the pain. She heard the explosion of the gun and felt the red-hot metal rip through her skull, but it all seemed far away.

Then she opened her eyes and saw a sky as clear and luminescent as she had imagined only heaven could be, more radiant than any she had ever seen, even in the Alps. She smelled grass and wildflowers and felt a soft carpet of moss cushion her skin. She heard the vibrant melodies of what must have been dozens of species of birds. The desperate ritual had taken her beyond the nightmare! She lay, her frozen pores drinking in the warmth of the air, without even wondering, since there was no sun in the sky, whence came the light. For what seemed like hours she remained deliciously still without thinking about anything, so wonderful it was to be without pain. Then she remembered, and the fury returned.

"Let it go for the moment and rest. Your anger will keep."

The voice was rich and deep, that of a man, or more than a man. It reached down into her heart, soothing, caressing, bringing it peace. But she did not want peace. She sat up and turned in the voice's direction, and at that moment its owner seemed to take shape right out of the air.

"I don't want you to forget," he said, as if he were privy to her thoughts. "I only want you to regain your strength."

He was tall and handsome, with skin the color of bronze and smooth, long muscles taut as steel. His hair fell in jet-black ringlets over his neck and brow. He wore a simple yet richly textured tunic the color of a crimson sunset. And his eyes, his eyes were cobalt fire! Such unearthly beauty might have frightened her had his voice not felt so reassuring.

"You'll need it for what's ahead."

She barely caught his meaning, so striking were his comeliness and calm self-assurance. Without intending it, she fell into a courtesy that had been natural to her only in another lifetime, the time before the horror. "Sir, would you be so kind as to tell me where I am and how I came to be here?"

"Think, Rachel!" he replied with sudden passion. "Where were you just before you arrived in this place? What was happening to you?"

His voice was now a knife cutting a path through the jungle of her despair, and yet still a balm upon the wound it inflicted. With a shock she realized that, even though she did not know him, she both wanted and feared this man. How could a stranger make her feel so much so fast? "I'm no fool," she said, with all the pride her tormented spirit could muster. "I know where I've been."

"You've been through death," he explained softly, as if to appease her. "Now you're on the other side."

"The other side of death?" she cried in wonder. "These flowers and birds and trees and radiant light? This is the other side of death?"

His eyes narrowed, as if he were gauging how much of the truth she could handle.

"Please, sir," she begged, "hold nothing back. I'm sick to death of lies!"

He nearly smiled at the unintended irony in her last remark, but then thought better of it and managed to compose his expression into one of grave concern. "Everyone who comes here is told that death is only a transition to a better place—this place."

"But you don't believe it?" She marveled at how easily she now attuned herself to the slightest inflection in his voice, the subtlest nuance in his facial expression, even the tiniest flicker of his eyes. She wondered if this keenness were a product of the struggle for survival in the camps, where success so often had depended upon an inmate's ability to read the moods and anticipate the desires of her tormentors, or if somehow it was part of the magic of this place.

"For the moment it seems to be true," he smiled broadly. "But then, appearances can be deceptive."

She returned the smile despite herself, and supposed this meant she trusted him. Still, even at the risk of seeming simple-minded, she could not resist the chance to point up his irony. "Is your appearance deceptive?"

He answered with sudden solemnity, as if he were a rabbi and the time for service had come. "That depends on what you see when you look at me."

Despite its face value, Rachel did not feel this reply was a romantic ploy, as such remarks had always been in any man-woman situation she had ever known. There were levels upon levels here whose reality she could sense well enough, but whose depth she could not fathom. "What did you mean before," she asked, thinking it best to change the subject, "when you talked about my anger? What anger?"

Again he smiled, a smile as warm and inviting as a summer breeze. "My dear, if you, who are newly come to this realm, can sense my thoughts and feelings, don't you think that I, a native to this place, am at least as capable of knowing yours?"

Strangely, the prospect of her soul standing naked before this stranger's gaze did not frighten her as, she knew, with someone else it would. "You are to the manner born?" she giggled, not at the literary allusion, but at the discovery that she could still make one.

"As much as anyone can be," he bowed low, at once the personification and caricature of gallantry, but then he turned sharp again. "But let's stick to the point. You've been through hell and we both know you're angry, so why not admit it?"

The sense of intimate communion was suddenly, brutally, shattered, and the larger universe came crashing into this meadow that hitherto had seemed a world of its own. Had she been wrong to trust him? But no, the greater reality could not be denied. "Yes, I'm angry," she admitted. "Why shouldn't I be? And what are you, some kind of rabbi who wishes me to forgive my fellow man?" She almost laughed when she compared him in her mind's eye to the rabbis she had known. "Well, I've got news for you. I'm not angry at my fellow man. I'm angry at God!"

He did not look the least surprised. "We've something in common then. Allow me to introduce myself." He drew himself up to his full and highly impressive stature. "I am the one known as the Light-Bearer."

"The Adversary!" she gasped. Rachel felt herself atingle with excitement and fear.

"Yes, I also go by that title."

"Am I...?"

"In hell? Look around you!" The birds still chirped, the air sparkled. "What does it look like to you?"

"Why are you here?" she asked warily.

"The prayers of the dying are especially holy," he replied, not a trace of irony in his manner or voice. "I've come in answer to your prayer."

"What do you mean?"

"You're angry at God," he explained. "You Jews have always been angry at God, and for good reason. You've even put him on trial once or twice, but what did such proceedings amount to but a handful of rabbis shaking their fists at the wind?" He came closer, so close that she felt his aura penetrate her soul. "As you know better than anyone else, the Almighty has much to answer for. How would you like to put him on trial for real?"

Rachel went rigid with mistrust. "What do you mean, that I know better than anyone?"

"It's no secret to him or me that, ever since you were old enough to speak his forbidden name, you've felt yourself on especially intimate terms with him. You've every right to hate the lover who's betrayed you. Not by taking another mistress. That would be trivial. No, but by taking the people he himself chose, your people, and dumping them on the trash heap of history. Yes, he chose you, alright, chose you for annihilation!"

Rachel drew back, turned away and buried her face in her hands. Hearing all this from another, from the Adversary, was not the same as saying it herself. Was this where her litany had brought her? Was she really at war with the Lord? But then she remembered all the pain, cruelty, horror and death. Even if it all ended here, in this idyllic refuge, that still did not make it right. Let the rest of her people fawn upon God. She would demand an accounting from the Lord, even if it took the help of the devil himself. "So be it!" she cried, turning to him with eyes shining and long midnight tresses waving in a sudden breeze.

There was nothing insincere in Lucifer's welcoming smile. He had no doubt that he had just fallen in love.

Chapter 2

After leaving Yeshua, Mara wandered through the meadows and forests, not seeing or caring where the spirit took her. The sky lightened the while, adding to her pain. Why could her moods not rule the atmosphere? Why could he not enjoy life? Would it be the end of the world if he laughed once in a while, joked once in a while, sang and danced once in a while? Always brooding, always bleeding misery, always carrying the weight of the world! Always shutting her out...

Of course she loved him. There was no one else like him. It was not his stature or looks. If he truly were the Lord Almighty, he surely had chosen a most unassuming form in which to manifest to his creation! But no one else had such spiritual nobility, such emotional power.

Of course, she did not believe he was God. She was not sure she believed in any god other than the one of whom the mystics spoke, the oneness of all being. But he believed it, she was certain of that. Was he crazy? She had often wondered that. Many if not all of the angels seemed to believe in him. They spoke of a time long ago when he had overseen the creation of the world! However, when Mara probed more deeply, they admitted that then he had not been in his present form. Clearly he had caught them up in the sheer force of his conviction. She herself was not so easily deluded, though he had still won her heart. But he was so difficult! Why did he have to be so difficult?

Her foot struck something hard, and she stumbled and nearly fell. Mara felt something almost akin to the physical pain so common in earthly life, but unknown to her in heaven. In the distance, whence she had just come, she saw the jagged peaks of the Mystical Mountains thrusting up through the blue empyrean, green and purple and white at the very top. She should have reached the Heavenly City by now.

She bent down and studied the ground. At her feet were hard little stones embedded in the path. She had roved all through these foothills for ages and never come upon such trouble. What could this mean?

She sat down in the middle of the trail, rubbing her foot and feeling a slight but distinct foreboding, like that of a child hurt while playing in a forbidden place. She looked up and to the side, as if someone had called her name from that direction, and there she saw a man sitting in what appeared to be deep meditation. He was tall and angular, thin and with pointy features, including his ears. No, it wasn't a man. It was one of the fallen ones. Azazael!

She leaped to her feet to flee but then stopped herself. Why should she be afraid? She thought him evil only because Yeshua said he was. Perhaps the time had come for her to start discerning the ways of the spirit-realm for herself.

Azazael smiled as if he could read her thoughts even in his meditation, and then opened his eyes. Yes, his appearance was striking rather than handsome, but in a comic way that Mara found refreshing. No sham or pretense here. As his amazingly purplish eyes engaged hers, she felt no fear at all, but rather a budding mirth. She returned his smile.

"My Lady!" he called, rising from his feet and, with surprising grace for one with such an ungainly appearance, bowing until his head nearly touched his feet. Even though he looked like a bent twig, she flushed in delight. "What is your pleasure, my lady?"

"What do you mean?" she asked in guilty curiosity.

"What about music?" He clapped his hands, and straightaway a dozen musicians ringed him who came, it seemed, out of nowhere. The twang of strings vied with the rumble of percussion instruments, and a horn both resonant and deep made harmony between them. Azazael himself joined in with a flute, high-pitched and sweet. The wind came up, as if in response to the music, and Mara found herself swaying in time to its exotic rhythms.

"Dance, My Lady?" Azazael asked, tossing his flute aside and taking her by the hand. Mara shrank and almost pulled away. This was a bigger step than she had looked for. Yet, it was only a dance. What harm could there be in that?

She nodded, laying her hand on his shoulder while he slipped his arm tightly around her waist. It felt soft and supple rather than bony, as she would have expected. They began slowly, as if deaf to the music, but bit by bit, as they got used to each other's step, they hopped and whirled with greater abandon until Mara could not tell whether they were dancing to the music or making it with their dance. She began to laugh furiously, hysterically, as if she were making up for all the ages she had gone without such merriment. As they spun madly around and around other couples appeared, again as if out of nowhere, and joined in the fun. They were dressed in the finery of every age and nation, from the tattooed nudity of tribal Africa to the silks and powdered wigs of aristocratic Europe. Each couple danced in its own style but all, miraculously, kept time to the music. As they whirled, a glorious, high-ceilinged hall of evanescent, multi-colored crystal formed around and above them, adding the luster of resounding echo and shimmering light to the intoxicating masque. The hall grew larger as more and more couples appeared at the ball, but the faster she and her partner whirled, the more they seemed to be alone in their own seductive world. She trembled with the sense of this intimacy. As she gazed into the impish eyes of Azazael—a being hitherto all but a stranger to her, glimpsed now and then by happenstance and without note—wonder took hold. The dance, she said to herself in alarm at her lack of alarm, had without question become more than a dance.

* * *

The sound of some outlandish stringed instrument, played at what Wendell could only think of as demonic tempo, screamed from the mouth of the otherwise desolate cavern into which James had just disappeared. Across a small ravine a party, perhaps a family, of some dark, sleek, and, to Wendell's eye, exceptionally longhaired apes studied the intruder with wary curiosity. The cry of some exotic relative of the eagle echoed periodically off the face of the silvery cliff below him, but the bird came nowhere in sight.

Wendell did not like this place, but what really bothered him was that he did not know why. He should have liked it. In his youth, mountain climbing in the Swiss Alps had given him a taste for the wild side of nature, especially in its elemental forms, and the present terrain was exemplary of the rugged, masculine beauty of the skeletal structure of the earth. The lines of the mountain upon whose bare side he perched were classic in their economy and grace. They reached for the highest heaven without switchbacks or curves, as if the obsidian rock of which they were made had crystallized instantaneously from lava poured by a supernatural hand from on high.

Perhaps it was too perfect, a counterfeit that lacked the inevitable flaws of the original. Or perhaps it was all the mystical hocus-pocus and mumbo-jumbo that had been James' preamble to bringing him to this place. Something about an authentic Indian fakir, a real Hindu holy man. For James it may as well have been Christmas!

The barbarous music, if such it deserved to be called, was not conducive to allaying his misgivings. Suddenly, as if in response to his irritation, all fell silent. Thank God!

"Why here?" he mumbled to himself, as he had mumbled to the professor when James told him they were going to this place. "Why a heathen snake-charmer?"

"He's not a snake-charmer," James had replied with that unflappable equanimity which, Wendell was certain, he had developed to so high an art in order to hide from some deep inner turmoil. "He's a Hindu saint, a sanyasi, to be precise. He has renounced the world so as to pursue spiritual liberation."

"Well, he's made it," Wendell had returned derisively, "so why doesn't he join the rest of us?"

"That's the interesting part," said James, warming to his subject, his eyes going all atwinkle and his nose twitching. "He doesn't think he's made it yet. He doesn't think this is it."

"Then where in heaven's name does he think we are?"

"I'll let him speak for himself," replied James, and after that Wendell could get no more out of him.

Of course, Wendell was under no obligation to accompany his friend on this spiritualistic quest. James had evinced neither means nor desire to coerce him. On the contrary, his manner just before they left for the mountains said unequivocally that he was going no matter what, and Wendell could do as he pleased. However, if one thought through to the heart of the matter and took into account Wendell's situation, as well as the probable politics of this spirit realm, did he really have a choice? At this point James was Wendell's only link with the heavenly power structure. He could not afford to do without him until he found something more reliable.

So they had gone to the mountains together, passing briefly en route through the Heavenly City. Oh, how Wendell longed to explore its cosmopolitan magnificence, filled as it was with the art and architecture, laws and customs of every period and nation on earth! In the quick glimpse their morning passage had afforded, he had noted that each people appeared to have its own sub-city. In what was obviously the Christian quarter stood cruciform and stately Romanesque churches, soaring and deceptively fragile-looking Gothic cathedrals, golden Byzantine domes of truly heroic proportions, and a hodgepodge of other houses of worship whose architectural style was eclectic at best and non-existent at worst. Naturally, there were also the secular structures, dwellings and theaters and museums and such. There was everything from hovels to castles, palaces to modern skyscrapers. Interspersed among these human artifacts were parks and gardens, mostly but not exclusively in the English style, with flowers and ponds and meandering paths that trailed off into sculpted woods.

This European section of heaven alone was enormous. Wendell judged it to be ten times the size of London, the largest city he had ever known, but without the problem of traffic. He had asked James why there were no carriages in the Heavenly City, let alone motorcars. The professor had smiled his mysterious smile and said only that transport was no problem. The urban skyline had filled the horizon, but off in the distance, jutting up like slender needles in the nooks and crannies, could be made out what Wendell supposed were the minarets of Islamic mosques. Given the variety of religions and cultures in the world, there had to be so much more, and Wendell wanted to see it all.

At long last, James emerged from the mouth of the cave. When he waved and shouted that everything was all right, whatever that meant, there appeared to be a circle of perspiration around his armpit. Wendell thought this odd, not only because the air was as bracingly cool as that of any mountain aerie he had ever known, but also because sweat somehow seemed out of place in the afterlife. Then he remembered what James had said about the spirit world's "increasing physicality." If his friend were right about that, as on earth he had been right about the existence of the spirit realm, Wendell thought ruefully, then perhaps there was something to this Hindu swami after all.

James beckoned Wendell to follow him back into the cave, and the latter obediently did so, for the moment his resentment in abeyance. Wendell noted how his eyes, whose sight had grown so dim in the twilight of his earthly sojourn, now shifted effortlessly from the brilliance of the open air, at this altitude as bright as if lit by three suns, to the brooding shadows of the cavern. He also wondered again why James had been sweating, for the air within was even cooler than that outside on the mountain ledge. All these thoughts abruptly came to a halt, however, when his gaze suddenly locked upon the most remarkable pair of eyes he had ever encountered.

One eyeball was screwed up to the top, the other sunk deep into the bottom of its respective socket, so that neither was wholly visible. As he watched, the upper globe lowered and the lower globe rose until they came level with each other. With a start, Wendell realized that they were now looking into his own eyes. Then they smiled. The eyes themselves smiled! Only then did Wendell notice that they had color, a kind of oceanic green, and that they belonged to a face that belonged to a body that belonged to the alleged holy man. "Why aren't his eyes brown?" Wendell muttered to James, despite his fascination.

"What?" asked James, evidently taken aback by what he considered Wendell's ill manners.

"I thought he was Hindu," Wendell persisted, causing James to turn florid with embarrassment. "Why are his eyes green?"

"That is a question I've often asked myself," said the holy man with a disarming chuckle. His voice had that Indian singsong lilt, oft encountered in London, that struck Wendell as insufferably ingratiating or enchantingly lyrical, depending upon circumstance and mood. "They once were brown. I think it came from staring too much at the sun."

Wendell did not know whether to be charmed or outraged by this silly remark. Then he realized that he was a guest in this man's home, however crude that home might be. James was right. Wendell had been rude. He decided it would be best to accept the pleasantry in the spirit in which it had been offered, so he returned the smile and held out his hand. "O. Wendell Holmes, Jr.," he formally introduced himself.

Though the holy man was sitting cross-legged on a mat on the cave's floor, the movement whereby he extended his hand upward as well as outward to take Wendell's own was not a bit lacking in grace. "You are most welcome!" he answered, indicating with his free hand that Wendell should sit opposite him on the mat.

Wendell was not accustomed to sitting on any floor, much less that of a cave, but for reasons he himself could not fathom he responded to the holy man's gesture as if it were an irresistible command. He silently admonished himself to be careful here. Obviously this "saint," for all the beauty of his smile and courtliness of his manner, had certain occult powers that bore watching.

"I am Sivananda," said the holy man bowing, and Wendell bowed in return. Also for some unfathomable reason, he just now noticed how absolutely naked this ascetic chap was, utterly bare save for a skimpy loincloth. His skin positively glowed in the gloom of the cave. Nevertheless, if this had not been the afterlife, Wendell was certain, the fakir would by now have caught his death of cold.

James also sat down, to Wendell's left, and proceeded to explain the purpose of their visit, leading Wendell to wonder what in God's name he had been doing all that time in the cave before fetching Wendell to join them. Or was this little speech for Wendell's benefit? At any rate, it contained nothing that Wendell did not already know. They were there, as far as James was concerned, to hear Sivananda's opinion as to the nature of the realm in which they presently found themselves. What exactly was the pleroma? Was it coterminous with the spirit world? If so, what of all the souls who were absent from its ranks? If not, what part of the spirit realm was it? And so on. James listed his queries as if he were introducing a research proposal. Always the professor! When he finished, Sivananda closed his eyes for a long moment, and then reopened them, fixing them first on James, then on Wendell. Finally he spoke.

"Long have I sought the answers to these questions," he sighed. "I can give only tentative hypotheses."

My God, thought Wendell, *he too talks like a college professor!*

"When I first came here, many centuries ago, I thought this was the akashic plane, the realm of psychic confusion, containing all the thoughts, emotions, personalities and events in the historical memory of the human race jumbled together in one cosmic slop."

Wendell leaned forward. The conversation was rapidly growing less academic.

"But you don't think that any longer?" James asked.

"Two things changed my mind," he replied. "Or rather, two persons."

"Yeshua and Lucifer?" guessed James.

"Yes," Sivananda nodded, "precisely! I met them for the first time in my meditations, and humbly requested each to honor my poor abode with a visit. Thereafter I spoke with them many times."

James looked skeptical. "You spoke with them together?"

Sivananda laughed, and his whole body, skin and bones that it was, quavered like the feathers of a shivering bird. "No, naturally not! Do you think they lacked the power to arrange separate interviews?"

"And what did you talk about?" asked James.

"That is not important." Sivananda's tone made it clear, that subject was off-limits. "The important thing is that both men, if I may use the term in a philosophical sense, are undoubtedly real. They are not figments of anyone's imagination. They are as real as anything can be that is not the great reality of Brahman, the infinite and absolute being."

"And the rest of us?" broke in Wendell. "Are we real?"

"My dear friend," Sivananda smiled, "reality is a relative concept. You and I are as real as we permit ourselves to be."

"How does one permit oneself to be real?" Wendell demanded.

"By living according to reality," Sivananda answered with disarming gentility. "By living according to the spirit."

"You're sidestepping the issue," Wendell insisted, sounding for all the world as if he were still sitting on the United States Supreme

Court. "Are we as real as Lucifer and... and..."

"Yeshua," James helpfully supplied. "Roughly speaking, that's 'Jesus' in Hebrew. He was referring to the Lord."

Wendell went on looking straight at Sivananda as if he had not even heard James. "Are we as real as Lucifer and Jesus?" he insisted.

"No," replied Sivananda without hesitation. "We are not as real as they, but some of us are closer than others."

"Which of us?" shot back Wendell.

Sivananda continued to smile, not at all perturbed by this hostile cross-examination. "That, my friend, is an ego-game I do not wish to play."

Wendell felt himself blush, as if he were a child about to throw a tantrum, but then he got control of himself. He could not force the hermit to answer questions he did not want to. After all, what did Sivananda owe him?

James managed to give Wendell a face-saving out. "Are we real?" he repeated Wendell's question, but in a humble tone, as if he were praying to God. The holy man looked at Wendell as if he had asked the question. "You and I are as real as any you and I on earth, only we live out of a different aspect of the totality of our being."

"Which aspect?" pressed James. "The spiritual aspect?"

"The spirit is present in all aspects," replied Sivananda, continuing to look at Wendell. "It is the thinker of all thought, the feeler of all emotion, the doer of all action. If you wish, call that aspect which those of this realm embody what everyone else here calls it—the soul."

"These are all abstractions," groaned Wendell, though this time without rancor. "What, then, is the soul?"

"It is the realm of values, of ideals, of fundamental emotions and one's basic sense of reality."

"The eternal in man!" cried James.

"Not exactly," Sivananda explained, finally turning to face the professor, "but that in man which goes to meet the eternal."

A prolonged silence followed in which the holy man and James seemed to be exchanging some profound, emotionally charged and infuriatingly wordless message. Wendell cleared his throat to indicate he was about to say something of importance. James and Sivananda turned their eyes upon him and waited. At length, he found words for his question. "My dear sir," he addressed Sivananda, "I'm sure that my friend here, who is of a metaphysical turn of mind, finds what you're saying fascinating. I myself, however, have always been a practical fellow. What, in plain terms, is the upshot of this idea?"

James regarded Wendell with what appeared to be pity. "My dear Holmes," he said, mimicking Wendell's manner, "it means we are all at war!"

"War?"

"Yes," confirmed Sivananda, "this is the second Kurukshetra."

"Whatever does he mean by that, Will?" queried Wendell. "What's Kurukshetra?"

Sivananda answered for himself. "Kurukshetra was the site of a great battle in ancient India between the devotees of God and the forces of darkness."

Wendell sat pondering. "I give up, Will. It's all beyond me."

"That's why Yeshua and Lucifer are both here," explained James, "as well as the rest of us. It's the war in heaven of which the biblical Book of Revelation speaks. That war is a war of values, a struggle to determine what is truly real."

Again Wendell pondered. "But such conflict takes place every day on earth. It seems to me that Occam's razor would be useful here. The hypothesis of some second battle in some shadowy spirit realm is utterly superfluous."

"Does it?" scoffed James, grabbing Wendell by the arm. Does such warfare really happen on earth?"

"Of course it does!" cried Wendell, jerking his arm away. "What about our own Civil War?" Any mention of that conflict could always be counted on to take James down a peg or two. He had always been ashamed of failing to enlist. Evidently, however, he had matured since Wendell knew him last, for this time he steadfastly held his ground.

"Was it such a war?" James reiterated. "Did the North fight that war to free the slaves and preserve the Union, or to maintain and increase its economic supremacy over the South?"

"A little of both, I dare say," rejoined Wendell. "Do you think the Great Emancipator was out only for 'economic supremacy'"?

"Certainly not he," Sivananda interjected, "for he was one of the avatars of God."

"Avatar?" echoed Wendell.

"An incarnation of God," whispered James. "He's saying that Lincoln was an incarnation of God!"

"Yes, an avatar," Sivananda confirmed, ignoring his guests' astonishment. "But the vast majority of souls on earth do not live according to moral and spiritual values, nor do they engage in any profound attempt to comprehend the meaning and purpose of their lives. They seek convenience and immediate gratification of the senses, that is all. Because they ignore that aspect of themselves which makes fundamental decisions as to the nature and meaning of life, it develops a life of its own, connected with the earthly life only, as you Westerners say, subliminally or subconsciously. This is the life," he concluded, gesturing with his hands to take in his surroundings and, by implication, the entire spirit realm, "that the soul has created for itself."

Both Wendell and James were struck dumb. At length Wendell asked, "How do you know all this?"

Sivananda's eyes twinkled, but only a hint of a smile played around his lips. "It is obvious to anyone with the time and leisure to inquire."

"You spoke of war," Wendell went on, though he had yet to digest all that had gone before. "What war? What are its nature, scope and purpose?"

Sivananda's face, hitherto so animated, now became a mask of impassivity. "I have told you all you need to hear from me," he said in a lifeless monotone. Then he assumed the posture in which he had been sitting when Wendell had entered the cave and went back to his cross-eyed meditation.

Wendell wanted more than anything to shout at him, shake him, do anything to get him to respond to further questions. Had James tried to forcibly restrain Holmes, he certainly would have raised a row. As it was, Will's gentle touch of his arm dispelled his fury. Without another word, he arose and followed his companion out of the cave. As they began their trek down the mountain, they heard once again the outlandish music coming from Sivananda's retreat. Though there was much to discuss, neither man spoke, preferring for the moment silent contemplation of all they had learned from what, for Wendell, was so surprising a source of knowledge.

* * *

Rachel took Satan's proffered hand and journeyed with him to what he called "The Heavenly City." They walked, and yet that walking was a floating, covering a vast expanse in half the time it would have taken the speediest automobile on earth and without haste or jarring. Strangest of all, this gliding did not feel strange to her but natural. It was like strolling in a dream. Perhaps this was a dream! After all, what was the world of a dream but the landscape of the soul?

At first, despite their unearthly beauty, she barely noticed the forests and meadows, lakes and streams over which they moved. Unearthly? No, they displayed the essence of earthly beauty, free of all hazards of time — no soil erosion, no dying flowers, no trees felled by lightning or charred by fire. More arresting, however, was the look Satan gave her as they left the meadow of her epiphany. She knew that look well, though she had not seen it on a man's face for over three years, since she first had arrived in the camps. Then she had still been young, plump and beautiful, her hair lustrous and streaming, her breasts swelling with the milk of life. She had been with child, though no one in her family had known it, and the freshness of youth had been magnified by the radiance of pregnancy.

The camps had changed all that, she had thought, forever. Starvation, filth, backbreaking labor and lack of sleep, coupled with occasional rape and the daily spectacle of Nazi brutality, put an end to her pregnancy in short order. She had a miscarriage while "defecating" with no one else the wiser. It had been as simple and, she thought sardonically, as painless as that. Indeed, it had been a relief emotionally as well as physically, not only because pregnant women automatically were selected for the "showers," but also because it let stand the fiction among her fellow inmates of the "virtuous" Rachel. So her baby had become one more victim of the shit pit.

Strange, when it had meant nothing to her at the university, how much she cared for her reputation in the camps, especially since she was repeatedly the object of the forced attentions of the kapos, the Ukrainian guards, an occasional German enlisted man, and once even a furtive German officer. But rape was different. Though Rachel knew plenty of women who blamed themselves, no one could blame you for what was beyond your control. Conceiving out of wedlock was another matter. No woman, unless she was a well-fed Nazi pet, could possibly get pregnant in the camps. On the outside it had never mattered to her what she did, but it mattered in the camps, perhaps because there the appearance of self-respect was all one had left in an utterly humiliating world. As she followed Satan's lead, she marveled at how she could remember the horror now with almost clinical detachment. But then, she realized with the psychological acumen for which she had been notorious among her peers at the university, that was merely her way of dissociating. She was not really remembering at all.

The regimen of the camps also put an end to her looks. The beautiful tresses had been shaved and the full, supple figure reduced to a skeleton. She had also had no doubt that the light in her eye—about which not only men remarked, but also her parents, siblings, friends, and roommates at the university—had been forever put out. Now, however, the way Satan looked at her made her realize that not only her hair had been restored, but everything else as well, including the habitual white linen knee-length shift in which, according to her lovers, she looked by contrast so exotic. Everything but her child...

She was not sure how she felt about this turn of events. Given her experience of men, perhaps she would be better off had she remained a repulsive hag.

As they neared the city, Rachel paid more attention to the sights around her. The sky was no longer blue, but darkening into twilight gray enlivened by random splotches of shimmering and evanescent oranges, pinks, purples and reds. The spectacle far surpassed any sunset she had seen on earth. The massive city loomed against the sky in a welter of building materials and architectural styles that nevertheless, at least from a distance, appeared harmonious, even sublime. As they drew nearer, she saw that the city was really a number of cities surrounding a huge central park. "So there are ghettos even in heaven," she said, not caring what effect such a remark might have upon her companion, coming as it did after so long a silence.

"Yes," he smiled. "Yes, you could say that, for all that the divisions here are self-imposed."

Rachel was not at all surprised. Having been born and raised in Baden, a small town barely thirty kilometers outside of supposedly cosmopolitan Vienna, she knew well that urban sophistication was just another mask for tribalism.

They descended, floating like mist through the trees of the park. As they came near a clearing, Rachel was astonished to see a magnificent palace at the park's center. Its design was not like any she had glimpsed in their flight over the city, nor did its style have any earthly counterpart. It was all curves and spaces, one seamless undulation of a chartreuse, glass-like substance that so perfectly reflected its surroundings as to blend in with them almost completely, which doubtless was why she had failed to notice it until they were almost upon it. Nevertheless, it was unmistakably a dwelling, and a dwelling of such scale and grandeur that it could only be a palace, the home of a glorious emperor or king. "Is this the Lord's house, Satan?" she asked sharply. "Do you dare to bring me here?"

"Please, I prefer 'Lucifer,'" he said with equanimity. "And no, the Almighty has no need of such a place. This is my home."

As soon as they passed up the magnificent stone stairs and through the oak door, impressive but out of keeping with the style of the rest of the exterior, they touched down onto the solid floor. Had Lucifer stopped exerting some occult power, or was the building designed to be earth-like in its gravity, maybe to give its occupants a sense of order and stability?

He led her through a vast stone hall hung with richly brocaded tapestries from which light seemed to emanate. They depicted scenes of battle, but not like any battle ever fought on earth. Heavenly figures resembling Satan (or rather, "Lucifer") in their power and beauty, some dressed like him and some robed in white, but all surrounded by multicolored orbs of light, appeared locked in struggle, but without the use of weapons or even physical force. In one scene victory went to one side, in another to the other, but the tapestries did not make clear who had won in the end. "So," she whistled, "there was a war!"

"Yes," he said as he led her into a chamber off the hall, much smaller and more intimate, even though the wall facing the outside was the green glass looking out upon a rose garden. For some reason, perhaps because it was night and the room was dimly lit, Rachel did not feel exposed.

"Who won?" she asked, as he sat her down upon a couch of satin and lace. He took a gold comb from a side-table and gently passed it through her hair. She did not object.

"That depends upon your point of view," he replied. "It was a war between two factions of angels."

She arched her eyebrows. "One led by you and the other by Mikael?"

"You've heard the legends," he grimaced. Lucifer clearly had no taste for the exaggerations and half-truths of mortals.

She nodded, causing her hair to pull in his hands, but she felt little pain. "And according to the legends," she found herself teasing him, "Mikael won."

"He won heaven," Lucifer admitted, "but we won the chance to rule on earth."

She jumped up, tearing her hair out of the comb, turned swiftly and fixed her accusing eyes upon him. "So, you're just like them, after all! You're just another Nazi!"

He looked so hurt at this attack that she knew it could not be true. "I want to rule over earth, yes," he said, "but only so that men like Hitler will no longer be possible." He took her head in his hands and tenderly eased her back down, massaging her temples and scalp. She moaned softly with pleasure, but her quest for understanding was not to be denied. "What did you mean," she asked, gently but firmly, "when you said that we would put God on trial for real?"

He chuckled quietly as he continued the massage. "I didn't mean we would literally put God on trial, of course," he explained. "God is in each and every one of us. We are all God. I meant that we would arraign the one who's been playing God all these many centuries and leading us all to disaster, the one known to you by two names: Yahweh and Yeshua."

"Yahweh *and* Yeshua?" she gasped, again leaping up, this time in amazement. Again, he eased her back down.

"Yes, they're the same!" he proclaimed. "The tribal god of the Israelites who claimed to be the only God and the man who started the three-ring circus known as 'Christianity' are one and the same.

It's time to put an end to this travesty of majesty!"

She felt the bitterness in him, and the passion, calling out to her own. Now she took his head in her hands and drew him down on top of her. As if by magic, there were no longer any clothes in the way. She felt his hot, hard member enter her warm, moist opening like the sunrise in early spring, and thought with tears in her eyes how long it had been since a man had really loved her. She kissed his brow, his eyes, his cheeks, and then he placed his lips over hers and she felt his tongue reaching for her own. At that moment a searing pain pierced through her from the center of her heart. She stiffened and nearly screamed, tearing her mouth away from his as if he were smothering her.

"What is it?" he hissed with the impatience of a bottled-up volcano.

"I can't do that yet," she apologized. "I can't kiss that way just yet."

She felt his disappointment, but all he said, in the gentlest of tones, was, "We've time together. We have time."

"Lucifer," she asked like a playful kitten, revolving her hips slowly beneath him, "why did we see no people as we passed over the streets?"

"Because I arranged it that way," he replied. "I wanted us to be alone."

"I thought so," she smiled, drawing his lips to hers and kissing them lightly. "Be patient with me?" she asked.

In answer, he kissed her eyes and enfolded her once more with his surging warmth. The pain went back down to her heart's core, where for the moment she could ignore it, and once again she knew bliss.

* * *

"You know what's happening, My Lord!"

Uriel spoke with the gravity of a physician informing her patient that his disease was terminal. Her aura deepened to a rich royal blue. Yeshua again sat on the edge of the precipice, as still as a sentinel, looking down upon the enshrouded earth that glowed softly like a crystal ball swathed in black but translucent satin. Or had he not moved since she had left him half the night ago? The stars shone so brightly that they painted the sky a milky white, and yet they did not disturb the dark peace of the night. From off in the distance came the exploratory hooting of an owl, and the crickets had begun their nightly concert, chirping, it seemed, only for him. He took a long time to answer, causing her to wonder if he had heard, though she knew he had.

"Yes," he sighed. "Now that the latest war is over, more people are dying of starvation and disease than were killed by bombs and guns."

Why must he so often be so deliberately·obtuse? "My Lord," she exclaimed, "a conspiracy is afoot! As first act, Lucifer is bedding a new arrival who could make great trouble for you, and Azazael is seducing your queen!"

Yeshua regarded her with abstract interest, as if her appearance were of greater import than any news she might bring. "What do you expect me to do, Uriel?" he said wearily. "Each soul is free to make its own choices, especially now."

"Why especially now?" Uriel asked.

"Because now is the time of testing!" he proclaimed with an enthusiasm unsuited to the situation. He leaped up and capered on the very edge of the cliff. She had never seen him so excited. "It's all coming together, Uriel! Haven't you noticed? This realm is becoming more like earth, earth is becoming more like here—it's all coming together!"

Uriel flew backwards as if he had struck her. Was he mad? He went after her, taking her hands and dancing her in a circle as if they were children.

"Don't you see, my ancient friend?" he laughed. "It had to be. Sooner or later it all had to come together. I'd almost given up on the possibility, almost resigned myself to the torment of a lonely existence in an eternally schizoid universe. But it had to happen!"

As they danced, or rather, he danced and she let him drag her along, she felt her spirit brighten. Whatever possessed him now, she decided, it was not the demon of insanity. Finally he stood still and, without letting go her hands, looked straight into her eyes. "You don't believe me, do you?" he asked sadly.

"My Lord," she protested, "how can I believe or disbelieve when I don't even know what you're talking about?"

He smiled as comprehension came into his eyes. "I see," he said. "Well, then, ask me! What don't you understand?"

She felt like saying "Everything!" but then she realized that he had never been more serious. Perhaps something was happening, something new and momentous and of cosmic proportions. She felt a flutter of hope in her heart—the heart that, less than a day past, had been ready to resign itself to its own emptiness. "You said that everything is coming together, My Lord. What did you mean?"

She sensed his excitement rise at the question and wondered if an even more dizzying dance were in the offing, but now he seemed more interested in talking than dancing. "Haven't you heard me speak of the marriage of heaven and earth?" he asked.

"Yes, My Lord, many times."

"What do you think I meant by that?"

Uriel felt some impatience, but she was accustomed to Yeshua's habit of answering a question with a question, so she replied. "You spoke of it in many ways: sometimes in general terms, as a spiritual ideal each soul had to achieve for itself; sometimes specifically, as your incarnation as man or your marriage with the Lady Mara."

"Yes, and all these things are part of this sacred marriage," he said. "I'm not taking anything back. But suppose"—his eyes took fire—"all these things were to consummate in a real and literal marriage? Suppose the two realms were to be rejoined?"

Uriel thought for a moment. "Rejoined, My Lord?"

"Think back, my faithful Uriel, to the very creation of the world! Was it then as it is now?"

"Of course not!" she answered. "That was before sin."

"And what is sin?" he asked.

"Sin, My Lord? Why, disobedience to you."

"If sin is disobedience to me," he teased, "you've been guilty of it more than once." Uriel's aura flushed crimson. "No, sin is disobedience to the law of life! It's violation of the integrity of life, and the integrity of life is love."

For the first time since this crazy conversation began, Uriel was catching a glimmer of his meaning. "So," she said tentatively, "sin is disruption of life."

"Exactly!" he cried, as if praising his star pupil. "Sin is tearing asunder what God has joined together. Ultimately, there is neither spirit realm nor earth realm. There is only the realm of life! For a season, an unimaginably long season, my Father has permitted this division, this wound..."

"Why, My Lord?" she interrupted.

"I'm not sure," he admitted. "That will be clear only in the light of its healing. Perhaps it's because the wound had to be brought into the awareness of the wounded before it could be treated." He hesitated, and she knew a new insight was coming. No other mind in heaven or on earth worked quite like his. "Or, perhaps, that is the treatment! To bring the wound into the awareness of the wounded, to have them meet their own insanity face to face, is to heal it!"

Would that it were so easy," Uriel whispered to herself, but knowing he would hear.

"You think that's easy," he said. "In all creation and the uncreated, there's nothing more difficult!"

Uriel knew better than to argue with him. When it came to such issues as the human capacity for self-deception, he had lifetimes more experience and was infinitely wiser than she. Instead, she chose to return to the previous subject which, though not of such cosmic import as the marriage of heaven and earth, was of less speculative a nature and more immediate urgency. "My Lord, they do mean to make trouble for you."

The excitement drained from his face, leaving only what of late had become his accustomed expression, a look of quiet suffering. "My friend, when do Lucifer and Azazael not mean me trouble?"

"But this time they really can do it!" It was her turn to be excited. "This time they really can hurt you!"

"What, turn the denizens of heaven against me?" he scoffed ironically, knowing that Uriel knew he had nothing but contempt for politics. "There's a sizable plurality of Christians, and the rest are badly divided among themselves. How can Lucifer hurt me?"

"He can take your queen," she said, knowing her words would be knives in his heart but feeling obliged to force him to face the truth. "She's ripe for the plucking!"

"No, he can't," he countered. "Whatever happens, she's responsible for herself." Obviously, he had already considered this possibility. "I'll be hurt if she turns away, but I will survive."

"You may think yourself secure," she persisted, "and so may all who follow you, but Lucifer knows something no one else knows, not even you."

"And what's that?" he asked.

"That you are your own worst enemy!"

He did not seem at all surprised at what she said, but only gave a sad smile and turned his face once again toward the earth. Evidently he had also considered this possibility. Dread turned Uriel's aura a deep purple, almost one with the night.

* * *

Will sat in the armchair of Holmes' bedroom, too exhausted to return to his own cottage, too excited to sleep. Luckily, upon their return Holmes had asked him nothing about the afternoon adventure, wanting only to snack, bathe, and lose himself in sleep. Despite his eagle-like visage and habit of command, the newcomer was like a baby in his mindless contentment with creature comforts, and Will found himself wanting to protect him like a baby. The grandfather clock ticked away at the edge of Will's consciousness, and the candle on the night table cast eerie shadows wherever it threw its sputtering light. Nevertheless, even though the surface of his awareness was very much in the room watching over his sleeping friend, the kernel of his mind was back in Sivananda's cave.

Before fetching Holmes, Will and the sanyasi had sat in silent meditation, as they always did at the start of one of Will's visits. But this meditation was different. Instead of emptying Will's mind of tension and strain, it had filled it with troubling, perplexing, even nightmarish images. They were faces, that was all—a parade of faces, each going through all the emotions known to humanity, and some Will had never known any human to have had. He felt, in some small way, that he was feeling at least the echo of these emotions as he looked on. It was the extremity of it all that had been so trying! Nothing was done by halves. Everything was all or nothing. How could anyone sustain such intensity? Then Will realized whom he was seeing. In all those faces there was but one soul. It was Yeshua! No one else was capable of such abandon. So that was the secret even the angels were forbidden to utter. These were Yeshua's past lives! Sivananda had said Lincoln. Lincoln and who else? Will watched in wonder as the drama of Yeshua's multiple incarnations unfolded before his mind's eye: great sages, poets, artists, statesmen, prophets, martyrs, saints. There were only faces, true enough, but the faces told everything.

Now Will did not merely remember the experience in the cave; he relived it, if possible more intensely than before. When it was over—and Will had no idea whether minutes or hours had passed—he reflected fearfully upon what he had seen. If these were truly Yeshua's past lives, then his gift of himself to the world took on dimensions Will's mind could never encompass. If these were truly Yeshua's past lives, then his humanity was as broad and deep as his divinity, and far broader and deeper than that of the rest of the human race put together. If these were truly Yeshua's past lives, then he was more naked and exposed to life's maelstrom than any of us. If these were truly Yeshua's past lives, then he had been with us throughout the wretched history of our pathetic strivings to wrest the helm of creation into our hands, waiting in an anguish Will could not even begin to fathom for us to surrender to the mystery of grace he embodied. If these were truly Yeshua's past lives, then Will and his fellow men were guilty of a spiritual myopia bordering on total blindness. If these were truly Yeshua's past lives...

This suppositious litany went on until sleep mercifully relieved Will, for a time, of the burden of consciousness.

* * *

"He's acting strangely." Uriel spoke in a whisper, but still the empty council chamber, its concave obsidian walls gleaming shadowless with a preternatural light, echoed with her words. "He goes from one extreme to another. At one moment, he's in the deepest despair. A few hours later, he's dancing with joy at the very edge of the precipice!"

Mikael listened intently, his aura splendid in gold and white. Uriel had summoned him to a private meeting in the middle of the rest period, but long practice had enabled him to make the transition from repose to vigilance instantly and effortlessly. Doubtless thinking that no one would suspect a secret rendezvous in so public a place, she had asked him to join her in the massive hall where the twelve archangels held both their open and restricted forums. Or perhaps it was simply because the council chamber, like the worship places of mortals, was designed to overawe and humble rather than comfort and cheer. Its dark, smooth surfaces hosted no organic life, and no ornamentation or furniture softened its uniform majesty. It was only an empty space, a hall of dusky crystal that produced a glorious spectacle of multicolored light whenever the auras of Mikael and his fellows played within it. Even the magnificent angels of light felt out of place here, and perhaps meeting here was just another of Uriel's tricks to shake him, the chief of the angels, out of his supposed complacency.

"He says a great change is coming," Uriel continued. "Something about the marriage, the literal marriage, of heaven and earth. He also says it will be a withering time, a time of severe testing."

Mikael bowed his head in thought and then looked up at Uriel seriously, but not with the alarm she had expected her words to awaken in him. "It fits the pattern," he said judiciously. "Just before any major development, it has always been so. The tensions that generate change seem to originate in the depths of his soul. Only after he's wrestled with them and tamed their fire, it seems, are they let loose upon the rest of us."

Uriel could not believe what she was hearing. She had come seeking sympathy, even aid, for the one they loved above all. Instead Mikael was giving her metaphysics! "So, we should just leave him to his own devices?"

"Uriel, my dear," Mikael smiled tenderly, "I know it's hard, but by now you should know that none of us can really help him."

"And what about Lucifer's and Azazael's mischief?" she cried. "By now they've both succeeded in bedding their victims. Are we to leave that business to settle itself as well?"

Mikael's aura took on a hard metallic sheen, but his voice remained gentle. "We'll keep a watchful eye," he replied, "but we can't bring the issue up in council tomorrow. It's too private, too personal, and tomorrow we will have visitors."

"Can't they be put off to another day?" Uriel pleaded, her aura thin and pale as watery mist. "Isn't the Lord's business more important than entertaining two earth-souls?"

Mikael tried not to look amused. Uriel was a clever one, but her tricks became embarrassingly obvious when passion carried her away. "The visitors are the Lord's business," he reminded her whose memory was like a photographic plate. "Yeshua expressly requested their admission to our deliberations."

"Why not another day?" Uriel persisted, but Mikael was unyielding.

"He specifically said tomorrow."

"If they attend, then I will not," she declared, and instantly she was gone.

Mikael lingered in contemplation. Her message had a much more profound effect on him than he at first realized. Something was going to happen tomorrow, he was sure of it, something for which the Lord wanted the two earth-souls present and Uriel absent. Mikael spent the rest of the dark-period meditating in the council chamber, feeling out with his spirit all the possibilities inherent in the time and situation, so he would be able to do his part in taking things in the direction the Lord wished them to go.

* * *

Yeshua lay in the sylvan bower on the bed of thick green moss that he always shared with Mara at this late hour, but she was not there. He felt a dull ache in his heart and rising waves of something akin to nausea in his stomach and head, the combination of which every so often forced a tear or two to well up in his eyes. He stared up through the boughs of silvery, long-needled pine at the cold and uncomprehending stars. He was numb, and he wondered what the pain would be like when the numbness wore away.

He had not known he could feel like this. In all the eons he had walked the way of the cross, he had felt nothing like this. Misery was now the medium of his existence.

Mara had come to the pleroma toward the end of the first revolt against Rome, a fair-haired Galilean maiden whom Roman soldiers had raped and murdered in one of their mopping-up operations. She had been drawn to him, he felt, not on account of his supposed power and glory, nor because the angels who were still angels hailed him as their lord, but out of an affinity of soul. While on earth Mara had done what she could to aid the rebellion, not in the spirit of nationalism or religious fervor, both of which were foreign to her temperament, but simply because she hated Roman oppression. She had a zeal for justice, and that, more than anything else, had drawn the two of them together. In recent times, however, he had begun to wonder if being the consort of the king of heaven might not have gone to her head. Now he knew. It really meant nothing to her. "Why, Father?" he whispered through clenched teeth. "Why did it have to come to this?"

He did not know how long after that she came in. Time seemed to have stopped. Perhaps thinking he was not awake, she settled herself next to him as if to sleep. He turned and touched her gently on the cheek, but she drew back as if she had been slapped. "Why did you come back?" he asked.

There was neither hesitation nor contrition in her reply. "I owe you at least a goodbye."

Tears swam in his eyes. Or was it the pain that so distorted her image in his mind? "So, it's settled then. All decided, just like that."

"No, not 'just like that!'" she mocked, her voice fraught with pent-up bitterness. "How long did you think I could go on with a union that was no union? When I first knew you, you were different somehow. Of course you were always serious, and every so often you'd have your fits of abstraction. And you never left room for doubt that you carried the weight of the universe on your shoulders. I respected your sense of duty, to be sure. It was part of why I loved you..."

"Loved?" he interjected.

"If you don't want to hear this..."

He cut her short with a gesture that said please go on. She took a deep breath and then continued.

"But it wasn't enough. It was the moments when you managed to push all the duty and responsibility aside, to dance and laugh and sing, that I lived for. When was the last such moment? I can hardly remember. Now you're brooding always. And I've asked myself more than once if it's really the plight of the world that throws you into such depression, or me."

"You?" he queried, though perhaps not as sharply as he should have.

"I've felt so lonely!" she suddenly sobbed. "It seems to me that you've felt lonely too. Perhaps we're simply not meant to be together. Perhaps it's time I set you free to find your true love."

"You are my true love," he said quietly.

"Of course you have to say that!" she cried, her tears flowing freely. "Perhaps, right now, you even have to believe that." Her voice faded to a whisper. "But it's not true. I know in my heart that it's not true."

Despite his own pain he wanted to take her in his arms and comfort her, but the distance between them had now become an impassable chasm. He lay back and stared up into the empyrean. All was breathless with the transition from nighttime to morning. She arose and kissed him on the forehead. "Goodbye, Yeshua," she said. Then she glided silently away into the dawning light. As the birds began to sing, Yeshua felt himself buffeted by wave after wave of a pain that was more than physical, more than emotional, a pain endless in scope and infinite in intensity. At that moment he realized something he hitherto had failed to understand: how much he loved Mara, and how much he could hate her.

Chapter 3

Wendell awoke after what seemed the soundest sleep, he thought ironically, in his life. The light shone soft and enticing, the air in the room blew fresh despite the closed windows, and the grandfather clock ticked reassuringly in the corner. A hearty breakfast of eggs, biscuits, sausage and coffee sat invitingly upon the night table, its aroma alone almost rich enough to satisfy his appetite. When James finally appeared, Wendell was indulging in an after-meal cigar. "Look here, Will," he asked boisterously as he puffed away with relish, "what's the meaning of all this corporeality in the spirit world?"

James flashed a quick smile and then settled himself in the easy chair next to the bed on which his friend lay like a voluptuous feline. "I've already told you that the physicality of the pleroma is growing," he reminded Wendell. "But all that aside, it's different for each soul. The period of transition, I mean. The pleroma is a place of great spiritual intensity. The recently earth-bound soul, it seems, must cushion itself from that intensity until it becomes accustomed to it. Some souls take refuge in natural beauty, others in relations with the opposite sex. You, it appears, find insulation in the grosser pleasures of the flesh."

Wendell grimaced at the playful insult, but quickly recovered his good humor. "What do you mean by 'relations with the opposite sex?'" he asked eagerly. "Do you mean the souls of heaven engage in lovemaking?"

"With little exception," James replied, "everything one finds on earth, one finds in the pleroma. Only there's no need for any of it here. If you didn't eat, your body wouldn't waste away. If you didn't sleep, you wouldn't drop from exhaustion or go insane. If there were no sexual congress, the population wouldn't diminish. Here souls engage in the pleasures of the 'flesh' simply because they want to; and since these pleasures are really of the imagination, their side-effects are purely spiritual."

"In other words," Wendell hazarded, "no bed sores or obesity, no indigestion or heart-burn, no pregnancy or venereal disease?"

James nodded.

"Then this is heaven indeed!"

"Perhaps," James said warily. "I'll leave you to judge for yourself." He helped himself to a biscuit and cup of coffee.

Wendell put his tray aside, stood up, stretched his well-proportioned frame, and paced about the room as much as space allowed. James' words, and even more his manner, made him restless. "I feel like I'm twenty-six again!" he proclaimed with satisfaction.

"Naturally," said James. "The soul doesn't age."

"Then why do I still look like Methuselah?" Wendell whined.

"Why do *you* still look like Methuselah?"

James smiled. "I don't know. Some who come here at an advanced age regain the appearance of youth; others do not. Perhaps it has something to do with subjective age."

"Subjective age?"

"How old one feels."

Wendell extended his arms and tried a few knee-bends. "I'm living disproof of your theory, Professor," he declared. "I feel as if I could climb the Matterhorn! I suppose we'll have to add this age business to our list of baffling mysteries." Then, suddenly serious, he sat back down on the edge of the bed and looked at his companion eye to eye. "We didn't really talk about what your Hindu holy man said yesterday."

"No, we didn't," agreed James in his confoundedly evasive equanimity. "Is there something to talk about?"

"You know there is! This 'war in heaven' business—you seem to know a lot more about that than you're letting on."

James munched contentedly on his biscuit. "I've no idea what you mean."

"Come now, Will!" Wendell cried, his cheeks warming. "You picked up on the old fakir's meaning straightaway. Even made me feel like a fool for not following suit. What's it all about?"

"My dear Wendell," said James, "I don't know why you get upset when I don't explain my 'metaphysical nonsense' to you. You've never thought it worth your while."

Wendell felt properly humbled. "I plead guilty as charged. I've not given the devil his due!" he suddenly laughed, pinching James' cheek and turning on his considerable charm. "But, after all, my dear chap, you did say that *he* wants you to be my guide through this place, which I presume means he wishes for you to give me your best counsel in spite of myself."

James looked thoughtful as he swallowed the last bit of his biscuit. "Alright, Holmes, here it is," he said at length, setting down his breakfast. "I'll give it to you as I understand it. I can do no other, and I make no guarantees."

Wendell nodded.

"What is the root of all human behavior?" commenced James. "That's a question whose answer I've sought all my life. Some men say we're nothing but machines, acting strictly according to the laws of physical science, our movements no more the result of conscious volition than those of the planets or stars. Others say the motions of those planets and stars govern us, which amounts pretty much to the same thing. A third party admits consciousness as a determining factor, but one that is itself determined by preconscious psychological forces like drives and instincts. As you know, my friend," James said with a warmth such theoretical discourse could engender only in him, "I've always believed that we actually have free will."

Wendell knew for a fact that James had not always believed in free will, but he decided it would be more politic not to remind the professor of his more philosophically orthodox salad days. Besides, James had bought into this idea early enough in his career to cash in his stock for a hefty profit now. Back then Wendell had thought it one of his more eccentric superstitions. Now he was not so sure.

"Actual decision, real choice, a new beginning at every moment— that's what's at the heart of all human behavior!" James enthused. "Of course, I'll grant that we have habits, reflexes, automatisms, impulses," he added, as if in anticipation of an objection from Wendell that had not, in fact, been forthcoming. "But I'm more convinced than ever that the will ultimately governs even these psychological mechanisms. We choose to put ourselves on automatic, so to speak, because we choose not to take full responsibility for ourselves at every moment of life."

James paused, not so much to let what he had said thus far sink in, Wendell felt, as to scrutinize his auditor for any sign of inattention. He evidently found none.

"When we do act consciously, we do so not as a result of antecedent causes, but in accordance with certain goals and principles that may be said to govern our acts, but only because we choose to let them. These goals and principles are our *values*."

James smiled, as if fully aware that he had just taken a long and roundabout route to explain something extremely simple. Wendell waited patiently for the remarkable insight he hoped was to result from all this circumlocution.

"Now take what I just said and think of it not merely as psychology, but also ontology—that is to say, as defining the very structure of reality, the constitution of being. In other words, think of mind and matter as coterminous. Then every automatism in the psyche is an automatism in nature."

"I'm not sure I follow here," Wendell said in gross understatement.

"The hard places of the soul are the rocks and clay of nature," James explained, "the consternation and anger of the soul are the violence and storms of nature, and so on. I'm not saying that the mechanisms of nature mirror those of the soul. I'm saying that the mechanisms of nature *are* the mechanisms of the soul!"

Wendell would at once have dismissed James' thesis as utter nonsense were it not so obvious that the professor fully expected him to do just that, so he made an unaccustomed leap over his own intellectual assumptions in an attempt to land in this strange new universe of James' devising. "But then each of us would inhabit his own little universe, which would be indistinguishable from his body."

James regarded Wendell with what the latter hoped was more respect than tolerance. "Not if we were all part of a larger collective soul, the soul of the world."

"Yes, Aristotle said something of the kind," remarked Wendell, pondering. "So, if what you say is true," he went on guardedly, "then when we take responsibility for ourselves, deautomatize our souls, so to speak, we deautomatize nature."

"Bravo, Holmes!" applauded James. "I would not have wagered a plug nickel that you were capable of such metaphysical daring-do!" He suddenly sobered, as if remembering something serious. "But perhaps now is the time when we all must make a leap of faith."

Wendell smiled ruefully. James' point was well taken.

"To bring the lesson home," James continued, "nature is not the great enemy, as scientific-technological man would have it. We are our own enemy. The universe is ours to design, if we would but first deal with our own soul. Assuming, however, that we finally learn, or perhaps are forced to do so, what kind of a world will we create?"

"That's where the war of values comes in?" Wendell queried.

"Precisely!" affirmed James. "And it seems, my dear Holmes, that you and I have been chosen to bear witness to this war. Unless, of course, *he* has some more active role for us in mind."

James' last remark aroused in Wendell some disquiet, but he thought it best not to pursue the topic. At this point it was all he could do to keep up with what was actually happening. He had neither the energy nor, he had to admit to himself, the courage to add what might or might not occur in the future to his growing list of concerns. With a brief smile of gratitude indicating, he hoped, that he had taken in all that James had said and would now need time to digest it, Wendell leaped from the bed and proceeded to dress. As he knotted his tie he said cheerily, "What's on the agenda, today, Will?"

James smiled in return, as if he understood. "A walking tour of the city, if that's to your liking," he replied with gusto. "And, this afternoon, a visit to the Angelic Council."

The day seemed promising to Wendell, very promising indeed.

* * *

At bright mid-morning she found him, dark-skinned, turbaned and half-naked, in the crowded and twisting alleys of the low-slung Hindu quarter. Barefoot and bejeweled women carried babies in slings at their sides or balanced baskets of food on their heads. Deep-eyed yogis with unkempt beards and matted hair demonstrated their supernatural power by plunging iron stakes into their limbs. Vendors hawked their wares in voices so loud they seemed to carry for miles. Naked children ran screaming and laughing, not caring whom they shoved or whose toes they trampled. Shaven-headed priests strode calmly, oblivious to the tumult, their dignity born of the conviction of their spiritual superiority. From every quarter emanated cooking odors of grease and curry whose sum-total would have put the most ravenous stranger off his appetite. "Slumming, My Lord?" she asked.

Yeshua winced as if Uriel had slapped him. She immediately regretted her sarcasm, but she could not really be sorry. Ever since the coming of the light she had been searching for him, her feeling moving from concern through alarm to irritation and finally anger. He had not been at any of his accustomed haunts. Now, to find him strolling in disguise through the foul, narrow alleys of this damnable human ghetto... It was too much for even an angel to bear!

"Who made you their judge?" Yeshua shot back, every bit as angry as she. "And who made you my governess?"

"My Lord," she knelt before him in mock contrition, knowing such telltale reverence would be the last thing he wanted, "I humbly beg your pardon." But, instead of taking her hand and lifting her to her feet, as she expected, he smartly turned on his heel, just like a martinet, and strode quickly away. She arose and rushed after him. "I'm sorry, Lord," she said earnestly, all sarcasm bled out of her by the realization that he only grew so angry when he was in tremendous pain.

"Don't call me 'Lord!'" he snapped. "Not here. Not now."

She took his hands and held them until he stopped trying to pull away, and then looked into his eyes. She tuned in to his aura and found it to be the color of a lowering sky at sunset, all crimson and black. She felt his agony almost as if it were her own, and knew it was not time for the lecture she had planned to give him. It was not time for lectures at all. She released one hand but held fast to the other, going on with him in the direction he had been walking. "There's a Council meeting today," she said offhandedly, as if commenting upon the weather.

He managed a twisted smile. "Yes, there are always council

meetings. Meetings make them feel like they're doing something."

"They?" she queried. She had never heard him speak with contempt of the Angelic Council.

He waved his arm around, vaguely indicating the souls about him. "They," he reiterated, as if his meaning were obvious. "All of them."

"You mean, 'All of *us*?'" she asked, a hint of anger returning.

"Yes, all of you, angels and humans," he affirmed. "All of you!"

She had no chance to reply, for at that moment a skeletal *sadhu* with long, tangled hair and wild black eyes fell in adoration in Yeshua's path, chanting some hideous Sanskrit mantra. Yeshua looked upon the devotee calmly, almost with affection, and then, as only he could do, melted into the crowd. At once Uriel raised her vibration and shot into the empyrean. She had had enough of humanity for the moment, even the humanity of her Lord.

* * *

Rachel did not sleep right away. She basked in the warmth of Lucifer's passion, but finally closed her eyes and began to dream. At first she dreamed of all the natural beauty, the birds and flowers, mountains and forests, meadows, lakes and stars she had seen since coming to the pleroma. But then the incandescent horror that had taken possession of the core of her being burned away the tissue of self-deception and gave her over to vivid images of the atrocities in the camps: incessant and senseless whippings, hangings, beatings and shootings; the ripping of parent from child, sibling from sibling, husband from wife; never-ending roll-calls in the bitter frost and chilling rain; merciless and inescapable hunger, thirst and exhaustion; and the shame of having to wallow in one's own excrement. Worst of all was the fighting among the inmates themselves. It was not only that the Nazis, by giving them too little bread and regularly selecting the weakest to be gassed, made each of them feel as if every other inmate were a rival in the struggle for survival. No, it was also that, when it was impossible to strike out at one's tormentors because they were too strong, one kicked whoever was weak and at hand.

When she finally managed to master her pain—or, perhaps, when whatever power that governed such things decided she had received the night's quota of grief, guilt and despair—she opened her eyes. A soft light infiltrated the glass wall and softly illuminated the room. The roses in the garden, all red and white, bloomed under its benign influence. It took her a moment to remember that she had not been alone when she lay down, that she had had a bedmate who was no longer with her. Lucifer had gone. She was not sorry for his absence. Her eyes were wet with crying and she did not like to display her weakness before anyone, let alone a lover. Besides, it was all she could do to deal with her own emotions. If their intimacy remained purely sensual at this point, she realized, that would be all right with her.

She got up, not thinking about washing or breaking her fast, perhaps because she was neither hungry nor sweaty as she had always been after nights of lovemaking on earth. Instead, she was eager to roam through the city, preferably on her own. She liked Lucifer, but disliked being led about like a child. As she slipped out of the chamber and moved quickly but silently through the great hall and out the huge oak doors, she noted without surprise that she was once again clothed, but now in a chiffon-blue sari-like garment that, she hoped, would enable her to blend in with the denizens of the city.

The atmosphere was twilight when she set out, but brightened as the day came into full flower. She found herself at first in a Muslim quarter, where her bare head and shoulders gave her the opposite of anonymity. There were a number of other non-Muslims passing through, however, some of them women also with no veil. No one seemed to care. It appeared the inhabitants of the Heavenly City, unlike their counterparts on earth, tolerated one another's ways, even those they found personally offensive.

This part of the city reminded Rachel very much of Istanbul, which she had visited with her parents as a teenager, with its proliferation of mosques and bazaars, food carts and colorfully robed people; only here everything was cleaner, the colors shone brighter, and all the odors were enticing. The noises likewise were similar: the hearty invitations of merchants to sample their wares; the laughing, shouting and crying of children; the low, earnest hum of the devout engaged in prayer. The lyrical beauty of Arabic, Turkish, Persian, and other Oriental languages whose names she did not know wove all these sounds into a musical bouquet, only now Rachel understood all that was said and much, it seemed, that was not said. There were, it appeared, no language barriers in heaven.

Rachel had no idea where she wanted to go. Aimlessly she passed into a more modern, Western part of the city, replete with skyscrapers and motorcars. She had no desire to visit any of the numerous museums or theaters, nor to linger in any of the shops, though she told herself she would have to ask Lucifer what place buying and selling had in the pleroma where, he had told her, the substance of life was the imagination and individual souls could create whatever they desired. Perhaps these were more like galleries than stores, designed to influence taste rather than market goods. Or perhaps most of the souls of heaven, just like their counterparts on earth, found creativity too much of a bother.

Whatever the case, she was in no mood to window-shop. An undercurrent of emotion drew her on, at times almost insensibly but always irresistibly, to a destination beyond her ken. She did not stop to chat with anyone, no matter how interesting the person might appear. At most, she exchanged pleasantries as she floated down the river of an unnamed desire.

Gradually she realized there was no need of talk anyway. All she had to do was look into a person's eyes, and then she could feel what he was feeling and, in a vague way, sense what he was thinking. Or so it seemed to her. Rachel had always possessed profound empathy as well as keen intuition, so what she experienced now was an extension of, not an addition to, her natural state of being. Nevertheless, she found it remarkable, despite her experience with Lucifer yesterday in the meadow. Where passion was involved, she had never had any difficulty reading another person's mind. Today's intimacy with absolute strangers had nothing to do with passion. It was of a totally different order. Or was it? She had the humility to admit to herself that she was in uncharted territory here, and none of her accustomed categories need apply.

"Rachel!"

Rachel knew the voice, but could not place it in her memory. She looked up to see two deep-blue smiling eyes meet hers, and then she saw the face. "Lily!" she cried, and the two women rushed to embrace.

Lily was a *shiksa* who had converted when she married Daniel Reuben a few years before the Anschluss. When the Germans took over Austria, she had refused to renounce her new husband or faith, and had been deported to the camps even before Rachel and her family. Lily was a perfect Aryan type—tall, blonde, athletic, and beautiful—so the Nazis had regarded her as a particularly heinous traitor to her race. Through the grapevine, Rachel had heard that Lily had been brutally and repeatedly raped by S.S. officers who, unlike the enlisted men, dared not violate Hitler's injunction against sexual relations with Jews and so found the beautiful gentile a godsend. It was rumored that Lily had wanted to die, but held on until news came of her husband's death. Then she had thrown herself on the wire.

As Rachel hugged Lily she knew, without knowing how, that everything she had heard was true. Lily's wounds ran deep. Heaven, it seemed, had done nothing to heal them.

"That feels wonderful, Rachel," Lily murmured. "Thank you."

"For what?" Rachel asked softly.

"For the gift you just gave me!" Lily laughed. "Haven't you learned that empathy is healing?"

Rachel stepped back and held Lily at arm's length, looking into her eyes. "I only just got here yesterday," she said lamely, feeling no words could do justice to the emotion between them.

"It isn't true just here!" Lily said knowingly. "But, since you arrived so recently, I guess it would be stupid to think you might have seen Daniel?" Her tone rose at the end of this statement, turning it into a pathetic interrogatory. It was all Rachel could do to keep herself from breaking down into sobs. So it had always been with her. Her own pain she could hide from others and, if need be, from herself. That of others was another matter. Rachel finally managed to give a little shake of her head.

"Yes, it was foolish of me to ask." Lily thought for a moment, biting her lip until, had she been on earth, it certainly would have bled. "So, where have you been so far?"

Rachel felt it best not to tell Lily about Lucifer. "I've seen the Muslim quarter."

"Why were you in the Muslim quarter?" Lily asked with more than mild curiosity. "You're not thinking of converting, are you? I hope not, but after all we've been through, no one could blame you!"

Rachel then realized that she had just crossed over into a part of the city inhabited by her own people. "No!" Rachel laughed. "If I could not stand to be a good little Jewish hausfrau, how do you think I'd get along as a Muslim concubine?"

Out of sheer joy at seeing her, Lily hugged Rachel again and then, arms locked together, they strolled deeper into the Jewish section. Except for an occasional synagogue rather than mosque, this part of the Jewish quarter did not look much different from the Muslim sector. The houses were mostly one- or two-storied, flat-roofed and made of dried mud or brick. These, she realized, were the accommodations of the Middle Eastern, mostly Sephardic Jews. She had just passed through the Jewish "business" district. Farther ahead she could make out more modern buildings, high-rise apartments and single-family houses in the American style, as well as European villas and mansions. It seemed the poor of heaven were like the poor of the world, providing a buffer so the rich could forget the shameful ways they earned their wealth when they were at rest. "So, even here there's scenic poverty," she said.

Lily smiled. Her friend had not changed. "Here people can have whatever accommodations they desire. Earth habits die hard." Then a look at once wistful and earnest came into her face. "Are you sure you haven't seen Daniel?" she repeated apologetically. "I just want to find him before I move on."

"Move on?" Rachel echoed, shaking her head. She was so surprised that she stopped in the middle of the street.

"This isn't the end of the line," Lily explained, drawing her companion to one of the many little parks nearby and seating Rachel and herself in the grass. "At least, not for everybody. In fact, not everybody comes here to begin with. It's all very mysterious. No one has ever been able to figure out why some come here and others do not, nor why some stay and others leave." From her tone it was clear she wished she could give Rachel a better explanation.

Rachel turned away from Lily's probing eyes, for the moment wanting to focus solely upon this new information. "But you talk as if you could simply decide to leave whenever you please!" she said at length. "And where would you go?"

A wave of sadness came over Lily, palpable to Rachel even when she wasn't looking at her. "I know I'm destined to leave," Lily said quietly. "I don't know where I'll be going," she added, then stifled a sob. Rachel took her in her arms. "But I don't want to go without Daniel!" The tears flowed freely now from both women's eyes. "That's why I came here," she said passionately, "to be with him!"

They held each other for a long time, giving and receiving solace for their pain. But then the strange force that had been leading Rachel on once again became irresistible. She rose, sharing with Lily one last, lingering look. Lily nodded as if she understood, and Rachel went on her way.

* * *

Azazael waited in the ghostly Hall of Communion, for him all the gloomier because of its boring symmetry and the hackneyed splendor of the golden-lit globe at its center. "Today is the day!" he chattered nervously to himself. "We'll never have a chance like this again. If Lucifer bungles it! This Jewess is surely sweet, and Lucifer doubtless likes to linger in his pleasure, but business must come first. Especially in wartime, personal concerns must always come last. And no mistake about it, this is war!"

Azazael could not sit still, but pacing was not his style. So he flitted about from shadow to shadow and then in and out of the hemisphere, never leaving the hall for more than an instant lest Lucifer arrive and miss him. Finally, on a return trip, he encountered his master sitting upon a grand throne as if he had been there waiting all along. So, Lucifer's lovemaking had put him in an imperial mood. "Sleep late this morning, My Lord?" he asked, the innocence of his tone more cutting than a leer. Lucifer, however, was untouched.

"That's my business," he replied evenly, implicitly warning Azazael to remember his place. "How does it stand with our erstwhile queen?"

Azazael smiled, held out an open palm, and then slowly made a clenched fist. "She's in my grasp."

Surprisingly, Lucifer did not question his lieutenant's appraisal of the situation. "Yes," he said, as much to himself as to Azazael, "I didn't think she'd give you much trouble."

Azazael bowed, the mockery in his movement all the more

obvious because it displayed no mockery. "Your trust in me, My Lord, is most gratifying!" But again Lucifer went on as if he had noticed nothing.

"Have you broached the subject with her?" he asked, his neutral tone almost beguiling Azazael into believing that the Light-Bearer had complete confidence in his henchman's judgment in this matter.

"Indirectly," Azazael replied. "I've no doubt she'll come round to our side when the time comes." Then he added, in a voice fraught with sincere and deep concern, "She's suffered so much at his hands."

Lucifer smiled at Azazael's antics. "She'll be of some use," he said.

"And yet," Azazael went on, "she's not our main weapon. What of the Jewess?"

"As anticipated, she's ready to take the 'Almighty' to task for the suffering of her people." Lucifer smiled again, a pleasant memory from last night flashing across his face. "She's out exploring the city," he mused.

"Is that wise?" Azazael queried, careful to mute the irritation in his voice lest Lucifer regard the question as intolerably insubordinate.

"She's not like Mara," Lucifer continued his musing, "always needing someone or something to prop her up and make her whole. No, Rachel is wild and free." Again came the fleeting smile. "Give her an inkling that she's penned in, and she'll fly away."

"'The spirit blows where it wills,'" quoted Azazael without any further attempt to mask his sarcasm. In his present mood, Lucifer was no danger. "By the way, speaking of spirit, a little cherub told me that the grand and glorious Angelic Council meets today."

"Not until after mid-day," said Lucifer.

"Do you at least know where she is?"

"I'll have no difficulty finding her," Lucifer answered with absolute assurance. "She and I, we're connected."

Azazael drew back in alarm. Lucifer was in love! His affection for this Jewess could ruin everything! But then he began to consider the situation from a different angle. To be in love was a weakness. As he took his leave, he pondered how he might turn his master's vulnerability to his own advantage.

* * *

Wendell and James had been on their tour of the Heavenly City for about two hours when the former cut his friend off in the middle of an observation concerning the decadence of late Roman architecture. "My dear James," he declared acidly, "the day is beautiful, the buildings and people picturesque, and the exercise invigorating, but I'm afraid I expected to find something special here. We've been traipsing about this town for the better part of the morning, and I've seen nothing of real interest except for a magnificent Arab horseman who almost ran us down."

"That was Muhammad," James commented, "and he would have trampled us if he had wished. He's not so dangerous as those mighty ones who run amok in more emotional ways, like Mara, Yeshua's self-styled queen."

Wendell bridled at this non sequitur, but then he sensed that Will was airing some personal grudge and had no wish to get involved. Nor did he want to discuss Muhammad, either. "I wasn't complaining about that bit of adventure at all," Wendell continued, refusing to be sidetracked despite his natural curiosity about the founder of one of the largest and most influential religious traditions in the world. "That was exciting. Everything else has been..."

"Bland?" interjected James, sweeping the horizon with a gesture that took in the well nigh infinite multiplicity of human types, national costumes, architectural styles and cultural trimmings. "Monotonous?"

"I'll grant you, we've seen tremendous variety," said Wendell, "and the Japanese pagodas and Hindu temples were especially charming. But when you get right down to the heart of the place, no matter how exotic the outward trappings, it's all merely a sanitized version of an earthly city."

"An amalgam of earthly cities," James corrected.

"Alright, an amalgam!" Wendell huffed. "But quantity doesn't make up for quality, and variety is a poor substitute for the grit of reality. In fact, it seems to me that it's the dirt, crime and poverty on earth that make its cities so much more fascinating!"

James regarded Wendell with irony. "I dare say you would not find crime or poverty so 'fascinating' were you their victim."

Wendell blushed. "You're right of course, Will, but you know what I mean. I've seen nothing of spiritual grandeur here, nothing to challenge the powers of the soul, nothing to engage the heart. Perhaps this really is hell!"

"If that's the way you feel," James remarked with a cheeriness belying the import of his words, "then perhaps it's time you had a taste of what heaven and hell are all about. Follow me!"

James led Wendell into one of the many art galleries lining the heavenly avenues—not the nearest, but one he singled out from the rest, perhaps because it had the least charm: a gigantic glass-and-concrete box. The paintings, set in full light because there was no danger of decomposition in the pleroma, were strange, even outlandish to Wendell's eye. In the last years of his life he had seen something like them in the catalogs sent by various museums seeking his patronage, but he had never felt any desire to study them firsthand. And now here they were, or at least paintings very much like them, as well as their cousins, children, and grandchildren. The more traditional compositions had hints of organic forms, even faces, but for the most part Wendell could make out only a jumble of slapdash colors and geometric shapes. Some canvasses looked as if the artist had simply dribbled paint down them, others as if the paint had been splattered. In fact, Wendell wondered if the title of artist applied here at all. Any child, it seemed, could have produced the same effect with far less affectation.

James left Wendell to wander around a bit before calling his attention to a particular picture, a simple reddish-orange square outlined in yellow against a black, empty-feeling space. "This was a throwaway," James informed him. "It's by a famous artist, but he thought it unworthy of display."

Wendell looked at the signature in the lower left corner of the canvass, but it meant nothing to him. It could have been German, Austrian, Swiss, or even American. "Imagine that!" he said, a little too loudly for the sarcastic effect he intended.

"Yes, if he hadn't destroyed it, it—or rather, its earthly original— would be worth a fortune today." James took a moment to look upon the painting the way one would the casket of a loved one prematurely dead. "Now, you wanted to know what's so special about the pleroma. Stand directly in front of this painting."

Though he did not like taking orders from his friend, Wendell did as he was told.

"Now, let your mind be filled by what you see."

"What is this, Will, some kind of mesmerism?" Wendell queried.

James calmly insisted. "Let your mind be filled by the painting."

Wendell did his best to obey. He allowed his imagination to take up the fiery rectangle and dwell upon its every detail against the backdrop of blackest night. He was not sure exactly when it happened, but suddenly he realized the painting was no longer in his mind, his mind was in the painting! The canvass became a universe all its own, his universe. It remained the same picture he had seen from a distance, but now it was his world. The vibrancy of the bold and fiery colors was intensified a thousand fold, and he not only saw them but heard, felt, smelled, and even tasted them. The simple lines became the lineaments of his body. The dark backdrop became the constant and ever real threat of his annihilation. There was something frightening but also intensely pleasurable in it all until Wendell panicked, wondering if and how he would return to his accustomed mode of being. Instantly he found himself as before, standing in front of the canvass with James at his side.

"Are you back?" James asked uncertainly.

"Of course," Wendell said dreamily, a part of him still in the world of the painting. "Can't you see?" Wendell immediately realized how foolish this question was. To the onlooker, he must have been standing there all along.

"Good!" James proclaimed. "Now we'll visit a different museum." He took Wendell's hand and walked toward the exit, but without so much as stepping into the street they suddenly found themselves in another building, much older looking and more Gothic than modern in style. The ceilings were vaulted and the stone walls perforated with stained glass. It seemed more like a church than a museum. Even the air was musty. Its somber, candle-lit halls were filled with an entirely different type of art, much more familiar to Wendell than that they had just seen, but for different reasons equally to his distaste.

"This is a museum in the specifically Christian quarter," James explained.

"As opposed to the generically Christian quarter?" quipped Wendell. "How did we get here?" he asked absentmindedly. He was much more curious about James' reason for bringing him than the manner of their conveyance.

"In the pleroma a soul can go wherever it wants and however it wishes to get there."

It wasn't much of an explanation, but it satisfied Wendell for the moment. "And why are we here?" he continued.

"I've something I want to show you," said James, his nose reddening with excitement. He led Wendell toward a dark corner where a painting had been mounted in such a way as to make it nearly inaccessible. "Do you recognize it?" James asked.

From a distance, Wendell could only make out a welter of deep earth tones highlighted by splotches of scarlet, silver and gold. Once he managed to worm himself into the tight space directly before the painting, the colors delineated themselves into definite objects and figures. He took a moment to position himself and search his memory, and then he did indeed recognize it. "Why, that's a Rembrandt!" he exclaimed. "Not one of my favorites, mind you. I've always been partial to his landscapes."

"Of the female form?" teased James.

Wendell smiled. "Those too." He cupped his chin in his hand and thoughtfully studied the canvass. "It's *The Preaching of John the Baptist*, isn't it? I guess the fire-eater never could work a crowd the way Jesus did. Only..."

"What?" James encouraged him to voice his thought.

"Only, he doesn't look like much of a fire-eater here. I've never had much time for religious art, as you know, so I've never thought seriously about this work before..."

"What are you trying to say?" coaxed James.

"This may be blasphemy," Wendell finally let it out, "but why did Rembrandt make his Baptist look so much like Jesus?"

"Why is that blasphemy?"

"Not blasphemy against God," Wendell grinned. "Blasphemy against Rembrandt!"

James returned the smile. "Would you like to enter into this painting?"

Wendell felt eager to try. "Same way as before?" he asked. James nodded. "So be it!" Once again Wendell allowed the canvass to fill his imagination, and once again the canvass, and even more than the canvass, became his world: the cool, brooding, eternally gray Dutch sky; the public square filled with townspeople and surrounded by a stately array of stone and brick mansions and public buildings, interspersed by the small but well-kept clapboard houses which were all that the workingmen could afford; and, off in the distance, visible not in but from the painting, the chill, green, steep-waved ocean insecurely guarded by puny-looking sea-walls.

He found himself in the picture the way he had, as a child, imagined God in the world — a free-floating, ghostly being who could tune into the thoughts and feelings of any of its occupants at will. John seemed the most intriguing focal point, not only because he was the only one dressed as a first-century Jew rather than a seventeenth-century Netherlander, but also as it was obvious what everyone else was about. A few people were paying attention to what the prophet was saying, but most were engaged in personal affairs, evidently here because it was the place currently fashionable to be seen, in the company of an authentic holy man. The burghers of the town discussed business and politics, the housewives gossiped, the street urchins scampered about fighting and playing, the old men quietly snored, and again, a few people actually listened. So Wendell fixed his concentration upon John, who was saying something about the coming of God's kingdom in the hearts of men, and then found himself 'inside' the figure, so to speak, thinking and feeling what he was thinking and feeling. At that moment, Wendell realized that the preacher was indeed Jesus rather than the Baptist! He it was whom Rembrandt had painted, regardless of how the artist had titled the composition.

Wendell felt Jesus' strong temptation, indeed almost overwhelming urge, to give up. The crowd did not want to hear him and had no concern for the spiritual issues of life. He and they were in two different worlds. Even those who made the effort to listen understood next to nothing of what he was saying. He had always been alone and always would be alone.

Yet, beneath this layer of despair, which went considerably deeper than a veneer but still failed to penetrate to the core of the man, lay an iron determination to follow his path to the end, whatever that might mean. It was born of the realization that it had to be this way, that he had to spend himself in words before something more than words could wake them from their sleep. He was the farmer sowing seeds, and he had faith that his heavenly Father would bring them to fruition.

Wendell was startled to find that Jesus had faced such indifference, and even more startled to discover in him such deep despair coincident with such profound faith.

But were these discoveries authentic? Perhaps Rembrandt, as artists were wont to do, had simply projected his own experience with the general public onto Jesus. Nevertheless, it all rang true, very true indeed, leading Wendell to explore the psyches of a few of the other figures before leaving the painting. He found that, on the whole, his *prima facie* impressions had been correct, but only superficially. As he plumbed the depths beneath their apparent heedlessness, he learned that something in each and every one of them, from the sophisticated mayor to the thoughtless brat, delighted in Jesus' presence, fed off his spiritual substance, so to speak, a substance they themselves lacked. He also discovered that, because Jesus possessed something no one else had, they feared him more than an accursed murderer or bloodthirsty tyrant. Could all this be Rembrandt's invention?

When Wendell returned, he went straight to the point. "What exactly is this world of the picture, Will? Is it the artist's imagination entirely, or is there something beyond that?"

James mused. "You mean, is there a truth to it that bears upon the real world? There are all sorts of opinions on that question. I can only give you my own."

Wendell nodded the go-ahead.

"An artistic work is a marriage of creativity and truth. It's too artificial to say that an artist causes one to see a timeless truth in a new way. In a sense, the artist actually creates truth. Yet, it is also misleading to think that the truth of a work is only imminent to the artist and his experience. Any truth is something far beyond any of us, much bigger than any of us, even if one happens to be an artist. To put it more prosaically, did Rembrandt here give us merely his own version of John?"

"Jesus," corrected Wendell. "The subject of the picture is Jesus."

James nudged him conspiratorially, as if Wendell had just passed an initiation into a secret society. "As I say, did Rembrandt give us merely his own Jesus? Yes, if one omits the word 'merely,' for his Jesus doubtless is the product of genuine insight into the real Jesus."

Despite the excess verbiage, Wendell grasped James' point and it caused him to ponder. Rembrandt's Christ certainly was not the Jesus about whom he had been taught, not even in his liberal New England Transcendentalist youth. "If he meant it to be about Jesus," he asked, "why did Rembrandt call this *The Preaching of John the Baptist?*"

"The answer should be obvious to you now," James replied. "He was afraid of what the religious authorities of conservative Amsterdam would have done to him, or it, had he revealed its true subject."

Wendell nodded. It was obvious. Another matter, however, also puzzled him. Turning to face James, he said meaningfully, "So, is this the gateway to infinity in this place — art?"

In a way only he could do, James nodded and shook his head at the same time. "Yes," he replied, "but not the only gate, nor even the most direct and profound, but perhaps, for most of us at least, the most accessible."

"What do you mean?" Wendell asked.

"Love is the real gate," James answered solemnly, "but most are afraid to go that route. Take you, for example."

"Me?" Wendell vaguely felt as if he should take offense.

"You've been here some time now..."

"Less than two days!" Wendell objected.

James waved his hand as if to say, "More than enough!" Wendell felt humiliated, but managed to hold his temper. "You've been here some time," the professor went on, "but this is the only hole you've discovered in a realm that's more porous than the heads of Harvard freshmen!"

"What in heaven's name are you talking about?" Wendell demanded, oblivious to the unintended irony in his choice of expletive.

James did not smile either. "For one thing, you saw a lot of different people this morning and said not a word to any of them."

Wendell was taken aback. Why had he behaved in such a fashion? "Well," he stammered, "I suppose I figured that the exotic ones wouldn't understand English, or at least, not modern English, and that the ones like us who would" — he winked coyly, a habit of his when he was personally, as opposed to professionally, on the spot — "probably weren't worth talking to."

"Is that the real reason?" James queried. "Wasn't it really because you were afraid they would understand you all too well?"

"What on earth are you talking about?" exclaimed Wendell.

"Didn't you sense what they were thinking as they spoke among themselves, even if it was in languages you didn't understand? And weren't you afraid that, if you opened your mouth, they would know your thoughts as well?"

"Are you saying there are no language barriers here?" Wendell asked in a vain attempt to shift the discussion onto a more theoretical plane.

"I'm saying there are no barriers of any sort save the ones we carry around in our own hearts. This place is not what it seems to you. It's not what it seems to any of us!"

"Then what is it?" Wendell asked.

"If I knew that," James sighed, "I would not be in the same plight as the rest, would I?"

Wendell sank to the floor, his back against the wall. For a time he stared listlessly into space. Then, his voice flat, he said to James, "If you are in the same boat, if you can't see past appearances either, how do you know they're appearances? Maybe there's nothing more to it all than what we see."

"Do you believe that?" James said sharply, hovering over him. "After what you just experienced?"

"No," Wendell admitted. "How can I?"

"Well, then," said James with mixed frustration and satisfaction, "I've one other item to show you. It's something I did myself. I keep it out at my place. Will you come?" Without another word, he stepped out of the museum, obviously assuming Wendell would follow.

Wendell continued to sit in the corner, weighed down by the sheer mystery of this universe. He was accustomed to dealing with manageable problems and enjoying everything else as an aesthetic observer, as if the world were a museum through which he might wander, intrigued but untouched. Here even the museums were not safe! What had he gotten himself into? Then again, what choice did he have? One thing was certain; James was in his element here, and Wendell far removed from his.

Upon this realization, panic once more swept over him and he jumped up and went off after his companion. Outside the museum, however, where the narrow and winding alleys reminded him of the medieval quarter of a European city, James was nowhere in sight. Everything was normal, as far as the newcomer could tell. The day was bright even without a sun, and people in a great variety of dress, from antiquated robes to modern business suits, were strolling about as earlier. Occasionally, despite to all appearances the complete absence of wildlife from the city, he even thought he could hear a birdcall. He seemed to be in no danger, but his alarm grew. He was distressed at losing James, but even more distressed at needing him so much. He almost collapsed then and there, but then he sensed another, deeper feeling underlying his despair. Or was it a sensation? At any rate, the more attention he paid it, the stronger it grew, and with it the overwhelming certainty that it would take him to his friend. He gave himself up to this "spirit-possession," and in a twinkling found himself at the doorstep of what was for a certainty James' home. There was no mistaking it. It was identical, in form and feeling, to the charming oak-shingled, weather-beaten farmhouse James and his family had summered in for so many years. The surrounding flora, including spruce pine, red maple, pickerel weed, and English primrose, also looked as if it had been transplanted from rural New England. Wendell took a deep breath. Even the air seemed fresher out here.

The natural thing would have been for Wendell to open the door before him and enter, but he still felt the strange sensation of being taken by the hand by some invisible power, though now it was not so strong — not, it seemed, because it was fading away, but because he had become more responsive and it could afford to be more subtle. At its prompting, he walked to the other side of the house and into a storage shed. Only, it turned out to be no shed! If anything, it was a shrine, for all it contained was a sculpture, about seven feet high, with candles burning around it. It was Christ crucified between the two thieves.

Now the unseen hand left and the panic returned. Wendell looked about, but James was nowhere to be found. What was he to do? Surely he was not to enter into such a work as this! He was not ready, he would never be ready for that. But James' absence, as well as that of the guidance, was like an implacable finger pointing out the road he must take. Without further hesitation, which undoubtedly would have deepened into paralysis, Wendell placed himself squarely before the cross of Christ and allowed his mind to be filled by the eerily realistic scene. Almost immediately, the objet d'art became his world.

Wendell expected terror, perhaps even pain. Instead, a profound peace came over him. After all, he reassured himself, he was still an observer. When he had entered into the figures of the Rembrandt painting, their thoughts, feelings and sensations had remained clearly their own. This recollection fortified him. Nevertheless, he decided to deal with the thieves before tackling Jesus.

One thief was tall and angular, the other short and chunky, but they both had full beards and long, disheveled hair. They looked like they were in a great deal of pain, and that proved to be the case. One was angry and defiant, the other resigned and reaching out for death, but the souls of both men seemed half asleep, already with one foot, so to speak, on the other side. If their discomfort was not so terrible, Wendell reasoned, then how bad could Christ's suffering be? After all, he was a spiritually realized being, whatever else he might be, not carrying the burden of a guilty conscience and filled with a deep and unshakable conviction in the purpose and meaning of his death.

Before entering into the figure of Jesus, Wendell took a moment to examine his face. It was not that of the handsome and regularly featured Christ of European iconography but possessed the large nose, narrow eyes and thick lips conventionally associated with the Semitic type. Once again, the man was caught up in contradiction. The expression upon his visage could have been an impassive mask, or the manifestation of an anguish so profound and encompassing that it left no room for variation. The paradox shook Wendell's self-confidence, making him realize how fragile it was. Nevertheless, he decided, curiosity would never let him rest if he backed down now, so he made the plunge. What happened next was over in an instant, but its memory lived with him forever after.

There was pain. In a way, that was all there was. There was no distinguishing between physical and emotional pain, the torment of the flesh and the agony of the spirit. It was all one, because he who was suffering it was one. He was not divided up into a lot of little compartments in which the pain could be shunted to and fro, and thus he could not escape the pain. Neither could Wendell, any more than one who looks at the sun can escape blindness. The pain was of utter loneliness and rejection, of one who gives himself entirely because others cannot do without him, and yet is regarded by those same others as a fool, a madman, a prince of evil. Jesus seemed held by some spiritual force, it was true, but that only intensified his suffering beyond endurance, fixing his soul to the cross as surely as the nails fastened his body. If God were truly holding him, the victim wondered, why was God permitting him to suffer so? Even the Almighty seemed on the side of his tormentors. All this Wendell noted in a split second. It was imprinted on his memory by the spiritual equivalent of a massive electrical charge running through his psyche. Then, mercifully, he was released and lost consciousness. When he came to, James was kneeling at his side, looking down upon him with just a hint of anxiety in his face, which was more alarming to Wendell than if his friend had been distraught. When he saw that Wendell had opened his eyes, however, he smiled. "All will be well," he said, a trifle complacently.

Wendell sat up and discovered he was no longer in the shed but on a sofa in the farmhouse parlor. "Where'd you go, Will?" he demanded hoarsely.

James rose, poured a cup of tea from a kettle hanging over the flaming hearth, and offered it to Wendell. "It was the only way," he explained, not at all contrite. "You had to find it on your own. Otherwise, you wouldn't have been ready."

Not at all in the mood for social amenities, Wendell refused the tea and rose shakily to his feet, but then immediately sank back down upon the divan. He tried to shout at James, but could only manage a whisper. "Is anybody ever ready for... that?" He straightened up. "How did you create such a thing?" he asked, his voice returning. "Is that how you experience life?"

"Me?" James echoed, evidently astonished that anyone should think such a thing. "No, of course not! I'm as weak and fragmented as anyone else. I simply provided the vehicle. *He* filled it with his spirit."

Wendell pondered. "There must be some wonderful, and terrible, art around this pleroma."

"There could be," agreed James, "but the curious thing is that hardly any souls, even those of famous artists, bother to make anything. All the works you'll find in the museums are replications of earth art."

"Why is that?" Wendell queried. "Why waste such tremendous opportunity?"

Now it was James' turn to ponder. "That's another one of those questions on which I've spent much thought, but no answer has readily presented itself."

"Have they grown lazy?" Wendell wondered.

"No, at least, not in the usual sense," James replied. "In terms of effort, artistic activity is so much easier here." For a minute he was lost in thought. "Perhaps that's why there's so little of it!" he suddenly cried, his face lighting as if the possibility had not occurred to him before.

"I sort of see what you mean, old fellow," Wendell said, "but I don't quite get it."

"Art," James explained, "is born of passion. Passion builds against resistance. Where there is no resistance, passion dissipates." He sat on the divan next to Wendell and put a reassuring arm around his shoulders. "But we don't have time for philosophizing now, my friend," he said cheerily. "Are you sure you're alright?"

Wendell nodded.

"Good. We have to go."

Wendell stared at him blankly.

"Don't you remember," laughed James, "or did your experience take your memory away?"

The experience! Wendell had allowed himself to be sidetracked from the experience! There was something about it he had badly wanted to ask James, but it had slipped away. Now he did not know with whom he was more angry, James or himself.

James seemed oblivious to Wendell's sudden surge of emotion.

He either misread it or chose to ignore it. "The Angelic Council!" he declared. "It's a great honor to be invited, so few human beings are. We mustn't be late."

Wendell allowed himself to be swept up by James' enthusiasm, but he was still angry, and still searching for that question.

* * *

Dressed in the coarse brown robe of a mendicant friar, a knotted cord around his waist and the hood pulled up over his head, Yeshua knelt in the candle-lit, almost empty nave of the massive cathedral. It was modeled after St. Peter's in Rome, and its dome dominated the skyline of the Roman Catholic section of the Christian quarter. On earth its counterpart was filled from Matins to Vespers with hundreds of tourists and pilgrims. The tourists were here as well, though more in the tens than hundreds, but the pilgrims had mostly disappeared. Since they had already made it to heaven, there was no need. Or so they surmised. Little did they know, Yeshua thought sardonically.

Still, old habits die hard, and so members of various religious orders continued to perform the daily devotions and celebrate mass right on schedule. He had borrowed the body of one such monk, for if he was likely to be recognized in his own form anywhere in the Heavenly City, it was here. Through their spiritual discipline, these religious had developed the ability to see his image in their own souls. Ironic, he thought bitterly, how his reality still eluded them.

For the last forty-five minutes there had been no peace. The monks and nuns had joined a fat old bishop, richly caparisoned in the gold and white vestments of his trade, in singing a high mass. Ordinarily Yeshua enjoyed the Catholic chants and hymns, so much more tuneful than their Protestant counterparts, even if he did choke on the smoke of the incense. This morning he found the entire business tedious and distracting. At the moment, however, all was quiet. The bishop had just finished the benediction and there would not be another service for at least half an hour. Yeshua blended in with the rest of the monks by bowing his head in silent contemplation.

He did not know what he was doing here. He certainly did not feel like praying. But the bitterness, anger and pain welled up within him, and he could not help whispering to his Father, "Why? Why did you take Mara from me? Why did you make it impossible for us to be together? Why were you always coming between us? Why, why, why?"

At that moment Yeshua hated his Father, hated himself, hated life for bringing him to this anguish. His breathing was labored and tears flowed down his cheeks, like rivulets losing themselves in the underbrush of his beard. He would rather have been crucified a thousand times over than have suffered the loss of Mara's love.

Yet, he was too honest to think that was the whole of it. That Mara could leave him only by rushing into another man's arms meant she was using men to avoid herself. That she would turn to a mountebank like Azazael meant she would use any man who would allow himself to be used. How could she not see that Azazael was pandering to her for his own ends, none of which had to do with love? It became clear to Yeshua, now that he let himself see it, that she was worse than a sleepwalker, those heedless of their inner depth. She was a hypocrite who staked out her ego-territory and built around it an impenetrable wall against everything else in her being, including her own heart.

His fury subsided as he realized that, given Mara's spiritual condition, their parting was inevitable; but the anger flared anew as he reminded himself that there was nothing inevitable about that condition. It was her choice. Why did she choose the way of self-deception? Why had his Father not brought him together with someone of real courage? Why did she fear love, fear life?

"Everyone," he muttered bitterly, "is afraid." Everyone was afraid of life. He had not encountered one individual, in heaven or on earth, who did not serve fear in one way or another. Was he always and forever to be alone?

He tore the suffocating hood from his head and leaped to his feet. Even this cathedral was a bribe to God to escape damnation. He could not stand being in this "holy" place, this supreme monument to human fear, one second longer.

As he turned to go, he saw her. She was staring at him. He had no idea how long she had been staring at him. She had long, jet-black curls and limpid, dark-brown eyes, and as soon as he saw her, he felt himself sinking into those eyes. His heart nearly burst within him, and he wondered what kind of trick was being played here, or what kind of fool he was for falling so swiftly in love with another after losing Mara. Then he sensed *his* presence. He broke off from her gaze, looked to the rear of the nave and saw Lucifer enter. Of course! Now it all made perfect sense. Yeshua had no desire to trade barbed pleasantries with his fallen brother, or to let him see how nearly his little stratagem had succeeded. He summoned the monk whose form he had borrowed to return from the ether, and in a twinkling he himself was gone.

* * *

The council building stood upon a rise outside the city proper. There were no walls to this Heavenly City, as Wendell remembered it having been portrayed in Biblical fantasy. Rather, the urban environment shaded insensibly into an indefinite expanse of breathtaking wilderness containing, it seemed to Wendell, every kind of forest, jungle, mountain, valley, lake and river known to man, and some that were known only to man's imagination. Wendell wondered why he had not appreciated its wild beauty before, on the excursion to Sivananda's retreat. Then it had seemed too perfect, too tame. Was he changing or it changing? Or perhaps it was just the viewing of it from a different angle. Here was another question to add to his list of imponderables.

The Angelic Council held its meetings in a monumental structure on a butte at the very edge of this wilderness, but the building appeared so natural it could have been an outcropping of the hilltop. Despite the geometric symmetry of their placement, the pillars and central dome looked like red rock formations and the windows like crystalline openings to brightly lit caves. Wendell had never seen so effective an integration of artifice and nature. Architects on earth, he mused, had much to learn from their angelic brethren, if such they could be called.

The interior of the building was thoroughly consonant with the exterior style and equally impressive. There was no clutter of statuary or furniture to mar the spacious symmetry. "Majestic" was the word that came to mind, but not uncomfortably so, as were so many of the gargantuan edifices of worship Wendell had visited as a tourist on earth. It took him a moment to realize that it was something more than the soft glow of the pale walls, the warm light flooding the high-ceilinged chambers, and the reassuring clarity of the atmosphere that made him feel at home here. There was an aura of power—not the wanton power flaunted by a tyrant, but the concerted, deliberate, responsible power Wendell himself had wielded while sitting on the United States Supreme Court. As he and James sat in what Wendell took to be the visitors' gallery—a small and unobtrusive corner bench, surprisingly comfortable despite its composition of stone—he felt a stab of envy, even self-pity, that he who had once been in the thick of it all was here only to observe.

Wendell still struggled to remember the vital question he had wanted to ask James, but he was content to forget, at least for a time, everything else he had experienced that morning. It was not that it had all been such a torment. He could take the pain without too much trauma. It was that a door had opened in his universe where he had never, in his wildest fancies, imagined one to be. A door? No, rather a cavernous, gaping maw threatening to swallow up his sanity. He was happy to have the excuse of the council meeting to let all that go, to leave it for later. Perhaps with the distance of time he could make some sense of what, in its immediacy, stretched beyond the compass of reason.

Today, James had explained on their way over, which had been something between ordinary walking and the instantaneous transport Wendell had experienced earlier, was a meeting only of the High Council, consisting of the twelve elders who had been with the Lord from the very dawn of creation. What they had seen and experienced was beyond any human's imagining! Wendell asked about Lucifer, whom Sivananda had mentioned. James admitted that, yes, there had originally been thirteen elders, but was not forthcoming with details, and Wendell had not been in the mood to coax them out of him.

At any rate, the twelve were gathering today to discuss the worsening situation on earth. Mankind, Wendell was not all that surprised to learn, had developed the means of unraveling matter and so destroying not only itself, but all life on the planet. Some of those who would be present today had aided earth's democracies in inventing this weapon of preternatural proportions, lest the minions of the soulless Hitler do so first. Others had opposed this strategy but not obstructed it. The Lord had been disconcertingly silent about it all. Angels always felt uncomfortable when they had to go it alone. Now they were meeting to see if the Lord would grant them clearer guidance and, if not, whether they might formulate a unified policy in the face of such a devastating threat to earth, the crown jewel of all creation.

When the time came for the meeting to begin, the angels did not file in, as did the justices of the Supreme Court. They simply appeared, forming a circle at the center of the great hall. There were eleven of them, not twelve as James had said there would be, but a place at the foot of the circle was left vacant. There were no tables and chairs. The angels stood. Nevertheless, insofar as Wendell could tell, they seemed amply at ease.

He studied them closely, since he had never seen an angel before. In truth, he could not make out much, because not only was each surrounded by a radiance of variable or indeterminate hue, but also they themselves actually seemed composed of shimmering light. No wonder earth's myths and legends offered so many divergent descriptions of angels. Human beings, even those gifted with spiritual sight, could not see them clearly enough to note with accuracy characteristics like gender, let alone details of gesture and facial expression. Only two facts were clear from his observation: in stature they were well above the average human, and they had no wings that he could see.

The angel at the head of the circle, apparently the leader, commented little upon James' and Wendell's presence. He merely gestured toward them and said, "It's the Lord's will," and everyone bowed in acquiescence.

"That's Mikael," James whispered.

"I should have guessed as much," Wendell returned, his voice sounding unconscionably loud, amplified by the cavernous space. From now on he too would whisper.

"Now Raphael will speak," James informed him. "He's the angel of healing."

Wendell wondered if his friend had been slipped a program. If Mikael were at twelve o'clock, the aura of the angel at nine o'clock composed itself into a delicate, pale-green hue, and then he gave his report. His words were few and to the point. Wendell had the feeling they were for the visitors' benefit, and that most of the communication with his fellow angels was from mind to mind.

"For the first time in her history, the earth itself is in need of healing, and the future bodes even worse. As we all know, the human race itself is the problem. Until this time, men were small in numbers and lacked the means to bring great harm upon themselves and their fellow creatures. They had no power to violate the integrity of the earth. Now all that has changed."

Raphael's light returned to kaleidoscopic indeterminacy, what Wendell supposed was the angelic method of relinquishing the floor. The aura of the angel opposite, at three o'clock, now settled into a median blue. "She's Gabriel, the messenger," James told him. Wendell was less irritated by this remark than by James' earlier comments, for he never could have guessed the gender of an angel.

"There's more, if not worse, on the horizon," Gabriel warned. "Even now earth laboratories are testing the prototypes of deadly chemicals that will bring great abundance in the short run, but deplete the fruits of the earth, indeed the earth itself, of their nurturing substance. The human race will poison itself with its food and fill its belly with starvation."

Then followed a long and, it seemed to Wendell, embarrassed silence. "It's Uriel's turn," whispered James, "but she's the one who's missing." Finally, Mikael took up the slack.

"It's our sister Uriel's part to recommend a course of action. I ask you all to let me speak in her place."

Wendell saw no change in their auras and detected no other sign of communication, but evidently they gave their assent. Perhaps Mikael's request was merely a formality since he was, after all, their leader; or perhaps silence indicated agreement. In any event, Mikael continued.

"As you all know, but at least one of our guests does not, we are mandated by divine law not to interfere with the course of human history. We may offer guidance, and even succor, when requested by a pure heart, and through our presence we may somewhat lighten the increasingly darker aura of the earth; but we may not force, seduce, or otherwise manipulate humankind, no matter how strongly we believe such intervention would be for its own good.

Those among us who violated this law have fallen from angelic status."

So, that was it! The Promethean myth was not far off the mark.

"It's our duty now to uphold the law as our Lord handed it down from the beginning. We will continue to help as we have always done. In addition, we will watch and wait."

"That's what I always liked about you, Mikael. You're a man of action!"

The voice was heard before its proprietor could be seen. As its sarcasm infected the pristine atmosphere like the mustard gas used by the Huns in the Great War, an individual markedly different from the angels Wendell had yet seen materialized in the empty space where Uriel should have been. "Lucifer!" James gasped. Obviously this epiphany was not on the agenda.

Satan looked far more human than angelic. No radiance streamed from him, no blinding light obscured his handsome face and muscular, well-proportioned, unmistakably masculine form. He wore a scarlet tunic and golden sandals, the simple attire offsetting and thereby enhancing his natural dignity. To Wendell it was refreshing to see a man in the midst of all these strange and supernatural beings, especially one who displayed the human form to such advantage. The atmosphere darkened slightly and the general mood grew even weightier, but otherwise there was no indication that the angelic elders were perturbed by Lucifer's advent.

"Welcome, brother," Mikael said calmly, refusing to take Lucifer's bait. "What brings you to our gathering?"

Lucifer smiled. If this was the devil, he certainly lived up to his reputation of being a charmer. Then his smile went crooked. "The world is on the brink of self-destruction," he declared acidly, "yet you continue to advocate a do-nothing policy. Why have I come? Unlike you, my brother, I'm not afraid to shoulder the responsibility of power. Something needs to be done, and you're incapable of doing it. It's time for a new administration around here!"

The ensuing silence was more eloquent of the shock Lucifer's last remark engendered than would have been a general commotion. At length, the angel stationed at seven o'clock, immediately to Lucifer's left, managed to speak. James was too flustered, it seemed, to tell Wendell his name. "It's not Mikael you are attacking, Lucifer," he said ominously.

"You're right, Zadkiel," Lucifer readily admitted. "You were always quick to see where the real conflict lies. My quarrel is with *him.*"

Again there was silence. "Lucifer," Mikael finally said, his words measured, his tone mild, "all of heaven and earth knows your quarrel is with our Lord, but..."

"*Your* lord!" Lucifer cut him off.

"Yes, my Lord," Mikael resumed without annoyance, "and your Lord too, whether you like it or not."

"We'll see," Lucifer retorted meaningfully, his muscles strained and shining with the sweat of his passion.

Mikael's radiance flickered and then steadied. "So far you've brought nothing new to this meeting. If you've no business here, will you have the decency to let us get about ours?"

"I have business, sir!" came a feminine voice from a somber recess of the hall. Even the angels turned to see to whom it belonged.

It was that of a young woman, brunette and very pretty, even beautiful according to some tastes, Wendell was certain, who apparently had tiptoed in unnoticed while Lucifer distracted attention. Now, as Lucifer stepped aside, she strode forward into the very center of the angelic circle. Was she a fallen angel, that she displayed such audacity? Or was she merely a foolish mortal whose boldness was born of ignorance? Or, perhaps, was there really nothing to fear? Was ignorance the mother of Wendell's own caution? Perhaps, but he doubted it. The angels had power, there was no question of that, and it was always wise to respect power. The girl had power too, however. The anxiety in the hall intensified as soon as she spoke, and James and Wendell were not its only source.

The girl was a slip of a thing, but she drew herself up to her full height and, as much as is possible for a human to do to an angel, looked Mikael straight in the eye. "I am Rachel, late of earth, more specifically Auschwitz. I've seen what the world has become, what this 'Lord God' has allowed it to become. I've experienced the abyss of its horror in my own soul. I refuse to accept this abortion of a universe any longer. If he won't or can't make it right, then we should be ruled by someone who will."

Gabriel, who Wendell sensed was more accustomed to intercourse with humans than the others, answered for the Council. "You don't know what you're asking, my sister. The Creator's authority is inalienable in the strictest sense of the word. It can't be taken from him because it is what he is. He *is* his authority."

"I'm not talking about the Creator," she rejoined. "I'm talking about him who claims to be his only begotten son."

"But he too is his authority. You can't..."

"Enough!" Mikael intervened. "Daughter, we all know the torture you've endured, not only in your own person, but in the persons of those you love. Your pain is the measure of your love." As Mikael said this, Wendell thought the girl's eyes shined with unshed tears. "Rachel, your love is great. The anguished plea of so pure a heart cannot go unanswered. He whom you blame for all your woes has agreed to go on trial. All the human souls of the pleroma will be his judges."

"What about us?" queried Lucifer, looking as if taken off guard. He was speaking, Wendell supposed, for his angelic brethren, or at least the fallen ones.

"Anyone may give argument at the trial, but no angel may take part in deciding the verdict. Do you agree to these terms?"

Lucifer was clearly wary. The opposition, it seemed, had caved in much more rapidly than expected. Doubtless he feared a trap. Nevertheless, what could he say? Mikael's conditions were eminently fair, given that angels were merely observers of the human condition. Only those who knew first-hand its joys and agonies could justly judge its architect.

"Yes, if you will clarify one point for me," Lucifer finally replied. "The stakes. What will he do if found guilty?"

"That's simple," answered Mikael evenly. "He will relinquish all his authority to you."

These words sent a shock wave through the hall. The only one who appeared unwavering was the girl. Truly, it had to be out of ignorance.

"And what if he's found innocent?" Zadkiel demanded.

"Why," said Mikael, "then he will be free to go about his business as he always has."

"No consequences for the accuser?"

Wendell could not see, but nevertheless could distinctly feel,

Zadkiel glare at the girl.

"She's not on trial," Mikael declared conclusively. "As you may have guessed by now, Lucifer, the Lord foresaw this development and has made provision for the proceedings, as well as for a smooth transfer of power should he lose. He has given me full authority to speak on his behalf. If it is agreeable to you, we shall retire to a private place to work out the details."

Lucifer still seemed uneasy. "What about my ward?" he asked, waving a hand toward the girl.

"If you like," said Mikael, "I'll have an angelic escort see her back to your palace."

"I can find my own way," Rachel demurred, as Wendell had an inkling she would. "I'm getting to know the city quite well, and there's no danger — certainly nothing to compare with what's to be found on earth."

Lucifer looked even uneasier. For a creature who was supposed to be the father of lies, Wendell chuckled to himself, he certainly wore his heart on his sleeve. He glanced at Rachel, their eyes met, and then she turned and strode out of the hall. The fallen one had no choice but to accompany Mikael to one of the inner chambers. The rest of the angels disappeared as they had come. Then Wendell suddenly felt that something was wrong with his friend. He studied James, who sat with unnatural stillness staring at the space the angels had just vacated. He could see the tension break in him, and Will began to sob. Wendell tentatively patted his hand, then put his arm around him the way he had around many a soul-weary comrade during the war. The two men sat thus for what must have been hours, until the day turned into night.

Chapter 4

Uriel found Mikael in closed conference with Zadkiel in one of the lesser chambers of the council building. Like everything else in the building, the room was all of stone. No door barred her entry, but the miscreants had fashioned their auras into a luminescent globe encompassing them both. The circumference of such a globe could not be penetrated by any save another angel of light, and no angel had ever failed to respect the privacy it invoked. But she no longer cared about protocol or decorum. She broke in on them.

"How could you?" she demanded of Mikael. "How could you agree to such a trial? Are you now to play the role of Pontius Pilate to Lucifer's Caiaphas, and are the rest of us to be your legionnaires?" Her aura flared in the riotous color of fire just before dying out. Zadkiel was about to devastate her with a withering rebuttal—he was always the fierce one—but she was ready for him. "And you, Zadkiel, where is your honor? We're supposed to stand up for our Lord, not hand him over for thirty pieces of silver!"

Zadkiel moved as if to strike, something unheard of since the beginning of the world. Angels, even fallen angels, fought with the weapons of the spirit, not brute force. Mikael did not like what he was seeing. "Hold, Zadkiel!" he commanded. Zadkiel hesitated on the verge of an act that would relieve his frustration but open the door to chaos. He drew back. "And you, Uriel," Mikael continued, "please curb your acid tongue. You can see that none of us here is having an easy time of it."

Uriel turned her attention inward in order to establish some semblance of calm. "I'm ready," she said at length. "Give me your explanation, if you have one."

"You know there can be only one explanation," Mikael answered. "It's *his* will."

"But we're not his robots!" she shot back, her aura flaring again. "He says so himself!"

"No, we're not," Mikael replied gently, as if speaking to a child, "but I trust his sense of things more than I trust yours, or my own."

She eyed him haughtily. "Have you considered the possibility that he's so distraught at the loss of his queen that he doesn't know what he's doing?"

"You know better than anyone else what he suffered in the past. Your faith never wavered then."

"Those were different times," she said, "and he was a different man."

"But the same Christ!" Mikael proclaimed. "Or have even you come to doubt that?"

"No," she said quietly after a moment of self-searching. "I don't doubt that. But things are not as they were. The old order is passing, and who knows what is required of us in the new?"

A solemn silence fell over them. Uriel had not meant to say that. When an angel spoke in that way, without forethought or intention, the message was usually oracular. In her words all three heard the voice of God, and it drew them together as nothing else could. It was time for them to share their deepest fears.

"Politically, it's not an unwise move," Mikael observed. "Christians do have a sizable plurality in heaven as well as on earth."

"And the Hindus and Buddhists will most likely abstain," added Zadkiel, like a general marshaling his forces. "Of course, there's no love lost between the Muslims and Christians, but when it comes down to it, would Muhammad really join forces with Lucifer?"

"The Jews are negligible in number," Mikael continued the tally, "and the atheists and agnostics can be expected to be neutral."

"Do you really believe what you're saying?" Uriel exclaimed. "You know as well as I that if *his* hand is in this, it has nothing to do with politics!"

Mikael bowed his head. "You're right, of course," he admitted. "There's no telling where this business might lead."

"Oh, yes there is!" Uriel cried. "There's only one place it can lead — the cross! And I'm sick of it. I'm sick of standing by watching his agony. Have you ever thought that maybe there is no way to save the world, that maybe his creation is irredeemably corrupt but he's too much in love with it to destroy it?"

Mikael studied her intently. "So, you think he wants it to destroy him?"

Uriel was in tears. "I think it may be that this time our task is to save him, especially from himself."

"That can't be!" Zadkiel protested. "If we start doubting him, then whose authority are we to obey?"

"Perhaps no one's," replied Uriel. "Perhaps only that of our own hearts."

"Chaos!" Zadkiel whispered, dejectedly withdrawing into himself. Uriel likewise did not want to argue anymore. She hurried out of the council building and shot up into the blue empyrean where her tears could fall freely, her heart overflow in anguish without false hope, and her mind ponder the next move in a game that suddenly seemed without any rules.

* * *

When Rachel left the council chamber she had no idea where she was going. This was her first full day in the pleroma. She looked up from the chiseled escarpment to the azure sky, and her thoughts seemed to float like the cottony puffs of clouds that wafted across the horizon. She had no desire to return to the palace just yet, especially since there was no telling how long Lucifer would be closeted with Mikael, and the bustle of the Heavenly City did not suit her mood. So she wandered off in the direction of the mountains, their serene and majestic solitude beckoning to her troubled spirit.

For troubled she was, despite her show of strength before the Council. It had nothing to do with the upcoming trial. It was that monk! Or rather, to be more precise, it was his eyes. There was nothing particularly special about them. They were a common brown, and neither unusually large nor small. They were not the kind of eyes she would ordinarily have noticed. But at that instant, when the monk's eyes met hers, they were aflame with an intensity she had never seen in anyone's eyes before. Not even in those of the victims of Nazi torture. Not even in the eyes of those rare heroes who had sacrificed their own lives merely on the chance that doing so might help another to survive. There were no defenses at all in that monk's eyes. Then, upon sensing Lucifer's presence, she had looked away. When she looked back, there was nothing. It was still the same monk, at least to all appearances, and the eyes were still the same eyes; but the fire had gone out. Looking a little dazed, the friar excused himself as he slipped past and left the cathedral. Rachel had wanted to go after him, to ask him something, she didn't know what; but Lucifer was ready to take her to the Angelic Council and at the time that had seemed far more important.

Now, in her heart, she wasn't so sure. She ambled through a field of regal foxglove, scented like the chamomile tea her grandmother used to serve. The shiny, purple, bell-shaped flowers shone so metallic it seemed that they would chime. As she drifted toward the iris-hued mountains whose snow-frosted peaks, defying the laws of thermodynamics and gravity, jabbed like upside-down icicles into the warm and brilliant sky, she remembered those eyes again and felt a pang of fear. Was she afraid she would never encounter them again, or of what might happen if she did?

She still felt the emotional undercurrent leading her on. What could be out there? Was it simply her own spirit taking her to much needed solitude, or was it perhaps the holy spirit of the Almighty leading her to her destiny? But how could that be? Had she not just ranged herself on the side of the Adversary?

Then an amazing thought occurred to her. It was not the Lord she was fighting, it was a usurper. She was the true servant of the Lord, not all those pious mumbo-jumbos (the term she and her sister had coined in their childhood for the strictly observant and extremely self-righteous Jews of Baden). They had been taken in by the supreme con artist of all time! So she told herself, and all of a sudden did most firmly believe; but it seemed as yet impossible for her to feel it.

As she walked, the mountains disappeared behind a forest of weeping willows that seemed to spring up around her, their long, languid branches reaching out to her as if in sympathy for the plight of the lonely rebel she had become—no, that she had been all her life. Then the trees, the sky, everything vanished. It was as if she were in a trance, fixated upon those burning eyes. And then, miraculously, the eyes into which she had been melting were no longer in her imagination. They were right before her, as real, more real, than anything she had ever known. She could tell because they were no longer burning. Instead, they had become translucent pools of soft brown light into which she desired to sink and never return.

"Hello, Rachel," a voice said softly. It took her a moment to realize that the voice belonged to the owner of the eyes. And now she saw him, slight of build and short of stature, with fine, straight brown hair flowing over his shoulders and a light brown beard. His voice, though not deep, was resonant. His face was striking rather than handsome, broad, furrowed and deeply tanned, with high cheekbones like the ones she had seen in picture books on the American Indians. All this she noted quickly and then turned away. "How do you know my name?" she demanded.

"Everyone knows your name," he replied, amused. "You're the one who's put God on trial."

"Not the Lord," she objected, turning back to him. "Only one who wrongly claims to be the Lord."

"I don't rightly understand that," he said, a sliver of sarcasm, shocking by contrast, embedded in his otherwise gentle voice. "I thought you were after the one responsible for the genocide of our people."

She nodded soberly. "I am."

"I thought that you held God responsible because all power is in his hands, and therefore nothing happens in this universe without his permission."

Again she nodded, seeing where his logic was leading but unable to find a flaw in it.

"Then what is this about a usurper?" he queried. "Your grievance is against the one in charge, not one who only pretends to be."

"What if no one is in charge?" she rejoined. "What if God is not a person? What if we are all God?"

He turned his eyes away, considering. "So this usurper, in claiming to be the Lord, perhaps even in believing himself to be the Lord, lays a foundation of self-deception upon which the edifice of evil stands and will continue to stand until the foundation itself is destroyed. Is that it?"

Rachel suddenly felt ashamed. "You're laughing at me, sir. You show how little thought I've given to so weighty a matter."

"On the contrary," he answered with a smile of pure and disconcerting affection. "I simply put into words the logic of your actions. I offer clarification, that's all. When one lives from one's heart, no justification is possible or necessary."

She felt herself blush, but she did not avert her gaze.

"What brings you this way?" he asked, graciously changing the subject. "Out here visitors are a rarity."

These words caused Rachel to instinctively look around, and for the first time she noticed her surroundings and wondered how she could not have noticed them before. They were in a green, mossy field, here and there dotted by bright yellow dandelions, bordered on one side by an oak and birch tree forest, and on the other by an abrupt drop-off. She glanced over the edge and saw a steep cliff-face whose termination was shrouded in mist. Then she remembered her manners. "I'm sorry if I've intruded upon your solitude," she said, moving as if to leave. "In truth, I was seeking solitude myself."

He took her hand to prevent her going, sat her unresisting body down opposite him, and looked deeply into her eyes. "Perhaps we can be solitary together."

In very truth, she did not want to leave.

"I've seen you before," he said, as if plucking the words from her mind. "Today, in the cathedral."

"That *was* you!" she marveled. "And yet, it wasn't you."

"You're exactly right!" he laughed. "It was and was not me."

"But, how...?" she started to ask.

"I have my little tricks," he interjected. "We all of us here have our little tricks. Even you."

She bowed her head, feeling embarrassed, though she did not know why.

"You were with Lucifer, weren't you?" he asked, too nonchalantly.

"Yes," she replied, raising her head to look at him again, though not quite directly. For some reason, the question made her feel uncomfortable. "We're together."

"Is he here, too?" he asked, vaguely looking around.

"I meant that I'm staying with him, living with him." Again she blushed, though she had no idea why. It certainly was nothing of which she need feel ashamed.

"I see," he said, a hint of sadness in his voice. "So, you wish to be alone now?" he asked, rising. Now it was her turn to take his hand and reassure him.

"No, I like being here. I like... being with you. I feel I can trust you, that you're someone I can talk to." She had not known she was going to say that until it came out, and then she realized that it was true.

"So," he resumed the former topic, "you're putting God, I mean the usurper, on trial.".

She felt herself blush once more, something she never did, not since childhood. "You believe he is God, don't you?" she said. "You must think me awfully wicked."

"Not at all," he replied. "Merely honest. After all, you know the story of Job, don't you?"

"The man whom God tested," she said. "The one who wouldn't question or curse the Lord no matter what happened to him. That's not me!"

"On the contrary, that is you," he asserted, "if you only knew the story."

"Really?" she laughed, her eyes twinkling. "Tell me!"

"It's a serious story," he admonished in mock solemnity.

She managed what she hoped was an expression of appropriate gravity.

"Job was the wealthiest man in the East, and the most righteous. He had everything—huge flocks of sheep, goats, horses and camels, as well as seven handsome sons and three beautiful daughters."

"Why only three daughters?" she asked.

"Back then that was the optimum number," he replied. "Just enough to take care of the household without becoming a financial burden. Remember, Job had to provide their dowries when they married."

She was not sure this explanation satisfied her; but as nothing of great consequence hinged on the point, she nodded for him to continue. Though she knew the story already, it was refreshing to hear it told as a story and not a religious lesson.

"As I said," he went on, "Job was also righteous. No one ever had any complaints against him, and he had an open and charitable hand. He was so careful for the welfare of others that, when his children banqueted, as they did quite often, he would sacrifice to the Lord in atonement for sins they might have committed!"

Rachel smiled, and then suddenly sobered. "I had a grandfather who was like that," she said, feeling as if there were no need to add that he had perished in the camps. Her companion regarded her sorrowfully in silent communion. She felt the balm of his sympathy soothe her spirit. Then he continued the story.

"One day the Lord was looking down from Heaven when Satan returned from roaming about the earth."

"Lucifer," Rachel interrupted dutifully. "He prefers to be called Lucifer."

"Assuming we're talking about the same individual," he said.

"Aren't we?" she asked, her curiosity piqued.

"That's something you must decide for yourself," he answered. "This Satan was not the devil of the later tradition, but something like the chief prosecutor in the heavenly court. The Hebrew *shaitan* does mean 'adversary,' but here he's not the adversary of God, though he may be the adversary of man. He has a job to do, and he's doing it."

"Testing faith?" she hazarded.

"Something like that."

In his voice Rachel detected a slight but unmistakable note of impatience, as if he would rather she were silent and let the story unfold before her. She decided to be a little more sparing of questions, but she would not let him intimidate her.

"The Lord," he resumed, "asked Satan if in all his wanderings he had come upon anyone as faithful and righteous as Job. Satan said that Job was faithful only because the Lord had given him everything a man could want and planted around his blessed life an impenetrable hedge of protection. So the Lord permitted Satan to do anything to Job's family or possessions he pleased, only not to touch Job's person."

"A wager!" Rachel cried in a mixture of awe and anger. She jumped to her feet and turned away.

"Surely you knew that part of the story," his voice followed her softly. In the ensuing silence, from high off in the distance, she heard an eagle cry, piercing her heart. Tears coming to her eyes, she turned back round, seeking comfort. He put his arms around her and drew her to him. She had never felt so pure an embrace, not even from a child, and its innocence awakened her desire. She held her mouth up to his. "You can't escape your pain that way," he whispered. Coming from anyone else, such a remark would have struck her as patronizing and made of its speaker an eternal enemy. From him, it was the simple truth. She sat down once again, opposite him as before, only this time her hands in his. She still wanted to hold him, but even more to look into his eyes. "Do you think that's what God was doing with my people?" she asked, her eyes still wet but her voice steady. "Making a bet with the devil?"

"I think if that's what God was doing," he answered sternly, "then not only should he be tried, but flogged and crucified."

She listened closely, but heard no trace of humor or irony in his voice. "Then why did he do that to Job?" she insisted. "How could anyone worship such a monster?"

"It's a story," he replied. "What it's about, the pain and loss we all experience in life, is real enough; but the story itself, including the part about God making a bet with Satan, is fiction."

"But it's in the Bible!" she exclaimed, resisting the urge to rise and turn away again, but still letting go of his hands. "How can you say that? I thought you were a believer!"

He regarded her coolly, objectively, as if she were a psychological case study. Then he unexpectedly, provocatively, infuriatingly smiled. "The Greek word *biblia* means 'books.' The Bible contains many genres: history, poetry, moral philosophy, apocalyptic, even fiction. The Book of Job is fiction. But why does this upset you so?" he added earnestly, reclaiming her hand. "I thought you weren't a believer!"

"I'm a rebel, not an infidel," she declared, finding it impossible to keep pride out of her voice.

"I see," he said, his insufferable grin returning. "And you don't wish to be a rebel without a tyrant."

"You don't understand at all!" she cried contemptuously, on her feet before she realized it.

"I don't understand," he challenged, "or I don't agree?"

He slowly rose to his feet, the very movement saying to her that she was being as senseless as a jack-in-the-box. She could not take any more of his impudence, but she also could not leave him with the final word. As she glared at him, searching for the most hurtful rejoinder she could make before leaving and never seeing him again, she realized that was not really what she wanted at all. She wanted to stay with him, but why in heaven's name did he have to make her so angry? "Why should I agree to some outlandish theory just because you advocate it?" she blurted out acidly.

"Don't," he replied. "Look at the evidence." He began pacing back and forth, stopping every so often and stabbing a finger into the air for emphasis, the lawyer arguing his case before a jury of one. "One! Every historical book of the Bible locates itself in time, like *Exodus*, which begins four-hundred-and-something-odd-years after Joseph. Not so with Job. It begins like a fairy tale: "There once was a man in the land of Uz whose name was Job..."

He went on pacing without looking at her.

"Two! The book has a highly symmetrical structure, a poetic middle neatly sandwiched between a prose beginning and a prose ending in which all loose ends are neatly tied. History, by its very nature, is messy. Any ending in history is arbitrary. It's natural to wonder what happened to Moses and the Israelites after they received the *Torah* and built the sanctuary. Did they reach the promised land? Did they rebel again against the Lord? There's no question what happened to Job. He lived happily ever after, and there is nothing..."

She stopped him by taking his hand. "How can I judge what you're saying," she asked gently, "when I don't know the book?"

"How about this reason, then?" he said, looking into her eyes in mock defiance and smiling once again. "Who went up to the Court of Heaven to listen in on this little tête-à-tête between God and Satan?"

"But if God dictated the Bible..."

"That's what you believe?" he demanded scornfully.

"I never thought about it," she admitted, feeling at sea. He certainly could get worked up over little things!

"Oh, it means nothing to you," he said sarcastically, as if responding to her thought rather than her words. "You, who just a moment ago were ready to walk away."

Before this compelling truth she bowed her head, ready to listen to anything he had to say, no matter how offensive she found it. She had never met anyone who so insisted upon pointing out the obvious, nor who used the obvious to arrive at such surprising conclusions. It was terrifying, but also exciting. The world suddenly took on a whole new character. She did not know what depth of revelation might appear in anything and everything she had previously taken for granted. She let him take her hands again and sit her down.

"Alright," she said, "the Book of Job is fiction. What difference does that make? God still inflicts suffering upon innocent people."

"You don't know that," he replied.

Again she was angry, but she willed herself to remain still and let the power of her feeling come out in her voice. "I don't know that?" she exclaimed. "I've seen friends, family, little children, even babies tortured, beaten, shot, gassed, and immolated or thrown into mass graves! I don't know that?"

"You think the Nazis were taking orders from God?" he asked.

"They thought so!" she replied.

"But do you?"

"Of course not!" she admitted. "But he permitted the carnage. What's the difference?"

He was about to answer, but then caught himself and smiled. "You're right," he said. "God is responsible for what goes on in his universe. Perhaps there are mitigating or even justifying circumstances, but you must come to see that for yourself. The only point I wanted to make is that we don't have to take the bet seriously to take the book seriously. Clearly, you already know that."

He paused, his face a question mark. She nodded for him to continue.

"Job lost everything: his wealth, children and health. Job's friends came to comfort him. But when Job cried out to God that he'd done nothing to deserve these troubles, that God didn't give a damn about justice, that he even laughed at the suffering of the innocent, it was too much for them."

"Job said that?" she asked, marveling.

"Read the book," he said.

"Why was I never told that?" she wondered, as much to herself as to him.

"People hear what they want to hear and read what they want to read. Hardly anyone sees what's really there."

He looked deep into her eyes as he said this, and she returned his gaze. It was so different, so much more than seeing into the inner life of the people she had encountered in the Heavenly City. She felt as if she were diving into a bottomless ocean of light.

"Job's friends leap to God's defense," he resumed, not turning his eyes away. "At first they're polite, suggesting that his misfortunes are the result of his children's transgressions. But soon they find his complaints against the Almighty intolerable. They declare the Lord has only visited on him the punishment his sins deserve."

"I thought you said he was righteous," she said.

"God knows that, Satan knows that, and the reader knows that," he replied, "but Job's friends don't know that. Besides, what do you expect from the lowly mortals? If Job is right, if he's done nothing to deserve his fate, then the same thing could happen to them. Then there's no rhyme or reason to life, all is moral chaos, and the abyss opens beneath their feet."

He paused as if he knew the telling effect these words would have on her. Just like in the camps, she could feel her heart pounding in her chest like a jackhammer. "Doesn't the Lord favor Job in the end?" she finally managed to say.

"Yes," he replied, "but not before he gives his faithful servant a good drubbing. In response to Job's complaint, the Lord appears to him in a terrifying vision, displaying his limitless power and challenging Job to match his strength. In the most beautiful poetry of the entire book, and its most exquisite sarcasm, he beats Job down, reducing him to groveling for forgiveness for having dared to question divine justice."

"The omnipotent bully!" she cried.

"Yes," he suddenly frowned, "or simply the author's way of saying that, whether we like it or not, we're utterly at the mercy of the living God."

"I refuse to debase myself before him, no matter what he does to me!" she declared, her dark eyes flashing like black lightning. "So how am I like Job?"

"Do you remember the end of the story?" he asked.

"Job got everything back in the end, and then some," she replied.

"I won't be bribed!"

"That's the interesting part," he said. "It wasn't a bribe, or a reward for repenting. The Lord scolded the three friends for not speaking rightly of him, *as his servant Job had done.*"

She pondered. "But Job's friends defended God, while Job attacked him."

"Precisely!" He smiled again.

"So the book contradicts itself," she concluded.

They fell silent, looking into each other's eyes, and she felt that what passed between them in that boundless moment had nothing to do with Job.

"Not necessarily," he finally answered, but now she felt two lines of communication open between them, one through words and the other through their eyes, and both conversations could be carried on at the same time without one getting mixed up with the other. "My rule of thumb is that, whenever one encounters something that doesn't make sense on the face of it, always search for the deepest meaning the text, situation, person or whatever will bear. And Job himself points the way. Earlier in the debate he proclaims that not only is he not godless for questioning the Lord's justice, but his friends are godless for defending the Lord with falsehood and without understanding."

Again, he gave her time to think.

"So, even in God's own eyes, Job is right for attacking God and his friends are wrong for defending God? It makes no sense!"

"Doesn't it?" he countered, his own eyes flashing now. "Suppose a couple has an argument, and the husband goes away in a huff. While he's gone, a few of his friends drop by, notice the wife is upset and ask her what's wrong. She explains, and they comfort her by saying she has nothing to worry about because her husband couldn't have been serious and really didn't mean it. Upon his return she embraces him lovingly, he looks at her quizzically, and she tells him what his friends told her. How would you feel if you were that man?"

"Angry," she replied.

"I wager you would." Again that lovely, infuriating grin. "And why?"

"Because, even if they were right, they had no business speaking for him, especially to his wife."

"I agree," he said. "Who is anyone to insert himself into this most intimate of human relationships, that of husband and wife? But the relationship between God and one of his children is even more intimate. So who is anyone, friend of Job or otherwise, to insert himself between any of us and God?"

From far away again came the eagle's cry, almost as if the bird were purposely supplying dramatic emphasis.

"I see," she mumbled, and then fell into deep thought. Her mind was racing to make connections so quickly that she herself could not keep track of its movements. "But that's what religious people do all the time!" she cried as it hit her. "Even the rabbis!"

"*Even* the rabbis?" he asked sharply.

"Especially the rabbis," she corrected herself.

"And not just rabbis," he continued, drawing out the logic of the story of Job to its simple, inexorable, and yet startling conclusion, "but also priests, ministers, and all manner of evangelical so-and-sos. Don't they regard it as their sacred duty to defend God no matter what, to personally make sure that people think the right way and feel the right way about God?"

She nodded, dumbstruck not so much by his argument, as by the fact that it was coming from the lips of a believer—far more of a believer, she sensed, than she herself had ever been, even in her pious childhood, even before the camps.

"And what's the result?" he cried, his voice full of profound anger and contempt, though not, she was certain, for her. "Suppose you were about to marry, and you vowed to yourself never to have an unkind thought or feeling about your new husband..."

She laughed, despite the gravity of the subject. That certainly was not her!

"...and you kept the vow. What would happen to your marriage?"

"It certainly would not work!" she laughed again.

"It would be still-born, dead before it ever came to be," he declared, almost as if she had not answered at all. Never, she thought with carefully guarded amusement, not even among the undergraduate philosophy students at the university, had she seen anyone display such passion for an abstract point of logic. Or, she realized with sudden sobriety, was it so abstract?

"Why?" he went on rhetorically. "Because you would not be relating to your husband, but to your idea of how you should relate to your husband, and that's altogether different. You could imagine your husband doing the most outrageous things simply to get from you a genuinely personal response. Children do that to their parents all the time because parents, as a rule, do not relate to their children, but to their idea of how they should relate to their children, and that's not the same thing at all."

"And so too with God?" she offered.

"And so too with God. People form an idea of God in their heads so they don't have to deal with the reality of God in their lives."

"And Job refuses to do that?" she added.

"Yes, Job refuses to do that," he affirmed, "and so do you."

"One thing I've noticed," she said quietly, inwardly reveling in this new-found intellectual intimacy, "is that people would rather decide in their heads that life is all caviar and champagne, or nothing but a stinking cesspool, than live the mystery of life as it unfolds before them."

He looked at her with such undisguised admiration that she wondered if he were falling in love with her. But no, that could not be. He was so infinitely wise and deep and she so merely clever — what could he see in her?

"And within them," he added softly.

They gazed long into each other's eyes. She knew she should be going, but she could not bring herself to leave. The sweetness, the peace, the communion was too deep. Gradually, however, as the day passed into twilight and the twilight into night, her eyes grew heavy and she slipped away into sleep. When she awoke, she lay upon the couch where she and Lucifer had spent the night before and the Light-Bearer was smiling down upon her. She felt the warmth of his passion and drew him to her. As they made love, again only with the briefest of kisses, she tried to keep her eyes open, for when she closed them she saw *his* eyes, only this time they were filled with unspeakable sorrow.

* * *

When James had composed himself sufficiently, he arose and led the way out of what now seemed the cavernous jaws of the council building, through a tunnel-like, deserted path whose black walls were made of the night, back to Wendell's townhouse. Neither man said a word, and neither sought nor wished to intrude upon the other's thoughts. Foreboding stifled all other emotion. When they arrived, Wendell left James in the study, performed his nightly ablutions, put on his nightshirt, and settled into bed with a book he picked randomly from the shelves. It turned out to be a dime-novel mystery by an author of whom he had never heard, but the blend of off-color, back-alley witticisms and fast-paced, predictable melodrama suited his mood perfectly. He was already half way through the volume when James appeared in the doorway. He had not even unbuttoned his collar.

"They're here," he said.

For an instant Wendell thought James was referring to the heavies in the novel. Then he felt irritation. Confound it! Perhaps these little rituals of daily life, like eating, bathing, and relaxing before bedtime, were not necessary in the pleroma, but they damn well made life here a whole lot more tolerable. Why did something always have to be going on? Were there no limits?

The ticking of the grandfather clock soothed his nerves, enabling Wendell to keep his complaints to himself, or so he thought. But when he lifted his eyes from the book, James looked as if he had just been slapped. Not for the first time since his arrival, Wendell thought that whoever had brought him here had made a ghastly mistake.

"*Who* is here?" he asked, mustering at least a show of concern for his friend's all-too-evident anxiety.

"Lucifer and Mikael," James replied stiffly, the weathervane nose blushing red, mouth open and one eye twitching. The poor chap was petrified.

Wendell knew that, if those two were involved, the matter was important. He laid the book down immediately, not bothering to mark his place, changed back into his suit, and followed James down to the parlor. Mikael was planted in the center of the room, his violet aura almost blinding to Wendell, though it did not seem to bother anyone else. Lucifer, on the other hand, reclined casually on the sofa, one arm crooked back so that his hand could support his head, the other draped lazily over the side and resting on the floor. Once again Wendell noted how infernally attractive the devil was, if indeed that term could properly be applied to one so manifestly human.

As soon as James and Wendell entered, Mikael spoke. It seemed that angels were accustomed to coming immediately, even brutally, to the point. This was a trait Wendell had always admired in himself but found hard to stomach in others, perhaps because their points were usually at odds with his own and it left no time for formulating a defensive strategy.

"We've worked out the details of the trial," the chief of the angels declared. "Our agreement includes a role for each of you. You," he said softly, his aura reaching out to James, "already know your part."

"No, I do not!" protested James. "I know nothing about any of it."

Wendell thought he could actually see a sad and knowing smile illumine Mikael's countenance. "You have been told," he insisted gently, as if he would let James forget about it if only he could.

"He was joking!" James declared with a vehemence Wendell never imagined the professor would permit himself in talking with an angel.

"You know he was not," Mikael asserted.

"But why me?" James cried. "Why not Kierkegaard, or Pascal, or Dostoevsky, if you want somebody modern? I, for one think too much is made of modernity. Why not Augustine, or even Paul? For that matter, why doesn't he defend himself?" James turned his back on Mikael and threw himself into an easy chair.

"He will speak when his time comes," the chief of the angels replied, "but he will never defend himself."

"My brother was always expert at logic-chopping," Lucifer remarked.

Mikael ignored him. "Those whom you've named have developed a greater philosophical depth, it's true," he said to James, "but at the cost of intellectual flexibility."

"In other words," Lucifer added, without moving any part of his splendid anatomy other than his lips, "he wants someone who can dance around the issues."

Mikael refused to grace Lucifer's sarcasm with so much as a glance, but it was clear the barb had struck home. He continued to speak to James, but his aura flashed sharply at Lucifer. "He wants someone who won't gouge deeper the ruts humans have worked into their minds, but who will strike out into new territory. You must think as no man has ever thought."

Lucifer smiled sardonically. "To successfully defend your client," he said to James, "you must think as no man ever could."

"Client?" Wendell echoed, not solely out of curiosity but also to relieve the tension building between the angel of light and the fallen one.

"The Lord has asked William to speak on his behalf at the trial," Mikael explained.

"You mean to conduct his defense?" Wendell said in astonishment. "But he has no legal training!"

James sank more deeply into the easy chair, as if he wished to be lost in it forever. "That's what I told him," he said, his voice eloquent of misery. "I'm not fit for the task. I am not worthy of the honor."

Mikael moved closer to James and embraced him with his radiance, which now was flecked with a sparkling green. The effect was subtle but undeniable. James perked up immediately. "Why not let him be the judge of that?" the angel said tenderly.

"Yes, he too said that," James answered calmly, the blood no longer gushing from an open wound. "But Holmes here seems to be of a different mind. Perhaps we should all defer to him." He smiled at Wendell. "After all, he's the professional."

Wendell was too pleased at the lift in his friend's spirits to take offense at the sarcasm. He went to James and took his hand. "This isn't earth," he said. "Given your acute and industrious mind, you probably understand as much about the mysteries of this place as anyone. I'm sure you'll do a fine job."

James regarded Wendell quizzically, as if searching out the irony hidden in this praise; but when it became clear that no punch line was in the offing he squeezed Wendell's hand in gratitude. "It will be the greatest ordeal I've ever faced," he whispered.

"It will be an honor to face so brilliant an opponent," Lucifer chimed in unexpectedly, rising to a sitting position apparently out of respect. No sarcasm was to be found here either. Evidently the dark angel really meant it. His contempt was reserved, it seemed, for the angel of light. The better Wendell got to know Lucifer, the more his respect for him grew. He knew James felt otherwise, but for the life of him he could not understand why. At any rate, except for a brief honeymoon as young men, he and James had rarely seen eye to eye about anything. Maybe this trial was not such a bad thing after all. Change was the very medium of progress on earth. Why should it be any different in the pleroma? Furthermore, as far as leaders went—and he had known quite a few in his day—one could do a lot worse than Lucifer.

As if tracking Wendell's thoughts, Lucifer now turned to him. "Professor James will be defense counsel," he said, "and I the prosecuting attorney. The souls of heaven will be the jury, but our court still lacks something."

Wendell knew that tone of voice. He had heard it before every great advancement in his life. "I have neither experience nor knowledge of your judicial system," he said evenly.

"And Professor James has no legal experience whatsoever," Lucifer countered. If we require no curriculum vitae in his case, why should we in yours? Besides, we have no judicial system here. We've no system of any sort. All is 'divine providence.' That's wishful thinking for haphazard and chance. This administrative chaos is one of the things this trial is intended to remedy."

Now that he had been elevated to the level of judicial impartiality, Wendell felt obliged to ignore this partisan jibe. "How much time do I have to prepare?" he asked, not the slightest doubt in his mind that he would be up to the task of officiating at the heavenly tribunal.

"Prepare?" Lucifer laughed good-naturedly. What is there to prepare?"

"Proceedings begin in the morning," Mikael proclaimed. "We simply ask that you draw upon the wisdom you've gleaned from decades of judicial experience to ensure a fair and orderly trial. There are no hard and fast rules of evidence, nor any set protocol."

Lucifer laughed even louder. "Yes, you make up the rules as you go along! That's a magistrate's dream, is it not?"

Or a magistrate's nightmare, Wendell almost replied. "I will have supreme authority over the conduct of the trial?" he answered instead, not asking a question but stating a condition.

"Absolutely," assured Mikael, his aura passing from purple to a deep blue. Lucifer likewise nodded his assent.

"You don't think it irregular that the presiding magistrate and defense counsel are close friends?" Wendell queried.

"My dear Holmes," Lucifer replied in a bright and intimate tone, "I like to think of you both as my friends as well. So shall we keep it all in the family?"

Wendell hesitated. Was Lucifer hoping that the regard in which Wendell obviously held him would bias the judge in favor of the prosecution? Or rather, was bringing up their mutual admiration Lucifer's way of setting it aside so that each could concentrate upon his role in the upcoming drama that was far bigger than them both? Finally, he nodded in acquiescence.

"It's settled, then." Mikael pronounced the words like a benediction.

After exchanging a few more pleasantries with their hosts, the angels departed. Once again Wendell bade James good night, and then retired to his bedroom and the dime novel. There was much he would have liked to discuss with the professor, much he should have discussed already had the latter not been so obstinate in his mind-set. Under the circumstances, however, he felt it improper to have any but absolutely necessary communication with his friend. Professional ethics now came down like a wall between them. He hoped James understood.

* * *

Will left Holmes' townhouse right after Mikael and Lucifer. He was grateful that Holmes had not tried to engage him in further conversation. He felt that, instead of words, he would have produced only tears. His friend was still caught up in his earthly habits and obviously felt he needed a good night's sleep before taking on the momentous business of the morrow.

The night was soft and brooding, the empyrean distantly brilliant. There was an odor of honeysuckle in the air. Or was that merely nostalgia for his youth? In the pleroma, Will could never be sure what came from himself and what from outside of himself. He could have flashed immediately to his farm, but he felt too keyed up to do anything but walk. So he headed for the mountains that, except for the interruption of a crystalline lake, nearly surrounded the Heavenly City. He walked for what seemed like hours before coming to the foothills. One could do that in the pleroma: make a journey in an instant that on earth would have taken days, and stretch out what ordinarily would have been a stroll into a prolonged hike.

Will breathed in the air with pleasure. It was actually crisp, like the invigorating New England autumnal atmosphere. Change was definitely coming to the pleroma. His heart teeter-tottered between excitement and foreboding.

Will did not hear *him* approach — probably there had been nothing to hear — but he knew when he arrived. "Why are you afraid?" came his voice from behind, tinged with sad amusement. "You're so much more brilliant than I!"

Will halted but hesitated to turn around. He knew that if he did he would melt into those eyes, and there would be nothing more to say. He had to guard himself against those loving eyes. "You always ask the hardest thing, don't you?" he finally managed to whisper, his voice breaking with emotion.

A long silence. What could the Lord answer to that? That it was true and not true? That his Father always asked the hardest thing of him? Will turned around. Yeshua smiled and squatted in the middle of the path, with his hands inviting Will to follow suit. Will sat cross-legged on the earth. The ground was hard, harder than it had ever felt before. Will finally broke the silence. "For now, forget about how I feel. You're making a great error, entrusting your fate to my hands."

"There's only one to whom I entrust my fate," Yeshua replied, as Will knew he would.

Then He is in error, Will felt like saying, but he dared not. "I've no choice then," he sighed, hating himself for the self-pity he was unable not to feel.

Yeshua smiled again, but the smile did not dispel his air of sadness. "Of course you have a choice," he affirmed. "Each and every one of us has a choice."

"You know I could never refuse you!" cried Will, rising to his feet in anger. He glared at Yeshua. For the first time he understood how people could hate this man.

Yeshua also arose, though much more slowly, not flinching or even blinking at Will's furious gaze. "That's exactly what you're working yourself up to do now," he remarked evenly. The truth in what he said only stoked Will's fire.

"I won't do it!" he shouted. "I can't do it! I can't bear such a burden. I'm a thinker, a theoretician. I've never been a man of action. With all the great saints up here at your beck and call, there's no need for me!"

Yeshua lowered his head and whispered, almost inaudibly, "You can't know how great the need!" Then, as if remembering himself, he looked straight into Will's eyes. The sweetness of honeysuckle came to him again, and the stars were all of a sudden unbearably bright against the black backdrop of the mountain-pierced sky. "Remember," Yeshua said earnestly, "if tomorrow you choose to help me, my spirit will be with you. Remember also, when you find yourself lost in confusion and doubt, that forever and in all things, here and everywhere, it always has been and eternally will be about love. Love, and nothing but love."

This pronouncement made Will angry again. "If it's about love," he spat out bitterly, "then why have you fixed upon me? I'm no exemplar of love! If anything, I'm a walking textbook on failure in love."

"In some ways," Yeshua replied quietly, "the failure knows more than the exemplar."

"Hogwash!" Will cried, but then, all unexpectedly, a profound peace settled over his heart.

"You're right," said Yeshua. "You can only go so far." He clasped Will's hands and looked into his eyes. "But when you've gone as far as you can—which, by the way, will be much further than you think—I'll come to complete the work."

Will knelt and bowed his head, the dark earth unusually rugged against his knees. Yeshua placed a hand upon Will's crown, and he felt the blessing come into his heart. His anger melted away in the warmth of Yeshua's trust. "But why not do it yourself from the beginning?" he asked meekly. "Then you would be assured of its being done right."

"You know I never defend myself," he replied. "If you wish to defend me, do so. If not, not. When it's time to go on the offensive," he smiled, "I'll be there." And with that, he was gone.

Will sank back against the gnarled trunk of an oak and sat for a long time in utter stillness, not one thought passing through his head.

Then he arose and spent the rest of the night wandering through the mountains. Owls hooted, stars twinkled, and a capricious breeze played in the branches of the trees, but he hardly noticed his surroundings. Idea after idea welled up from the inner recesses of his heart. He was beginning to understand the why and wherefore of it all. He was also beginning to realize that he was not, never had been, and never would be alone.

PART II: THE TRIAL

Chapter 5

From its beginning—if indeed it had a beginning, lost in the abyss of time—the pleroma had never had a dawning such as this one of the day of judgment. *There was a sun.* As it came creeping over the mountains in a jagged crimson line, word spread rapidly, so that everyone, even those who had been sleeping or otherwise engaged, beheld the splendor of its advent.

Wendell too saw the glory of aurora's coming. He had slept very little, and yet felt rested and alert. Since everything in the pleroma was new to him, he was not particularly surprised at the colorful spectacle of the sunrise or the climactic appearance of the flaming yellow orb in the sky. But when he learned of its novelty, he understood why everyone else was. What interested him now, however, was the fact that he could gaze upon it without perceptible damage to his organs of vision. He made the discovery quite by accident as he drank in the beauty of the dawn, something he had done often while on earth, and suddenly realized that the sun was well up over the horizon. He had been looking at it for some time without noticing because it caused no discomfort to his eyes. Just another indication, he mused, of the relativity of natural law.

As the pulsating light flooded the atmosphere, Wendell remembered that he was to be in court that day—a court unlike any over which he had presided on earth, unlike any the universe had ever known. He decided that, no matter how atypical the proceedings promised to be, his morning ritual was still in order. So he bathed, clipped his moustache and shaved his whiskers, and dressed in his dark-gray suit. These things were not necessary—he could have stepped out the door and in a supernatural twinkling become equally presentable—but they initiated the psychological process whereby every workday on earth he had metamorphosed from the shy, sensitive and insecure Wendell, Jr. to the magisterial Justice Holmes.

He was just completing his toilet and wondering, since James was nowhere in sight, how he was to find his way to the court, when he felt their presence in the parlor and immediately went down to see. Half-a-dozen angels had been detailed as his escort. Wendell was flattered, but also a bit uncomfortable with all the attention. He was accustomed to walking to work with at most a secretary or fellow justice to keep him company. Nevertheless, he could not very well refuse, especially since he had no idea where to go.

Once outside, he found himself floating above the city in the midst of these heavenly beings. Surprisingly, he felt no fear of falling, a sensation with which he had become intimately acquainted while mountain-climbing in his youth. He was also surprised to see that the city was bordered on one side by a "lake," he supposed it could be called, though it was far more regular in shape than any natural body of water he had ever seen, as well as much bluer. It was almost a perfect square, with the part extending away from the city slightly longer. Or perhaps that was just a trick of perspective. What amazed Wendell the most was that this sizable landmark had hitherto escaped his notice. Was this another lesson in the relativity of perception? The angels headed straight out over the lake, in the middle of which there suddenly appeared an island. Wendell did not see it until they were almost upon it. Had it, and perhaps the lake as well, materialized out of thin air, or had he simply overlooked it? He regarded both hypotheses as equally preposterous until he reminded himself that he was in a place where literally anything could happen.

The island, rocky and wooded on the fringe but one vast, green meadow in the interior, seemed to grow as they drew nigh, and this was definitely not a trick of perspective. When the center of the grassy field lay directly below them and they were yet what Wendell judged to be two thousand feet high, the island filled the entire horizon. The Heavenly City could no longer be seen, if indeed it still

THE JUDGMENT OF CHRIST

existed. The discomfiting thought crossed Wendell's mind that the entire population of the pleroma was to be marooned on this vast, water-bound plain until the business for which they gathered was brought to a conclusion.

As he and his escort glided slowly to the ground, Wendell could see that indeed all the souls of the pleroma must have been there. The size of the crowd was staggering. Even if attendance were not compulsory, he reflected, certainly no one wished to miss the show since, as far as Wendell could gather from his short time in the pleroma, nothing much ever really happened here. James had mentioned that occasionally there would be a new arrival or departure, a soul disappearing and going no one knew where, if anywhere. For the most part, however, people went about doing whatever they felt like doing and letting everyone else do likewise. There was never any crime, since everyone could have whatever he wanted simply by wishing for it, and one could enter hallucinatorily into any film or artwork to satisfy one's craving for adventure. There had never been a legal proceeding of any sort, let alone one in which the defendant was the Lord himself, in all the history of the pleroma. Wendell could tell from the air of festive excitement that, if they were trapped on this protean landmass, no one really cared.

Protean, indeed! As Wendell and his escort touched down, the spot where they landed sank, creating a gently concave amphitheater that enabled everyone to see what went on at center-stage. The earth was matted with soft, spongy grass, enlivened here and there with a riot of wildflowers from every quarter, it seemed, of the globe. Wendell could make out delicate white jasmine, as much by its fragrance as form; hearty, fiery Himalayan cinquefoil, which he had gotten to know in the Alps; evanescent morning glory, whose trumpeting petals, at least on earth, rarely lasted more than a day; and a host of other flora whose names he did not know, mixed in with the common dandelion, lily, and wild rose. There was also an occasional shrub or tree, mostly hardwood like maple or oak, possibly because, unlike numerous pines, these grew upward in bulk, thus not obscuring anyone's view, and also because they were more accommodating to those who wished to climb and witness the proceedings from a high perch. The effect was one of artfully artless and wholly natural beauty.

Everywhere people lounged about in this spontaneously generated, geometrically shaped English garden, keeping mostly to their own kind. Those of modern Western attire, though many in absolute numerical terms, were in a distinct minority, as were the almost naked savages. Between these two cultural extremes Wendell spotted, among others, desert nomads hooded in white or dark burnooses, men of the eastern Mediterranean dressed in ankle-length caftans, European peasants in the colorful folk dress worn these days only on holiday, East Indian women in their enticing saris, and sub-Saharan tribesmen sporting ferocious or mysterious looking masks and brightly colored feathers. There were also aristocratic Europeans, quite a few as a matter of fact, dressed in the hose and doublets, gowns and lace of a more innocently ostentatious era. Neither dress nor period alone, however, could account entirely for the pattern of association. Larger groupings were also evident, but without apparent rhyme or reason. Wendell was certain they had something to do with a common faith, but except in the case of the Westerners, he could not say how. What were exquisitely manicured Chinese mandarins, for example, doing with straw-hatted, barefoot Indochinese peasants? Why were so many abundantly dressed Arabs consorting with Negroes clothed mostly in body paint?

James would have been of great help here in sorting out the various cultural and religious traditions. Unfortunately, religion had been a subject whose study Wendell had thought a waste of time. That was one of the differences that drove Will and him apart in the first place. Right now Wendell would have literally sold his soul to know what these diverse members of *Homo sapiens*, ranging from naked and tattooed aborigines with rings around their women's necks and bones through their noses to elegantly turbaned and bejeweled sheiks and Continental dandies in hose and powdered wigs, were thinking. He had an almost overpowering desire to leave the center and wander through the crowd. But it was not his part, Wendell reminded himself, to pander to the populace, even if they were the jury. They were to follow his rules, not he theirs.

But what rules?

He had spent a considerable part of the night thinking about the issue. Mikael and Lucifer had given him carte blanche. One thing of which he was certain was that standard judicial procedure would not do here, and neither would standard rules of evidence. No artificial bounds could be placed upon the vast issues at stake. Lucifer's sarcasm had not been wide of the mark. Wendell would have to make up the rules as he went along. With that realization came an almost unbearable excitement. When James finally appeared and tried to mumble conspiratorially something about one of Lucifer's lieutenants and his liaison with the queen of heaven, Wendell caught the names and descriptions but then stopped his ears to any further gossip. He could not allow his magisterial disinterest to be compromised. For the first time in a long and distinguished judicial career, he need concern himself with only one thing: justice!

* * *

The moss felt deliciously chill against the warm earth, and the early morning air blew fresh and clean upon her tingling skin. Veiled and anonymous, Mara sat among her own people in the midst of the crowd, but for the first time since leaving Yeshua she was alone. Even when Azazael was away from his estate, there were always attendants with whom to gossip and frolic—delightful little imps whose spontaneous impulses, like those of Azazael, magically complemented her own. Never had she imagined that life could be so rich, so full! With Yeshua she had always felt like an emotional leper, a spiritual lightweight, always lacking in some inner depth that lay forever beyond her reach. Now she knew that it had all been a sham, that this "king of heaven" was a charlatan—the most contemptible charlatan of all, because he had succeeded in fooling not only most of the souls of the pleroma, but also himself.

Now Azazael had a crucial part to play in the unmasking of this pretender, and she was proud of him. It was only fitting that he engage in this glorious crusade with his entire entourage accompanying him. He had asked if she wished him to leave a few of the littler ones behind for her company and amusement, but she had declined the offer. Besides, she wanted to be free to concentrate upon whatever emotions the trial brought up in her, as she knew it would. There was still a great deal of feeling for her former mate, no matter how distant they had grown from each other, and she needed to experience it so as to be finally free.

Everyone around her was talking about the sun. She herself was surprised at how little surprise she felt at its appearance. A new day was dawning, so why not a new sun? Like Yeshua, the pleroma had been closed in upon itself long enough. It was time for everyone and everything to open to the cleansing forces of nature, the only real God. She welcomed the prospect of wind and rain, thunder and storm unconnected with the moods and whims of any being. There was something bracing and liberating in it all, and she had Azazael and his comrade Lucifer to thank!

* * *

Attired in an old-fashioned business suit rather than judge's robes, and looking increasingly hot and uncomfortable as the sun climbed higher into the sky, the Honorable Oliver Wendell Holmes stood at the concave center of the bowl-shaped field surveying the assembly with a calm and noble bearing. As if at a prearranged signal, as he opened his mouth to speak everyone fell silent. Protocol appeared to be no problem here in the pleroma. Everyone seemed to know what each moment required.

Rachel, by contrast, was dressed for the weather, though that had not been her intention. She was once again clothed in a sari, this one of a lavender hue. This time she had chosen, or rather, with Lucifer's technical assistance, designed it herself so that she could hide out among the south Asian women, away from her own people, who she knew would give her no peace. The slender, brown-skinned women had been chatting excitedly among themselves about the possibility of seeing their beloved Krishna this day. They kept their distance from the fair-skinned stranger, and that suited Rachel well. She did not wish to be distracted. As Holmes began to speak, she listened intently. She was not going to miss any part of this trial, and she would be ready to say her piece when the time arrived. She felt as if the fate of the entire universe were at stake here today. Judging from the instant silence and unwavering attention of the audience, so did everyone else.

The great American magistrate spoke simply, even humbly, of his duty to ensure the fairness and order of any judicial proceeding, but especially of this one in which the defendant had voluntarily submitted to the judgment of his fellow citizens of the pleroma. On the other hand, he declared, the case must be judged on its own merits, without regard for concerns extraneous to the issues at hand. In other words, it did not matter how much one liked or even worshiped the defendant, or for that matter hated and despised him. Everyone who had substantive testimony or pertinent argument to give would have the opportunity to do so, but he would not tolerate one iota of empty rhetoric in his court.

Moreover, insofar as they were unnecessary for the maintenance of order and decorum, the judge had also decided to dispense with the legal forms and customs with which he was familiar. For one thing, there were souls on the jury—and everyone except the defendant, angels and officers of the court was part of the jury— from every place and time in the history of the world. To adopt a particular type of legal proceeding from a particular culture, no matter how much the presiding magistrate held it in favor, doubtless would cause incalculable confusion. More importantly, legal forms were designed to demarcate a case, to extract from all the minutiae of actual human existence the judicially relevant details. Since the present court was dealing with issues not only of time and circumstance but also of destiny and eternity, any attempt to place an arbitrary definition upon the topics and manner of discussion would turn the trial into a cosmic farce. No, as judge he would have to rule *ad hoc*. If anyone objected to this approach, he would step down and let someone abler and wiser take his place. No one objected. Indeed, as far as Rachel could tell, if anyone had felt misgivings about the appointment of this American jurist, they were now put to rest.

Next Lucifer rose to speak and Justice Holmes acknowledged him with a nod. "Your Honor," Lucifer bowed, "the prosecution is ready to conduct its case, but would like to put a question to the defense counsel just to be certain that there is no confusion as to the identity of the defendant."

Both Lucifer and the magistrate looked toward a full-bearded, white-haired, red-nosed man sitting near them, dressed in the same mildly archaic style as Justice Holmes, but the object of their sudden attention remained impassive. "Professor James," the judge prompted the man, "is defense counsel ready to proceed?"

So this was the famous William James! Rachel had read his work as a student, even though by then it was considered outdated, and found its clarity and humanity a relief from the pontificating textbooks penned by her professors. So, he was defense counsel! She wondered if he really sided with the impostor, or if he had taken the case only because no one else would. She had not known he was a barrister as well as psychologist. As she looked at him, however, with his rosy complexion, wintry beard and kind, thoughtful, almost opalescent eyes, he seemed like an ascetic version of the Dutch Saint Nick whose annual visitation the Christian children of the world so eagerly awaited. He certainly was not the type to play devil's advocate, especially in a trial like this. His face was too honest, his entire manner too vulnerable. He was not, never had been, and never could be a lawyer.

Professor James finally stood up and faced Lucifer. "What's your question?" he asked, his confident voice belying the insecurity—or was it anxiety? – in his eyes.

"Since, for the moment at least, the defendant is being tried *in absentia*," — Lucifer's voice clearly insinuated that the impostor was too cowardly to appear—"I wish to confirm the terms of the trial as well as the extent of the actions for which he accepts responsibility."

Professor James nodded him on.

"The defendant admits that he is the one known to history both as Yahweh, lord of the Israelites, and as Jesus Christ, alleged incarnation of the creator god?"

"Yes, that's so," Professor James readily replied.

Rachel did not have to see the Jewish section of the crowd to know how her people were taking this admission, although everyone else, including the non-Christians, seemed to accept it as a matter of course.

"And the defendant agrees to abandon any pretense to being lord of heaven, or lord of anything, if the verdict goes against him?"

"Yes, that's also so," James assented.

The psychic equivalent of a murmur ran through the crowd. No one actually said anything, but the astonishment was palpable. Everyone had heard that the pretender had staked his authority on this trial, but now no one had any choice but to believe it. After all, was not the great Mikael himself, along with the rest of the Angelic Council and its attendants, hovering over the field of judgment without a sign of objection?

"Let everyone remember what the scales of justice hold in the balance here today!" Lucifer cried. Justice Holmes' face darkened and his mouth opened as if he were about to rebuke the chief prosecutor for such an outburst, but then he seemed to think better of it and remained silent. "Let everyone also remember," Lucifer continued in a more restrained manner, "that the prosecution's willingness to do battle with the defendant on his own terms in no way implies that we accept his claim to spiritual authority, past or present. In the interest of maintaining peace and unity within the pleroma, we simply feel that the best way to dethrone this tyrant is to reduce him, by his very own logic, to absurdity."

"And what if you lose, Satan?" thundered an angry voice from the mammoth Christian section of the crowd. Rachel turned and saw a thin, red-bearded, imperious man with close-cropped hair wearing, incongruously to her eye, a white-and-blue Jewish prayer shawl over a finely made Greek toga. Though unusually thin, his body had the tensile strength of a willow wand.

"My dear Paul," Lucifer responded coolly and without sarcasm, "by the end of this affair you may realize that you and I have so much more in common than you ever could have dreamed. However that may be, if I lose, though nothing has been demanded of me by the opposition, I will accept the pretender's authority, if for no other reason than that he shall have won it over me by his greater skill at deception."

Paul, who Rachel assumed was the famous St. Paul of the Christians, glared at Lucifer, and no doubt would have let loose with a volley of invective belying his sanctity had not Justice Holmes intervened.

"Gentlemen," he called out, "now that we're publicly agreed on the stakes of this trial, shall we get down to the business at hand? I believe it's the place of the prosecution to set forth a preliminary argument, then the defense may answer, and we will proceed from there."

Paul held his tongue and sat back down, while Lucifer accepted the magistrate's invitation. "Let's begin at the very beginning," he said, addressing the entire assembly in a conversational tone that nevertheless easily reached the ears on the outskirts of the crowd. "I could tell you what I remember of that time before time; but then my former comrades, who now so thoughtfully provide us with shade from the new-born sun, might wish to present their own version of those primordial events, and we would end up wrangling over a history of which none of you members of the jury have any first-hand knowledge. Therefore I'll stick to the public record."

Rachel wondered what Lucifer meant by "public record," but no one asked him to clarify.

"Modern science tells us that the earth began several billions of years ago, and life on earth hundreds of millions of years ago, and that human beings evolved from lower, or at least simpler and less sentient, forms of life. But what of that? Science can't know the whole truth. After all, it denies that this spirit-realm and all we souls who inhabit it exist! On the other hand, it's asking of a rational being a bit much to regard the mutually contradictory creation myths bruited about by the world's various religious traditions as literally true. Nevertheless, to give both sides in this legal contest some evidentiary common ground, let us assume some truth to the charming Judaeo-Christian story of Adam and Eve in the garden. Does the defense grant that much?"

So that's what he meant, Rachel thought. *Fight the pious with their own weapons.*

"Some truth," James agreed, "but its nature and extent remain open to question."

Lucifer gave him a look as if to say that Professor James was much wilier a legal fox than anyone would have guessed, but he said nothing on that score, most likely for fear of upsetting the magistrate. "Would you at least admit that your client purports to be the Lord God mentioned in the story?"

"Yes and no," answered James, causing Lucifer visible irritation. "Why don't you tell your version of the story; then I will tell mine."

"And let the jury make up their own minds?" Lucifer extrapolated, finally recognizing that James would not be anyone's straw man. "Your suggestion is in keeping with the spirit of this trial," he said, a note of unmistakable sincerity in his voice, "and I shall follow it." He bowed without any sarcastic flourish and James returned the courtesy. Lucifer looked to Holmes, and the magistrate nodded for him to continue.

"This 'Lord God' allegedly creates the universe, making himself responsible, let everyone take note, for all that happens therein. He creates the first man and woman and places them within an idyllic garden, filled with all sorts of beautiful trees bearing all sorts of luscious fruit. New to existence, this Adam and Eve, they are children in adult form, innocently romping through the playground of life. The 'Lord God' places one restriction upon them. What is it?"

Lucifer paused and scanned the crowd, appearing to look into the eyes of each individual therein.

"This 'divine legislator' feels the need to make a rule, so what rule does he make? Does he tell this first human couple not to maim or kill each other or any of their animal companions? No, they don't need such a rule, because harming anyone or anything is the furthest thing from their minds. Does he tell them not to lie or cheat or steal? No, because they are much too innocent to even dream of committing such crimes. He forbids them to eat of the fruit of the Tree of the Knowledge of Good and Evil."

Again Lucifer paused, gauging the temper of the crowd. As in the split-second between the rise and fall of a headsman's axe, the silence was absolute.

"And why does he forbid them to eat of this fruit? Because if they do, they will become like him. He doesn't want the competition!"

"Blasphemy!" Paul thundered. He did not have the floor, but there was no denying his passion. "Why do we sit here and endure this sacrilege from the Evil One?"

"Because," Holmes took it upon himself to answer the rhetorical question in his most imperious tone, "that is what all major parties to the dispute have agreed upon, including the one, I believe, whom you acknowledge as your Lord."

Ignoring the judge's rebuke, Paul lifted his eyes to the heavens, gathering within himself a raw but tremendous spiritual force that no one in the assembly doubted he would shortly unleash against Lucifer. The Prince of Darkness, for his part, looked more than ready to dispense with legal niceties and do battle with Paul with weapons of the saint's choosing, however barbaric those weapons might be. As for the assembly, like dogs hearkening to their masters' voices, the religious sided with Paul and the irreligious with Lucifer, and there was no doubt that they would fight if the principals fought. At this point the trial might have escalated into a riot, a spectacle that Rachel was certain had yet to grace the pleroma, had not Azazael, Lucifer's lieutenant whom she had briefly met that morning, stepped in.

* * *

Wendell wondered if his tenure as magistrate in the Heavenly City was to end before counsel got through opening arguments, when Azazael—about whom James, despite Wendell's wall of professional silence, had given specific if epigrammatic warning—provided the crowd with a vaudevillian diversion. Wendell well knew the type. Ever the clown whose oozing charm was the proverbial oil over troubled waters, he leaped to his feet with an astounded smirk, shouting to get everyone's attention, "I've seen the light!" Then he raised a finger into the air and, as finishing touch to his comic masterpiece, conjured the apparition of a gigantic light bulb over his head. There was a moment of astonished silence, and then everyone in the crowd broke into laughter. Azazael lowered his finger, the light bulb burst into a thousand corpuscles of light, and he opened his mouth to speak. The laughter died away. "I have a simple suggestion," he declared, "that the court is under no obligation to accept." He bowed to Holmes.

"That goes without saying," the magistrate responded with dour authority. He did not like this creature for whom all the world was a stage and he its comic player. Men like him had no depth, no integrity, no concern but their own advantage. Nevertheless, Wendell could hardly refuse him a hearing, since the fundamental principle upon which he was basing the conduct of these proceedings was that anyone who wished could speak. "What is your suggestion?" Holmes finally inquired.

Azazael smiled more brightly, as if his good cheer fed upon contempt. "Why not let the blessed St. Paul provide a third point of view, a salutary corrective to that of defense counsel? After all, Professor James is widely reputed to hold an opinion or two that many of Yeshua's most devoted followers find a wee bit heretical

And given what's known of the good counselor's temperament, he's highly unlikely not to permit these opinions to influence his defense strategy."

Wendell actually liked the idea, but he would not give the mountebank the satisfaction of knowing it. "That would be most irregular," he huffed, thinking that, regardless of the merit of the suggestion, it was more important to maintain the dignity of the court by putting the jackanapes in his place. For Wendell that would have been the end of it, but Azazael now received support from an unexpected quarter.

"The entire trial is irregular," James declared, "as you yourself pointed out when we started, Your Honor. I personally have no objection to the apostle lending his views as counterbalance to my own."

Wendell felt backstabbed. "Your personal preferences have no bearing upon the question," he answered severely, sensing his control over the trial slipping away.

"If my client objected," James grinned condescendingly, "I'm sure he would make his opinion known."

James' air of familiarity infuriated Holmes. The professor had never been able to conquer the habit of contaminating his professional affairs with his personal life. *My God,* Wendell thought, *am I the only one in the entire spirit-realm who realizes this is a court of law, or for that matter has any respect for the law?* Nevertheless, he knew he could only go so far in bucking the tide. "So be it!" he finally proclaimed. "If neither the defense nor the prosecution has any objection," — Holmes looked to Lucifer, who nodded his head in consent — "I hereby appoint Paul of Tarsus an officer of the court, to serve as supplementary counsel for the defense. You may now come forward and add your voice to these proceedings."

Everyone cheered, even those who a moment before had been ready to slit the saint's throat, were such a thing possible in the pleroma.

"But he must wait to speak," Holmes added in a tone that brooked no opposition, "until the chief prosecutor has finished his statement."

"If it please Your Honor," Lucifer smiled, "before I continue, I would like to know exactly what the saint finds so objectionable."

"As if you didn't already know!" Holmes muttered under his

breath. *Is everyone, even Lucifer, laughing at me?* Exerting every ounce of self-control he possessed, Wendell signaled with a wave of the hand that Paul, who had arrived at the center of the field, should speak his piece.

"You accuse the almighty God of testing his creatures beyond their strength," the saint began, facing the assembly but rhetorically addressing Lucifer. "But who is any of us to question the Lord's ways? He gave our original parents everything—love, health, beauty, peace, happiness, and life itself. He gave them something greater than life. He made them after his own image and likeness. He made men rational. Through reason, men came to know God, not merely as the one who cared for them in the garden, but also as the supreme Lord of heaven and earth, the omnipotent creator of the universe. Then the Lord presented them with one little test to see if they would obey him in all things, big and small. They had every reason to trust him, and yet they perversely rejected his beneficent rule over their lives. Thereafter they suffered the just and inevitable consequences of their rebellion."

"Which was it, just or inevitable?" Lucifer interjected.

"Both!" Paul affirmed.

"How can it be both? If one heats water to the boiling point, it inevitably evaporates into steam. If a mortal fires a bullet into his own head, he inevitably dies. But if a mortal fires a bullet into another mortal's head, the murderer does not inevitably die. The court may not require his execution, or he may be pardoned by a higher power. His punishment may be just, but it is hardly inevitable."

"Divine justice is not like human justice," Paul readily retorted, not at all taken aback by Lucifer's objection.

Lucifer smiled. "I agree with you wholeheartedly," he gibed, "but in what way do you mean that, exactly?"

"Human justice is an ideal man strives to approximate," explained Paul, the rabbi in him coming out. "In human existence, there is a separation between will and ideal. Divine being knows no such division. God always and everywhere wills the ideal. In human existence, there is a separation between will and goal. Man does not always accomplish what he wills. In God there is no such distinction. God always and everywhere achieves what he wills."

Now Lucifer was truly delighted. "So God willed that Adam and

Eve sin against God?"

Again Paul did not hesitate. "Of course!" he affirmed. "Nothing comes to pass in heaven or on earth apart from the will of the Lord."

"So," Lucifer continued, "God wills that we put his alleged son on trial?"

"Nothing comes to pass without God's will," Paul reiterated.

"And God willed that this same 'son' be crucified?"

"It was a necessary sacrifice for our sin," Paul replied.

Lucifer held a finger to his lips in contemplation. "And God willed," he said at length, "that the Jewish people be sacrificed in the Nazi extermination camps?"

"Nothing happens," said Paul in complete yet not complacent equanimity, his voice heavy with the terrible purport of his words, "unless God wills it."

Lucifer smiled darkly. "If this were all the pretender had to offer in his own defense, there would be no need for further argument."

Paul scowled. "To the world the Gospel is folly and offense!" he retorted.

"For good reason," Lucifer said acidly, and once again the air was electric with tension. Then there came a flash, as of lightning, and the entire field was magically transformed.

Justice Holmes now sat on a brightly polished, ornately carved gilt bench that could have done duty as a throne. The designs were geometric, reminiscent of Islamic art, cleverly if not brilliantly interwoven with conventional symbols of justice and cosmic balance, such as the Hebrew Star of David, the Chinese *yin-yang*, and of course the Greco-Roman goddess Themis, complete with sword, scales and blindfold. The magistrate's dress was also changed. The well-worn, habitual frock coat gave way to magnificent ermine judicial robes and powdered wig after the British fashion. The clothes of the other court officials remained as they were; but the center of the field, hitherto entirely *au naturel*, took on the look and feel of a Western-style courtroom, though not so definably as to be recognizably Continental or Anglo-American. There were a witness box and tables for the prosecution and defense, the whole enclosed by railings with entry-points at the four corners. Most notably, the judge's bench was elevated above the rest. Moreover, benches and chairs had sprung up throughout the field, apparently to accommodate those among the assembly who were culturally unaccustomed to lounging upon the bare earth. Equally important, the field was transformed into a giant semi-circular amphitheater, so that Wendell and the other principals no longer had to perform in the round, but could face the entire assembly at all times. The effect was to focus attention upon the magistrate, as well as to give outward reminder to the assembly that they were all here to engage in the solemn and serious business of legal deliberation. It seemed to Wendell that, if his dissatisfaction with the way the trial had been going were translated into a prayer, that prayer had now been answered.

"But that's not all the defense has to offer," declared Holmes, admirably retaining the thread of the discussion through the transformation. "Is it, Counselor James?"

The question recalled Will from a moment of understandable disorientation. He rose from the chair in which he now sat while Lucifer, to all appearances in complete self-possession, seated himself gracefully at the prosecutor's table. Paul however remained standing, as if frozen in indecision as to whether this sudden metamorphosis was demonic in origin or divine.

"Not at all, Your Honor!" said Will heartily, as if to make up for coming late on cue. "But before I begin, I wish to make it clear to the court that, for reasons which will shortly be plain, I cannot accept the esteemed apostle"—he bowed to Paul—"as my colleague. The line of argument I feel conscience-bound to pursue is, in significant part, quite different from, and in many ways counter to, that of St. Paul."

"This is no difficulty," Holmes assured him. "The jury has one simple question before it: whether or not the defendant has been derelict in his duty as the Lord God, and therefore whether or not he should be removed from office."

At this point Wendell's eyes met Will's, and Wendell realized that two crucial details had been overlooked in arranging the trial: one, what kind of vote would be needed to convict—a simple majority, unanimity, or something in between, or, given a sufficient number of abstentions, a plurality; and two, whether the citizens of the pleroma would accept the agreement between Lucifer and Mikael that, should the defendant lose, Lucifer would succeed to his office.

Wendell had the distinct feeling that James had been struck by the same thoughts at the same time. If so, his failure to raise these questions before proceeding probably meant he had also come to another realization: given the moodiness and changeability of the crowd, as well as Lucifer's unpredictability, it would be disastrous to bring these issues to public attention now. Better to wait and hope they resolved themselves.

"It doesn't matter how many different lines of argument are heard," Holmes finally resumed, "as long as everyone keeps firmly in mind the fundamental question before us."

Will nodded in understanding both of what Wendell had said and, it seemed to Wendell, what he had not said. "First of all," the professor addressed the assembly much as if they were his students, "I should like to make it clear that my argument will rest on the presupposition that human beings have free will, even in relation to God, and that not even the Almighty can foresee, let alone determine, another's free decision."

"Why, such an idea would permit chaos!" interjected Paul, now torn from his fit of abstraction by the prospect of a more immediate battle to fight.

"I submit," James rejoined, his eyes twinkling mischievously, "that chaos has flourished without my permission from time immemorial. However, while I have your ear, sir, may I ask you a question? Why, in your opinion, did God create us?"

"Out of love, of course," Paul replied.

"And he has given us a world filled with torment and suffering out of love?"

Paul looked around at his numerous supporters as if to say that no one involved in this blasphemous trial except they and himself had kept the faith. "Who is the pot to tell the potter what he is to do with the work of his own hands?"

"I've read your Epistle to the Romans, so I'm familiar with the argument," said James. "But I don't find it convincing. 'Not even a sparrow falls to the earth without the knowledge of your heavenly Father' is more to my liking."

"Are you opposing me to Christ?" Paul cried, a note of hatred in his voice that had not been there even when he had confronted Lucifer.

"You do that very well yourself," retorted James, leaving no doubt that he and the saint were now engaged in total war. "Lest we try the patience of the court," James added quickly, "I had best proceed with my argument."

Paul surprised everyone by sitting down without another word. Everyone, that is, but Wendell. He knew the kind of wrath that ran so white-hot and deep that it would never loose itself blindly but always wait for the perfect moment, the moment it could consummate itself in full and unadulterated revenge. Wendell feared for his friend. Though Will certainly was clever in his own way, here he seemed like a lamb among wolves.

"God is love," James declared solemnly. "My client intends to stand or fall with the truth of this proposition. If it can be shown that he has violated love in any way, then he will gladly, even gratefully, relinquish whatever hold he has upon your hearts. If not, then you will not be able to eject him from your hearts."

There was a stirring among the irreligious in the crowd. The defense counsel seemed to be usurping for the defendant the authority of the jury. Lucifer, however, remained silent. He was tired, Wendell surmised, of quibbling over technicalities. James went on, apparently oblivious to the disturbance he had aroused.

"There are but two ways to understand this first sin of Adam and Eve: either they are flouting God's authority or they are betraying God's love. If one chooses the former interpretation, then all that's left to decide is whether the undeniably all-powerful God is to be worshiped or despised. Furthermore, not much is left to say about the history of divine revelation. One can argue over the details, but obedience to the divine will becomes the cornerstone of life."

There were unsuspecting murmurs of assent throughout the crowd, especially from the Christians and Muslims. Clearly, Wendell thought, they failed to see where James was taking his argument.

"My client has no desire to be the divine dictator in the sky," continued James. "He regards any defense that would acquit him simply because he is God as special pleading. He himself would never obey such a dictator, no matter if the penalty were eternal damnation."

Now, more appropriately, thought Wendell, barely concealing an ironic smile, there were cries of "Blasphemy!" and "Heresy!"

Predictably, Paul once again seized the floor. "I submit to the court that, while the honorable Professor James may follow whatever line of falsehood and delusion he pleases, he has no right to put his loathsome harlotry into the mouth of our savior."

"It's my understanding that Counselor James was so commissioned," replied Holmes.

"Your Honor," queried Paul, "were you witness to the commission?"

Holmes took a moment to reflect. "Suppose we resolve the issue this way," he suggested. "Since the defendant is not here right now to speak for himself, why not have each of you" — with a gesture he indicated Paul and James — "propose his own version of the defendant's motivation. If and when the defendant appears he may, if he wishes, validate one interpretation or the other. If not, the jury may decide for itself which argument is more convincing."

"In other words," Lucifer raised his voice in assent, "let's agree to extend some tolerance to one another. Let's agree to listen to what each of us has to say. Otherwise, this trial could go on for eternity and settle nothing. It should be clear to us all that the earth can't wait that long!"

The assembly was shamed into silence. Paul, clearly not one wit abashed but certainly recognizing that he must bide his time or risk losing all opportunity to expose the pernicious falsehoods that beset him from all sides, resumed his seat. Wendell nodded gratefully to Lucifer and then told James he should go on.

"The facts to which the defense stipulates are these: that God created Adam and Eve in his own image and likeness, endowing them with reason and free will, with the attendant moral and spiritual responsibility; that God placed them in a 'garden,' the fruit of whose trees represent all the wonderful possibilities of life; that in this garden there was no violence, suffering, or death; that the first man and woman enjoyed personal relationship with the animals, with each other as husband and wife, and with God, who 'walked and talked' with them; that Adam and Eve lost this idyllic existence when they ate of the fruit of the Tree of the Knowledge of Good and Evil; and finally, that suffering and death entered the world, not just for humans but for all creatures, through this first sin. All parties to the dispute agree upon these facts, even if in actuality some, like the prosecution, hold such 'facts' to have no factual validity, and others, as the defense maintains, think that they are mythical in character."

"This is beyond endurance!" Paul objected. "Say what you have to say, no matter how false and benighted, and if you wish call it *a* defense, but don't have the temerity to call it *the* defense!"

"The apostle's point is well taken," Holmes interceded. He had anticipated this objection. "However, in order to avoid awkward and unnatural circumlocutions that might detract from the clarity of presentation, the court recommends that both you and Counselor James be permitted to use the term 'the defense,' and in accordance with our earlier ruling, pending the appearance of the defendant, that the jury be trusted to make its own distinctions."

Again Paul clearly did not like Wendell's decision, but at this point he was just as clearly in no position to contest it. "Your Honor," he asked, "may I put a question of clarification to Professor James?"

Holmes nodded.

"What, sir, do you mean by 'mythical?'"

"It's unimportant whether these events actually happened," James elucidated, as if fielding a question from an eager and inquisitive graduate student. "The story is not about what some prehistoric couple did thousands or millions of years ago, but what we are doing here and now. It's not about how sin began, but what sin essentially is."

Paul showed unexpected restraint. "So, what do you mean," he asked calmly, "when you say that the defense, your defense, stipulates to these 'mythical' facts?"

"I mean that I'm perfectly willing to discuss these events as actual up to a point in order to discover their deeper meaning."

"This is the worst sort of equivocation!" objected Lucifer, leaping to his feet.

"Not at all!" retorted James. "You yourself give no credence whatsoever to the Biblical story, but you will accept its 'factuality' for the sake of argument if by doing so you can gain a conviction. Your equivocation is more extreme than mine."

Recognizing the validity of James' argument, Lucifer sat back down. Wendell had seen that look on lawyers' faces before. This American academic was more formidable an opponent than the

Light-Bearer had anticipated. Nevertheless, Wendell was certain, a new strategy was forming in his mind, and the fiercer the battle the sweeter the victory.

Paul threw up his hands. "I will leave you to your convolutions. You're bound to trip yourself up in the end."

James barely waited for Paul to resume his seat. "The key question," he went on, addressing the assembly, "is what did Adam and Eve expect to get from eating the forbidden fruit."

"No!" objected Lucifer. "The key question is why was the fruit forbidden in the first place."

James smiled. "I stand corrected," he said. "I don't know if what the prosecution proposes is the key question, but it certainly is a logically prior one. I suggest that the Tree of the Knowledge of Good and Evil represents the possibility of doing evil—in other words, the fact that human beings have free will."

"Then why not call it 'The Tree of Good and Evil?'" pressed Lucifer. "Why 'Knowledge of Good and Evil?'"

"What do Adam and Eve expect to gain by eating its fruit?" James reiterated his original question.

"The serpent promises them that they will become like God, knowing good and evil," answered Paul, who in his own mind, as well as that of most Christians in the audience, was the Biblical expert in residence.

"If I gave you some fruit," James said sharply, addressing himself directly to Lucifer, "and told you that, by eating it, you would become like God, would it be knowledge that tempted you?"

Lucifer hesitated. "The book says knowledge."

"Would it be knowledge that tempted you?" James repeated even more sharply.

"Power," Lucifer admitted, almost ruefully. "I'd be after power."

"There you have sin in a nutshell," proclaimed the professor with, however, no triumph in his voice. "Knowledge, the turning of reality into an objective system that can be studied and manipulated, is but means to an end. Adam and Eve rip themselves out of the divine embrace, which is the very nexus of life, in order to pursue the illusion of power."

"Why 'illusion?'" asked Lucifer.

"Because genuine power is power with responsibility," answered

James, his spirit burning hotly. "This is the power God exercises in forming and nurturing creation. It's the power entrusted to Adam and Eve when the Lord places the rest of creation under their dominion. What the serpent offers the first humans in the way of power, what you and I and all humans ever since have sinfully pursued as power, is power without responsibility—to be able to do whatever one pleases and face no consequences. Such power does not exist. It's a lie, the oldest and most dangerous lie in the universe."

Profound silence fell over the assembly, a silence as much of shame as contemplation.

"But isn't that the lie upon which the defendant himself has been feeding?" said Lucifer, finally breaking the silence.

"That's precisely what is here to be determined," replied James. "You accuse the Lord God of toying with his creation, of tempting Adam and Eve beyond their ability to endure. This is a convenient excuse for all creaturely wrongdoing since time began. As Paul said, we are given everything—life, love, the opportunity to do meaningful and creative work—and yet we persist in chasing the chimera of absolute power. In doing so, we betray love. No man can serve two masters; in betraying love, which is the very integrity of life, we violate life itself. We unravel the fabric of existence, and then complain because all has become death and chaos."

Paul looked upon the professor with grudging respect. "You're saying, then, that God did not exile us from the garden?"

"Precisely!" affirmed James. "We exiled ourselves."

"That's hardly in keeping with the text," observed Lucifer.

"Books are not reality," James retorted. "Books are written by men, and subject to the same foibles. If I may bring a bit of psychology to bear upon the story, here we have a classic case of displacement and projection. Through their choice of power over love, Adam and Eve tear themselves from the very substance of life. They become observers and manipulators. Instead of *being* themselves, they now *see* themselves, and so feel naked and vulnerable, guilty and ashamed. The Lord God confronts them with their iniquity, and what happens? The man blames the woman; the woman blames the serpent; and, if the serpent were given equal time, no doubt the serpent would blame God for being the creator of human and serpentine nature."

"And it would be right to do so!" a woman interjected, jumping up, throwing off a veil as if she had been in disguise and swiftly coming to the fore, her fair hair fiery in the sunlight. "One doesn't give a lit torch to a child!"

Wendell would immediately have intervened had not James seemed abnormally disturbed by the interruption. His chin quivered and his form went so limp that he almost slouched back down into his chair. He studied the woman as if she were a bomb in need of defusing and he was not sure which fuse to pull. He looked out into the audience and then up into the sky, as if in search of succor. Then, perhaps realizing that no help was at hand and there was nothing for it but to handle the creature himself, he straightened up, took a deep breath to stop the tremors, and went on with to all appearances as much assurance as heretofore.

"There is choice every step of the way," he said, "even for the Lord. You liken the gift of free will to that of a lit torch. A child can very well exist without a lit torch in its hands. No human being, or angel for that matter, can exist without free will. One can't introduce free will to a man who already exists and then teach him how to use it. Without free will, the man would not exist!"

James turned away from the woman as if to say that *that* point was settled, but her eyes flashed with an anger that could only be so terrible in one who was used to being treated as royalty. Wendell now was certain of her identity. She was undoubtedly the Mara about whom James had not long ago given him offhand warning. "As treacherous as Mara, queen of heaven," he had remarked when Wendell had stumbled down a steep incline on the way back from Sivananda's retreat. He remembered it well, because his failure to ask for an explanation had told him how little he had been in a talking mood. "What you're saying is nonsense!" the queen retorted now.

By keeping his back to her, James publicly returned her contempt. His face flushed and his eyes went wild. Wendell had never seen his friend in such a state, as if he were a newly active volcano. Doubtless, Will had a history with this woman. "At every step of the way there is choice, even for God," he insisted, looking at no one in particular. The quiet intensity of his voice indicated to Wendell that he was hearing a confession of faith, or perhaps, in some unfathomable sense, an admission of guilt. "If God had wanted a universe of puppets with himself pulling the strings, doubtless he could have created one."

"How can you be so sure he did not?" Lucifer asked. "After all, the good apostle here seems to think so."

James looked at Lucifer as if he himself had wondered that very thing countless times. "Because," he replied at length, "I can see no reason for it, none whatsoever. There are reasons for everything men do, even when those reasons are hidden at the bottom of their souls."

"For what Hitler did?" Lucifer queried.

"Yes, even for what Hitler did," James said wearily, "as one of your wide-ranging experience should well know. But I see no reason, not even the ghost of a reason, for God to create a universe of puppets and then cause them to behave the way we behave, especially if those puppets have feeling. It would be utterly insane."

Lucifer bowed to James with a flourish of his arm. "Counselor," he said, "I rest my case."

"On the other hand," James continued, ignoring the riposte, "I can well understand why God might risk creating a universe of free individuals, of genuine selves, in order to establish with them a relationship of love."

"Love?" Mara cried with a contempt so powerful the sky seemed to darken. "Endless toil, the agony of childbirth, constant worry over oneself and one's children—that's all love?"

Once again, however, the guileless James managed to turn the attack back upon his assailant. He calmly faced Mara, and with a scorn as menacingly subtle as it was overwhelming, said, "My dear woman, are you always this dull? I have explained to you that, from my perspective, all such evils are the inevitable consequence of our betrayal and disruption of the relationship with God, which in essence is indeed the betrayal and disruption of all relationship. Next, you challenged my line of reasoning—quite astutely, I must say, to give the devil her due—by maintaining that God is culpable for bestowing upon us the dangerous gift of free will. I was in the middle of answering this charge when Lucifer, with whom, I presume, you are well acquainted,"—Mara turned livid at the sexual innuendo—"mistook a hypothetical statement for a categorical one. Now that

I've set him straight, do you think we might return to the real point at issue?"

James' convoluted wit was wasted on the crowd, but Wendell barely stifled a snigger, and he could see that even Lucifer, that master of diplomacy, was having trouble keeping a straight face. Mara looked lost in rage and confusion. James deliberately mistook her silence for assent.

"My point is a simple one," he continued. "Free will is what makes us individuals. Without it, a human being would not be human, a person would not be a person. For example, if you, my former queen, invented a magic potion that would place a man entirely in your power,"—here James' voice once more took on an edge—"then that man would no longer be his own person, but an extension of you."

"What if we are ourselves in what we experience and God's puppets in what we do?" countered Mara, reminding everyone that she was no fool. "What if God causes our actions, but the thoughts we think, the emotions and sensations we feel, are our own? After all, didn't you yourself all but say that so it is with animals?"

"Animals aren't rational," said James.

"Aren't they?" Mara pressed. "Animals don't kill their own kind. They don't take more than they need. They care for nature as if she were their loving mother. None of this could be said of man!"

"I didn't say animals were irrational," James retorted, now facing his opponent in a stance so strained it was as if he and Mara were locked in an invisible wrestlers' embrace. "One can't be rational unless it's possible for one to be irrational. One can't be good unless one can also be evil. It's a choice, and animals don't have that choice."

"Now who's dull?" Mara laughed scornfully. "Stick to the point, Professor. Is it possible for a creature to suffer without having free will? If so, then it's possible for a creature to be a person without having free will, at least in its own mind. If that's so, mightn't we all be under the illusion that we have free will because we experience ourselves as persons?" As it became clear he had no answer to her argument, Mara looked upon James with growing triumph.

"But we talk!" a voice came from the midst of the crowd. It was vaguely familiar to him, but Wendell was so intent upon the exchange between James and Mara that he did not bother to try placing it. "If you think you have something worth adding to the debate," he called into the assembly, "stand and come to the fore!" A diminutive figure moved timidly toward the center. At first Wendell did not recognize her, though he was certain he had seen her before. At the Angelic Council, of course, the Jewish girl who had started all this! Now she seemed so shy, so quiet, quite a different person.

"If it please Your Honor..." she began when she arrived at the railing.

"Your name, miss?" Wendell asked kindly.

"Rachel," she replied, relaxing a bit. "If it please Your Honor, it seems Her Majesty has overlooked one bit of evidence favorable to Professor James."

"And what's that?" Mara asked, obviously amused at the newcomer's temerity.

"The difference between thought and speech," said Rachel. "I've thought about it a great deal since coming here. Simply by looking into each other's eyes we can divine one another's thoughts, yet for the most part we choose to communicate through speech."

"There's nothing remarkable about that," Mara declared. "Speech is more definite and precise."

"Yes, but why is that?" Rachel persisted. "On earth we communicated through sounds, but here speech is merely an occasion for transmission of thought. That's why, though you're speaking Aramaic and I, German, we've no difficulty understanding each other."

No linguistic difficulty, thought Wendell.

"In either case," said Mara, "the result is the same. Through speech one focuses one's thought and directs it to others."

"I agree with you entirely," affirmed Rachel. "That's exactly my point. It seems to me that most thought happens to people. They experience it; they do not produce it. We live in a sea of consciousness, and each of us is a little island in that sea. Waves of thought, feeling and sensation wash over us, but we aren't entirely passive. Some thought we originate, or at least make our own, and speech is the way in which we decide what of consciousness belongs to us and what does not. When we talk we are saying, to ourselves as well as to others, 'This is who I am.'"

Everyone was still except Mara. "And animals have no speech?"

she challenged. "According to Genesis, the serpent certainly had a glib tongue!"

The girl did not seem at all intimidated. "I was also thinking," she continued, "that maybe animals and humans aren't so different after all, that perhaps the difference is of degree rather than kind. Perhaps animals are like islands partly or wholly immersed in the ocean. They make no distinction between what they experience and who they are, so they never come to the point of deciding or saying who they are. They signal and sign, but they don't speak."

These words cast a spell on everyone. Wendell felt as he imagined the rabbis and scribes must have felt when the prepubescent Jesus displayed his wisdom in the temple. "Counselor James," he said, breaking what was threatening to become an oppressive silence, "the court grants you permission to pursue your 'free will' defense, just as it allows Paul his 'authority' defense. The prosecution may attack both defenses in whatever ways it pleases, just so long as it keeps the two distinct and separate."

Lucifer bowed. "We haven't much more to say concerning the argument from authority," he smiled, "though I believe Mr. James will deal it a few more blows before he's through. This free will argument, on the other hand, intrigues us. With your permission, we should like to make it the focal point of further debate."

"You can't rid yourself of me so easily," said Paul, rising with dignity. "You know that scholar isn't your real enemy."

"Yes, I know that," rejoined Lucifer with equal dignity, "but despite your sanctity, neither are you. Before this is over, Paul, you will recognize me as undeniably the lesser of two evils."

Without another word, Paul turned and strode back to his original seat among his fellow Christians, the crowd parting, Wendell could not help thinking, like the waters of the Red Sea before Moses. The new sun was low on the horizon, bathing the sky in crimson light. Wendell had never experienced so short a day, or one so long. It was just like a day of battle, only more so. "It's late!" he announced. "If it be agreeable to all parties, this court will recess until tomorrow at sunrise."

Wendell had no idea what, if anything, would happen when he put an end to the day's proceedings. After all, they were on an island with nowhere to go. However, as his magisterial voice faded in the twilight — still as good, he thought with pride, as the rap of any gavel — lights came up all around the 'island,' which now all unbeknownst had turned into a huge field in the center of a city. The Heavenly City, of course! What other city was there in these parts? Only now it seemed more expansive. The alleyways had become streets, the streets boulevards, and the parks tracts of jungle, prairie and forest where one could well imagine livestock pasturing and wild animals roaming, were any such to be found in the pleroma. By contrast the buildings also seemed more imposing, and at the same time more sharply defined — not just the cathedrals and temples, the mosques and palaces and pagodas, but also the homes, shops, houses and hovels. The trees were budding, and the savor of lilac and apple-blossom filled the air. The country had come to the city, and spring had come to a place that had hitherto been seasonless. Everyone seemed to relish the change. The assembly grew light-hearted, even festive, and people laughed and chatted as they sauntered back into town.

Nevertheless, Wendell noted with a sinking feeling, most souls still stuck to their own kind. This evidence of bigotry and insularity in heaven disheartened him. Was Lucifer right? Had divine mismanagement brought about this atmosphere of division and latent strife? An unaccustomed and distinctly unpleasant feeling of bitterness suddenly took possession of him. Ever the practical jurist, he immediately searched himself for its source.

Wendell resented the unmanageable proportions of the issues this trial was raising... No, that was not it. The problem was not that the issues were so large, but that they were so nebulous. On earth, no matter how momentous or complicated the case, everything had been so much more tangible.

"Brooding doesn't suit you."

Wendell would have been startled were he not already accustomed to having that voice interrupt his thoughts. "Counselor James," he teased, "you acquitted yourself well today!"

Will's eyes twinkled. "For an amateur," he chuckled.

"It's well that you're an amateur," Wendell returned, suddenly serious. "I don't know one certified lawyer who could have risen to the occasion."

"No, I suppose not," Will agreed matter-of-factly as he took a seat in the witness box. "They're trapped in their professional personae."

Wendell nodded, looking off into the fading sunset and feeling far older, and far less wise, than he had ever felt on earth. After an indeterminate time, during which the twilight remained unchanging as in the summer in northern climes, he started with recollection. "I felt you should have nothing to do with me until after the trial," he explained apologetically.

Will sighed, more in weariness than discontent. The air was still as death.

"At the time it seemed like a proper and necessary precaution," Wendell went on.

"Against what?" Will smiled. "Muddying the waters?"

"It's professional ethics!" Wendell snorted, irked by Will's dismissive manner despite his relief at having his friend back. "Counsel must have no personal contact with the presiding magistrate lest personal feelings influence the latter's judgment."

"But that's just it!" James replied excitedly, like a thunderstorm whipping in off a lake on a hot summer day. "This trial is all about personal feelings! By its end none of us will be able to hide his true mettle."

"You make it sound as if we're all on trial," Wendell remarked.

"No, you make it sound like a war!"

"Remember the war in heaven?" James asked.

"I'd almost forgotten about that," replied Wendell.

"I suppose you're so tired you only wish to return home and retire," said Will in apparent non sequitur.

"You've something else in mind!" cried Wendell, surprising himself with the eagerness with which he took the bait. "I am incredibly weary, but I doubt it's the kind of exhaustion sleep would remedy. Look here, Will, it's not another of your Oriental fakirs!"

James' failure to reply, along with the knowing look on his face, was confirmation enough that indeed was what he had in mind, or at least something along those lines. Wendell slowly returned the smile with a grin that brightened his entire disposition. "I'll be damned if you don't make a metaphysician of me yet!"

Chapter 6

As the infant sun died its first death, Rachel drifted vaguely toward Lucifer's palace. She was so overwhelmed by the plethora of ideas thrown about in the trial that she could not think a thought of her own. Strange how a full mind could feel exactly the same as an empty one.

She looked up, not at the horizon, but at the wisps of pink and blue-gray clouds swirling around the newly twinkling stars, and stood transfixed by the beauty of the early evening sky. Then she heard a voice, a once familiar voice, calling her name. It was Lily. For some reason, Rachel was not surprised to see her.

"I've come to invite you to Shabbat!" Lily exclaimed brightly, but beneath her good cheer was disquiet, even fear.

"I had no idea what day of the week it was," replied Rachel evenly.

"We keep track," explained Lily.

"We?" There was more disappointment than contempt in Rachel's voice.

Lily lowered her eyes. "They want to talk to you, Rachel."

"Of course they do!" Rachel cried. "No one greets me when I arrive, but now they want to talk to me!"

"It won't hurt to talk," Lily pleaded, and Rachel suddenly realized that her friend was as disturbed by the train of events Rachel had set in motion as *they* undoubtedly were. In point of fact, no one could be more upset by it all than Rachel herself, so yes, why not talk? Rachel nodded and they set out for the Jewish quarter, Lily walking slightly ahead in order to lead the way.

The part of the quarter to which Lily brought her was notable only in being so very nondescript. Even in heaven, it seemed, her people liked to keep a low profile. Most proudly stood a two-story white-brick synagogue that, from without, could easily have been mistaken for a town hall. Around it huddled a potpourri of low-slung dwellings with yellow brick chimneys, but otherwise mostly composed of some combination of wood and stone. Everything was clean, as it was throughout the Heavenly City. Nevertheless, the lack of self-expression in these dwellings, the architectural anti-style that Rachel instantly christened "anonymous humility," made it all seem grimy and cheap. Not even in the Viennese ghetto had Jews appeared so ashamed of being Jews.

And yet, when she looked at the people themselves, this did not seem to be the case at all. Their dress was as varied as that of Jews on earth. Traditional long robes and floor-length dresses vied with modern business suits and evening attire, but everywhere one could see yarmulkes and veils, prayer shawls and phylacteries. Everyone was recognizably Jewish, and all seemed proud of who and what they were.

The Shabbat ritual meal only sharpened the contradiction between the people and their surroundings. It was held in a bare, sparsely furnished room inside the synagogue. Besides Lily, Rachel recognized only one other person: Rabbi Aeschermann, whom she had known as a child, presided, but his wife was nowhere to be seen, and neither was Lily's Daniel. If there were any inmates from the camps in attendance, she did not recognize them, as doubtless they did not recognize her, since none of them were any longer half-starved scarecrows with shaved heads and eyes so large they seemed to swallow everything they saw. And, as elsewhere in the Heavenly City, there were no children. In other words, this was definitely not the family gathering Shabbat was supposed to be. Also, from what Rachel remembered, the prayers were drawn from a variety of sources, not only the various Sabbath ceremonies in the home but also those in the synagogue, and some had even been turned into Christian-like hymns. It was as if this single meal had to do service for the entire day, and for a bastardized Judaism to boot. The fervor with which this company of fellow Jews intoned the Kaddish and recited the Havdalah could not disguise the artificiality of the occasion.

Rachel ate the bit of challah Lily offered her and then waited for the meal to end. She was only curious about one thing: would the rabbi take her aside or would he talk to her before the congregation? She did not care one way or the other. She was simply curious.

Finally it was over, and then the sixty-odd participants extended to one another the traditional wish of peace and all but a half-dozen left. Two younger men pulled a table out of the large square that had been eating surface for the crowd, and those who stayed sat around it. On one side of this inquisitional tribunal hunched a young, lanky yeshiva student with unruly facial hair. His neighbor looked to be one of those stylishly dressed rabbis *a la Viennese*, but Rachel could not be sure — a well fed, well heeled, self-satisfied man who, if one averaged out the wrinkled skin and dark straight beard, would fall just on the windward side of middle age. At the corner, with back as straight as that of her chair, perched a thin, severe, and equally middle-aged woman with a bluish, filmy complexion. On the other side sat Lily and a short, fastidious, wavy-haired man in business attire who sported an expensive-looking pair of eyeglasses, and who made up for his below-average stature by taking up twice as much space at the table as anyone else. Rabbi Aeschermann, looking more than ever as she had always imagined Moses, with chiseled features, burning eyes and a tangled, dark brown beard that, unlike his head, refused to turn gray, took the place at the head of the table. Feeling like the loser in a game of musical chairs, Rachel waited until everyone else was seated and then, without protest, lowered herself into the only vacant chair remaining, that at the foot. The rabbi extended his arms, and the small group — half the size of a witches' coven, Rachel thought sardonically — linked hands to form a circle. Lily sat to Rachel's left. Her hand was warm and comforting, as Rachel remembered it in life. The hand of the scarecrow yeshiva student to her right, however, was cold, clammy and trembling, as if he had just stepped out of a premature grave. Since the rabbi sat opposite Rachel, instead of bowing her head she stared directly at him as he began a prayer she knew would be about her.

"Lord of all the heavens and the earth," he intoned earnestly, his hoary head bowed in extravagant humility, "we are grateful to thee for bringing our people through yet another trial, as well as for the opportunity to bear witness to thy glory and righteousness before all the nations. But there are some among us who are angry for having been given this test. Soften their hearts, Lord, so they may cease their self-destructive rebellion. Open their minds so that they, like thy servant Job, may perceive the wisdom in accepting whatever comes to us from thy hand, thou who art Lord of death as well as life."

"Job did no such thing!" Rachel interjected, and a current of shock passed through the circle. The rabbinical student released her hand, contemptuously it seemed, yet also with a touch of fear, but Lily grasped the other even more tightly.

The rabbi raised his head and looked with patronizing tenderness into her eyes. "Job railed against the Almighty, it's true," he said, "but in the end he made his peace with God and received his reward."

"No!" Rachel shot back. "God beat him down until he did what Job predicted he'd do, convict Job out of his own mouth! Well," she declared, her dark eyes turning black and flashing like meteorites, "you won't beat me down!"

Cries of "How dare you!" and "What a thing to say to the rabbi!" came from everyone at the table but Lily. Rabbi Aeschermann, however, spread and lowered his hands in a gesture for patience and silence. "We're here to reason with you, child," he said calmly, even kindly, "not to beat you down."

"Then reason with me!" returned Rachel. "Say what you have to say." She released Lily's hand and folded her arms, at once open and defiant. She took some deep breaths to calm herself, but they did little good. Despite its size, the room felt close and airless.

"You're angry at the Lord for permitting the murder of so many of our brothers and sisters," began the rabbi.

Rachel nodded.

"I, too, am angry," he continued, "but not at God." His eyes were soft and understanding. "I'm angry at the wicked men who once again have used our people to avoid confronting the evil in themselves."

The rabbi paused, inviting a response, but Rachel did not speak. Nevertheless, she began to listen more intently.

"No doubt you think we've gathered together this Shabbat evening to condemn the rebellious path you've chosen. I tell you quite frankly, my daughter, that there's much in what you're doing that I don't like, and even more that I consider dangerous. If the majority of our people were to have their way, you'd be silenced."

"How is that possible?" Rachel spoke softly, matter-of-factly. Defiance hardly seemed appropriate in face of the rabbi's gentle demeanor.

"There are ways."

"Even though I'm under Lucifer's protection?"

"The reason you haven't been stopped before now is not because you're under *Lucifer's* protection."

"What do you mean?" she asked, bewildered.

Before the rabbi could answer, the yeshiva student, who now struck Rachel as so ungainly as to look like he belonged in the fields rather than a seminary, broke in. "How is it possible, Rabbi Aeschermann? How can she be under the protection of his spirit and not even know it?"

"Haven't you noticed by now, Jacob?" replied the rabbi without turning his eyes away from Rachel. "She's an innocent in every way. His protection goes unnoticed because it's been with her all her life."

"Whose protection?" Rachel demanded, rising from her seat in mounting exasperation.

"That of the Holy One of Israel!" cried Jacob. "Are you so unaware?"

Rachel broke into laughter, nearly falling back into her chair. When the rabbi continued to look kindly upon her and no one else laughed, she sobered. "How can you tell?" she asked.

"There is no 'how,'" said the rabbi. "Those who have eyes to see simply see."

"Why would God protect someone who hates him so much?" Rachel lowered her eyes to the table, but then realized she had no reason for shame and met the rabbi's gaze straight on. He smiled. "What's so funny?" she queried.

"I just remembered a Hindu proverb," he chuckled. "They say it takes a man who loves God ten lifetimes to reach him, but a man who hates God three, because a man who hates God thinks about him all the time!"

"I've had only one lifetime," Rachel retorted, "and quite a short one, too." Then, realizing she was being perverse, she fell silent.

"In any event," the rabbi declared with conviction, "you are under the Lord's protection, he alone knows why."

There followed a long and, for Rachel, awkward silence, though no one else seemed discomfited. Throughout the rabbi held her gaze. He reminded her of the man she had met in the mountains, and suddenly she had a burning desire to see him again. Nevertheless, she felt powerfully that it was not yet time to leave. "What did you mean," she found herself asking the rabbi, "when you said the Gentiles were using us?"

"To avoid themselves," he added.

"Yes, to avoid the evil in themselves."

Aeschermann pounced upon the opportunity to explain his idea. "We are a people who, for all our faults, have ever been mindful of the goodness of all God's creation, and that means everything within ourselves as well. We've sought to serve God with our 'evil' tendencies, our passions and appetites, rather than overcome and root out those tendencies, because we knew they came from God."

"What do you mean?" asked Rachel, deeply interested and vaguely remembering him preaching on this theme when she had been a child and not at all interested. "I mean, I think I may know what you mean, but I'm not sure."

"The goyim tear themselves into two parts. One part they consider good and the other part evil. The evil part they throw away, or think they throw away. In reality, one can never throw away any part of oneself."

With a start of recognition, Rachel realized that Aeschermann was talking about what Sigmund Freud and other psychologists called "repression." It was refreshing to hear the idea put so simply and directly, without the distracting costume of scientific jargon.

"The pagan devotees of Cybele did this by castrating themselves, the Christian monks by practicing asceticism. These are relatively harmless methods because they are so obvious. Today's Gentile does it in a far more insidious way. He castrates himself in his head. Whatever he regards as evil in himself, he disowns. Awareness is a powerful weapon, for good or for evil. He shrinks his awareness to a tiny but highly concentrated pinpoint of light. Thus he avoids

THE JUDGMENT OF CHRIST

taking responsibility for those parts of himself he finds inconvenient, those parts that don't fit with the way he likes to see himself."

"But why would anyone do such a thing?" Rachel asked, though she well knew the answer.

"Man is lonely," replied the rabbi, his voice almost comically saturated with pity. "He wants to belong. He is afraid when all by himself, so he must join a herd. The herd requires its members to possess qualities of character that will strengthen the herd, or at least give the herd the illusion of strength. Any qualities that undermine this illusion are branded evil. Man disowns the 'evil' part of himself so he will fit in with the herd."

He paused until Rachel indicated with a nod that she had taken in this idea and was ready for more.

"As I was saying," the rabbi continued, "to do so he must shrink his awareness to a pinpoint of blinding light. He resides within that light, while everything else within him is thrown into correspondingly black and infernal darkness. Within the light he is king, king of the abstraction into which he has magically changed himself. He is an abstraction who deals only with abstractions. Opinions, which in truth are worth nothing, become to him everything. He chooses who he is by choosing his opinions. Opinions have nothing to do with reality but everything to do with the way men see themselves. That's why people fight so passionately over them."

"Because they're fighting over nothing?" asked Rachel.

The rabbi nodded, smiling sadly. "Everything that's not included within this pinpoint of light..."

"Everything that's real in the person," Rachel interjected, just as she had been in the habit of doing with her professors. Just like her professors, Aeschermann seemed delighted with the astute interpolation.

"Yes," he agreed, "everything real, everything that doesn't fall within the chosen system of ideas, is thrown into the denied and neglected inner night where, robbed of the civilizing radiance of spirit, it takes on a monstrous life of its own. This refused and abandoned vitality haunts man, the way an amputated leg haunts a cripple. Man feels it lurking in the shadows, but he does not and will not see it. Therefore he fears it, and this fear poisons his emotional life. Feeling is our link with other beings. If one corrupts one's feeling, one corrupts one's relations with others. The surest way to corrupt one's feeling is to shirk responsibility for whatever in oneself one happens, for whatever reason, to dislike. If man lives in fear, he must also live in hate."

"What do you mean, Rabbi?" asked a disturbed Lily. "How can feeling be corrupted?"

The rabbi turned his kindly eyes toward her. "Those parts of himself that man casts into the darkness now haunt him like ghosts. They threaten him like monsters, dream monsters. They've been exiled from their native land, and now they fight to return. He doesn't wish them to return, he wants no part of them, so he fights to keep them out. He can't accept them as parts of himself, yet he can't deny their reality. He has no other choice but to see them as parts of others. Therefore he hates others for having the hateful qualities from which he's freed himself."

"But not really freed," observed Rachel.

"Of course not," the rabbi shook his head dolefully.

"What are these 'hateful qualities?'" asked the bespectacled, professional-looking man sitting on Lily's left. He was somewhere between Jacob's and Aeschermann's ages, and seemed irritated by what the rabbi was saying.

"Whatever makes one vulnerable, of course!" replied the rabbi with a harshness of tone of which Rachel hitherto would have thought him incapable. He and the man seemed to share an intimate enmity.

"And what's that?" persisted the man.

"Why, you know as well as I!" replied the rabbi with more than a hint of scorn. "Sexuality and individuality."

"Always sexuality and individuality," the man echoed. "I'm weary of hearing the same old song. Would you at least explain yourself for a change?"

The rabbi studied his antagonist closely. "Not for you, Samuel," he said at length. "I've explained myself to you before, over and over again, and you've no will to understand. I'll explain for the sake of our visitor, even though"—here he smiled and winked at Rachel—"she probably understands more about these things than the rest of us put together."

"I understand," said Rachel, "that you're talking about what psychologists call repression and projection."

"I'm talking about promiscuity as well, my child," returned the rabbi. "They're all wrapped up in the same stinking miasma."

"Promiscuity?" said Rachel. "I don't understand."

"Listen carefully!" Samuel admonished, shifting in his seat and putting his feet up on the table, boots and all. At that point Rachel realized that Samuel could only be the rabbi's son. "This is his favorite tune. Only, don't expect it to make any sense."

The rabbi did his best to ignore Samuel. "Like fish out of water, we spend our lives flip-flopping back and forth between repression and promiscuity. We work hard and play by the rules so we won't get into trouble, but after work we go on drunken binges or squander our spiritual substance in idle entertainment. In the end, what does it all amount to? Nothing!"

"He's talking about me!" declared Samuel. "I supported him in his old age, and this is how he repays me."

The rabbi continued, speaking directly to Rachel. "People get married, then they get bored with their mates, divorce, and marry someone else, get bored, divorce, and so on."

"That's me as well," said Samuel in what struck Rachel as perverse pride. "I was married three times. Of course," he added, downing his wine, "none of my wives was any good. No woman is."

"How dare you blaspheme against life!" the rabbi exploded. "Weren't you born of a woman, or did I misapprehend when you sprang directly from the hand of God?"

Samuel sobered. "Mama was different," he said, lowering his feet to the floor.

"Mothers are always different," said the rabbi, a bit more gently. "What you must realize is that every woman, even if she never gives birth in the flesh, is a mother in her soul. Yet, in most cultures down through history, woman has been regarded as the incarnation of evil. That's because men have been in charge. Woman represents to man his own sexuality, and man is afraid of his sexuality because it's his vulnerability. So he denies it and casts it upon woman, seeing in her all the weakness he tries to root out of himself but never can. He both loves and hates her because he can't do without her. He worships her, but when she fails to live up to the impossibly exalted and saintly ideal he sets for her, he calls her witch and burns her at the stake."

There was a moment of brooding quiet as the candles flickered and a breeze, as if bearing witness to the truth of the rabbi's speech, came from Rachel knew not where. She relished the silence, but she was too stirred up in every way, emotionally as well as intellectually, to leave the discussion there.

"But there's quite a different attitude toward sex in the modern world," she finally remarked.

"Yes, very different," conceded the rabbi. "Sex is no longer something dirty that must be done only for procreation. Within the commonly accepted limits of privacy and decency, consenting adults are free to take their pleasure whenever and with whomever they please. Furthermore, no longer must sex be talked about only in whispers. Now we may discuss sex openly, scientifically. It's a natural function, just like respiration, digestion and defecation."

"See how he goes on!" laughed Samuel. "You shouldn't get him started."

"Before sex was kept in the dark," the rabbi continued, seemingly oblivious to Samuel's gibes. "Now it's exposed to the light of the laboratory, a light brighter than that of day. But, in truth, one way of hiding from it is as good as another."

"I still don't understand," said Rachel, once again bewildered.

"One's sexuality is one's vulnerability. It's purpose, as is clear from the Song of Solomon, is the penultimate intimacy, that between man and woman. To regard it as anything less is eating one's cake and keeping it too. It can't be done! One can't experience the true joy of intimacy without the risk and the pain. Yet that's what we keep trying to do. So the more sex people get, the less satisfied they are."

Rachel pondered, and even Samuel was silent.

"You called it the penultimate intimacy," she finally said, returning the rabbi's gaze with matching intensity. "What's the ultimate intimacy?"

He replied without hesitation. "Why, of course, that between the soul and God."

Rachel looked away. She suddenly felt empty. Though as a child she had deluded herself about God, in truth she had never experienced either intimacy.

"This is all very edifying, but when will you come to the real reason we're gathered here?"

It was one of the two people at the table who had not yet spoken, the portly man with the aged, wrinkly face and the incongruously jet-black beard. From the tone of his voice Rachel was now certain that he, too, was a rabbi.

"I thought we were here to celebrate Shabbat," Rabbi Aeschermann answered.

"Oh come now!" said the other rabbi. "As our guest no doubt has surmised, we've no way of knowing whether this is Shabbat any more than she does!"

"Every day in God's kingdom is Shabbat," proclaimed Aeschermann.

"We don't know that this is God's kingdom, either," rejoined the rabbi. "But if you insist upon deliberate naiveté, I'll take it upon myself to tell the girl what the council charged you to say." He turned to Rachel. "My dear, the Rabbinical Council forbids you to take any further part in this blasphemous 'Trial of God!'"

"How is it blasphemous?" Rachel asked, her voice calmer than she felt.

"I won't dignify that silly question with an answer," said the rabbi. "It must be obvious even to you. But I must also say that your conduct has placed our community in danger." The pale, sharp-featured woman sitting next to him regarded Rachel gravely and nodded in agreement. *She must be his sister*, thought Rachel, *or even his wife*.

"How so?" queried Rachel.

"We're a minority here, as we are everywhere. Our only hope lies in unity. This judicial farce has left us hopelessly divided. Among our own people, mind you, there are as many different opinions as logical possibilities, all because you took it upon yourself to accept the premise that the god allegedly incarnate in Yeshua of Nazareth was the same God as that of Abraham, Isaac and Jacob!"

Rachel felt her cheeks flush. "That's just a legal ploy," she mumbled, not even managing to convince herself.

"Be that as it may," retorted the rabbi, "have you considered the consequences? What side in this affair is a Jew to be on? If we defend our God, we defend the Christian god as well. If we attack the Christian god, we attack our God. If we remain silent, then we allow our God to go defenseless."

"Perhaps God can perfectly well defend himself!" declared Rabbi Aeschermann. "Don't forget the example of Job's friends whom the Lord condemned for defending him with lies!"

"Who talks of defending the Lord with lies?" rejoined the rabbi. "Besides, you used that argument before the council and the majority rejected it."

"I'm not answerable to the majority!" proclaimed Aeschermann. "I'm answerable only to God."

"So are we all," said the rabbi, "only the rest of us don't claim a monopoly upon divine inspiration."

Rabbi Aeschermann sighed deeply. "She's protected by the Lord," he said softly. "Nothing you can do will change that."

"So you say, though no one else can perceive this alleged protection." The rabbi again addressed Rachel. "The Rabbinical Council sympathizes with the suffering you've endured as a Jew in the death camps..."

"As a human being," Rachel whispered.

"What was that?" asked the rabbi. When it was clear no answer would be forthcoming, he went on. "As I say, we all appreciate your suffering. Many of the council members went through the camps themselves. No one condemns you for an extreme reaction to unbearable trauma. Nevertheless, it's time to come to your senses and realize what's at stake if you continue to participate in these unholy proceedings. The Rabbinical Council hereby orders you to withdraw your charges and so put an end to this affair. If you refuse, you'll be cast out from among your own people."

Rachel felt shock, but no surprise, like stepping from an overheated house into the winter cold.

"What makes you think anything this girl did now could stop the trial?" Rabbi Aeschermann asked sharply. "Lucifer will go on without her."

"But many others won't," rejoined the rabbi. "We've conducted an informal canvass. This girl is Lucifer's trump card. Without her, the rest of the pleroma would soon sink back into its accustomed apathy."

"You think that's desirable, Mendelssohn?" Aeschermann pressed, giving a name to this incarnation of Rachel's fear.

"What I think doesn't matter," said Rabbi Mendelssohn. "The council has decided. Though, if you must know, I personally happen to concur with its decision. The people must survive!"

"At any cost?" Aeschermann queried.

Mendelssohn looked at him meaningfully but did not answer. He then turned to the woman and said, "Eva, it's time for us to go!" Without giving anyone the wish of peace or even a word of farewell, the Mendelssohn's, whether brother and sister or husband and wife Rachel would never bother to learn, solemnly marched out of the synagogue. Samuel and Jacob followed.

"Is Samuel your son, then?" asked Rachel, grasping at the commonplaces of everyday life as a drowning person seizes upon any bit of flotsam that comes within reach. The rabbi sat head-bent and still as if he had not heard. Then, as Rachel made up her mind to leave because it seemed he wished to be alone, he said, "Don't go, child, not just yet. As a favor. Your presence is a comfort to a lonely old man."

"You live alone, Rabbi?"

The rabbi looked up. "Samuel is my son and Jacob my student. Lily is my nephew's wife. And yes, I live alone. Until I'm called," he added, his eyes once more cast down upon the table, his jaw working out the tension the clash had left hanging in the air. "Lily keeps me company from time to time."

"The council doesn't like that either," Lily smiled blushingly, rising and placing her hand tenderly upon the nape of Aeschermann's neck.

"Yes," the rabbi muttered, "the council doesn't like much of anything that might make us look bad."

"Called?" asked Rachel, as if she had heard nothing else.

"To move on," said the rabbi.

"Where?" At the moment Rachel could manage only monosyllables.

"No one knows, really," said Lily, answering for the Rabbi. "Many from the East, of course, think it's to be reborn on earth. Others believe it's to a heaven higher than this one, or even to complete absorption into the divine essence."

"Whatever it is," added Aeschermann with quiet but intense conviction, "it's not the end. It's a new beginning. That's what we all need," he added after a moment in which no one else spoke, "a new beginning." The rabbi raised his eyes to Rachel. "So, you're to be an outcast."

"I don't know." Rachel felt as if she were floating above everything and none of it really mattered. "I suppose so."

"We won't abandon you!" pledged Lily, taking Rachel's hands.

Rachel felt as if she had been brought back down to earth. At Lily's touch she suddenly experienced tremendous pain, along with an infusion of strength. "Why not abandon me?" she asked matter-of-factly. "You don't believe in what I'm doing, do you?"

"I don't know about that," Lily smiled warmly, tears coming into her eyes, "but I do believe in you. And Rabbi Aeschermann knows that you're specially chosen by God!"

"That I don't understand." Rachel gently released her hands, arose and looked down upon the rabbi. She felt like she very soon would have to leave. "Why would the Lord protect a blasphemer like me?"

Now the rabbi also smiled. "Perhaps because he wants a woman with the chutzpah to meet him eye to eye! Please sit down, my daughter. I've one more thing to say to you. Then you may go."

Without hesitation, Rachel returned to her chair.

"Remember what we were discussing before Mendelssohn intruded?" Aeschermann asked, a twinkle of mischief in his eyes.

"The spiritual meaning of sexuality," answered Rachel. As a student of psychology she was not at all embarrassed by the subject. Nor did she feel threatened by the rabbi, who was behaving like nothing so much as a playful grandfather.

"Yes," he went on excitedly, "but it was in connection with the subject of insanity, the insanity of tearing asunder what God has joined together, of disowning any part of oneself."

"I remember," Rachel nodded.

"Well, we were distracted from the topic, but Rabbi Mendelssohn put me in mind of the other part of the self that people tend to disown—individuality. In fact, selfhood itself!"

Rachel said nothing, but nodded for him to continue.

"What two things do men fear most of all?" he asked rhetorically. "Vulnerability and responsibility. And these are precisely the two things that make us what we are, that make us human. Men fear their own humanity. To be human is to be totally vulnerable and yet absolutely responsible."

"That's not fair!" cried Rachel, at last finding solid ground in a sea of uncertainties. "Why should we be held accountable when we're so weak?"

"We're not weak!" the rabbi declared. "Man's fear of his vulnerability is also fear of his own strength! We have the power to create ourselves. We just have to be willing to suffer whatever it takes. It's like eating. In vulnerability one takes in the raw materials, and in responsibility one forges out of those raw materials the self. We fear our own strength!"

Rachel found herself rocking slowly back and forth in her chair, trying to absorb the meaning in the rabbi's words.

"What I have to say now, my daughter," Aeschermann went on, "is absolutely vital for you to hear." He waited until Rachel's eyes met his. "The man who denies his own selfhood sees everyone who does not as a criminal. That's why this judgment of excommunication has been brought against you."

"I know you have your differences," said Rachel, "but isn't Rabbi Mendelssohn only living up to his duty as a council member?"

"That means nothing!" Rabbi Aeschermann rejoined contemptuously. "There's no such duty. Councils, committees, assemblies—they're all so many ways of not living up to one's responsibility as a human being."

Rachel agreed, but did not know why she agreed. "Once again," she sighed, "I don't understand."

"Don't get me wrong!" said the rabbi. "I'm not advocating fascism. But, as the Greek sage Aristotle put it, the perversion of the best is the worst. Of course, he thought monarchy the best form of government. I don't agree with him on that point, though at times I wish I could, but on the general principle. A council is a gathering of men. If those men take advantage of the gathering to pool their wisdom in order to arrive at the best possible policy, we are all well served. If, however, those men use the fiction of group responsibility to avoid the reality of individual responsibility, all they do is reach the lowest common denominator, a policy based on fear. They choose the safest course of action, and therefore the most dangerous. They're willing to destroy the flowers to rid themselves of the weeds."

"But these are good men!" Lily whispered in troubled amazement.

"Yes, good!" echoed the rabbi. "They follow all the laws. They shrink their absolute and infinite responsibility to manageable proportions by reducing it to a list of rules, and then they follow those rules. Yes, they are good!"

Rachel pondered. "But you yourself condemned me as a rebel!" she exclaimed, remembering back to when she first arrived at the Shabbat meal, so long ago in another age when she was yet only herself and not a communal symbol.

"And so do I still!" said the rabbi with an incongruous laugh. "You know what you're against, but not what you are for. As long as that's so, you will continue to ally yourself with anyone who's against what you're against, even if he's also against what you are for."

Rachel could not gainsay this charge, so she cast down her eyes in silence. The rabbi stood up and approached her, putting an arm around her shoulders.

"Don't worry, my daughter, you'll find your way," he said gently, his compassion like a cooling summer rain falling upon her feverish soul. "We Jews are the archetypal outcasts. We carry the sins of the world. Now you are the outcast of the outcasts. You carry our sins. It's a lonely and painful task, but it's also holy and blessed. Even if your own people despise you, *he* will hold you in his embrace."

These words had a magical effect. The floodgates opened, and all the tears Rachel had been holding inside from the day she was taken to the camps came forth in what seemed like an endless torrent. For once, she did not care. For once, Rachel abandoned herself to the exquisite luxury of shedding tears on her own behalf.

* * *

"Where's your upstart princess, Lucifer?" demanded the fair-haired, shapely, self-righteous Mara, imperious as she had ever been when Yeshua's consort. Clearly this erstwhile matriarch was having difficulty surrendering her ersatz office. *So be it*, Lucifer thought mockingly. Yeshua derived a perverse pleasure from carrying crosses. The Light-Bearer would never take such a harridan to wife. To bed, perhaps, but not to wife.

"I've told you already, Mara, that she won't be here this evening."

Lucifer, Mara and Azazael were gathered in a war council at the Hall of Communion, where all this business had begun. Out of deference to the newcomer, the interior was more brightly illumined than usual, though still dark enough to be conducive to contemplation. Out of discretion, Lucifer had cloaked the globe of vision from the mortal soul's eyes. He could place a certain trust in Azazael, knowing that he would always act in his perceived self-interest. Driven by emotions great and petty, his current bedmate, on the other hand, was not so predictable. Or rather, she was all too predictable. If she caught sight of the globe, she would immediately want to play with the new toy, and there was no knowing where such dabbling in forces beyond her ken might take them all.

Mara had insisted that Rachel be present, why he had no idea, unless she thought that the immediate contrast would show her to advantage. He almost laughed aloud at the thought. At any rate, when Rachel failed to appear, Mara demanded that the three of them combine their considerable force of will to summon her. They had been concentrating on doing just that for some time now, and Lucifer was making an effort in good faith, but they could get no fix on her. Rachel was beyond his monitoring, not to mention his control. This fact alarmed Mara and disturbed Lucifer, but he kept his worry to himself. As did Azazael, if indeed he felt any. Ever the one to pour sleaze over troubled waters, he advised Mara that they make the best of a bad situation and get down to business. Mara protested, arguing that Lucifer himself had said that the girl's unusual combination of passion and innocence, more than anything else, was keeping the considerable opposition to the trial "in principle" from becoming opposition in fact. "They think this is some trick on Yeshua's part," she declared with a bitterness born of what Lucifer sensed was fear that "they" might have hit upon the truth. "They say Yeshua is using her to reveal some new depth."

"It's possible," Lucifer said evenly.

Mara's sea-green eyes glinted with a hint of the savagery that was the thing in her he had always found most arousing. "I tell you, I lived with him for ages and there's no hidden depth! He's just like you and me, with the same needs, the same appetites, the same desires. The only thing that makes him different is his megalomania. No wonder the fools believe in him! Who could doubt someone so infernally sure of himself?"

Mara was on the edge of hysteria, but Lucifer did not care. "A prophet is not without honor..." he baited her.

Mara regarded him with insulting pity. "And will you continue to quote him in your own defense when he wins and puts you on trial?"

"That's not going to happen," Lucifer replied.

"Why not?" she persisted. "Because he gave his word? You forget, I know him. His word is nothing. No doubt he means it. His sincerity is famous, and one of the things that make him shine. But as times change, he changes. He calls it 'the freedom of the spirit!'"

"No, it's not going to happen because I'm not going to lose," Lucifer declared with a calm assurance that he could almost convince himself he felt.

"James is being more of a nuisance than we anticipated, My Lord," Azazael broke in before Mara could respond.

"True," agreed Lucifer, reminded that the hawk-like Azazael's greatest value lay in his uncompromising realism. "But perhaps we can turn that to our advantage."

"How so, My Lord?"

Now Lucifer was also reminded that the chief reason he did not trust Azazael was his unfailing sycophancy. There was something mocking, or at the very least ironic, in the perfection of his obsequiousness. Ordinarily Lucifer would have masked his suspicions and straightforwardly expounded his ideas. But now, just as he had baited Mara, so too would he bait Azazael. On the eve of battle it was only prudent to test the loyalty of his closest subordinates. "I was hoping you might have something in mind."

The only sign of surprise on the part of Azazael was a slow, involuntary blink. "But I'm sure My Lord's idea is vastly superior to my own," he managed to say, quite neatly.

"Of course," returned Lucifer, smiling broadly. "Nevertheless, I'd like to hear yours first."

Azazael bowed. "They've claimed the spiritual high ground of 'love.' We need only demonstrate that their brand of love is so far above everything else that it has no place in reality."

"An excellent strategy," commended Lucifer, "but premature. We may need to fall back upon that position sooner or later, but first we must hazard a more forward line of defense."

"Why all these martial metaphors?" queried Mara. "This is a trial, not a war."

Lucifer smiled condescendingly. "I see you don't have much experience in legal affairs. A trial is a war—a war with rules but no honor."

"My dear," Azazael hastened to soothe Mara's petulance, "you must remember that our master is, first of all, a man of arms. What matters the metaphor," he grinned cajolingly, "as long as we're agreed upon the desired outcome?"

"The overthrow of Yeshua," she said after a moment's silence and to no one in particular, as if only upon speaking these words had she become aware of her deep-seated ambivalence regarding the issue. Azazael chose to overlook her uncertainty, and again, when it came to anything having to do with Mara, Lucifer simply did not care.

"My Lord," said Azazael, "what do you have in mind?"

Lucifer's flair for the dramatic now got the better of him. So what if Mara saw the globe? She was powerless to use it without Azazael. With Azazael, who was almost as intimately acquainted with the globe's secrets as Lucifer himself, his knowledge would be hers. *Together they plot, and together they fall.* Lucifer made the magic gesture, the globe appeared, and the story of Job began to play itself out before them.

"If we bring up the Flood," Lucifer explained, "Paul will say that the evildoers deserved it, and James that man is projecting onto God the consequences of his own sin. Neither argument applies to Job."

"But, My Lord," cried Azazael in what struck Lucifer as feigned alarm, "the assembly might identify you with the Satan of the story, and that would be disastrous!"

Disastrous for me, Lucifer thought, *but do you believe it would be disastrous for you?*

"Besides," Mara joined in, "it's obviously just a story. I've heard Yeshua speak of it a thousand times."

Even though he had anticipated these objections, Lucifer turned away from his henchmen as if to consider what they were saying. Then, turning back, he waved his hand and Job, writhing in agony while his wife bade him curse God and die, vanished, to be replaced by the Egyptians mourning their dead on that first Passover over three millennia ago.

"Of course," cried Azazael, this time in genuine delight, "the Exodus!"

Mara did not look so enchanted. She beheld with obvious distaste the graphic depiction of grief, torment and death. "The Egyptians doubtless suffered terribly at the hands of the Lord," she said, "but didn't they get what they deserved?"

"Perhaps some of them did," replied Lucifer with a patience he did not feel, "but what about the innocent among them? What about the children, the babies?"

"'He visits punishment upon the wicked and their offspring, even unto the fourth generation,'" intoned Mara, her eyes as round, limpid and lifeless as those of any oracle.

"That's precisely the point, darling!" chortled Azazael, smacking his hands together in glee. "He punishes the innocent! Who would call that love?"

"Then we are agreed upon the next step?" asked Lucifer, keeping his eyes fixed upon the airy images that magically conveyed the illusion that they were real. He was beginning to feel that his plan was more than a gambit. What kind of monster would slaughter the first-born of an entire people, especially so masterful and civilized a people? One that, at any cost, had to be stopped!

Azazael took Mara's hand to forestall objection. "We concur, Lord!" he declared. "Your idea is brilliant in its simplicity. There may be no need for my overly subtle strategy after all."

Lucifer was not deaf to the implied insult, but he was used to such parting shots from Azazael. Nevertheless, he knew without a doubt that he must keep a close watch upon his lieutenant, especially now that he was allied with the willful and high-strung Mara. The combination was volatile, and he had to take care that it exploded only if and when it would profit his cause.

After they left, Lucifer summoned up images from other episodes in the tormented history of the world. There were barbarian horsemen overrunning the newly Christianized and thereby emasculated Roman Empire and bringing its magnificence to ruin. There was the burning at the stake of Europe's finest minds in the Christian witch-hunts and Inquisition. There was the devastation of Germany, the heartland of Western civilization, wrought by the fighting of Protestant against Catholic in the Thirty Years War. All this meaningless destruction and more could be laid directly at Yeshua's door. The horror of it all convinced him ever more deeply that the earth's salvation lay in wresting control from the pretender and taking it firmly into his own hands. After all, what needed to be done was patent. Only he had the courage and strength of will to do it. Tears of pity and joy welled up in his eyes, pity and joy he felt for the entire human race. "Your time of salvation is at hand," he whispered. "I am coming soon."

* * *

Wendell wearily closed his eyes and wondered exactly how far into the murky depths of the human imagination Will would dare take him. More to the point, how far would he be insane enough to go?

After court adjourned, James led Wendell once more into the mountains, only this time they descended into a valley shrouded in mist and filled, no doubt thanks to Will's silence, with an air of mystery. Always the professional, Wendell worried over how long they could stay and still return for the trial's resumption in the morning. He thought of raising the issue with James. At least it would serve as excuse for conversation. But then Will was an old hand here compared to Wendell, and it would seem perverse to question his competency in such mundane matters as keeping to schedule. Besides, there were too many variables unknown to him. He had experienced instantaneous travel, though for some reason they had not come to the valley by such a convenient means. Moreover, time here behaved differently. He would not have been all that surprised if this excursion, which on earth would have been difficult to squeeze into a full day, took no more than a few hours of heavenly time.

At the floor of the valley, nestled in what by moonlight appeared to be emerald-green hills along the banks of a crystal-blue stream, sat a temple. At least, Wendell had no idea what else the white stone obelisk-shaped structure might be. Surrounding the temple in artless (or perhaps exceedingly artful) beauty were hundreds of exotic plants, many of which were in riotous flower, their open, richly hued petals drinking in the moonlight. None of these could Wendell recall ever seeing before, not even in Europe, except for the proud, star-shaped lotus with which he had become acquainted during the visit to Sivananda. And again, as upon that outing, music wafted from within the temple, only this time it was not the wild rhythms of what Will had told him was the Indian sitar, but the quiet, brooding, sometimes plaintive breath of a simple wooden flute.

Without hesitation, Will led the way into the interior, where Wendell discovered that the obelisk was merely the tip of the proverbial iceberg. Down, down they went, their way lighted by a soft luminescence with no visible source. As the passageway leveled out, Wendell found himself in a chamber brilliantly lit by hundreds of white, finely tapered candles, with an altar at the center: an uncarved block of a smooth, marble-like stone, only so white that on earth it would have been blinding. Flanking the altar on either side were equally white divans. Will turned to Wendell and indicated that he should recline upon one of the couches. He wanted to ask his friend why everything was white, but in this inner sanctum silence seemed imperative. From a tabernacle hallowing the center of the altar Will withdrew a chalice of crystalline glass. He gently raised Wendell's head and put the cup to his lips. He had no chance to try a taste. James made sure that he downed the tart, syrupy liquid in a single draft.

What happened next was unlike anything Wendell had ever experienced, on earth or in heaven. He would never have thought it possible. He would never have thought it, period! Even now, now that he had returned, he could grasp very little of it with his rational mind, and put even less into coherent concepts, let alone words.

At first he felt himself shaking. No, that was not quite it. He was shivering, vibrating at so tremendous a speed that he feared he would be jolted out of his skin. And then that was exactly what happened! Never had he known such pain, not even when he had been wounded during the war, not even when he had entered into James' sculpture. There was no way to withdraw from the shivering, not even mentally. It encompassed his entire being, shaking him right down to the roots of his soul. If God were a gardener and he a weed embedded deeply in the earth, this was precisely what God would do to work him free.

Finally the quivering was over. Wendell wanted to raise himself from the couch and ask Will why in God's name he had poisoned a man who, if he had not always thought kindly of the professor, at least had tolerated his foibles more than most. That, however, was not possible. Not only could Wendell not move. At the moment at least, the whole concept of motion was meaningless. Everything seemed to be turned inside out. He no longer was in space. Space was in him, and the sanctuary had disappeared. It was as if his consciousness had become an infinite sphere, an unlimited limit outside of which nothing existed, or rather, in relation to which the notion of an outside made no sense. In his earthly life there had been moments in dreams when perhaps he had felt somewhat this way; but then again, this was not at all the same, because now he was not floating in sleep. Everything affected him viscerally, as if he were a gargantuan, hypersensitive stomach. The sensation, or rather, agglomeration of sensations, was disturbing in the extreme, and he had no idea how long he would be able to stand it. But then, of course, he had no choice in the matter.

In hindsight, perhaps the most peculiar aspect of the entire experience was that it brought his awareness to a point of supreme confusion, or integration, he was not sure which. Not only were taste, touch, sight, sound and smell all heightened in intensity to the point of pain, but they were also indistinguishable from one another. And not only were his senses fused, but his other faculties as well. There was no telling thought from feeling from sensation, and no way to discriminate between perception and imagination. It was insufferable, but there was no help for it.

At first Wendell's private, interior universe roiled and gurgled in cosmic indigestion. But then he instinctively struggled to focus, and the more one-pointed his consciousness became, the more articulated became its contents. He was its contents, in all the different roles he had played, all the different selves he had been throughout his life: the self-conscious son of a great liberal who rebelled by becoming his father's straight-arrow obverse; the romantic and charmingly naive lover; the steadfast, sometimes daring, but never really courageous soldier; the by-turns affectionate and distant but unfailingly courteous husband; the larger-than-life magistrate who confidently took the fate of individuals, corporations, and the nation into his hands. These actors and more strutted and fretted upon the stage of Wendell's remarkably unitary consciousness. He did not know how he was able to hold them all together without losing himself in one role or another, but he was.

At first the experience was like a theater, with himself as audience. These vignettes could have involved anyone, and the feeling they evoked was inchoate and evanescent. Gradually, however, he became more of a participant without, paradoxically, ceasing to be an observer. His awareness was like a thread sewing them all together, or a sponge soaking them in. No metaphor could do the experience justice. Gradually his consciousness achieved an indescribable multiplicity-in-unity whereby he became each of these Wendells simultaneously while yet transcending them all. He felt each Wendell feeling himself the one and only Wendell, but at the same time he knew indubitably that each was not. This inescapable awareness of the fragmentation of his being clamped down like a vise upon his soul. He now knew what men feared more than death. He wondered if the trial of God (Imagine him presiding as judge in such a trial!) had been a delusion, the ultimate fantasy of an egomaniac who was now being consigned, on account of his solipsism, to eternal torment in the hell he had created for himself, the hell of a thoroughly lukewarm, hypocritical, self-regarding and disintegrated self.

My God, have mercy upon me!

Initially this prayer—or was it merely a curse masquerading as prayer on the chance it might bring some relief?—had no effect. At length, however, even though nothing actually changed, the assurance came to Wendell that, though there was no way out of this impossible experience, there was a way through it. He felt more and more certain that he was being helped, not punished, if only he would have the courage to accept that help.

He was not sure why or how he knew, but it was clear there was only one thing to do. He had to become, fully and without holding back, each and every one of these Wendells. He had to surrender his transcendence. At the same time, he had to live out each scenario as if he still possessed that transcendence! How was such a thing possible? But then Wendell realized, again without knowing how or why, that the acceptance of such an impossibility was precisely what was meant by faith.

Yes, Lord, let me take up my cross and follow you.

Wendell expected to spend an indefinite period of time, perhaps all eternity, gluing together the bits and pieces of the fractured being his Creator had originally made one and whole. The process, however, turned out to be much simpler than anticipated, and infinitely more painful. It all happened at once, and he found it overwhelming, so much so that he lost consciousness of everything but the pain. As the inner walls came tumbling down, as the musty rooms of his dark and lonesome psyche were exposed to the light of his own spirit, he found there was nothing for him to do. That was the excruciating part, that he could only suffer the process, if such it was, that he could not control it. In a way, it would have been preferable to engage in the Sisyphean task of tackling each cul-de-sac in succession, even if it took forever. There would have been a perverse pleasure, like picking a scab, in reliving each and every neurotic episode and this time doing things right.

He undoubtedly would have chosen that route had he had a choice, but then he realized why. It would not have worked. He would have gone that way because it could never have worked. On the contrary, it would have been the most diabolically clever form of self-protection of all, the ultimate self-deception. While consciously breaking down one wall, he would have subconsciously used its debris to build another wall. In fact, that was precisely how all these walls had come into existence in the first place! In breaking through to manhood he had walled off his childhood, in breaking through to professional maturity he had walled off his romantic youth, and so on. Now, by merely reversing the process, he would not become like the little child who, his father had been so fond of reminding him, alone could enter the kingdom of heaven. He would become a simpering babe, cringing in terror before all those forces of the universe whose intimidating presence had inspired him to turn his being into a fortress-like prison in the first place. No, his true self was not to be found in the past, nor would he have found it in the future had he kept on with the game. All these little selves were not pieces of a puzzle. They were ingredients in an alchemical brew. They all had to be melted down, purified, and integrated simultaneously. There was no way around this immolation. The authentic self was not to be discovered, but forged.

That was the last thought, feeling, or whatever that Wendell remembered before being taken up into a great, bright something to which the word "pain" hardly did justice. Almost immediately he blacked out. When he came to, Will was at his side, looking down into his face with as much curiosity as concern.

"I feel wonderful!" said Wendell, realizing with surprise that it was true. Will's eyes narrowed as if noting the subconscious irony in this statement, but he said nothing. "How was your journey?" Wendell asked cheerily.

The corners of Will's mouth turned up in the merest hint of a smile. "I didn't drink," he answered. "I kept an eye on you instead."

"Awfully thoughtful of you!" enthused Wendell, this time the irony not at all subconscious. He wondered what Will could have done had things become unbearable. In fact, he wondered how much more unbearable it could possibly have been!

Will took Wendell's hand and helped him to his feet. "There is an antidote," he said, as if in answer to Wendell's unspoken question.

"An antidote to salvation?" Wendell laughed, but then he realized the remark was something less than half in jest.

Will's nose flashed crimson. "Do you think it's as simple as taking a draft, even from that chalice?"

Wendell was in no mood to back down. "See here, Will, there was nothing simple about what I just went through!" He patted his pockets, looking for his pipe, as James wearily sank to the divan.

"You won't find it," he said. "All intoxicants have disappeared from the pleroma."

"Tobacco's no intoxicant!" Wendell insisted. He realized as he said it that he was behaving like a child deprived of its candy.

"Like alcohol, tobacco is a means of avoidance," pronounced James, a bit sententiously it seemed to Wendell.

"Avoidance of what?" he returned. "But this is absurd!" he added before James could answer. "You enjoy a good cigar as much as the next man!"

Will closed his eyes and let his head find its own way to the couch. "I wasn't being superior," he sighed. "I was simply stating a fact."

"Avoidance of what?" Wendell repeated less stridently.

"Life. Intensity. Oneself..." Will's voice trailed off as if he were falling asleep. Wendell could not comprehend why his friend was so exhausted when he himself had done all the work. "At any rate," James added at length, "you won't be able to conjure up your brandy, cigars, or pipe now. From this point on, none of us will."

Wendell wanted to ask Will how he could be so cocksure, but felt they were wandering so far afield that, if he indulged his friend in these side-issues any longer, they would never get back to the point of chief importance. "So that's what's wrong with us," he hypothesized. "We're divided against ourselves."

"It's the other way around," Will responded without opening his eyes. "We're divided against ourselves because we run away from life. Certainly, we put on a good show. Soldiers dress up in uniform, parade about, and charge to their deaths to prove to themselves and everyone that they have what it takes. Holy men spend their lives in the desert, fasting and praying and whipping their flesh into submission to prove to themselves and an alien God that they're worthy of acceptance. At the other extreme ordinary, everyday people sentimentally make being everyday and ordinary the ultimate virtue. They're the salt of the earth because they do their jobs and don't meddle in other people's affairs."

Wendell winced. James had to be aware of how close to home landed his barbs. Except for the bit about the holy men, these were Wendell's own modes of being. And was not his single-minded devotion to his studies at law school a species of asceticism? "You're saying that all human existence is a sham?" he asked in a whisper, already knowing the answer.

"Only as a means to an end," replied James, opening his eyes. Not at all remarkably, his interest in the conversation seemed to grow as Wendell's resistance to what he was saying waned. "At bottom, it's all about avoidance."

At first Wendell was too deflated to speak, but then he regained the thread of his original argument. "But that's just my point!" he said with renewed enthusiasm. "One sip from the chalice and you have to face it all. It leaves you no choice!"

A look of pity came into Will's face. "Aye, that's its value," he assented, "and its limitation. The well can be purified, but what's to prevent its pollution again?"

Wendell pondered. "If we only face life when we must," he said, as if repeating a lesson, "then we run from it when we can?"

"Precisely!" exclaimed James, the mentor encouraging his apt protégée. "This holy chalice can force you to confront yourself, but no magic, no matter how powerful, can cause you to choose to confront yourself. That's something you must do on your own."

Again Wendell pondered. "But I don't see why not. Magic by definition is doing the impossible. Why can't magic, at least in principle, make one want to face oneself?"

"Magic is not doing the impossible!" James snorted. "It's simply a technology beyond our current grasp, or a power of the soul we have repressed, forgotten, or have yet to discover. The impossible is the impossible because it can't be done!"

Wendell recalled James making a similar argument at the trial. He had not been overly impressed by it then, either. But since this was obviously an *idée fixe* with his philosophical friend, he decided there was no point in butting heads over it. An indirect approach seemed advisable. "Then there really is no hope, is there?" said Wendell coyly, turning away.

This stratagem, however, did not have the effect Wendell intended. Instead of decisively asserting that yes, indeed, there was hope, and then proceeding to explain why, Will covered his face with his hands as if to stifle an impulse to weep. Then, allowing his arms to drop like dishrags to his side, he stared dully into space and said tonelessly, "That's what I struggle with every day."

Suddenly Wendell wanted to comfort his friend, but had no idea how. It would have been presumptuous in the extreme to think that an arm around his shoulders could ease so deep and spiritual a sorrow, and he could think of nothing to say that Will certainly had not thought of already.

"That's what *he* must struggle with every day," Will finally added, a wee bit of life entering into his voice. "The ultimate paradox! Or is it the ultimate contradiction? The cross upon which all life is crucified. The cross upon which we crucify life!"

Now it was Wendell's turn to sink to the divan. In all this business of the trial of God, he realized, somehow it had never mattered to him what he himself felt. Will was the emotional rock that kept him steady and sure-footed. Now he faced the possibility that the rock was crumbling, that his friend was losing faith in the cause for which he hitherto had been willing to sacrifice both his mortal and immortal life. Wendell's professionalism had always seen him through such moments of despair, but James, he knew, required something deeper. Now that Will had gotten to the bottom of it all and found it to be nothing but corruption, whence would he draw his strength?

* * *

Wandering, once again wandering...

Lily and Rabbi Aeschermann had invited Rachel to spend the night with them, keeping vigil, as the rabbi put it. Their warmth tempted her, but once again she felt that inexplicable draw, taking her she knew not where. *To him, perhaps?* Besides, she did not feel quite at home there. Indeed, since arriving in the pleroma, she did not feel at home anywhere. It was strange, because on earth, no matter how foreign or new the situation, she had never felt she belonged nowhere until she had been thrown into the death camps.

She had nowhere in particular to go, but she had somewhere not to go. Lucifer had been wonderful to her, but she could not return to his palace, not for all the world. At least, not just yet. The night had grown mild. The leafy, overarching branches of the familiar elms and the unfamiliar, silver-flashing aspens felt like so many tender arms reaching out to embrace her. The soft moonlight upon her skin and the cool grass beneath her feet were soothing, healing even, though for what wounds she could not say. The stars no longer seemed alien, but were so many smiling eyes twinkling down upon her. Out here, wherever here was, she felt free. Back there with Lucifer and the rest, or even with Lily and the rabbi, she was a counter in a game — a vastly significant game of cosmic proportions, but a game nonetheless. Out in these mountains, which seemed to go on endlessly, her soul could breathe, as if she were floating through a dream.

Once again she did not know how it happened. She was not aware of his presence until she found herself sitting and looking into his eyes.

"You had quite a day in court," he smiled.

She caught her breath. "Me? I did nothing."

His smile broadened into a grin. "That's what I mean."

She struck out at him in irritation. "Aren't you ever serious?" she cried in exasperation, but then she laughed too. Their eyes joined in ocular embrace. "Besides," she added, "how would you know? I didn't see you there!"

"You don't see everything," he replied, and she remembered the monk in the cathedral.

"So, you're a master of disguise! How do I know that you're not in disguise even now?"

His eyes fell to the ground and his brow furrowed slightly, as if he were giving weighty consideration to her question. Never had she known anyone with so paradoxical a combination of calm and vitality. "We all wear many disguises," he finally said, looking up. "Even you."

"Are you always so full of riddles?" she asked, punctuating her question with an involuntary giggle.

He was about to say something, but then caught himself, his face once again transfigured by that amazing grin.

"What is it?" she coaxed.

"Life itself is a riddle!"

Rachel bent over laughing, and her mouth came tantalizingly close to his. Alarmed by her own temerity, she jumped up and strutted about, as if to investigate the locale. "Why do you keep to these lonely, out-of-the-way places?" she asked. "Is it because you wish to be free?"

He too rose, but made no move to follow her. "You think loneliness is freedom?" he queried.

She laughed again. "Now I know why you're by yourself! You say things people don't want to hear."

"Then why are you here?" he asked, not a trace of irony in his tone.

"Because I like it!" she smiled. "It's refreshing. All the hypocrites and charlatans bore me."

"Are they all hypocrites and charlatans?" he asked meaningfully, taking a step toward her.

She turned away, not wanting him to see the tears that had come suddenly to her eyes. She had always been ashamed of crying and other displays of feminine weakness. She had allowed herself to weep at Rabbi Aeschermann's only because she had hoped to get the tears over with once and for all, all the tears that life had distilled in her heart. Now she faced the distasteful possibility that those tears would never end. "In the camps they weren't," she finally answered, managing to keep her voice even. "They changed in the camps."

"But at what a terrible price," he said, echoing her very thought. He embraced her from behind. She was not at all startled, as she thought she should have been. On the contrary, it seemed natural and right. She turned and returned his embrace. Never had she felt such comfort, such warmth. It was neither stifling nor smothering. Rather, it danced like heated moonbeams in and around her. After holding each other motionless for the longest time, her lips sought his and they sank to the welcoming earth and became one, as they had always, it seemed, been meant to be.

* * *

As Mara and Azazael left the Hall of Communion, they paused at the marble portico, gazing in astonishment at the huge white orb in the night sky from which a pale light emanated. A moon! Along with the new sun had come a new moon! "These are indeed wondrous times!" Azazael murmured, taking Mara's hand. Mara pulled away, leapt down the broad, faintly gleaming steps and sped along the silvery, tree-lined boulevard leading to the more thickly populated part of the Heavenly City as if she desired nothing more than to leave her lover behind. "My love, what's wrong?" cried Azazael, racing after her.

She turned on him in one of her increasingly frequent rages. "These truly are wondrous times, when the Light-Bearer can be hoodwinked by a slip of a girl merely because she let him squirm between her legs! When you made me vow not to mention Rachel's little defection in court today, I only agreed because I never dreamt that Lucifer would fail to raise the issue himself. How blind can our great lord and master be?"

"Hush, my love!" Azazael's voice permitted no defiance. "We must discuss these matters somewhere more private." He took her arm and they moved swiftly through the dark, deserted, unusually quiet streets almost as if they were flying. Doubtless, thought Azazael, the honorable citizens of the pleroma had been tuckered out by the unaccustomed mental exertion of following the trial. They had grown stupid and weak by wasting what they thought was their eternal time indulging in the pleasures in whose pursuit they had also wasted themselves on earth. With the exception of a few hearty souls, they never appeared to wonder just what this pleroma was really about.

Azazael and Mara left the city behind and made their way into the mountains. "Privacy may be necessary," cried Mara, her voice shattering the stillness of the night, "but don't you think this is going a bit too far?"

"My love," said Azazael, squeezing her hand and coming to a halt, "I have my reasons. All will be revealed presently. Trust me!"

"I do," she said, though she was beginning to wonder if she could trust anyone. "But why did you insist that I make that stupid promise? Why are you protecting the girl?" Upon saying this, Mara realized that her suspicion of Rachel was tinged with jealousy. She had the fresh innocence of a newly hatched soul, whereas Mara, though beautiful, bore the heavy aura of age-old experience. Why shouldn't Azazael gravitate toward the girl?

"My love," replied Azazael, looking into her eyes, "do you really believe I could find any woman as ravishing as you? I'm not protecting the wench; I'm using her to our advantage. You called Lucifer our lord and master, but why should that be so?" He paused to let her absorb his meaning. "He may be the Light-Bearer, our spiritual progenitor, but no cosmic law forbids children outshining their parents! Rachel is Lucifer's weakness, and a grave weakness it is. If I read the situation aright—and, as you know, I'm very seldom wrong about such things—he would stop at nothing to keep her, and he would destroy everything if he could not have her!"

"But why?" Mara wondered. "What does he see in her?"

Azazael stepped back as if to give space to the gargantuan thought to which he was about to give utterance, and then confronted her with arms akimbo. "Why, nothing less than the justification of his rebellion against God."

"Justification?" Mara echoed in the same wondering tone. "Why? To whom?"

Azazael smiled and gently took her hand. "To himself, of course. Despite his reputation, our lord and master has an extremely delicate moral sensibility. He has to convince himself that all he does is for the good of the human and angelic races—indeed, that of all creation!"

"I still don't see," said Mara. "How does Rachel satisfy his conscience?"

"If he wins the love of a pure and courageous chit like her, then he himself must be pure."

Mara pondered. "Do you think she's pure and innocent?"

"Of course," answered Azazael gently. "She's also conceited, stuck-up, and full of herself. She's precisely the kind of pretentious hussy I love to deflate." He embraced her. "If we play out this hand wisely, my love, Lucifer and Rachel will destroy Yeshua, and then they'll destroy each other."

Mara wriggled playfully in his arms. "Leaving only us?"

"Leaving only us," he affirmed.

Mara held him tightly, lost in dreams of glory. "And we're what is best for everyone, aren't we?" she asked, a cloud of doubt casting a shadow over her bright horizon.

"My love, you know your heart, and you know my heart. Can there be any question?"

In reply, she kissed him long and deeply and then sank to the earth, drawing him after. But he was immovable.

"We must save that for later, love," he said. "We've important business at hand."

"What could be more important?" she pouted, nevertheless returning to her feet.

"Everything we just discussed, the future of all creation, hinges upon it!" He led the way and she followed obediently, deeper into the mountains.

* * *

Having passed through the oak wood that set the estate apart from the rest of the Heavenly City, Uriel paused to study Lucifer's palace against the backdrop of the silver-orbed night. She had never been to this place, not in all the eons in which it had been so formidably a part of her world. There were no guards, as she had expected, indeed no pomp or panoply at all. Nevertheless the structure, looking like nothing so much as a gigantic, sensuously undulating glass serpent, was impressive enough, at least according to worldly standards. It was, however, too ornate for her taste, lacking in the simple majesty of the few buildings erected by the angels of light in which to conduct business too delicate to be bandied about in public. Strange how attractive seemed by demonic contrast what until now Uriel had regarded as the cold and foreboding angelic architecture.

She glided up the marble steps, feeling as if she were wading through pools of moonlight. In answer to her mental summons, Lucifer awaited her at the entrance. He smiled politely enough, and without a word ushered her into his palace. They passed through a great hall that belied the airy promise of the glass exterior. It was faced with stone, lit by flickering torches and hung with tapestries depicting the mythical war between the angels. Uriel barely repressed a derogatory comment concerning her host's taste in art. Toward the end of the hall they passed under an archway into a smaller room, one wall of which formed a gentle concavity of green-tinted glass looking out upon a garden of tulips of every color imaginable. Bookshelves lined the other three walls. So, here was one of the many libraries for which Lucifer's palace was famous! The volumes were ornately, even gaudily bound, but it was clear from their aura that they were not merely for show. There was no doubt that Lucifer had read them. There was also no doubt that Lucifer spent much time in this room. He became noticeably more at ease upon entering it. It was sparsely but comfortably furnished in blue and green brocades, so much more soothing than the red and gold or black and white of the hall and the rooms she had glimpsed in passing. Also, there was a refreshment bar in an unobtrusive but easily accessible nook. So, Uriel thought, Lucifer had become domesticated! Not only did he confine himself to his palace most of the time but, she would wager, hardly ever did he venture forth from this room.

Lucifer motioned to her to make herself comfortable upon one of the divans, but she ignored the invitation.

"Are you alone?" she asked, deliberately avoiding any amenities. It was bad enough she had stooped so low as to traffic with the enemy. She did not have to pretend they were friends.

For some reason, the question set off in her host momentary but intense consternation. Then he covered it over with an air of smooth civility. "I'm at your service," he bowed, a cold, ironic smile playing about his mouth. "But why this air of secrecy?" he asked, the smile deepening. "Have you finally seen reason and decided to come over to my much maligned but truly noble cause?"

Though she automatically replied with a look of disdain, she was surprised to see, from looking into his eyes, that there was genuine hope at the heart of his seemingly playful query. She marveled at his sincerity. Now she knew that the pesky intuition that had brought her here was more than her spirit's natural defense against despair. Beneath the proud sophistication and cynical wit, Lucifer had a purpose that, at least in his own mind, was lofty and heroic. If she could convince him that his present course of action ran counter to that purpose, she would have a chance.

"Then why are you here?" he asked, more offended, she could tell, than he was willing to admit, even to himself.

"Why are you doing this, Lucifer?" she implored. "When has he ever treated you with anything but the utmost love and kindness?"

Lucifer laughed as he crossed to the bar, took a green glass bottle from the cabinet, and poured its blood-red contents into a silver chalice. He did not bother to offer her some. "I had forgotten how refreshing you are, dear sister. Always right to the point!" He took a sip from the chalice, swilled the liquid about in his mouth, and swallowed. His face puckering in distaste, he set the chalice down so hard upon the marble counter that she would not have been surprised had the smooth stone cracked, the impact sounded so very much like thunder. Clearly the liquid was not what he had hoped it would be, and neither was she. "What would you have me do?" he pleaded, equally direct.

"Stop this farcical trial!" she replied.

Lucifer turned swiftly as if to attack her, but then willed himself into an eerie calm. "You're concerned for his welfare," he said quietly. "That's as it should be. You love him. But if this trial is really a farce, why worry?"

"It's a dangerous farce!" she exclaimed, her aura leaping out and her eyes boring into his, but Lucifer did not flinch.

"It's dangerous, that's true," he said judiciously, "as any worthwhile quest must be. But I assure you, though farcical elements may obtrude from time to time—pathetic creatures that they are, mortal souls will have their comic relief—this trial is the most serious business to be transacted in the pleroma since the creation of the world!"

"Business?" Uriel echoed with contempt.

"Of course!" said Lucifer, as if he were talking to a child. "It's all business of one sort or another. One may call them families, castes, classes, religions, tribes or nations, but the human race is organized into millions of corporations, big and small, each seeking to maximize profits for its shareholders."

"I don't understand!" Uriel broke in. "Profits?"

"Surely even you, though pristine in your purity, aren't that naive!" The ironic smile returned to Lucifer's lips. "Profit is for humans what you say love is for the angels. It gives their lives meaning. It governs everything they do. They're willing to go through hell if the odds are even that they'll come out ahead."

Uriel wondered if Lucifer could really be so simple-minded. "Not every human is driven by greed. The love of money is not the guiding light of every earth-soul's life!"

Lucifer laughed. "My dear Uriel, you define profit much too narrowly! Profit goes far beyond the accumulation of economic counters. Most seek treasures of the material sort, it's true, but some seek the riches of the mind. An elect few savor the wealth of the spirit. In the end, however, it all boils down to profit."

Uriel reflected. "Suppose what you say is true. What does it have to do with this trial?"

Lucifer's eyes flashed and his skin glowed with a sudden surge of vitality. He was in his element, expounding his most cherished ideas to one hitherto unexposed to the truth. He strutted up and down before her, preening himself. "It has everything to do with this trial!" he proclaimed. "Until now, conflict has been the medium in which human culture has grown. On the whole, it's been a nourishing medium, weeding out the weak and exercising the strong.

Yeshua's governance fostered this conflict."

"How can you say that he encouraged conflict?" Uriel protested. "He's done nothing but preach, teach and live love!"

"My sister," said Lucifer, placing a hand upon her shoulder. It was meant to be a reassuring gesture, but she found it disquieting. "Don't let emotion cloud your judgment. I'm not attacking him. On the contrary," he smiled, winking in conspiratorial mischief, "I'm giving the devil his due. I'm admitting that, despite his impossibly high-minded ideals, on the whole Yeshua is leaving the world a better place."

"*You* are the devil," Uriel said pointedly. "And isn't talk of Yeshua leaving a bit premature?"

"I apologize if my candor has introduced discord into the heavenly harmony of your being." Lucifer's deliberately warm smile was eloquent of his contempt. Uriel now knew that he hated her, though whether this hatred was personal or categorical, having to do with something she had done or simply on account of her being one of the unfallen, she could not tell. "I'll strive for greater tact." He bowed his head as if contemplating how to proceed. Uriel suddenly felt it useless to go on. If Lucifer harbored such ill feeling toward her, she could imagine the depth of his malice toward Yeshua.

The Dark Lord raised his head and resumed his peroration. "Competition has been the seed-bed of civilization. It's forced savage tribes to stop frittering away their restless energies in appeasing non-existent gods and fleeing ghosts and shadows, and to come to grips with the hard facts of the objective world. Had it survived, the Garden of Eden would have been the death of the human spirit. But now mankind is ready to take the next step, to graduate from competition to cooperation. Yeshua's brand of creative chaos, to put it in charitable terms, hasn't merely become a hindrance. It now threatens the survival of life on earth!"

"You talk of disorder," said Uriel thoughtfully, having forgotten her discomfort in following the logic of his discourse, "but I still don't see what love has to do with chaos."

Once again she felt the chill flash of his hate. "Love, emotion, whatever you wish to call it, is nothing but chaos! Until recently humans understood this and regarded love as a luxury rather than a necessity, a luxury whose traffic had to be strictly regulated. Marriages were arranged with a view toward social equilibrium. Children submitted to parental authority and citizens to government authority, and those who did not suffered the consequences."

"Most of the world is still as you describe it," said Uriel. "You think it desirable, this condition of blind servility?"

"It's a matter of priorities," replied Lucifer. "Intelligent obedience is always preferable to unthinking submission. It makes the difference between civilization and barbarism. But barbarism is superior to savage chaos, and that's precisely the condition to which mankind will return if it continues to take this business of love seriously. The seeds of this chaos are already sprouting in that land of the brave and the free whose democratic ideals are so dear to Yeshua's heart. I readily grant you that romanticism gives a tinge of excitement and passion to what otherwise would be a drab and colorless existence. But to seriously advocate it as a way of life—indeed, as the only way of life—is criminal!"

Lucifer paused, inviting comment, but Uriel remained mournfully silent.

"So you see," he concluded, "that's why we're having this little trial. To allow Yeshua to continue down his path of 'love' is unthinkable. He must be stopped before civilization, indeed creation itself, comes undone!"

"And how would you hold it together?" asked Uriel, her voice soft and fragile, her aura sinking into a purple so deep it was almost black.

Lucifer studied her as if gauging her sincerity. "As I said, competition has outlived its utility. Cooperation is the key to climbing to a higher plateau. The human race can't make this climb unaided. It needs a guide. All corporations must now be merged into one supracorporate entity with one executive to oversee and coordinate all its operations."

Uriel now did something foreign to her—she lowered her gaze. "And doubtless," she asked evenly, "you're the one best qualified to fill this position?"

"It certainly isn't Yeshua!" rejoined Lucifer. "For one thing, it's not at all his style. And for another, he's obsessed with this idea of love. Can you think of anyone else with the qualities such a position of supreme leadership requires?"

Uriel once again looked into Lucifer's eyes, this time searching for some depth of soul to which she could appeal. She found none. "Now I understand," she finally said. "All your nobility is a smokescreen for your lust for power. The terrible thing is that you even fool yourself."

Lucifer recoiled as if struck. "I open my heart to you as a brother, and this is how you repay me?"

"On the contrary," Uriel smiled derisively, "you brag to the enemy about your brilliant strategy because you're so certain of your victory. Well, Satan, the war isn't over yet!"

Lucifer seethed at the hated alias. His body melted into liquid fire. "I could hurt you!" he cried.

"We could hurt each other," she retorted, "but what would that accomplish? You and I both know that the real battle must be fought on a different level."

With what must have been a supreme act of will, Lucifer returned to his usual self. "It will all come down to this in the end, you know," he said in a contempt now laced with sadness. "It always does. He never permits it to go any other way."

Uriel turned away. She knew the truth in what he was saying all too painfully well. She felt a weakness that, had she never experienced it before, she might have regarded as weariness—a strange and yet familiar emptiness at her very center. "Why won't you stop this, Lucifer, before it grows into something no one can control? Aren't you the one who loves order?"

Though she was not facing him, she felt him look upon her with pity. "The sick body must be purged of its disease," he answered, "before a new equilibrium can be established. The bankruptcy of Yeshua's way must be impressed upon all before they will be willing to abandon their sentimental illusions and face reality. In comparison with the grave danger to be avoided and the tremendous good to be attained, an interim time of troubles is a small price to pay. The future of creation itself is at stake! Individuals count for nothing. Surely you can't object to that logic, not if you're a genuine disciple of Yeshua. He and I agree on this point. Not on anything else, but certainly on this. After all, what is his 'way of the cross' but a romanticizing of the necessity of sacrificing the individual for the sake of the whole?"

Uriel whirled back upon Lucifer with one last surge of hope. "The individual sacrificing himself, not being sacrificed!"

Lucifer's face darkened. "If Yeshua continues on his present course, he will be sacrificing himself."

"What does that mean?" she cried. "You started this trial, not he!"

"There's only one way for him to avert disaster," explained Lucifer, his manner uncharacteristically solemn. "He must abdicate."

Uriel felt as if she and Lucifer were in two different universes. "But how is that possible? He is who he is. It's not an office. It's him!"

Now it was Lucifer's turn to be amazed. "You really believe that, don't you? May I ask why?"

Uriel now understood that there would be no compromise, no accommodation. War with the fallen ones, in whatever form it came, would be to the death. "I simply know it, that's all, the way a child knows its mother. He is the source of our being."

"A child will call mother anything that sticks a tit in its mouth!" Lucifer retorted.

Uriel was no longer angry. Could one be angry with a blind man who stumbled over you? "Let's just say, then, that I prefer his sweet and nourishing milk to your bitter poison."

That remark ended it. Both knew there was nothing more to say. Strange paradox, Uriel noted, how the heat of impassioned conflict could produce such a chill in the air. She turned and swept through the arch, down the great hall, out the open doorway and down the no longer glistening marble steps. The moon had set. She wanted to fly off into the beckoning empyrean but was through with running away. Even though none of her comrades knew it, the war had begun in earnest. She would seek out her commander-in-chief and receive her marching orders.

* * *

Like huge yet slender and delicate hands reaching upward in prayer, the blue-green pines towered above them. The effect reminded Rachel of the Christian cathedral she had once visited at

THE JUDGMENT OF CHRIST

Chartres. She had been but a little girl on holiday with her parents, touring through Belgium and France, and perhaps because her father was uncomfortable with the religious atmosphere, they stepped in only for a moment, but she had never forgotten it. Later, in the camps, she wondered how the Gentiles could hold so much inspiration and so much hatred together in their souls.

The cathedral had towering buttresses that held up the sky, and magnificent stained-glass windows that transformed simple sunlight into poetry. The warmth of the colors had made her feel deliciously secure from all the terrors that the world, especially the modern world, held for a six-year-old girl. Later, in the camps, she would sometimes burst into fits of uncontrollable laughter remembering how frightened she had been of trains and motorcars and sirens and big, imperious-looking policemen. As it turned out, she had been right to be frightened, for these were the very things that brought her and her loved ones to annihilation.

But it had not been annihilation exactly, at least not for her, Lily, Rabbi Aeschermann, and the handful of other Jews she had met here who claimed to have come from the camps. And why would they lie? To have been "processed" through Auschwitz, Treblinka, Sobibor, or any of the hundreds of other hells created by the Nazis was no badge of honor. On the contrary, as far as she could tell, it meant having a soul that was, perhaps irremediably, darkened and crippled with horror.

Now, for the first time since arriving in this place, she did not feel crippled. Lying in the warmth of his arms did for the light of her spirit what that stained glass long ago had done for the light of the sun. The radiance of his being enfolded her. He was the only person she had ever known who did not seem divided against himself. In their lovemaking thought, feeling, and sensation became as one. It was exactly what Rabbi Aeschermann had been talking about! Passion and love melted together in a spiritual fire whose intensity came, she could tell, from him. Without having known it, he was what she had been searching for all her life. Lying here in his arms, she wished the entire universe would go away and leave them alone like this forever.

In sleep his breathing was regular and deep, like that of an untroubled child. She disengaged from his unconscious embrace, rolled over and studied his face. The moon had set long ago but a faint iridescence, which she could well believe had been generated by their lovemaking, illuminated his features.

To any casual observer his face, especially in repose, would certainly appear unremarkable. To love's eyes, however, it was filled with magic. The high cheekbones indicated delicacy of feeling. Even in sleep the prominent nose, set of the mouth and lightly bearded jaw betokened firmness, definition of character, and strength. The high forehead signified intelligence and nobility of spirit. The full lips and dark complexion revealed the sensual nature from which Rachel had drunk that night with such delight. The fine, soft brown hair enfolded the whole in an aura of gentle kindliness and tender vulnerability. All that was lacking were the now slumbering eyes that, despite their equally soft brown hue, suffused his waking face with animated fire.

A nightingale enlivened the silence with its sweet melody, and suddenly the eyes of which she had been thinking were before her. He did not move, but the deeply serious way in which he looked at her felt like a caress. "What is this place?" she asked him, as if he were the fount of all knowledge. He did not seem at all taken aback by the abrupt question. She felt then that she was right to look to him for answers.

"It's the point at which heaven is coming together with earth," he replied matter-of-factly.

"I don't understand," she said, withdrawing a bit in order to give space for the exercise of her intellect. "What is 'heaven'? For all that, I suppose I don't even know what you mean by 'earth!'"

He rose, swiftly yet smoothly, gently lifting her with him to her feet, and walked her over to the edge of the steep precipice. "Look!" he commanded.

She peered into what at first seemed a void. Gradually she made out a swirling of luminescent winds, currents and cross-currents of color and evanescent forms, shadow and light, together with echoes of voices and snatches of sound, vague rumblings and whisperings, callings and cries, but nothing that coalesced into definite form or word.

"Look deeper," he whispered, holding her from behind, his lips close to her ear.

She was not sure what he meant, but as she concentrated upon a particular vortex to which she felt drawn, it slowly materialized into a ramshackle tenement in the heart of a European city, from the sunny, colorful, grandiose and antiquated look of it Italian or Greek. Of course, Sicily! A young man, no more than twenty, was arguing wildly with a much older man, possibly his grandfather. The older man was telling him he had to go into hiding, or better yet, sail to America, where the *patrono* would never find him. The younger man, Rachel learned in the course of the argument, was in love with the *patrono's* mistress, and worse, she was in love with him. The younger man declared he would rather die than leave his beloved. The older man said that was all well and good for him, the romantic hero, but what about his mother? Didn't she depend on him for her bread, and didn't she dote on him as if he were more to her than her own life? How could he be so selfish as to think only of himself?

Rachel found herself engrossed in this battle of affections and wills. She felt as if the fate of the universe hung upon the young man's decision, which was most strange, since for one thing she had no idea which course was right, and for another she already knew that the question was moot because within an hour the *patrono's* gunmen would shoot him and his beloved dead. When the young man left for his ill-fated rendezvous without having made up his mind, Rachel felt cheated somehow, she did not understand why.

Her own lover remained still the whole time, but she knew that he saw what she saw. "Do you wish to see the end?" he asked, as the young man ran from the tenement into the bright morning light.

No, she did not.

"Do you wish to look elsewhere?"

Yes, she did.

This time she found herself drawn to a village in sub-Saharan Africa. It was late afternoon, and the people were holding a celebration. They had been engaged in a land-dispute with a European mining consortium. The survival of the village itself had been at stake. If the foreign corporation had been granted title to the land it wanted to strip-mine, the people would have had nowhere to grow the crops and graze the cattle that fed them and their children. After long months of harrowing litigation in which the wealth of the white men and the corruption of the local officials made defeat appear inevitable, rescue had come as if by the hand of God. A famous and saintly Belgian missionary had enlisted in the peasants' cause. He had come to live with the villagers and, as a last resort, gone on hunger strike. Under pressure of world opinion, the government had ruled against the miners. Now the people were releasing their fear in an exhalation of joy, and the missionary was rejoicing with them.

Throughout the day and into the twilight, they danced and sang hymns in a way that again reminded her of Rabbi Aeschermann's ideas, because never had she witnessed such a natural and spontaneous integration of the sensual and the spiritual. Then, as the moon rose, the people drifted away by families, couples, and individuals until the missionary — a tall, white-haired, wrinkled and plain-looking but nonetheless impressive man — was left alone in the midst of the dying bonfires, gazing up into the night sky. Looking up, Rachel almost felt, at her.

Then the thunder came.

Rachel had not anticipated it at all. She knew what it was, of course — machine gunfire, and the antiphonal screams of the wounded and dying. White mercenaries had surrounded the village and were systematically wiping it out. Rachel wanted to turn away, to turn it off, to turn herself off, but she could not. By sharing vicariously in their joy she had become so deeply enmeshed in the peasants' lives that she could not leave them now in their terror and pain.

Within a half-hour it was over, a half-hour that seemed the equivalent of eternal damnation. The soldiers-of-fortune left no one alive, not even the missionary, who had rushed to confront them when the shooting started and was among the first to die. No matter. The bodies would be burned, the official story would be that the village had fallen prey to plague, and the priest would be posthumously decorated with the nation's highest civilian service medal by the very man who had ordered the massacre. When the mercenaries completed their work, they melted into the jungle whence they came. With revulsion Rachel realized that, for everyone save the victims themselves, the slaughter was a business transaction—nothing less, nothing more.

"You're cold," he said, holding her still closer, enveloping her with tenderness. She felt herself shivering.

"Why have you shown me these things?" she broke away angrily.

"I've shown you nothing!" he declared, matching her sudden ire with his own. "You've seen for yourself."

"But you knew what I was seeing!" she cried, sinking weakly to her knees.

He was implacable. "Yes, but you chose what to see."

"Why would I choose such sights?" she retorted. "Haven't I already seen enough?"

He stood over her, looking down on her as if he were her judge. "Perhaps you needed reminder that no people has a monopoly upon suffering and death."

If he had heated a dagger until it was white and then slowly twisted it through her groin and belly and on up into her heart, he could not have caused her more pain. Nothing that the Nazis and their henchmen did to her in all her time in the camps, not even the brutal and repeated rapes, hurt half so much as this. She wanted to be angry, to strike out at him, to run away and never see him again, but there was no room for fury or anything else. The pain was all.

He squatted down so he could look into her eyes and placed his small, almost childlike hands gently upon her shoulders. Her pride told her she should be disgusted by his touch, but instead she found it comforting, more comforting than before, when there had been no pain or anger between them. *What could this mean?* They remained that way, almost motionless, for the longest time, and the pain remained as well. But then it began to change, to brighten into something even more unbearable because it was in the no-man's-land between agony and joy. As he gazed into her eyes, his look correspondingly deepened into one of pure love.

What was she to believe real, the pain or the ecstasy? Indeed, how could she make up her mind when the two were so damnably intertwined? It was all too much for her! It would have been too much for anyone. Slowly, and fighting for consciousness every inch of the way, her head sank to the enticingly soft green, and she slipped beneath all conflict into a dreamless slumber.

* * *

Through forest and meadow in the wakeful night, Mara trailed Azazael obediently up the winding mountain path, but she did not know if it was out of love or only because she had nowhere else to go. That she did love him she had no doubt, but this love was different from her love for Yeshua. That love had been all consuming, it was true, just as, according to the erotic poetry of her people's tradition, love was meant to be. But it had also been one-sided. She had never felt as if he loved her, at least not in the same way. He had been everything to her. She had been something to him, she supposed, since he had made her his queen, but she had not been everything.

She was also not everything to Azazael, obviously. In fact, though Yeshua and Azazael differed in most ways as cloud to sun and dark to light, they were the same in one important way. Both men were self-centered. Their own goals and ideals were more important to them than anything or anyone else. Yeshua, however, put on a show of caring for others. He was the consummate martyr. Azazael had no pretense. He was what he was. She found his lack of hypocrisy refreshing.

So she was not everything to Azazael; but even though she pretended to him and even herself at times, neither was Azazael everything to her. Really, now that she thought about it, the arrangement suited her perfectly, at least for the present. They could laugh together and cry alone. There were no demands and no show of commitment. She was free to be the self she had never been.

So why was she following him now? Perhaps because she did not know what that self was, and exploring in one direction was as good as exploring in any other. Or perhaps because he was the most intriguing of all the entities she had encountered in the pleroma through the nearly two millennia she had been confined to this realm. Or perhaps simply because she chose to. She did not have to settle on any one of these reasons. Nothing fateful hung upon her motives, as it had always done with Yeshua. She was following him, and that was good because *she* was doing it. What else mattered?

As they made their way deeper into the mountains, the going was not as easy as it used to be. Until now souls had glided effortlessly over the varied and beautiful landscape of the pleroma, not really touching, or being touched, by anything. The pains and pleasures of earthly flesh were here only the afflictions and delights of the imagination. Now, however, there was suddenly an edge to it all. The early morning mountain mist really *felt* cold. Moving over the rough terrain required a bit of effort. Her skin actually became moist and sticky, as if she were sweating!

The look and sound of things were also undergoing transformation. The soft, sourceless iridescence that hitherto had gently illumined the night now gave way to the harder, almost metallic sheen of the moonlight, and when the moon set the darkness was amazingly complete. The nocturnal hush in which the denizens of the pleroma had taken their rest was now broken by sounds too faint to be identified, but eerily reminiscent of the steady rhythm of frogs and cicadas, the mournful hooting of night-owls, and the low growls and shrill cries of animal predators and prey that punctuated the nights of earth.

Not only were there different sights and sounds, but also sound and sight themselves were different. By the end of the first day of the trial, Mara's ears were throbbing with pain from the unaccustomed pulsations. Her eyes burned from the glare of the newly hatched sun. Physicality was coming to the pleroma, and no matter how much it hurt, she loved it! Mara really did not mind that Azazael was unsure of his destination, and hence had to follow his nose rather than will them there. The journey was carnally delightful!

It was also delightful for another reason. Since she had only to follow her lover's lead, her mind was free for some needful contemplation. She wondered if the pleroma's transformation had anything to do with the spiritual revolution Azazael and Lucifer were spearheading. After all, was not the "fall" of these two angels simply the embrace of sensuality in all its myriad and wondrous forms? So perhaps now the souls of the pleroma were reaping the fruits of the rebels' pioneering efforts, the coming together of heaven and earth! Maybe that was why she was following Azazael, because he was a leader in a cause so much nobler than Yeshua's fleshless and anemic spirituality. What was this love of which the soon-to-be-deposed king of heaven constantly spoke if he could not give himself, body and soul, to his queen?

Azazael now interrupted Mara's reflections. He suddenly stopped and crouched low, signaling her with a squeeze of the hand to do likewise. They halted in some bushes not far from a clearing that was aglow with light from the still hidden rising sun. Mara peered intently into the glade, and after a moment she made out Yeshua in the company of another woman whom she could not see clearly but was certain was none other than Lucifer's beloved Rachel! She was sleeping, and Yeshua was holding her tenderly as satisfied lovers do, studying every detail of her face with seemingly endless fascination. Mara did not remember him ever looking at her that way. "Why have you brought me here?" she whispered to Azazael. Azazael did not answer. "It's quite astonishing," she went on, her tone neutral, even conversational, "how such a pure and innocent creature could manage in just a few days to make herself mistress of the two most powerful men in the universe."

The spasmodic jerk Azazael gave her hand revealed that the barb had struck home. "My love, we must be quiet!" he said in a low but commanding voice. "We must wait until Yeshua leaves."

Mara bit her lip and was amazed to taste blood. As the sky grew steadily lighter, she and Azazael waited. Then they heard a noise from behind and turned to behold a deer bounding through a thicket. Except for imaginary ones in paintings, she had never seen an animal in the pleroma! The deer bounded past them and slowed as it neared the clearing. When they looked back to where the lovers had been lying, Yeshua was gone.

"He always enjoyed his little theatricals," chuckled Azazael.

At first Mara's heart was too full of emotions she could not name to speak. She watched in bittersweet silence as the animal gingerly pawed its way up to the still sleeping Rachel and stood, almost protectively, over her. It was a large-horned buck, a magnificent beast, but it moved with the elegant grace of a doe.

"So, you really believe he has power over the animals!" she finally laughed.

"My dear," Azazael rejoined, "every spirit of any intelligence has power over the animals, if it wants it." He did not seem at all surprised by the deer's advent. "But right now that's of no importance. I've a plan that will require all our brains and daring. If it succeeds, Yeshua and Lucifer will no longer be lords of the manor. We will!"

Even though Mara found this reiteration as astonishing as Azazael's initial declaration, she could not turn away from the deer and the slumbering Rachel. "You keep saying you have a plan," she whispered in quiet intensity. "What is it?"

Azazael stepped back, as if anticipating her response to the answer he was about to give. "You must make friends with Rachel."

She turned to him with no change in mood or expression. "Will this lead to her downfall as well?"

Azazael smiled in relief and squeezed her hand. "Most assuredly, my love."

Mara returned his smile and then resumed her observation of Rachel. The sharp rays of the sun came shooting over the horizon as the buck licked her face and she awoke. It was time for Mara and Azazael to escort Rachel to the court.

Chapter 7

Yeshua leapt and danced through the forest, humming improvised melodies and marveling once again, as he had countless times through the ages, at how quickly life could vault from despair to joy. Squirrels and chipmunks chattered as they frolicked about him, and birds flew playfully over and around his head. As he settled into a rapid and pleasurable spin, something he had picked up from the dervishes long ago, he gave thanks to his Father for once again raising him from the pit.

Then he stopped. The pit, he knew, would come again, and again and again and again and again, and keep coming until all his brothers and sisters shouldered their own spiritual burdens instead of leaving them for him to carry. Through him the creative power of God flowed to all humanity, but through humanity it flowed to all creation. Though in moments of misery he had sought relief, he knew he would never drop his precious bundle of life until the others were willing to take it up. And here was one, the wondrous Rachel, who might carry it with him, by whom it might be received as blessing rather than avoided as curse! He began to spin again.

His memory held the history of endless days of loneliness through which he had stood fast, punctuated by climaxes of terror in which he had chosen torture and death rather than betray his Father's trust. Worst of all were the heart-wrenching dilemmas he had repeatedly confronted where to be faithful to life meant to give up life's promise of fulfillment. Every such experience filled his universe with a despair from which the only possible relief seemed total and eternal oblivion. Then, when all felt lost, new life awakened in his soul. It did not matter whether the life came from within or without. It was all one, all part of the same treasure he received from his heavenly Father and that was his to bestow upon all creation. In pouring himself out upon the world, he received himself back, and more. He opened up the possibility of love, of a sacred marriage between God and creation. He had looked to Mara for the consummation of that marriage, but she had never been able to accept the truth that the price of love was the cross. Now this novice, this Rachel, had taken the first step, a step Mara had refused to take in all the centuries she had been with him. *Truly, the last shall be first and the first last.*

Had he and Mara really been together? Yeshua's spinning slowed with the weight of remembrance. Mara's desertion had been worse than any execution. The pain had been his only reality. It had made every moment an unbearable eternity. Now, in memory, that pain was abstract, as if it had never been. Rachel had changed everything! "Father," he murmured, closing his eyes and falling to his knees in prayer, "I'll be grateful for all you've brought me through, the anguish as well as the joy, if only it leads me to her, if only she's mine in the end!" Even though he felt the gathering of spirits about him, he remained kneeling, his head bowed and body motionless, held in his Father's embrace. When he stood up at last, all the angels of the council were gathered before him and Uriel, not Mikael, came forward to speak.

"Lord," she said, all but prostrating herself before him, "the part I've chosen is too heavy for me to bear. I can't go against you, not even for your own sake. Forgive me for ever having doubted you!"

Yeshua took her by the hand and gently raised her to her feet, then looked into her eyes. He could see so deeply into her, much more deeply than she could see into herself, and what he saw made him smile. "You've not been fighting me," he said at length. "You've been fighting your way to me."

Uriel's tears flowed freely, glistening like dew on her cheeks. Her aura, at first slowly and tentatively but then, when she saw his smile broaden, strongly and assuredly, reached out to embrace him in a rainbow of love. "Lord, I will never abandon you again!" she proclaimed. "From this moment forth, I'm your faithful servant."

"Serve the love in your own heart," he said, "and you'll be serving me."

Uriel stood motionless, drinking in his presence. The other angels drew close around her to lend their affectionate support to their repentant sister. Even the animals hushed in honor of the tender sanctity of the moment. Then Uriel broke the silence. "He means to destroy you," she warned, and her words were like the rumbling of distant cannon.

"That he can never do," Yeshua reassured her.

"He can cause you great suffering," she continued, "and do so with the noblest of motives!"

No one could ever guess how deeply troubled he was by her words, nor how terrible that suffering would be. "It's what I'm here for," he declared, himself marveling at how such great assurance could coexist with such deeply rooted fear. Yet that was always the way it had been with him, and no one had been able to see it. Others either perceived the fear or the courage, but never both. Except for Mara. She had seen both and thought him a hypocrite, which meant that she had not really seen him at all. "It is the cross."

Uriel's auric embrace grew stronger, and a look of compassion came into her eyes. Did she see what he was about? More importantly, did she understand? "I pray that this time it need not come to that," she murmured.

"That's in my Father's hands," he replied, though he really meant it was in the hands of his fellow human beings, but that would become obvious soon enough. "But now," he went on, addressing the entire council, "you've a trial to watch over, and I must be about my Father's business." Yeshua returned Uriel's auric embrace by hugging her to him, something no angel had ever experienced before. After that he returned to his Father to rest in communion before the next stage of testing began. To the angels, he simply disappeared.

* * *

The atmosphere was no less sunny and filled with excitement at the opening of the second day of the trial than it had been at the first. The bright crimson dawn heralded a deep-blue, brightly lit and cloudless sky. The air wafted almost as fresh as any Wendell had breathed in the Alps, or even at Sivananda's mountain retreat.

This renewal of nature's vitality communicated itself with delightful infectiousness to the heavenly denizens who, it seemed, had so long been without it. As the citizens of the pleroma streamed into the field, which this time did not become an island except, perhaps, by way of metaphor, there was a buzz of animated talk concerning the new sun and moon, the increasing physicality, the disappearance of mentally addictive substances, and numerous sightings of animals and birds. Theories abounded as to the significance of these unprecedented events but everyone agreed upon one thing—they all had something to do with the trial. Wendell was enough of a student of modern philosophy in general, and David Hume in particular, to know that contiguity alone did not prove causality. Nevertheless, he himself had the strongest feeling that these proceedings betokened, whether for obvious or not so obvious reasons, a cosmic upheaval, perhaps even a revolution!

As the crowd gathered, it struck Wendell how homogeneous these mortal souls were becoming. Beneath the differences in language, garb, modes of self-expression and what have you, there was now a common purpose, or at least activity, that united everyone. For the most part, each continued to stick with those of his own cultural sort, but there was an unmistakable feeling of greater unity. There was no fumbling today. All took their proper places and waited for Wendell to pound his gavel. As soon as he did so, Lucifer arose and opened for the prosecution.

"All souls of the pleroma—indeed, all creatures throughout the universe—have a stake in what we do here today. All of you have heard the defense proclaim the alleged Lord God innocent of the evil and suffering in the world. He supposedly made the world, he presumably controls it, but he is not in the least responsible when things go wrong. We weak and finite beings, with our alleged free will, are the source of all its problems. He must allow us this free will, or else we would be nothing more than robots, not persons at all."

Lucifer took a moment to survey his audience, and what he saw seemed to satisfy him.

"But let's look at a case in which this excuse of laissez-faire can't hold."

Now he looked right at James, but the professor remained

undisturbed, his nose only slightly pink.

"According to the second book of the Judaeo-Christian Bible, to whose authenticity the defense has already, if conditionally, stipulated, the Lord allowed his chosen people, the Israelites, to fall into slavery in Egypt. They labored hard at making bricks for the pharaoh's building projects. When they multiplied—as underclasses are wont to do, having no other source of amusement—the Egyptians were alarmed, fearing the Hebrews would form a powerful fifth column were Egypt ever to face foreign invasion. Indeed, it may be that Egypt had succumbed to enemy armies in the past, and that the pharaoh who dealt so kindly with Jacob and his sons was not even Egyptian!

"Be that as it may, around the time of Moses' birth, the pharaoh ordered that every man-child born to a Hebrew be drowned in the Nile. Apparently he did not intend genocide, but the eventual absorption of the Hebrew females into Egyptian society, not a wholly unenlightened policy for its day. The Biblical account goes on to say that one Hebrew boy's life was spared due to his adoption by one of Pharaoh's own daughters. The tenderhearted princess took in this Moses like a stray pup. The text is lacking in details at this point, but undoubtedly the foundling was given every advantage—educational, social, and material—befitting his new station.

"Everyone must have known he was a Hebrew. For one thing, he was circumcised; and for another, the barbarian Israelites must have had racial characteristics distinguishing them from the civilized Egyptians. The Israelites themselves appear to have been conscious of their own inferiority, because the name they took for themselves, 'Hebrew,' comes from the ancient Egyptian word for barbarian."

"A Chaldean word," interjected James, neglecting the legal protocol for making an objection but in other respects, with his eyes fixed on the ground and his voice oozing with world-weariness, looking and sounding every bit the battle-tested attorney-at-law. "And the original meaning is uncertain. By the way, the Egyptians practiced circumcision. The Israelites may have gotten the custom from them."

Lucifer looked to the judge. "What the counselor says about circumcision only strengthens my point about the cultural inferiority of the Hebrews. And as for the derivation of the term *hebrew*, everything we're talking about is uncertain." He smiled at Holmes, as one adult to another, at the tricks of the childlike professor. "It might even have been originally Hebrew!" He turned back to James. "Will it satisfy our learned professor if I concede that he *may* be right?" James raised his hands as if to say that there was no point in fighting over trifles, and Lucifer continued.

"So, undoubtedly and undeservedly, Moses was given every privilege and comfort of an Egyptian prince of the blood royal. How does he repay his gracious benefactors? One day he sees an overseer dutifully administering corporal punishment to a recalcitrant slave and, in a fit of anger, kills the conscientious official. This was not simple murder, but an act of wild and heedless rebellion against the very fabric of Egyptian society. One may grant that Moses was young, perhaps emotionally still an adolescent, although the text says he was forty years old at the time. But this wanton crime was merely a harbinger of worse to come.

"The fugitive flees to Midian, a land of uncouth sheep-herders where doubtless he feels more at home. In keeping with his social status as a Levite, he marries a priest's daughter and settles down to tending his father-in-law's flocks. He probably would have spent the rest of his life in harmless obscurity—when a man voluntarily stays forty years in one profession in one location, it's reasonable to assume that he's settled and content—but the meddlesome 'Lord God,' the very same self-proclaimed deity on trial before you today, intervenes. He speaks to Moses from the midst of a bush that burns without being consumed—a mere parlor trick, but enough to impress a superstitious shepherd. He commissions Moses as his front man who is to go to Egypt and confront its ruler, demanding that he free the Hebrew slaves and permit them to emigrate back to the land of their ancestors.

"An extremely noble cause, one might say! But if this Lord God is omnipotent, as he certainly claims, why did he let his chosen people fall into slavery in the first place? He himself gives Moses the answer to this puzzling question. He desired to create an opportunity to show forth his power and glory. In other words, he set the Egyptians up! He suckers them into thinking he is weak and contemptible, a god who lets his people fall into slavery without even putting up a fight. And then, just as they feel themselves secure and supreme, he challenges them to a contest of wills, a contest whose stakes are life and death, a contest they can't possibly win. A real supernatural hustler!

"He starts small, turning staves into snakes and making healthy hands leprous and then whole again, luring his hapless prey into the trap. Then he pounces, poisoning their water supply, killing their livestock, polluting their air and destroying their crops. Finally, as the fitting capstone to this magnificent work of sadistic self-glorification, he murders all their first-born, from the lowing calves to the crown prince of the realm!

"In all the history of the human race, what crime can compare to this? What kind of a 'Lord God' would do such a thing? A monster, only a monster. If the devotees of this monster still wish us to think him a god of love, they're mad! And if he still maintains that he himself is a god of love, either he's a self-deluded hypocrite, or he thinks us the damnedest of fools!"

As Lucifer proudly and defiantly overlooked the crowd, shocked silence reigned. No one had ever heard such talk in the pleroma, not even from the Lord of Darkness. The brightness of the sun did nothing to stave off the pall of anxiety that spread over the assembly. Finally, Lucifer's eyes came to rest on Paul. The fiery saint was glaring back at him, and it was clear to everyone who would speak next. Though fury stormed in his eyes, Paul controlled himself magnificently, taking his place next to James as co-counsel for the defense and holding his tongue until Wendell nodded for him to begin. Then, instead of bursting into a tirade, he spoke calmly, like the gentle but steadily rising wind that announces the coming of a storm and holds the promise of thunder.

"The prosecution condemns the Lord for abusing his power by afflicting the Egyptians unjustly. I don't dispute the history set forth by my adversary. The Egyptians enslaved the Israelites, and the Lord demonstrated his supremacy over the gods of Egypt by turning the waters of the Nile into blood, blotting out the sun, slaughtering the Egyptian first-born, and several other acts of lesser portent. I also agree that the Lord's motive, as he himself set forth in the Torah, was to reveal his unsurpassable power and glory. But, as one would expect from the father of lies, the light Satan throws upon the meaning of the Lord's mighty acts is diabolically misleading. It's cast by the fires of hell."

Paul paused, bracing for the enemy counterattack, but the prosecution did not object. Wendell hoped both sides finally saw that the petty bickering marking yesterday's proceedings hardly befitted a contest whose stakes were so cosmically high. More likely, though, they simply did not wish to squander their rhetorical power on minor skirmishing. In any event, Wendell felt relieved. An uninterrupted presentation made it so much easier for everyone to follow the logic of the argument, as well as to keep all minds on the essential issues.

"He portrays the Egyptians as an eminently civilized people," Paul resumed. "Civilized, yes, if one judges only by their material wealth and technological achievements. Civilized as well, if one adds to those achievements the sophistication of their art, poetry and religion. What, however, of the spiritual substance of this people? What legacy did ancient Egypt leave the rest of the world?

"The Egyptians were a pagan people. They worshiped the works of their hands, idols they themselves formed out of wood, stone and clay. They even went further than most ancient peoples and worshiped their ruler as divine. In other words, they regarded themselves, in the person of their Pharaoh, as supreme over all the earth.

"Now there can be no doubt that civil authorities are appointed by God to keep social order in a fallen world; but when a king sets himself up as a god, he forfeits the legitimacy of his title by overstepping the bounds of his divine commission. There is no surer way to stray from the path of righteousness. An entire people deifying itself can bring nothing but chaos and destruction.

"What were Egypt's great accomplishments? The merciless use of slave labor to build immense rock heaps as monuments to the vanity of their pharaohs, the perversion of religion to mask and justify tyranny, and most splendid of all, the waging of bloody and ceaseless wars of conquest from Nubia to Palestine in the vain attempt to make reality correspond to the megalomania of the Egyptian imagination.

"The Lord would have been well within the right to destroy Egypt, but in his never-failing mercy to all his children he did not do so. On the contrary, he gave the Egyptians his own chosen ones, the keepers of the oracles of God, to show them the way out of darkness. For over four hundred years the Israelites lived among them. In that time, did the Egyptians study and learn from them the law of the one true God, the way of righteousness and peace? No, they took advantage of the Lord's loving kindness to bind his people into the cruelest slavery!

"So the Israelites labored for their Egyptian taskmasters for decades, perhaps centuries, the real builders of their architectural wonders. Egypt's became a slave economy. Without the toil of her human chattels, she doubtless would have fallen much sooner than she finally did. Why else would Pharaoh have been so desperate to keep the Hebrews, despite all the harm that befell his people on their account? But, morally and spiritually, the price the Egyptians paid for the extended life of their empire was far too high. Egypt could have learned from the Israelites the way of holiness. Instead, she fell into depravity and corruption.

"Satan speaks of the death of Egypt's first-born. It was but fitting redress for the slaughter of an entire generation of Hebrew men-children, the substance of a people's strength and wisdom! Yet the Lord is not a god of vengeance. That's why he says, 'Vengeance is mine,' because he would have us give up all thought of vengeance and place the final reckoning in his hands."

At this point Paul glanced meaningfully at Holmes, as if to make the magistrate aware that he too was subject to the authority of a higher tribunal. Wendell wondered if anyone else noticed this short, silent, but nonetheless unmistakable sermon, and marveled at the subtlety of the saint's expressive power.

"No, the Lord does not afflict Egypt in order to exact vengeance. Does he not also call the Egyptians his children? What father would make reprisal upon the fruit of his very own seed? No, he chastises Egypt for her own good that she might turn from death and take the path to life! For Egypt walked in the way of death, there can be no denial of that. She gave herself up to the worship of idols and to the service of her appetite for leisure, pleasure, power and glory. So far did she stray from the truth that she usurped the Creator's prerogative over life and death. In the vanity of a proud and puffed-up imagination, she came to fall at the feet of her rulers, to worship them as divine! Is it wonder that the Lord laid the hand of discipline upon her? Had she been left in her own filth, she would have drowned in it!

"No man can serve two masters—that's what our Lord Yeshua told us when he walked the earth nearly two millennia ago. One can't be slave to passion and appetite and still see the light of reason by which all men know the reality and righteousness of God. Idolatry is falsehood, and falsehood is death. Sin gives rise to moral chaos and spiritual degradation, disorders fatal to any society. When an extremity is infected, the physician simply cuts it off, leaving the rest of the otherwise sound body intact. But what is the doctor to do when the entire body is diseased, even if the whole be corrupted through the fault of only some of its members? He must apply purgatives that will distress the entire body, not merely the offending parts, in hope that the entire body may be healed. Justice is not the issue here. The Lord condemns in order to save. To be sound and whole, both the individual and society must live according to truth. If the creature does not acknowledge the true source of life in the creator, it looks for that life elsewhere where it cannot be found. Creation feeds off itself in an orgy of violence, promiscuity, betrayal and destruction!

"The Egyptians needed to be shaken from the complacency of power. They needed to be shown that their idols were symbols of their own false and presumptuous self-glorification. They needed to be called to account, both for their own sake and that of the world. For this reason the Lord permitted his chosen people, the instrument of his self-revelation, to fall from the honor they knew in Joseph's time into shame and servitude. He knew that their dishonor, in the fullness of time, would redound to his honor, and that, even though they had fallen from a great height, in lifting them up from degradation to an even greater height, he would show forth his light and life to a world that in folly had embraced darkness.

"The Lord doesn't traffic in conjecture and surmise. These are the tools whereby men seek to avoid the condemnation of sin, of course to no avail. When the Lord acts, he does so deliberately, surely, and irresistibly. Men worship many gods in the fruitless attempt to escape the righteous demands of the one God, so they convince themselves that whatever good befalls them comes from one of their own deities. If evil comes upon some of them, then the rest say the victims were evildoers whom their gods have justly punished. Only if evil overtakes an entire nation do its people even begin facing up to the rot at the core of their whole manner of being."

Paul paused, his look indicating that he included the present assembly within this breath-taking generalization, and then proceeded to the climax.

"Then how dare the evil one scorn the righteousness of the Holy One of Israel? How dare this fallen spirit, swollen in his own conceit, hold up corrupt and vainglorious Egypt as a model of civilization? How dare anyone, let alone this damned upstart, accuse the Almighty of injustice? You may be certain this 'trial of God' is a test whereby the Lord may separate the wheat from the chaff. Every soul here is on trial, and there can be no doubt that God will requite each and every one of us for what we say and do here. Satan and his cohorts are lost, but give over, the rest of you, to the worship of the one true God, the God of our Lord Yeshua the Christ, before it's too late and the day of judgment is upon you!"

As the echo of Paul's thunder faded away, the voices of approval and dissent pattered like the first drops of what promised to be a downpour. As a preventive measure, Wendell gave one loud rap of his gavel and the voices stopped, leaving a tense and volatile silence.

As if oblivious to the tension, James stood and faced the apostle. "I believe it's my turn to speak," he said in a provocatively flat and understated tone. No one in the assembly dared laugh, but here and there a face lit up in a brief smile. Paul glared at the strange bedfellow circumstance—or perhaps, in keeping with his theology, divine providence—had given him, but the high dudgeon he had evoked in his audience now swiftly dissipated. There was nothing left for him to do but relinquish the podium. He did so wordlessly, but also with a dignified grace that was the hallmark of his demeanor. James courteously waited until Paul was seated back among his followers, for the saint refused to acknowledge the authority of the court by behaving as if he were one of its officers, but then the professor wasted no breath on preliminaries. "There's much insight in what the apostle said," James began, "and even some truth in Lucifer's remarks, but my client instructs me that he can no more associate himself with the one than the other."

Wendell looked to Paul for a storm, or at the very least an

objection; but though the saint's face darkened, he said not a word. Meanwhile James went on without skipping a beat.

"Lucifer speaks of pride, civilization, and glory. Paul proclaims the Lord's dread might, unerring justice, and unrelenting discipline of the evildoer. My client affirms that love is his only defense. If it give not ground enough upon which he may stand, then he willingly falls."

Shouts of both yea and nay arose from the Christian camp, as well as most unchristian expletives. Badly splintered into quarreling sects and denominations, like so many varieties of termites, the followers of Christ were running true to form. In the best of circumstances one could not count on their unity, and especially not when their master was being represented by two very different and, it was beginning to appear, diametrically opposed defenses. James must have sensed this, Wendell noted, because he went on in as conciliatory a vein as, presumably, the scope of his commission allowed.

"There is one point upon which Paul and I are in solid agreement," James said, his eyes twinkling in gentle irony. "The Lord does whatever he does for the welfare of his children. We are spiritually crippled, and he's striving to make us whole. But our healing won't come through threats and promises. It can only happen through the restoration of personal relationship with each and every one of his children."

Now the infection of discord spread throughout the assembly. Cheers of approval vied with shouts of "Absurd!" and "Impossible!" Like a compass needle subjected to a powerful magnetic force, the heavenly denizens were being polarized along unaccustomed lines that cut across traditional ideological boundaries.

"The world depicted in Exodus is given over to the worship of power," James went on, seemingly oblivious to the impact of his words upon the audience. "As Paul pointed out, it's a world of pagan polytheism, and pagan polytheism, in a nutshell, is the worship of power. It's the pursuit of survival as the foundation of life, power as life's meaning, and glory as life's apotheosis. Pharaoh embodies the glory of his people. He is Egypt's lord of hosts, their protector god. He fights their wars, brings them victory, and exalts them above all other nations.

"Paul was absolutely right on one point. The Egyptians would not have understood the Lord God of the Israelites had he come to them in gentleness and peace. To get the attention of the human race, Yahweh had to speak in human language. And make no mistake, getting our attention was the first step in repairing the rift. We, all of us, had alienated ourselves from our loving Father. We had chosen to live in fear, seeking to control life even if we had to destroy it to do so. He had to speak to us in the language we had stupidly, tragically come to regard as our native tongue—power. Only after bringing us up short could he begin to reeducate us in the language of love."

James sat down. His presentation had been unexpectedly brief, more an outline than an argument. His opponents doubtless wondered if the brilliant beginning he had made yesterday had been only a flash in the pan. Both Paul and Lucifer leapt to their feet in silent petition for the floor. Wendell was more curious about what the saint had to say, but in an effort to establish some regularity in the proceedings, he let Lucifer speak first.

"Professor James is impressive in his rhetoric," the Light-Bearer began, "but disappointingly slim in substance. So far, all we have heard in answer to the charges is an array of possibilities. No, worse than that!" Lucifer's coal-black eyes smoldered with contempt. "Two mutually contradictory arrays of possibility! As a favor to the court, I will bring some order into this tangle the defense appears to regard as logic."

Lucifer looked directly at James as he fired this salvo, but the latter seemed unperturbed. Indeed, if Wendell was not mistaken, a hint of a smile danced in Will's eyes.

"Both prosecution and defense have stipulated to the alleged 'facts' of this case. They're laid out in the Bible for all to read. The prosecution contends that the facts speak for themselves. The defense argues mitigating circumstances. Motive is an important element in construing the moral significance of an act, it's true; but when the noblest of motives is used to justify the basest of crimes, we have nothing but rationalization. When those who set it forth pretend to believe this rationalization, we have hypocrisy. Our esteemed St. Paul maintains that the Egyptians deserved whatever they got, but his logic is patently circular. They received their 'just deserts' because they refused to worship the 'Lord God,' but whether this god is worthy of worship is the very point at issue! The Honorable Mr. James said that this Lord was speaking the only language the Egyptians understood, that of power, and after getting their attention would go on to teach them the language of love. Apart from the obvious question of how one teaches people one has killed, where is the evidence that Yahweh has ever spoken in any language other than naked might?"

"Objection!" James cried. This interruption of Lucifer's speech when it was on the verge of achieving climax was as startling as an explosion, especially since hitherto Will had been good-natured to a fault. Rising from his chair, James addressed Wendell directly, but he must have been aware, as everyone else certainly was, of Lucifer's displeasure.

"Your Honor, the prosecution is assuming that the defendant is guilty until proven innocent, thus violating a fundamental principle of criminal justice, that one is presumed innocent until proven guilty."

Wendell wondered if the audience noticed him wince. How could the learned professor be so ignorant? "That's a principle of Anglo-American justice, to be sure," he answered in what he hoped was a judicious tone, "but it certainly isn't a principle in every system of jurisprudence."

"In fact," Lucifer commented without waiting for Wendell's permission, "if this 'principle of justice' isn't needed in every judicial system, it can hardly be a principle at all. It is, rather, a rule of procedure. Since we are following no such rules, the objection cannot stand."

Now returned as if by the wave of a magic wand to his accustomed equanimity, James turned to Lucifer. "Exactly my point," he said.

Lucifer regarded the professor as if he were lost in dementia, but there was just enough of a question mark on his face to serve James as cue.

"If the presumption of innocence is a procedural rule rather than a principle of justice, so too is the presumption of guilt. If we're doing without such rules altogether, one is no more valid in this trial than the other. If there's presumption neither of guilt nor innocence, it's beyond the ability of the prosecution and defense to establish one or the other. All we can do is present our arguments and let the members of the jury" — here he waved a hand toward the assembly in a circular motion that seemed to point indefinitely beyond the pleroma — "decide for themselves."

James sat down. There was no need for Wendell to formally sustain Will's objection. Its logic was self-evident and irrefutable. Lucifer had been deftly weaving a web of legal intricacies in which he hoped to entrap his adversaries, and now one thrust by James and it had been demolished. Even Wendell had missed the duplicity in Lucifer's approach, but now it was glaring. He could no longer admire the Light-Bearer as a paragon of humanity and was beginning to understand how he had earned the epithet "father of lies." The fallen angel had fallen a bit lower.

Lucifer took the blow with surprising grace. He bowed in courtesy, as might an unhorsed knight to his jousting rival. Admitting to himself that he might merely be succumbing to the human penchant for trampling upon fallen idols, Wendell nevertheless suspected that this noble resignation in the face of humiliating defeat was something other than good sportsmanship. He wondered what Lucifer had up his sleeve. The Dark Lord surely knew that one battle was not the war. Once again, however, the judge had to master his curiosity, because it was Paul's turn to speak. The saint needed no prompting. He arose, implicitly bidding Lucifer to sit down, and calmly waited for everyone's full attention and then some. He certainly was, Wendell thought impiously, a master of showmanship.

"There's an insidious logic to Mr. James' discourse on love, but that makes his ideas all the more pernicious. I can agree with him only on one thing: he and I are in no real sense co-counsels, and the god he defends is entirely different from my Lord and God. His god is a puling baby, or worse, an insecure matron coaxing her unfaithful husband back into her bed. If he won't come, there's nothing she can do. My God is the lord and master of all creation! He waits upon no man, and his purposes are inexorably and irresistibly fulfilled. Yes, he is the bridegroom, but the royal bridegroom. No soul to which he reveals himself can fail to be enamored of his majesty and beauty!"

Paul paused, and from practically every quarter came applause and cheers. Then the way a high-pitched note, however soft, will make itself heard above the loudest bass, there sounded that feminine voice, sweet even in anger, that would let no one in the pleroma rest in peace. "Then let him show himself to me!" Rachel cried, stunning the assembly into silence. Everyone looked to Wendell, but all he did was give full attention to the girl whose rare combination of humility, impudence, mettle and beauty he had come in the course of the trial to very much admire.

"Was Auschwitz beautiful?" Rachel went on in sarcasm so scathing it fell like a shower of sulfuric acid. "Was Treblinka beautiful? And what about all the other Auschwitzes and Treblinkas in which they've slaughtered the innocents down through the ages? That's all I've seen of the face of God!" Rachel had begun her diatribe at the outer edge of the assembly, but as she spoke she drifted inward until, with these last words, she was standing right before Wendell, her countenance a terror to behold. Will was the first to dare intrude upon the silence following her impassioned protest.

"That's not so, my dear! You've seen other faces of God: the love your parents lavished upon you, the ecstasy of a lover's kiss, the radiance of a full moon upon a gentle summer's night, the satisfaction of understanding the profundity of a genuine thought..."

"My parents died in the camps," Rachel spat back at him. "My last 'lover' was a Ukrainian guard who squeezed my throat and entered me like a dog from the rear just as soon as he could rip open my rag of a dress, leaving me bloody and half-dead for his ten or more comrades who followed. On the last 'gentle summer's night' I remember, I held my best friend in my arms while she died of starvation. And as far as I'm concerned, the only profound idea that has withstood the test of time and experience is Nietzsche's 'God is dead.' I firmly believe that!"

She stopped, her eyes glazing over and her body trembling as if she had reached some limit, though to what Wendell could not tell.

"No," she resumed dully, "I wish to believe it." Again, she hesitated. "No, that's not true, either. I want God to be very much alive so I can spit in his face!"

Again her words were like thunder to which no answer could be forthcoming except, as it were, from more thunder. Nothing, however, not even Rachel's outburst, could have prepared the heavenly denizens for the shock of what followed. Lucifer stepped forward and put his arms tenderly around her. This public display of affection was disturbing enough, since it entailed the Dark Lord's tacit but clear admission of a more than professional relationship with this, the prosecution's star witness. It was out of character for so consummate a strategist, but everyone already knew he was smitten with the Jewess, and everyone also knew how love could make fools of us all. What was truly disconcerting, even brutal in its emotional violence, was the way the girl recoiled from her benefactor. Lucifer looked as if he were being disemboweled.

"You!" she hissed, breaking free from his embrace. "You, who pretend to be so understanding! You talk of my people as if they were dogs not worthy to lick your spittle. You're no different than the Nazis. You used me to get to *him*, that's all. You used me in other ways as well."

Her meaning was unmistakable. Lucifer should have been crimson with rage. Instead he hung his head, though it was impossible to tell if he did so in shame. The feelings of an angel, even a fallen angel, were not so easily intuited as those of a soul from earth. At least, so it seemed to Wendell. "I've done what I've done only for you, my love," he said, pain having induced in him a curious calm. "You know they aren't your people. You have no people."

Wendell had no idea what Lucifer meant, but his words were not without effect. Rachel stood paralyzed with grief. Then she laughed, and her laugh, surprisingly, rang light and true, like the tinkling of sleigh bells, without a trace of scorn. Nothing, Wendell was certain, could have been more hurtful to her hapless paramour. Lucifer remained still, but now his muscles tensed as if he carried some tremendous weight—the weight, Wendell well knew, of a mad and hopelessly unrequited love. The light from the midday sun gave a glaring edge to his agony.

"Now I see what's going on," Rachel said as her laughter subsided. "You want me to depend on you. You all want me to depend on you! That's what your love is—enslavement! I don't know what this place is, but I know it's not heaven. I don't know what this trial is about, but I know it's not justice!"

Perhaps Wendell should have cited the Jewess for contempt of court. However, as she was the very *raison d'etre* of the trial, he hardly thought such a move appropriate. Besides, here he felt much smaller in his judicial robes than he ever had on earth. Magistracy no longer entailed majesty, let alone moral superiority. "What do you wish, my daughter?" he asked in a tone far gentler than any he had ever used from his bench on earth, gentler even than any he had used in his personal life, even with Fanny.

Rachel fell to her knees in supplication, but she held her head up and her face hardened in resolution. "I want *him*," she said. "If there's a person behind the divine mask, let him show himself and speak to me. Let him show himself and fight with me. I'm tired of grappling with mists and vapors. Like my ancestor Jacob, I want to wrestle with God!"

Once more Rachel's words brought the assembly to silence. Who could answer this challenge but the one to whom it was issued? Wendell wondered if they were all going to continue sitting there for eternity, waiting for a God who would never come, when Mikael descended from his literal oversight of the proceedings, waited until all eyes were upon him, and then pronounced four simple words:

"Tomorrow he will come."

Wendell involuntarily sucked in a deep breath, and only then did he realize that after Rachel's audacious but, he had to admit, timely and relevant request, his breathing had stopped altogether. Now he felt like a slave about to be unshackled, like a little boy on Christmas Eve. He knew that Jesus would take charge when he came, and Wendell would be free of a responsibility he was finding nearly impossible to fathom, let alone shoulder. He also knew that now the truth would come to light and understanding dawn on them all. Even though the day was yet young, Judge Holmes smartly rapped his gavel and the crowd began to disperse. The Jewess went on kneeling, stony-faced, looking up at the archangel without giving any sign that she understood what he had said. "Oh well," Wendell said to himself, "she's not my problem." He would go back home for a sorely needed siesta.

* * *

Rachel had not planned her assault on the powers-that-be. She had not planned anything since her arrival in this place where the heavenly and the infernal were indistinguishable. Why was she kneeling? The posture had happened of itself, and certainly it did not suit her mood. Nevertheless, now that she found herself in this pose of submission so proudly and paradoxically erect, she was not about to move until the last soul left the field of judgment. She had no desire to meet anyone's eyes, let alone engage in conversation. Her pain and disgust gave her the shame of an outcast, and she would not put herself in a position where she might involuntarily cringe or cast down her eyes.

Yet, she asked herself angrily, why should she be ashamed? Why was it always the innocent, the victims, who felt they had no right to exist? Why were the cruel and the unjust so arrogant and self-assured? Tears trickled down her cheeks as if she were a sponge and sorrow was squeezing her dry. Then she felt *his* hand gently stroking her hair! She looked up into the eyes of the man who, in a few brief hours in this realm of souls, had given her greater joy and agony than anyone else in all her years on earth.

"How is that possible?" he whispered.

Rachel pulled away and rose to leave. "I know that we can read each other's minds if we try," she said, turning away, "but you might have the decency not to try; or failing that, the courtesy to pretend you haven't!"

He did not move. "If you can read my mind," he challenged, "do so now!"

Without choosing, she found herself looking into his eyes. "I sense nothing," she said. "I feel nothing."

"You're lying," he said evenly.

"I suppose you know what I feel better than I do!" she countered, her voice cracking. He stepped forward and took her hands. She did not resist. "Why?" she murmured. "Why did you say that to me?"

"Is it true?" he asked softly, but still with an edge to his voice.

"Of course it's true!" she cried, exasperated, her legs giving way under her. She plopped back down upon the now moist ground and he immediately followed her. "But why did you think I needed to hear it?" she demanded.

He smiled faintly, in sympathy rather than amusement, she hoped. "Because you're lost," he replied, "and when one is lost, only the truth can show the way."

"That's just it!" she rejoined, once again feeling her mettle. "It may be factual, but it's not true! Yes, many peoples have suffered, not just the Jews. But to say it the way you did, at the moment you did... You struck out at me when you had just made love to me! But that's not important, that's the way men are..."

"I don't want to be that way," he pleaded. "I'm sorry, I didn't mean to hurt you."

"You were so bent on the truth of the situation," she went on, "that you didn't see the truth of me."

He placed a hand upon her shoulder, and again she felt that eerily familiar sense of comfort he had brought her at their first tryst. "Why are you so certain you know the truth of yourself?" he countered tenderly, like a mother tigress deflecting the playful swipe of her cub.

"I'm not," she admitted. "But yes, I am! I suppose you think I'm not making any sense."

"On the contrary," he reassured her, "I think you're making perfect sense."

She studied him closely but could find no mockery in him. Gratefully, she continued. "Yes, there's a mystery to me, as there is to everyone and everything. We can't know all that we are. But at the same time..." She broke off and laughed.

"What is it?" he asked.

"You already know, if you can read my mind," she teased.

"You're wrong about that," he said. "I read hearts, not minds. That way, when I'm hearing a joke, I don't spoil the punch line." He grinned, and then they both laughed.

"It's just..." she stammered, feeling herself blush. "I was beginning to sound like one of those stuck-up intellectuals I couldn't stand at the university!"

He leaned back against a tree, and Rachel only then realized that she was no longer in the field but at his mountain retreat, in the little bower where they had spent that wonderful, terrible night together. Until that moment she had been so wrapped up in herself that she had barely noticed her surroundings. Yet she was not surprised, merely bemused. Was it her desire that had brought her there? She certainly could not dismiss that possibility. Or was he smoother of an operator than he seemed?

"Is it a sin to connect one thought with another," he asked, his disconcerting grin making another appearance, "or only to express yourself that way?"

Rachel smiled, and then remembered where she had left off. "I was going to say that to respect anybody, you must respect that person's sense of himself."

"Ah," he rejoined, "but is everyone's sense of self worthy of respect?"

"I said only if you are to respect someone!" she cried, the hurt coming back. "You're free to respect or scorn whomever you please!" Once more she was tempted to leave, but something held her there almost against her will.

"I respect you," he said, and then, before she knew it, he took her into his arms and gently rocked her. She let go, floating in the sea of his embrace. After a while, she did not know how, their mouths met. Then everything else in them became one, and she sank into the sultry forgetfulness of something deeper than passion.

* * *

Did you give my message to the holy prophet precisely as I spoke it to you?" asked Lucifer of his envoy, an angel who had played a not insignificant role in the liberation of North Africa and the Middle East from the pernicious influence of Christianity.

"Yes, My Lord," replied the messenger.

"And what did he say?" broke in Azazael, unable to restrain himself. Or did he merely wish to demonstrate to one of Lucifer's trusted aides how the Light-Bearer allowed him certain liberties no other fallen angel would dream of taking? If so, the lesson redounded to Azazael's edification, for the angel responded to his demand not at all, and waited silently on his master's pleasure.

"Did Muhammad make reply?" Lucifer asked quietly at measured length.

"He did, My Lord," the envoy answered promptly, heedless of the sparks of irritation thrown off by Azazael's aura. "He said that he would have no intercourse with the enemies of God. 'Let them fight among themselves!' were his exact words. 'The Almighty stirs up discord in their ranks so they may destroy one another. So it has always been. The way of evil is conflict. Only surrender to God brings peace.'"

The only sign Lucifer gave of his chagrin was a slight leaning forward, as if the unwelcome news upset his stomach, but he quickly straightened himself up. The flickering torchlight deepened the melancholy of his mood as he fixed his eyes upon the messenger. He had deliberately chosen to hold audience in his most private chamber to prove, to himself if nobody else, that he was under no one's power but his own. What did it matter that here was the sofa on which he and Rachel had coupled? What did it matter that she might never lie with him again? There were others, many others, eager to have him. He was what he had always been. No pain or loss could turn the Light-Bearer from his mission. "That will be all for this evening," Lucifer dismissed his aide.

"They all had the impudence to say the same thing, My Lord!" cried Azazael as soon as the underling had gone.

Lucifer only nodded.

"But of course, that's what we expected?" Azazael hazarded. "We were simply testing the waters?"

Again Lucifer nodded, though he did not feel so self-assured and he knew Azazael sensed as much. The Light-Bearer also knew that, if this court jester gave even a hint that he knew what Lucifer knew he knew, the clown would come to regret it.

"My Lord," brightened Azazael, prudently switching to a safer subject, "Mara is wholly within our power!"

Lucifer relaxed and let his mind drift. Mara was such a trivial matter. "And what use do you think we might make of that pawn?" he asked, humoring his lieutenant.

"I can only guess at what My Lord has in mind."

"Guess," said Lucifer curtly.

"Yeshua is still entangled with his former queen," affirmed Azazael.

"Is he?" Lucifer's tone was neutral, but his body sank more deeply into the gold-trimmed divan. From long observation, Azazael knew that Lucifer invariably made a show of relaxing whenever he heard something that truly interested him.

"Of course, My Lord's insight goes far deeper than mine, but it appears that way to me. More than once has he waylaid her in the mountains, begging her to come back to him."

"Begging?" echoed Lucifer, his voice a mixture of incredulity and scorn.

"Most unseemly for the alleged lord of the universe, but yes, it was so."

"And how did the trollop respond?" asked Lucifer.

"You must already know how she answered him, My Lord!" trumpeted Azazael in merry contempt, dancing a little jig around the couch. "She was in the mystics' seventh heaven! It does her tender heart good to know he's suffering the pangs of lost and unrequited love."

"Over Mara," said Lucifer mirthlessly.

"Just so!" crowed Azazael.

"Are you sure it's unrequited?"

"Absolutely, My Lord! It's simple economics. When the pain of emotional intimacy comes to outweigh the pleasure of physical intimacy, one looks for a way out. Mara reached that point centuries ago. She has no fond memories of Yeshua that are not off-set by ten heartbreaking ones."

"Simple economics, of course!" declared Lucifer, rousing himself from his stupor. "You're right, we must make use of her." He leapt to his feet and paced back and forth, a restless lion seeking his prey. Azazael nearly prostrated himself in mock adulation, for now the Dark Lord, amused, was himself again. "What do you propose, fool?" he asked heartily.

"Yeshua speaks tomorrow," replied Azazael, raising his head but still kneeling. "Let Mara cross-examine him. She knows his weaknesses better than anyone, the tiny emotional pressure points where minimum force produces maximum pain."

Lucifer sat on the edge of the couch, his expression betokening ordered and dispassionate thought. After a period of reflection he asked, "Do you really believe she's up to the task?"

Azazael grinned. "When it comes to theology and metaphysics she's no prizefighter, but that's to our advantage." He drew up his stick-figure frame and stood conspiratorially over his master. "We don't need brilliance. How many of the esteemed citizens of the pleroma are smart enough not to get tangled in a chain of reasoning with more than three links, let alone brave enough to take on an idea that might throw them into the deep unknown? We don't have to worry about Mara keeping it simple." He winked and pointed lewdly to his groin. "She'll pour her passion into hitting Yeshua where it hurts!"

"Yes," nodded Lucifer, a sardonic gleam in his eyes, "concentration of force at the enemy's weakest point is a time-honored strategy."

"Then you approve, My Lord?" asked Azazael. He seemed a trifle over-eager to his master, but that may have been only his understandable glee in anticipating Yeshua's destruction by the weapon he himself had fashioned.

"We'll try it," Lucifer answered, "but we'll not stake everything on a single throw of the dice."

"Of course not." Azazael sneered in his best stage-villain fashion. "The Jewess will yet carry the day!"

Lucifer slapped Azazael before either realized what the Light-Bearer was doing. Such a loss of control on Lucifer's part was unprecedented. In oily abasement as well as genuine fear, Azazael fell to the floor. "Take care, madcap," Lucifer warned in a voice deliberately modulated so as not to drown out the echo of the blow. "She's not your affair." Azazael remained face to the carpet, motionless except for an uncontrollable trembling. "Be gone!" shouted Lucifer, raising a leg to kick at his lieutenant's belly. Azazael disappeared just before the well-aimed blow would have hit home.

The Light-Bearer sank down upon the sofa and buried his face in one of its elegantly embroidered cushions. "Where could she be?" he wondered. Was *he* hiding her? Was that rascal Azazael telling the truth? Could Mara still enthrall Yeshua after Rachel had come to his attention? Of course, there was no logic to love. He had never understood what Yeshua had seen in Mara to begin with. Yet Azazael had been so keen... Too keen. It was almost as if he were pretending to be eager lest Lucifer think he was feigning indifference. On the other hand, Mara and Yeshua had been together for what might now seem to the latter an emotional eternity. An investment of attention on that order of magnitude was no small pledge; and Yeshua, whatever else might be said of him, was not in the habit of going back on a pledge. Yes, perhaps he was turning overly subtle in his suspicions as a result of his own heart's agony. Or, on the contrary, perhaps that agony had sharpened his intuition. Mara would lead Yeshua's cross-examination, but she and Azazael would bear close watching.

* * *

Wendell lay stretched on a beautifully woven hammock whose azure fabric felt as light and soft as the kiss of a summer's breeze. All around him grew exotic shrubs and trees, tropical from the look of them, bearing fruit the like of which he had never seen or tasted: crimson orbs too rich and sweet to be apples; long, slender fingers too golden to be bananas; and luscious melons of every hue and texture. Broad, flat, darkly green and unconscionably large leaves waved overhead, so dense as to render nearly impotent the shafts of searing heat emanating from the white desert sun. Completing Wendell's satisfaction was the gurgling of a limpid stream as it meandered through the oasis like a shimmering ribbon of translucent glass.

"That sun doesn't appear to be new," Wendell muttered, determined to be cantankerous despite his contentment.

"It's not," the ever-vigilant James confirmed. He was strolling about, by turns poking his walking stick into every nook and cranny and intently studying the horizon.

"I thought there was no sun in these parts until a few days ago," Wendell limply droned. "And besides, from the look of it when we left, it should have been down by now."

"I've explained all that to you," said Will in some irritation. "Why don't you go back to sleep? I'll wake you when they arrive."

Wendell would have asked who "they" were, but he had already done so several times on the way to the oasis and Will had held his ground. It was to be a surprise.

James had roused Wendell from his drawing-room nap in what appeared to be late afternoon, telling him they were invited to a conference he would find most interesting. For some ungodly reason, the professor had insisted on walking from the Heavenly City. The route led through what at first struck Wendell as spectacular terrain, all sand and multi-colored rocks piled up on one another in ways that defied Newton's gravitational formula—arid, lonely, and yet majestic in its by turns jagged and smooth lifelessness. Before long, however, it turned monotonous. To top it all off, there was no sign of a conference. Thus far the only living creatures to make an appearance were vultures, evidently appraising the newcomers as potential supper. Strange, this place felt so very earth-like! And strangely ironic that the most wildlife Wendell had seen since arriving in the pleroma, except at Sivananda's mountain lair, should be in a desert.

"They're coming," said James, looking out into the nothingness.

Wendell felt like ignoring him, but something cautionary in the tone of Will's voice impelled him to rise. He was not prepared for what he saw. Way off in the distance there was a rumple in the desert floor, or rather, as James mentioned earlier when they were traversing its length, that flat part of it called a wadi which, in the rainy season, turned into a river leading straight to the oasis. It was as if some invisible hand were lifting the sand like a carpet in order to smooth it out again, or as if some camouflaged eel the breadth of the wadi were rolling sideways in their direction. At first Wendell thought it might be a sandstorm or some other natural phenomenon peculiar to the desert, but from the slight elevation of the oasis he could see the dust settle behind the disturbance as it moved ever more swiftly forward. It had been many decades since, but Wendell had witnessed such an event before, though not so spectacular because it had not been in the desert. But this was essentially the same thing, and there was nothing natural about it. It was a body of horsemen advancing at the gallop, and the oasis was their objective.

"My God," Wendell exclaimed in wonder, "a cavalry charge!" Not only was such a development wholly unexpected, but he actually felt foreboding in the pit of his stomach. What, he wondered in a serendipitous moment of lucidity, did someone already dead have to fear?

Incongruous in their Western, turn-of-the-century linen and wool, the two Americans watched as if in suspended animation as the Arab horsemen, in motley but uniformly cut robes and headgear, descended upon the oasis, which Wendell now imagined would look to an overhead observer like a green, blinking eye in a desert storm. They were a full regiment at the least. As they neared their goal, they slowed to a cantor and the flanks enveloped the oasis gracefully, like the wings of a guardian angel enfolding its ward. If these Oriental cavalrymen carried weapons, they remained sheathed and holstered, hidden in their robes.

As the dust settled, Wendell marveled at the perfect discipline and expert horsemanship of the desert riders. Once halted, they held perfectly still, as did their mounts. Not a muscle twitched on horse or human. Of course, Wendell reminded himself, there was no sweat or grime to itch or distract, no jangled bowels to calm or bursting bladders to empty, nor even, in the solar furnace of the desert, a parched throat to moisten. Such physical discomforts were but memories in the pleroma. Yet, in a way, that made this self-control all the more impressive. When there was only the idea of standing firm to keep one in place, perhaps it was all the harder.

Now a lone horseman emerged from the center of the regiment's line and advanced toward them. Wendell did not have to wait until the man's features were discernible from the white background of his mantle to know who he was. His flamboyant yet dignified self-assurance, whether walking or riding, was signature enough. At once swift and stately, Muhammad, messenger of God, moved across the sands as if he and his horse were one. What most impressed Wendell, however, was the gallant and respectful familiarity with which he addressed the magistrate as soon as he dismounted. "How do you like our little world?" he smiled, and swept his arm from horizon to horizon.

On their journey hither, Will had explained to Wendell that this desert realm was the product of the coordinated and highly disciplined imaginations of the Arabs of the pleroma. In principle, the power that had created this "sub-world" was no different than that by which Wendell had literally entered into the space of various works of art, at one end of the creative spectrum, or the entire universe had come into existence, at the other. Creation, James said, was mind infusing itself into forms produced by mind's own imaging power, or imagination. Spirit, which originally meant "breath," was but another word for creative mind. The original mind, or God, was of course the most powerful, and had made all other minds, and therefore all other creation, possible. But working in unison and harmony, created minds could approximate at least some of the powers of the uncreated divine mind. Of all groups within the pleroma, the Muslims were the most unified, and the Arab Muslims the most unified among them. The Jews were negligible in numbers, the Christians divided into thousands of sects, and Hindus and Buddhists, for the most part, were intent upon achieving an individual enlightenment that had nothing to do with creating worlds. As for the secular and political groups, their scientific assumptions barred them from experiencing the essential plasticity of the phenomenal universe. In other words, they had no faith with which to move mountains.

James had also said that, as far as he knew, one could enter this particular world only on Muhammad's invitation. Wendell then asked how they had entered it, and James said he had just explained that it was by invitation. This had not satisfied Wendell, but by now he had learned that it would be fruitless to press the matter. Finally, Will had said that time in this desert realm was not necessarily in sync with that of the Heavenly City, so what was high noon here might be midnight there. Wisely, he had not done so until they had reached the oasis and he could offer Wendell the hammock in which to continue his nap. Wendell had no way of knowing how long ago that had been except by the position of the sun, to which he had felt like paying precious little attention. He had to admit, however, that now he felt rested and as ready to face the present challenge as he ever would.

Apparently desirous of getting about the business that had brought him here, Muhammad turned swiftly to James, and again Wendell marveled at how the prophet's movements, so quick and to the point, never seemed rude or abrupt. "Has he arrived yet?" Muhammad asked.

James answered with his schoolmasterly smile. "What makes you so certain he'll come?"

Muhammad laughed as if he were accustomed to Will's ways and so took no offense. "Has he arrived yet?" he repeated, certain and amused.

"He's in the grotto, as you well know."

Wendell started. He had no idea who "he" was or that there was any grotto for "him" to be in. Wendell would have sworn that Will had not left his company since they set out on their desert trek, so what opportunity had he had to ascertain "his" presence or whereabouts? Wendell had long since given up expecting any laws or rules to govern events in the pleroma, but now and then a bit of to-be-taken-for-granted regularity would have been comforting.

"Let us go," said the prophet, as if he were stating a fact rather than suggesting a course of action. He led the way, and of course James and Wendell followed. The grotto turned out to be a broad-mouthed cave about a ten-minute walk away along the brook that had purled so melodiously by Wendell's hammock. Indeed, the stream appeared to have its source in moisture condensing upon the cave's walls, a phenomenon he had no idea whether to regard as natural or supernatural. Before he remembered where he was, he told himself that next vacation he would make an expedition to the desert.

"Why have you asked me here?"

Because of the contrast between the desert sun and the grotto's shade, Wendell heard before seeing him. It was a voice with which he had only recently become acquainted, but nevertheless it was now almost as familiar to him as his own. It was addressed unmistakably to Muhammad. He did not reply immediately, but bowed respectfully to St. Paul and gazed openly into his eyes, inviting him to see, Wendell surmised, that he had nothing to hide. No one even so much as hinted at sitting down. Wendell felt as curious as he imagined Paul did to hear what the prophet had to say. He had to give the devil his due—James knew how to orchestrate these little dramas.

"You and I have seen each other as enemies, lo these many centuries," Muhammad finally spoke, "but now I wonder whether we are not like the sun and moon, each with its own sphere but shining with the one light."

Paul met this overture of peace with stony silence.

"Or rather," Muhammad smiled in concession, "God is the sun, and we both reflect in our own ways the one light."

Again Paul did not speak, but he nodded, almost imperceptibly, as if to say that he too from time to time had wondered the same thing.

"So I decided to study your writings, and to my amazement I discovered that you and I, though not identical in our thinking, are foals of the same sire."

In the protracted silence that followed this remarkable assertion, Wendell glanced at James to see what he thought. Will looked noncommittal, but Wendell knew the professor well enough to realize that he could maintain the appearance of neutrality in the face of such a claim only if he agreed with its substance. Wendell returned to the parley between the representatives of the two most powerful factions in the pleroma with measurably heightened interest.

"You have no faith in God's gracious gift of salvation!" Paul spat out the words, as if it were all he could do to keep from turning on his heel and walking away or, more likely in the pleroma, instantly disappearing.

"Then why don't you explain this faith to me?" Muhammad beseeched him. "Isn't that your calling, after all, to bear witness to Christ?"

Paul studied Muhammad closely, as if to satisfy himself that he was not being mocked. "I will do so under one condition," he finally said.

"What is it?" Muhammad's tone implied that nothing the saint demanded would be too high a price.

"That I be heard by all the men who accompanied you here today."

Muhammad smiled as if nothing could have pleased him more. "Even now they are on the way," he bowed. Sure enough, the riders began to appear, without their horses and in groups of two's and three's, outside the cave. In a matter of minutes they formed a sizable, respectful, attentive, and absolutely silent audience.

"Men of the desert," Paul began without hesitation, his prayer shawl lightly dancing with the soft desert wind, "like your leader, I'm a city-dweller born and bred. Yet I've traveled through these trackless sands, so I know something of your world. Nowhere else are the essentials of life more rightly valued, and nowhere else is life, any form of life, more precious, because nowhere else is the miraculous nature of life more plain."

Paul paused and scanned his audience, his close-cropped head resembling the proud eagle whose spirit Wendell had so often emulated. He looked briefly but deeply into each man's eyes and there found a grudging but growing respect.

"I know that every man here confesses the supremacy of the almighty God. I know that every man here is a soldier accustomed to discipline, and holds his highest duty in life to be obedience to God. Your leader"—Paul deliberately avoided calling Muhammad a prophet—"so far is right, that we agree on these points. I also know that you recognize the beneficence of God and realize that, without the Almighty's compassion, no one—no, not the strongest man— could stand."

As if at a signal, the heads of the desert warriors nodded in unison. Wendell found this synchronization of response uncanny, even unnerving.

"You believe that nothing happens without God's will, that God is the real doer of all that is done, and yet you persist in the delusion that your own efforts can bring you to paradise."

Again Paul paused, doubtless expecting some protest. None came.

"We are all under the judgment of the law," he resumed. Wendell felt, against all reason, that this statement was aimed directly at himself. "By whichever version of the law one lives, who among us mortals is without sin?" Paul looked pointedly at Muhammad as he asked this rhetorical question. "How many of you have never missed the appointed time of prayer? How many of you never succumbed to the desert heat and took a sip of water under the Ramadan sun? Which of you never dallied with a slave girl when you should have confined the satisfaction of your lust to your wife or wives?"

For some reason Wendell could not fathom, Paul again directed this last question toward Muhammad.

"How many of you have failed almost every night to obey God's command not to go to your own rest as long as there is one servant of God without enough to eat or a place to lay his head?"

Wendell could tell from the soldiers' eyes that they grew angrier with each of the saint's questions, but such was their discipline that they remained polite toward their enemy without Muhammad so much as having to give them a look. Doubtless Paul sensed their rising enmity, and it seemed to feed his fire.

"You claim to be servants of God. You hold, rightly, that God is infinitely above and we infinitely below, and yet you hate us Christians for claiming that salvation is the free gift of God through

Christ. Can't you see your self-contradiction? Why are you so blind to your own arrogance? Do you think that God's law is so loose and paltry a thing that it can be satisfied in so shabby and slipshod a fashion? Do you think the divine mind so confused and imprecise as to mistake your aping of righteousness for righteousness itself? Divine forgiveness is not divine idiocy! There's only one who is perfect, and we are accounted perfect through his grace. At stake here is nothing less than the majesty and authority of God. Either he is the Supreme Being, or he is not!"

Paul paused, daring his listeners to give him violence. Nothing could have been more eloquent of their desire to do just that than the tense immobility with which they maintained their impeccable discipline. Not a one so much as blinked.

"I know that you recognize God's absolute power over the destiny of every human being," Paul resumed in a more conciliatory tone. "I know that you accept the essential mystery of God's ways, and that no man can know what his judgment over any of us will be. I simply ask that you practice common sense and see what necessarily follows from the omnipotence of God. It's all in his hands, not only our fate on earth, but also in eternity. And if it's all in God's hands—and how could it not be? —then it is the vanity of vanities to think that we could change any part of our God-determined destiny, whether in time or eternity. Is God only lord over time? If, as you rightly believe, God is lord over time, how much more must he be lord over eternity! The temporal world is but a pale reflection of the eternal. Do you grant God's authority over the dark and confused realm and deny it over the eternal light, the light that emanates from him, that is substance of his substance?"

Paul looked straight at Muhammad and the prophet smiled, though in that smile was a glint of steely anger. "Of what do you accuse us, Christian? When has a servant of God placed a limit upon the Almighty? It's you who do so by thinking that the glory of the Infinite can be bounded by the form of a mere mortal."

Paul glared at Muhammad as the latter's smile broadened into a supercilious grin. It was clear that the prophet had struck a nerve, though Wendell could not for the life of him understand why until James, playing the part of the diplomat, chanced to clarify in the course of pouring oil over troubled waters.

"If I remember correctly," Will said to Muhammad, "nowhere in the Christian New Testament is there any unequivocal formulation of the doctrine of the Incarnation, and that includes the apostolic letters."

"I know well enough what the Christian holy book says," retorted Muhammad, bristling at what he evidently regarded as James' condescension. "What I don't know is where the apostle stands on this issue now."

Paul did not hesitate. "I stand now where I've always stood," he declared to the entire audience. "Christ is Lord of heaven and earth. Since there is but one Lord, you may draw the obvious conclusion."

This confession of faith led to the unsheathing of hitherto unseen swords and menacing shouts and gestures. Despite the knowledge that he was an immortal soul, Wendell could not help trembling with fear almost exactly as he had right before his first taste of combat nearly a century ago.

"I don't understand," Muhammad frowned, apparently put out by his failure to drive an ideological wedge between Paul and later Christianity. "There's no such proclamation in your writings. Perhaps if there were you Christians would have one less reason for squabbling among yourselves!"

"What do you mean?" Wendell blurted out despite his desire to keep a safe and neutral silence. Muhammad answered Wendell's question with an impatient look, as if he had no time for such ignorance. Paul likewise ignored Wendell. Evidently, both great religious leaders considered the eminent jurist a dunce when it came to what really mattered in life. James, however, with a look of pity in his eye that was more insulting to Wendell than the others' contempt, whispered, "Battles were fought among third-century Christians over the doctrine of the Incarnation."

"The first followers of Christ weren't ready for the full truth," Paul explained to Muhammad. "The Jews awaited the coming of the messiah, and the pagans could well appreciate the advent of a son of the gods, but neither could have understood, much less accepted, the idea that God became man. It would have been meat for babes. The Holy Spirit had to prepare men's hearts, and when the world was ready to receive the revelation of that aspect of Christ's glory, it was made known."

"How convenient," Muhammad sneered. "And were you yourself one of these babes?"

"Convenient?" Paul echoed, ignoring the other barb. "Yes, you of all men should know about convenience! In the 'holy book' you yourself 'recited,' God provides you with special dispensations to have thirteen wives, to sleep with a slave girl, to marry the divorcee' of your adopted son. Did God use you, Muhammad, or did you use God?"

Now Muhammad placed his hand upon the bejeweled hilt of a sword that, the moment he reached for it, magically appeared at his side. The apostle faced him without symptom of fear. The prophet unsheathed his weapon, and Wendell thought that he had not heard so unnerving a sound as that of this steel gliding across steel in all his existence, no, not even in the whiny of a musket ball, nor even the fearsome rebel yell. Then something in Muhammad eased. He dropped his hand to his side and the blade disappeared. His followers took this movement as a signal to put up their own swords, and now, even though the sound was not so very different from that of a moment before, Wendell found it comforting. "I didn't invite you to this place to quarrel," he told Paul, his tone at once soothing and proud. A cool breeze wafted over them from some mysterious source, and only now did Wendell realize that he was sweating. He looked for moisture on the others' foreheads but saw none, not even on Will's.

"Again I ask," said the apostle, sinking into a crevice in the grotto's wall with a weary sigh, "why did you invite me here?"

Muhammad squatted down on his haunches and his followers took this as a signal to disperse. In a matter of seconds, the four men were once again alone. Now, it seemed, the two principals were ready to get down to the real business for which this meeting had been arranged.

"Did you think we might form an alliance?" continued Paul. "Too much divides us, the cross and the lordship of Christ. To outsiders these points may seem small, but both you and I know that between us they are an abyss!"

Wendell wanted to ask what the apostle meant by saying that Muhammad rejected the cross of Christ, but he was not about to make another display of his ignorance. He would ask James later, when they were alone.

"Yes," Muhammad answered ruefully, "for a fool's moment I even imagined something more than an alliance. I dreamt of a shared creed!"

Paul gave the prophet a look that said he would not be mocked. "What do you desire?" he asked. "In so far as I can do so without betraying my Lord, I would be all things to all men."

"In order to bring them to Christ?" Muhammad said knowingly.

"In order to bring them to Christ," Paul admitted. "What do you propose?"

Muhammad looked up and around at Wendell and James, who were both still standing, as if to emphasize the gravity of what he was about to say before answering Paul directly. "That if we cannot join in a union of friendship, then at least we form an alliance of prudence, lest a common enemy take advantage of our disunion."

"I would first be persuaded that he is your enemy, and how is that possible when you refuse to accept Christ as Lord?"

"Hear me, Paul!" entreated Muhammad, though he was by no means begging. "You know what's at stake here as well as I. We regard Yeshua as the greatest of God's messengers. You believe him the Son of God. I admit there's a chasm here, perhaps an impassable one, at least for mortals like us. Tomorrow Yeshua himself speaks. We both have awaited this moment for well over a thousand years. Though the occasion itself is profane, we both know that this supposed trial of God is really a trial of man. Let us join together in this, that we prevent Satan and his minions from interfering with whatever the messiah may have to say."

"God can shut the mouths of his enemies without our feeble help!" declared Paul.

"Yes," agreed Muhammad, "but perhaps it's our blessing to see to it. After all, God needs nothing from us. It's for our own good that he uses us as instruments."

Paul pondered, as if weighing out the wisdom in the prophet's words. The scowl on his face, however, also showed that he was considering whether he was being led into a trap. At length his face cleared. He had come to a decision. "Naturally, my fellow Christians will keep strict decorum while our Lord is speaking."

Muhammad looked straight into the apostle's eyes. "I'm asking more than that."

"There shall be no interruption by the godless ones," Paul promised.

Muhammad held out his hand to seal the agreement with a clasp. Paul's hand remained at his side, but he added, "You have my word. Do I have yours?"

The prophet looked steadily into the apostle's eyes and then, smiling in satisfaction, said, "Yes, Christian, you have my word."

* * *

Azazael found Mara at the Fountain of Hope in the Heavenly City's central square hard by Lucifer's palace. She sat on its edge, dangling her feet in the water. Maybe she was lost in thought, but more likely as empty-headed as a bitch in heat. As had become their little custom, he crept up from behind and threw his arms around her, fondling her breasts as if testing the ripeness of melons. Surprisingly, she did not respond with the usual glee. She hardly responded at all. "Look at the play of moonlight upon the spray," she said in a low voice without turning around.

"What's troubling you, my sweet?" he asked in his most sensitive tone.

"Nothing, really," she replied, turning to look into his eyes. "I've suddenly been struck by the greatness of what we're doing. We're overthrowing a tyrant, the worst and mightiest tyrant of all!"

Azazael smiled. "We're doing more than that, gentle Mara. We're overthrowing the ultimate tyranny. When our work is done no longer will any of us, angel or human, be bound by the cowardly love of death that masquerades as holiness. No longer will the cross, that ugly instrument of torture and despair, hypnotize the world into thinking that bitter is sweet and darkness light. The music will play and the dancing begin. The festivities will commence, and they'll never come to an end!"

Then music reminiscent of that accompanying their first dance magically arose from the burbling of the high-arcing water. He took her hand and led her in a little dance around the fount. Azazael mistrusted reflection in anyone, even if for the moment it appeared to be serving his turn. Thought could lead a woman like Mara to a place beyond his control. When he set her down again, she was breathless and safely locked in the immediacy of her ambition and his charm.

"Our 'master' has agreed," Azazael informed her, taking her hand as if he owned it and licking up the salt on her sweaty palm. The pleroma was indeed becoming more and more physical, and Mara seemed the most affected of all. He liked it. He liked it very much indeed.

"Then I'll overwhelm him!" she cried, thrilling at the touch of Azazael's tongue.

"But you must also be cunning, my love," he cautioned, moving from her hand to her neck. "Make Yeshua think that you're still in love with him, still wallowing in the misery of a broken heart. Draw out his sympathy. Get him on your side."

Mara drew back a little, and Azazael looked quizzically into her eyes. There he saw a welter of uncertainty, confusion and doubt. Then she smiled and gave a little laugh. "It won't be easy," she said.

"No," agreed Azazael with no hint of irony, "it will be the hardest role of your life. But think of all that's gained if you succeed!"

Mara's gaze drifted back to the luminescent fountain. "Not only for us," she said solemnly.

"Of course not, my love," reassured Azazael. "For everyone."

"Even Yeshua," she added, her voice lowering to a whisper. "This is what he needs too."

"Of course," said Azazael, turning her chin toward him. "This is what everyone needs."

Then he kissed her deeply, passionately, the way Yeshua had not kissed her for so long. "I'm yours, my darling," she murmured. "Entirely yours."

With difficulty, Azazael held back his laughter. So it had been with every woman he had ever known. There was only one way to bring the lesson home. And why not take his pleasure of her while he may? Everything was set for the morrow, the evening had barely passed into night, and he knew now that Mara could not climb with him to the heights.

* * *

Shortly after the moon set, Running Dear awakened to the hooting of a great horned owl and the gentle sighing of the standing people as they swayed in the mountain breeze. He did not know whether these omens were favorable or not, but he roused himself and mentally prepared for the task Morning Star had given him that day, to ready the people for the joining. There was no need to hurry. In the spirit realm there was little to do in the way of lowering teepees and packing provisions. Whatever amenities the people had provided for themselves could be stored away in their minds with the same speed of thought with which they had been produced, and food was a pleasure or a crutch rather than a necessity. Rousing the people and gathering them together likewise was no burdensome chore. The souls who dwelt in this part of the spirit land had long ago learned to live in harmony and peace. They were attuned to one another's thoughts and moods, and aligned in their innermost being with the way of spirit. No, Running Deer arose so early not because his work required it, but because he could hardly contain the excitement in his breast. Today was the day of the great reunion!

Running Deer had come to the Heavenly Sphere almost two hundred winters past, a member of one of the aboriginal tribes that at the time had roamed freely over the plains of what the white man called North America. He had been a warrior and then a medicine man, known especially for his power to heal diseases of the soul. He could not help smiling whenever he remembered those days, when each tribe had thought itself the chosen one. Often had he quarreled with healers of other tribes over the fine points of herbal selection and preparation, the proper conduct of a purification lodge, the relative efficacy of various rituals and symbolic systems, and other technical issues that in the spirit realm had no real meaning. Gradually he had learned to respect differences and even profit from them, so that now, after so many moons, technique was no longer a matter of tribal custom but individual expression. Underlying the differences was a heartfelt and growing respect for the mystery and beauty of the life the Great Spirit had given us, all of us, as well as a clearer perception of how essential each creature was to the well-being of the whole. In other words, the accidental and peripheral had not worn away, but been recognized for what they were—the specific but not the only possible ways a healer tapped into the universal energy of life.

It all felt so inevitable now, this firm and sure guidance of the spirit, but it had seemed nothing like that in the early days. They had been thrown into the maelstrom, he and his fellow healers. They had been given the task of restoring the wounded souls that had lost all ability to heal themselves; and Running Deer had seen visible proof of what on earth he had always believed, that fear, greed, hatred and lust wound so much more deeply and lastingly than guns, arrows and knives.

When he had first arrived, most of the derelict souls were from the tribal people, those whom he now regarded as his own people, even if they were not of his own tribe. Perhaps this was the Great Spirit's way of easing the medicine men into their work, for it was easier to understand the souls with whom they had much in common. Then came the sun-ripened ones, who had been brought in chains from over the great sea to work the land for the white men of the south. Each of them, it seemed, had a different language, so Running Deer and his fellows had to speak to them through the medium of spirit, at first a much more difficult but in the end far more effective means of communication. Finally and most recently had come the victims of the terrible Holocaust, the most hopeless and broken of all souls with whom Running Deer had worked. The Europeans had killed the aborigines because they got in the way of settling the land. They had brutalized the Africans in the course of exploiting their labor. The destruction of the Jews, however, had been no by-product. Those who saw with the eyes of the spirit knew it to be the end to which all the Nazis' means had been unflinchingly, insanely, even self-defeatingly devoted. Ignorant people cynically observed that genocide was the result in all three cases, but the healers saw the difference in the woundedness of the victimized souls.

The war between good and evil was coming to a head—that was plain for all to see. Yesterday Morning Star, the one whom the wassichu worshiped as Lord Jesus Christ, had appeared in the moist coolness of the early dawn and bade Running Deer prepare the people. When the moon was full, the Holy One had said, a spirit hitherto unknown to him would come and lead them to the joining with the stalwart ones, and thence to the reuniting of heaven and earth.

The stalwart ones, of course, were those who had no need of healing from without, who were strong enough in their sense of themselves to stand alone. Running Deer, however, had no idea what Morning Star meant by the reuniting of heaven and earth. In the pride that was his besetting weakness, he had no wish to appear ignorant about what to the Holy One was so important a subject. Instead, he had asked with vexation why Healing Wings, or Raphael, could not guide them, since he had been their mentor from the beginning. Morning Star had smiled in his knowing way and said that, at the time of the full moon, she who was known to the peoples of the book as Uriel and to the tribal peoples as Holy Fire would clear the way for the rejuvenated souls to rejoin their brothers and sisters in the City of Light. Now Running Deer looked out from the edge of the forest onto the vast plain, where most of the people still slept in their lodges, and awaited the arrival of this Holy Fire.

The wispy clouds scudded low, driven by a wind that had come out of the east immediately after the stillness of the dying sun. The air was cool, fresh and alive with the singing of the creeping-crawling people and the birds of the night. Iris and wild rose, prickly pear and desert lily opened their blossoms as if in obedience to a voiceless command and filled the atmosphere with a riot of scent and color. Even the grasses of the plain brightened their brownish hues to a bluish green. Despite the absence of moonlight, the plants of the spirit land—a jumble of species bearing no necessary connection with the environment since they were the product not of nature, but of the subconscious desires of the human souls who inhabited it—glowed with a soft, warm light that appeared to emanate from their own vital juices. This was also true of the animals. Running Deer could see clearly the foxes, coyotes, bears and other creatures who liked to roam in the dark, as well as the humans who, like him, for one reason or another had no desire to sleep. Nevertheless, despite this preternatural radiance, the whole was paradoxically veiled in night's profound and solemn blackness.

Then Running Deer sensed a slight brightening of the heavens. Perhaps dawn was coming early, as it occasionally did in this spirit realm, which gave little heed to the creaturely desire for predictability and regularity. But no, he realized, the light was confined to that part of the horizon directly before him, and he was not facing east. Even the sun of the spirit realm had never been so capricious as to rise anywhere but in the east. This radiance was coming out of the north. Running Deer barely had time to remember that, according to Morning Star, Holy Fire was guardian of the north, before she appeared before him in all her glory.

At first the light blinded Running Deer, as always when encountering one of these mighty spirit-helpers, especially at night. Next he saw a sphere of radiance surrounding, or rather emanating from, a shaft of fire. Then his powerful eyes, long accustomed to searching out game and healing herbs in the dark forest and shimmering prairie, began to discern the spirit's features. What he saw then was even more blinding than the light that had first obscured them.

She was beautiful. That was true of all the spirit-helpers, of course, but her beauty was wild, untamed, free. Healing Wings radiated calm, as if his aura were an unguent of liquid light. Holy Fire was well named, for her intensity was surpassed only by that of Morning Star himself. And yet, in one respect, hers was greater. Morning Star's fire was held firmly in control by his will, but that of Holy Fire was the very essence of her being. She could no more restrain it, it seemed, than an animal could restrain its heartbeat. Accustomed to making instant appraisal of any creature's state of being, Running Deer intuited all this in the brief moment before Holy Fire spoke.

"You are Running Deer," she said. It was a statement rather than a question and needed no confirmation. Nevertheless, Running Deer bowed his head low in response. "You should awaken and ready your people," she continued, holding his gaze with her own, "for we are to arrive with the sun."

Again Running Deer bowed, thinking that the sun had already risen in his heart. He had had a wife on earth, but she put his things outside their lodge when he dedicated himself to healing. She said that she had no desire to be the widow of a living man. Though he had been angry and deeply pained, he could not really blame her. In the spirit realm he had mated with no one, telling himself he needed to devote all his energy to the task given him by the Great Spirit. Now, in a flash, he realized he had only been waiting for Holy Fire. Could a human mate with a spirit being? The question forced itself upon him as he basked in her fiery presence, but he banished it to the shadowland of longing. Right now it was not worth the asking. Whatever road his love for her could take, it would. His heart had spoken.

* * *

"Confound it, Will, why are you in such an all-fire hurry? On the way to the meeting, when there was precious little to talk about, we took our sweet time traipsing through the desert. Now that my head is bursting with questions, you rush us back here and bid me a not so much as by-your-leave goodnight!"

Wendell was not given to speaking in clichés, but James so tried his patience that he sapped his mental energy. Will was perched on the threshold of the study, like a sparrow about to take wing. Immediately upon their return just minutes before, Wendell had sunk heavily into the easy chair and fatigue shrouded him in its lassitude; so he was not being fair to his friend, but he could not help himself. Like an exhausted child, he was torn between weariness and the desire to stay up and see what life would bring him next. There was so much he wanted to understand, and James was his most available, if not only, resource.

"I thought you wanted to rest," said Will mildly, shifting his weight to a less dynamic posture.

"What do I look like to you, a bedpost?" exclaimed Wendell. "After all that transpired out there, do you think I can sleep?"

Will smiled, evidently pleased despite Wendell's gruff tone. "You want to talk?" he asked, settling himself comfortably upon the divan.

"I want you to talk," said Wendell.

James' smile broadened into a grin. "About what?"

"First of all," asked Wendell, "what did happen out there today? Why on earth did Muhammad think he could form an alliance with Paul? What common ground could there be between Islam and Christianity?"

James' eyes widened and his mouth took an incredulous twist. It seemed no one in this place, not even his closest friend, could help regarding Wendell as criminally benighted. "Islam is a branch of the same Semitic monotheistic tree," Will finally answered, as if this information were common knowledge.

"I didn't know," Wendell said, sounding foolish even to himself.

"Yes," James went on, "a Muslim would say that God used Muhammad to rectify and complete the revelation that Jews and Christians have corrupted."

"And what would a non-Muslim say?" queried Wendell.

"Ah, a non-Muslim!" answered James. "A non-Muslim might say that Muhammad took certain personages, themes and ideas from the Judaeo-Christian tradition and adapted them to suit his own purposes."

"Including Jesus?" asked Wendell more confidently. He felt he was starting to get the lay of the land.

"Including Jesus," confirmed James.

"How so?"

"According to the Qur'an, Jesus was a great prophet, in some ways greater than Muhammad. He healed the sick, raised the dead, walked on water..."

"Right now I wish he'd change some water into wine," muttered Wendell, looking longingly at the mantelpiece liquor bottles whose spirits had so recently and dearly departed.

"He never did that," said James.

"I may be unlearned in religious matters," Wendell protested, "but I know what I know! It says so right there in John, or Matthew, or one of those damned gospels. My God, man, it was one of Wendell, Sr.'s favorite texts!" *So*, Wendell thought, *when I'm worn out I wax profane as well as hackneyed.*

James sighed, no doubt feeling this little lesson would be more of a task than he had originally anticipated. "In the gospels, yes, but not in the Qur'an. The Qur'an strictly forbids wine, so no prophet of God would do such a thing."

Wendell sat up a bit, his body feeling more energetic as his mind became more engaged. "Evidence that the Bible is wrong, eh?"

James nodded. "But still, Islam holds that the Bible is right about a lot of things. The Qur'an says that Jesus was the messiah promised to the Jews by God, that he was born of the virgin Mariam, or Mary..."

"Born of a virgin?" interjected Wendell. "Why on earth would Muhammad teach that?"

"Frankly, I've wondered that myself," admitted Will. "I don't know for certain, but..."

"Why make a religion more unscientific than need be?" continued Wendell, as if Will had not spoken. "Seems to me it would stand a hell of a lot better chance of getting accepted if it kept the absurdities to a minimum."

"Yes," said James dryly, "if it were recruiting its seventh-century adherents from the ranks of modern Western intellectuals."

"Oh yes," Wendell mumbled, abashed. "Yes, I wasn't thinking. Of course."

"I imagine Muhammad was seeking to win over the Christians of his day by keeping as many of their beliefs as possible. For example, the Qur'an even says that Jesus is without sin, that even now he's at the right hand of God while Muhammad is in the grave awaiting resurrection with the rest of us lowly mortals, and that he will return at the end of the world to, among other things, let Christians know how wrong they've been!"

Wendell whistled. "So that's why all the fuss over Jesus' coming tomorrow!"

Once again James nodded but said nothing, waiting upon his friend. There were so many directions in which Wendell could take this line of questioning that he felt like the proverbial ass starving between equidistant bales of hay. "But if we're all rotting in the ground," he finally asked, "how do the Muslims explain this place?"

"The soul may have dreams while the body awaits resurrection," replied James.

Wendell pondered. "How convenient," he said at length. "In that fashion they can explain away any empirical evidence contradicting their beliefs."

Will suddenly looked sad and too choked up to speak. He took a moment to recover himself. Wendell nearly asked what was wrong, but then thought it best, since it was obviously nothing he had done or could undo, to let it go. "But we were talking about Jesus," Will finally said.

"Yes, I'm sorry," returned Wendell. "I do have a tendency to get sidetracked, especially when there's so much about this religion business that mystifies me. So, if I get you right, Jesus is awfully important in Islam—so important, it seems, that Muslims and

Christians should have no cause for fighting over him. Why then, in heaven's name, do they?"

"Because there are two things about Jesus that Christians down through the ages have adamantly affirmed and Muslims vehemently denied: that he was of divine substance, and that he was crucified."

Wendell needed a moment to gather his thoughts. "I more or less knew Muslims rejected Jesus' divinity," he said at length, "but his crucifixion? Why?"

"You of all people should know the answer to that!" replied James with a playful lilt to his voice. "You know the ways of the world. Suppose the Canadian government executed the American ambassador for whatever reason. What would Washington do?"

"Declare war instantly, of course," replied Wendell.

"Without taking time to consider and negotiate?" queried James. "Declare war upon a neighbor who is no military threat and with whom it's always had the best of relations?"

"Not always," corrected Wendell. "There was the War of 1812."

"Ancient history," said James. "In any event, I think you get my point. Why go to war with a nation so incapable of doing us harm?"

"You really are becoming a lawyer," chuckled Wendell. "You never ask a question to which you don't know the answer."

James joined in the laugh. "Lawyers aren't much different from college professors. But, whether this interrogation is more suited to a courtroom or a classroom, would you kindly answer my question?"

"What's done to the ambassador is done to the one he represents," said Wendell. "Insult one and you insult the other."

"So too with a messenger of God," concluded James. "God could not allow one of his prophets to die so humiliating a death without permitting himself to be dishonored. The very idea is blasphemy."

"As blasphemous as believing a man to be God?" asked Wendell.

"Close," answered James.

"But is crucifixion really so dishonorable a death? What of all those hymns about the glorious cross?"

"Later Christian hyper-romanticism," replied James. "In the Roman Empire, crucifixion was the nastiest and most degrading death possible. By law, a Roman citizen could not be crucified. It was a method of execution reserved for society's scum."

"That's why Paul was beheaded rather than crucified, wasn't

it?" observed Wendell. "Because he was a Roman citizen."

Will regarded Wendell with a flicker of new respect, and for the first time in his existence the latter actually felt grateful to his father for his table-talk concerning religion.

"Yes, ironic, isn't it?" said James. "Jesus could be crucified, but not Paul. And crucifixion was doubly, even triply humiliating for a Jew. Not only were the condemned put up naked—it's extremely shameful for a Jew to be seen naked—but it says in Deuteronomy, one of the books of Moses, the holiest and most authoritative part of the Jewish Bible, 'Cursed is he who is hanged upon a tree!'"

Wendell was amazed, not so much at the information Will was giving him as at the way it was effecting a dimly felt but unmistakably profound synthesis in his understanding of the issues that had confronted him since his arrival in the pleroma. "So," he managed to say, "the crucified Jew was specially hated by God."

James nodded.

"I see." Wendell fell into reverie. The ensuing silence was so deep that he actually became irritated by the ticking of the grandfather clock, a sound he ordinarily found comforting. Any disturbance of the quiet seemed a profanation. "But there's something else to this business," Wendell finally said, challenging James, "isn't there?"

"Muhammad was the last of God's four messengers, God's greatest prophets," answered James. "Before him had come Moses, David, and Jesus."

"David?" echoed Wendell.

"Yes," said James, "the little fellow who killed the giant Goliath."

"I don't know anything about his physical stature," Wendell went on, "but wasn't he king, and didn't he have another fellow named Uriah killed so he could keep Bathsheba, Uriah's wife?"

"It didn't happen," James replied.

"Oh, I see," said Wendell. "Another corruption of the original. No prophet of God would commit adultery and murder." Again Wendell lapsed into reverie. "I'm sorry," he roused himself, "what were you saying?"

James smiled sympathetically and then continued. "That Jesus was Muhammad's most immediate predecessor in the office of God's messenger."

"So," Wendell mused, "if Jesus died a martyr's death, people might think Muhammad should too."

"Exactly!" approved James, once again nodding, this time vigorously. "And in the volatile political situation of seventh-century Arabia, such expectations tended to be self-fulfilling. Muhammad never had any intention of being a martyr," he added, a note of contempt in his voice. "In fact, the Qur'an has God saying that if Muhammad were destroyed by his enemies, he could be no true prophet of God."

Now it was Wendell's turn to nod, and he did so slowly, thoughtfully. "You were awfully chummy with the fellow out there today," he remarked.

"I like Muhammad," said Will. "It's impossible not to like Muhammad. But he's no Yeshua."

Another prolonged hush followed, but this time the air was so saturated with unspoken fear that the clock was barely audible, or so it seemed to Wendell. After a time, the weight of the atmosphere became so unsupportable that Wendell had to speak or be crushed by it, so he said the first thing that came to mind.

"So, *he* is coming tomorrow."

James stirred a little, but that was all.

"What do you think he'll say?" Wendell persisted.

"But you're barking up the wrong tree," Will suddenly bethought himself, ignoring Wendell's chitchat. "Paul and Muhammad have a much deeper commonality than the figure of Jesus. They both define God in terms of power."

"I don't understand," said Wendell, genuinely perplexed. "In what other terms could God be defined?"

Will was once more stricken by what Wendell, borrowing a term from Holmes, Sr. of whose actual meaning he was not even certain, could only think of as transcendental melancholy. "If you don't yet know after all I've said in court..."

"But you've said almost nothing!" Wendell blurted out before he could catch himself.

Now, as was clear from Will's expression, hurt was piled upon sorrow in his heart, so much so that he was unable to speak. He arose from the couch, turned away, bent over almost double, took a few deep breaths, and apparently relaxed into the pain. Wendell could understand it in no other way. "He will make it clear," Will finally said in quiet but intense conviction. "They're all waiting for him to make things clear. Now you've a reason to wait for him too."

Wendell had no idea what to say, so he waited for Will to continue, but nothing more was forthcoming from that quarter. Will stretched out on the divan and closed his eyes. Presently his breathing slipped into the regular and sonorous rhythm of deep and badly needed sleep. There was more Wendell wanted to know, but his own fatigue was too much for him. He fell into dreamless oblivion.

Chapter 8

Once again Rachel awoke to find him gone. A magnificent deer gazed calmly into her eyes and the day dawned crimson through the trees, but he was nowhere to be seen. As on the morning before, Mara and Azazael appeared to guide her back to the Heavenly City. Although now she knew the way well, even in the dark, she was grateful for their company.

His disappearance did not upset her. On the contrary, it seemed fitting. He was on the side of the pretender, it was clear, while she had allied herself with Lucifer. Perhaps they should meet only in secret until the conflict was resolved. Or perhaps, given their differences, their love could never flower. The romantic in Rachel derived a certain tragic comfort from this idea, though she was enough of a realist to admit to herself that entertaining the possibility of not being with him was one thing, and suffering the reality quite another.

As the sky grew ever lighter, they walked in a silence punctuated only by the allegretto rhythm of their nearly flying footsteps. Mara especially seemed absorbed in thought. Rachel was too new to the pleroma to understand how wondrous was the sound of tramping feet to a long-time denizen like Mara. Finally, as they were approaching the plain from which the Heavenly City would come into sight, Mara spoke. "You seem to enjoy ranging about these mountains as much as we do!"

Sensing a note of irony, if not downright sarcasm, Rachel looked briefly but intently into Mara's eyes, but found no hidden meaning there. "Sometimes I want solitude," she answered. "My spirit needs to breathe freely."

"Yes, I too often find it stuffy back in the city," commented Azazael, who was walking on Rachel's left, "especially in Lucifer's palace. Our master is a wondrous being," he winked in comradely conspiracy, "but his ego does take up a great deal of space."

Before Rachel had a chance to respond to this disquieting remark, she found herself back in the palace standing before Lucifer, her companions of a moment ago nowhere to be seen. It was dark, despite the flaming torches. Lucifer reclined upon the couch where they had shared their passion, naked except for a simple loincloth. He was a magnificent man! Desire leapt in her just at the sight of him. She knew now, however, that he did not have her heart. "I'm not what you want me to be," she said in response to his unspoken question.

"I want you to be only yourself," he returned, looking mildly into her eyes. "Weren't you yourself the first time we shared this bed?"

With a supreme act of will, Rachel broke free from his gaze. "No," she whispered, but then realized how hollow this sounded. "I mean, yes, but that's not me anymore."

"Look at me!" Lucifer commanded, rising to his feet. "Look at me, and tell me you don't desire me!"

She tried to avert her gaze, but his words were like so many hands grabbing and turning her in his direction. She could not lie to him now. "Yes, I desire you," she admitted, and he took this as a signal to rush into her arms. It required all her moral strength to hold him back. "I desire you, but there's something deeper than desire."

Now it was Lucifer's turn to exercise self-control. Rachel could tell that he was used to having his way with women. However, instead of overpowering her, which he easily might have done, he relaxed and drew a bit apart. Nevertheless, he kept her hand in his and began planting delicate kisses upon her palm. It was all Rachel could do to keep herself from moaning with delight, indeed, from pushing Lucifer down onto the divan and leaping on top of him. Then she saw *his* eyes and remembered *his* touch. She could not betray something so deep and pure. She backed away from the Light-Bearer.

"I've not changed my mind about the trial," she told him in a friendly but firm tone. "I will see my commitment through. But you and I can no longer be lovers."

Rachel could not help feeling pity for Lucifer as he drew himself erect, too proud to beg, except with his eyes. Was it the pride that struck him mute, or the pain? Since she could think of nothing further to say, she turned and stepped through the door, all the while feeling the heat of his resentment upon her. She walked down the marble hall as softly as haste allowed, yet the echo of her staccato footsteps stabbed at her eardrums. Just as she was about to pass through the massive oaken doors out into the morning light, he spoke, quietly, but his words were like so many slaps. "There's someone else, then," he said.

She stopped but did not turn around for fear that he would see the truth in her face. "That's not what this is about," she replied, the schoolmistress correcting her childish pupil.

"I wonder how long it will be before you betray him, too," Lucifer persisted, unabashed.

"I'll do my part at the trial," Rachel reiterated. "I haven't changed my mind on that score."

In the ensuing silence, Rachel wondered if Lucifer were desolately sinking into the morass of unrequited love or coolly plotting out the strategy that would best serve his interests, given what for him must be this surprising turn of events. Probably both, she decided.

"We're still allies, you say?" he finally responded.

Now Rachel felt it safe to turn around. "Yes," she said, smiling into his eyes, grateful that he had given her this way to remain his friend. "Allies. I have no more liking for the pretender than you do."

"Shall I accompany you to the field of judgment?" he asked, walking up to her and holding out his arm. She curtsied playfully. "It would be most kind of you, sir!" Arm in arm, they strolled out into the quickening day.

* * *

Their angelic escort roused Will and Wendell early. Nevertheless, the field of judgment was already crowded by the time they arrived. The atmosphere was brooding and tense, and the rising sun, which ordinarily would have brightened the mood, only added a shade of foreboding. As always, the citizens of the pleroma were grouped according to their kind, but now there seemed to be more than a subconscious herd instinct at work. Indeed, the crowd's appearance was reminiscent of troops in mass formation, sinister in their warlike intent.

"The Christians and Muslims are ready for trouble," noted James as they landed in the central clearing near the judge's bench.

"I don't understand," said Wendell. "Last night we encountered those desert cavalrymen, and today you speak of trouble between Christians and Muslims, but what possible effect can weapons have upon those already dead?"

Wendell was offhandedly undergoing the transformation of his street clothes into judicial attire, as if the magical process were the most natural thing in the universe. James made a pretext of straightening the already perfectly draped magistrate's robe in order to continue the conversation, it seemed, without giving observers the impression they were engaged in *ex parte'* communication. Why he should bother with the stratagem Wendell could not imagine, since everyone surely knew that the judge and the co-counsel for the defense shared the same lodging, and since the ruse was itself as much a token of personal intimacy as any open conversation. Perhaps Will was trying to be considerate of Wendell's sense of professionalism, or perhaps he simply wished not to flaunt their friendship. Or perhaps there was no trick at all. Perhaps Will was merely nervous. Come to think of it, perhaps Wendell's suspicion of an ulterior motive was likewise just nerves.

"That's just it," replied James. "No one knows. Theoretically, here a weapon is merely a focus and symbol of the intent to do harm. It's the intent of a strong soul that can harm, and perhaps overthrow, a weaker soul. But with the increased physicality of the pleroma, the theoretical may approach the actual."

Wendell's eyes transmitted his puzzlement.

"Physicality is embodied thought that takes on a life of its own," explained James. "Its value lies in showing us, objectively and unmistakably, the consequences of our attitudes. At any rate, you misunderstood me. The Muslims and Christians may be ready for trouble, but they don't appear to be lying in wait for each other.

Muhammad seems to be getting at least part of what he was bargaining for."

What James said about physicality did little to dispel Wendell's perplexity, but on looking about once more, he could see that Will's observation about the Christians and Muslims was accurate. The Marxists, as well as the freethinkers and atheists (with whom, Wendell had to admit, he felt a certain affinity), were readily recognizable not only by their modern, Western-style dress, but also by the air of breezy detachment with which they regarded the proceedings. They had been broken up into pockets, each surrounded by a small but highly disciplined contingent of Muslims, as well as a larger group of more unruly Christians, each of whom wore a cross around his neck as if it were a uniform. If they had tried, however, neither the Muslims nor the Christians had been able to fragment the Jews, who with few exceptions had massed together near the field's center. Wendell feared no disruption from them. Throughout the trial they, who might be said to have the most at stake in this business, had been the quietest and best behaved of the lot. On the other hand, he wondered about the Hindus and Buddhists, whom the Muslims and Christians appeared to be ignoring. For these Orientals had been given to spontaneous outbursts of emotion that hitherto had been on a small enough scale to constitute only a nuisance, but which, if they grew, had the potential to disrupt the court entirely. Most of all, Wendell worried about the Muslims and Christians themselves. Neither side was likely to accept peaceably a Jesus contrary to its expectations.

Now all these concerns had to be put aside, however, for suddenly everyone's gaze was drawn, as if by invisible strings, toward the rising sun, and what they saw filled them with astonishment. A highway of golden light now stretched from the city to the mountains, and down that highway, heading straight for the field of judgment, streamed millions, if not billions, of glorious souls, recognizably human yet shining like the angels, accompanied by all sorts of animals and birds. Like those already in the pleroma, these people were of every conceivable period, race, religion and nationality. Of much greater interest to everyone, however, was the presence of children among them! They were singing many different songs simultaneously, though all seemed to harmonize into one grand hymn of glory, gratitude, and praise. A blazing angel led them in stately and measured tread, but they themselves danced and engaged in all sorts of acrobatics to express their joy. Wendell could not say whether they were fast or slow in coming, because time seemed suspended; but then they broke over the field like a wave, and what ensued was happy pandemonium. From every quarter came unrestrained shouts of incredulous joy. Almost every denizen of the pleroma rushed to embrace one or more of the newcomers, and then went a little apart with what was obviously a long-lost child, parent, spouse, relative, friend, lover, or what-have-you. The birds and animals chirped and shrieked and cried and wailed and gibbered, joining in the fun. The field seemed to expand to accommodate the massive influx of souls.

Wendell was not immune to the contagion of unbridled emotion. Though out of duty he remained in the vicinity of the magistrate's bench, he sought with his eyes for the beloved wife whose company, it seemed, he valued more in death than he ever had in life. She was nowhere to be seen.

* * *

Rachel heard the commotion long before she and Lucifer arrived at the field of judgment. Even though—or perhaps, especially because—it was a happy tumult, Lucifer tightened his grip upon her arm. Something, he evidently feared, had gone awry.

The newly risen sun already shone brightly, but the radiance Rachel beheld when they reached the jubilant crowd was something more than solar. "We're lost!" Lucifer muttered in angry resignation, but she was too excited to take much notice. They were here! She did not know how she picked them out immediately from the multitude, nor did she care. All that mattered was that they were here: aunts and uncles and cousins and nephews and nieces—not all, but certainly enough to make for a grand reunion! She waded into the midst of them, hugging dour Uncle Solomon and kissing willow-wand Grandmother Sarah and picking up plump little Bertha and twirling her around until they both sank giggling to the ground. And there, at last, in the middle of them all, stood her parents, looking exactly as they had the day they were all deported to the camps!

Only now, instead of fear and foreboding in their eyes, there was joy. Rachel flew to embrace them both, one in each arm, and sank to her knees in gratitude. Then she remembered.

"This doesn't make up for it," she whispered.

"Make up for what?" asked her father in his calm, self-assured voice. She could tell from his tone that he knew exactly what she meant.

She rose and drew a little apart so she could look into their eyes. "You really think it does, Papa?" she asked in equal parts sincerity and irony. "What about you, Mama? Are you ready now to forgive and forget?"

Her mother's sad, quiet smile said that she was. "We know what you're doing," she murmured to her daughter as if she were a schoolgirl. Her mother had never been stern or repressive, but always sensible, sometimes, as now, condescendingly so.

"Yes," chimed in her father, "all the souls throughout this far-flung spirit realm know what you're doing. They talk about little else. Even the Orientals are engrossed." Rachel thought she detected a hint of perverse pride in her father's cheery sarcasm. His little girl was universally notorious.

"Can't we forget about it, at least for a day?" her mother pleaded. "We've been given a great gift! Who would have thought we should ever be together again?" She wrung her hands as she had the day their world was torn apart. "Can't we at least be grateful for a day?"

Rachel studied them both with the intensity of acute indecision. They were resurrected, yes, but something was missing. Her father's tall, proudly refined figure was slightly bent and stooped, something she had never seen of the poised and successful theater-owner in life. Her mother's beautiful face was creased with some strain of supernatural origin, for it had always been wrinkle-free on earth. Perhaps the camps had done this to them, but she doubted it. Life in the ghetto, she had seen for herself, had not beaten them down, and she had it from several trustworthy sources that they had been taken in the first selection and thus spared the agony of death by attrition. They had entered the showers and that had been that. Something here, in the spirit realm, was subtly but perhaps terribly wrong.

Still they were here, and that was something for which to be grateful. Their eyes implored her, even more than their words, to let it go, to be thankful for what they had. That was the way they had always been, even in the ghetto, and Rachel had learned to live with it. Ordinarily — that is, back in the time before the camps, death, and *this place* — she would have granted them their day. But here, in the pleroma, especially with the rapid change everyone said it was undergoing, who knew what sin of omission might be committed even in one hour? Perhaps this was a test of her mettle. To slacken now might be to sink into the torpor that possessed so many of the souls here. To Rachel, that would be a fate worse than death. "Mama and Papa, forgive me," she finally said, "but I can't wait. You've always taught me to place truth before everything else."

Rachel stepped farther back, as if in surety of her decision. Her mother came close, however, and rested her hands, still as smooth as a baby's, tenderly upon Rachel's shoulders, while her father took one of her hands in his. "Are you so very certain you know the truth?" he asked.

"I know what I know!" Rachel declared. "If I don't hold by the truth I know, how will I ever find my way?"

Unexpectedly, her parents nodded agreement, and she could see in their eyes that they really understood. As the tension broke, she wrapped her arms once more around them and wept gently into her mother's breast. For a moment that seemed at once eternal and instantaneous, they remained in this embrace. Then, as if in response to some silent signal, Rachel released them and they moved away.

Her father smiled. "We've learned the hard way that each soul must do what it must do."

"Yes, my dear one," her mother added. "We're the parents only of your flesh, and of the form that flesh has imprinted upon your soul. You've given us far more than we've given you, and you owe us nothing. Now you must come to terms with the progenitor of your spirit."

Rachel nodded gravely. "That's something we all must do," she said, and then turned and made her way to the center of the field of judgment. "Your Honor!" she called as she approached the judge's bench, next to which Justice Holmes was standing and scanning the throng. When he saw her, he smiled.

"Yes, my child, we've no further need of this trial. You may rejoin your loved ones and enjoy the..." As what he saw in her eyes registered, he stopped in mid-sentence. "You wish to continue the proceedings?" he asked incredulously. "What in heaven's name for?"

Rachel was too intent upon answering the question to pay much mind to the small white dove that at this instant touched down upon her shoulder, but the startled magistrate looked as if God were suddenly speaking to him.

"*This*," she said with a gesture that took in all the joyous reunions now transpiring on the field of judgment, "does not make up for what happened *down there*. For what is happening *down there*."

Justice Holmes cocked his white head to one side, as if taking counsel from an invisible confidant, before replying. "My dear, this is how I see it. If pain, suffering and death were the end of human existence, then you would have a case. But, quite obviously, I would think," — he imitated, without exactly mimicking, the precedent sweep of Rachel's arm—"it's not. Why shouldn't we now regard the earth as a place where God tests the mettle of our souls, gives our spiritual muscles a workout, so to speak, before coming here to rest?"

Rachel had no good answer to this question, but something in her would not let go. Besides, the multitude of souls on the field had now fallen silent. They were listening to the discussion, and many were growing hostile to the troublemaker, especially the religious souls. Rachel understood and had no desire to spoil their happiness, but she could not help feeling that everything of real importance now hung in the balance. "This isn't right," she managed to mumble. "This is too easy."

"She's right!" called a voice from out of the crowd, soft yet resonant, reverberating with a force everyone felt yet few recognized. It was *he*! "This is too easy. You wish to suspend the trial? Then you're hallowing the ultimate insanity."

Justice Holmes mounted the judge's bench and rapped down his gavel, evidently feeling he needed to meet this latest challenge with all the prestige of his judicial authority. "Who speaks?" he cried. "Make yourself known! Present yourself before this court in a dignified manner, and not like some catcaller at the vaudeville."

For an instant, as the echo of the judge's voice died away, absolute silence reigned over the field. Even the birds and animals made no sound. Then there appeared in the witness box, without anyone being able to tell exactly how he got there, a finely bearded man, small in stature but of erect and confident posture. He wore a robe, something like a monk's cassock, with a hood that hid much of his head. Something about him was different, Rachel felt, though she could not say what, but she had no doubt it was *he*.

However he felt about this unexpected advent, Justice Holmes maintained his composure. "If you have an argument to present before this court," he warned sternly, "then please do so with no more theatricals. This tribunal has been established by the very highest authority, and will permit no one to make mock of it!"

He bowed his head solemnly. "Rachel is right, Your Honor," he reiterated. "Nothing is settled by this reunion. It doesn't take away what's already happened, not unless it can ensure that none of it will happen again. Are you prepared to make that determination without hearing further testimony?"

He looked straight into Justice Holmes' eyes. The magistrate did not flinch, it was true, but yet looked disquieted. He was obviously at a loss for words, and seemed relieved when someone else took up the challenge.

"I don't see the point of continuing this parody of justice!" declared Paul, bringing the full brunt of his apostolic displeasure to bear upon *him*. Rachel wanted to protect him, to cry out to the saint that he was really on his side, but she was unable to speak. He turned to Paul, not at all perturbed.

"Nothing's been settled," he said. "The world is still what it was."

"Yes, the world is what it was," echoed Paul, "but those who did not believe in the Lord's promise of salvation now see that they were wrong."

"Do they?" he asked. "Where is this salvation?"

"Are you blind, stranger?" Paul's rejoinder was the paradigm of carefully modulated sarcasm. "We've been reunited with our loved ones. What matter how long or difficult the journey, as long as one finds one's way home?"

"So, you think this the end of the journey." It was *his* turn to be sarcastic. "Do you have any idea what's happening on earth right now? Do you think a world divided against itself into earth and heaven, or a person into body and soul, can possibly stand? Do you honestly believe that the living God's idea of salvation is the provision of a desert wherein all may hide their heads in the sand?"

"Enough, My Lord!" came a cry from one of the angels.

Rachel looked up and saw that the twelve brightest angels, the leaders, she surmised, had gathered in cruciform formation directly over *his* head. Now their light grew brighter than the sun, drawing the attention of all the assembled souls. The one interrupting the argument was the one who had led the procession of souls. This fiery spirit now descended and knelt before *him*. Rachel was not certain what this meant, but she felt now as she had the day she had been turned away from the university. No, she knew exactly what it meant, only she did not wish to face the truth. He was the pretender! The angel spoke softly, but Rachel was near enough to catch her meaning. "My Lord, how far will you take this unseemly masque? He is your own apostle!"

He regarded the angel with a melancholy smile. "I'm sorry it's not to your liking, Uriel. You'll discover how far in due time."

Rachel wondered abstractly how Paul was taking this strange turn of events. She almost turned around to study the play of emotion upon his fiercely expressive face. But she could not take her eyes from *him*, the one who wielded the knife that now was slowly, exquisitely, torturously cutting its way through her heart.

* * *

Shortly after Yeshua made his appearance, Will placed himself at Holmes' side. He recognized the Lord immediately, of course, but at first was paralyzed with fascination at everyone else's blindness. They really did not know who he was! Not even Paul! Not even Paul...

After Uriel had her predictable lapse of discipline, Will said to the distracted Holmes, in as much of a whisper as the height of the judge's bench would permit, "If the defendant himself wishes to go on with the trial, I think we'd better proceed."

Holmes roused himself. "Counsel approach!" he cried imperiously, but with a note of desperation as well. Will stood there already and Lucifer obeyed instantly, but Paul was frozen in disbelief. Will wondered if he were doubting his own sanctity or

Yeshua's authenticity. Given what he knew of the saint, he would bet on the latter.

Holmes seemed unconcerned, perhaps even relieved, by the apostle's absence from the conference. He looked intently at Lucifer and Will. "Do you concur that this man is in fact Jesus?" he asked, his tone clearly indicating that he would tolerate only a yes-or-no answer.

"It is he," Lucifer affirmed, and Will nodded in agreement.

"In other words," Holmes hypothesized, "in this quaint and roundabout fashion, he's saying that he wants the opportunity to present his side of the argument."

Will blinked stupidly, or so he himself felt, trying to comprehend what Holmes was *not* saying, while Lucifer remained impassive. Then he understood that Holmes was trying to make legal sense of the defendant's refusal to accept a dismissal of charges. Will also realized that all Holmes was asking of Lucifer and him was not to challenge this construction. Though Lucifer must have had his misgivings, he obviously had sense enough to see that the prosecution could not look this particular gift horse in the mouth without reducing the entire trial to a farce. But could the defense fail to make a mockery of the proceedings if it did not challenge the motion to continue, even if the defendant himself made it?

Had Will been an actual attorney, perhaps he would have answered this question by asserting that the decision to dismiss lay with the court, not the defendant; and that nothing anyone said, the defendant included, could alter the fact that this latest development, this reunion of souls, even if it did not involve all souls, pointed to a God who would make good on the suffering of his creatures. What more could justice, in all reason, require? But Will was not an attorney and this was not a regular trial. "Now we all know," he declared, "even if some of us did not before, that this trial will proceed according to *his* timetable. Unlike Uriel, I've no desire to fight the inevitable."

* * *

Even with the help of Yeshua's lackeys, it took some time for the crowd to settle down once again to the business of the trial. Puffs of white cloud in a deep blue sky added to a festive air that hardly encouraged serious deliberation. Despite the fact that he had no idea how he could have countered Yeshua's stratagem of the reunion, Lucifer made a mental note to find and punish whoever among his lieutenants was responsible for this lapse in the Light-Bearer's intelligence network.

On the credit side, the enemy now characteristically threw away whatever advantage his unforeseen tactic had gained. Since Yeshua was, technically speaking, the defendant appearing in his own behalf, his counsel had the right, one might even say the duty, to elicit from him as plausible an account of his divine tenure as human ingenuity could concoct. Paul, however, seemed to be lost in catatonia. Lucifer had to give Yeshua his due. He never would have believed that anything could stop up the mouth of that infernal saint! And Professor James neatly announced that, in accordance with the terms of his employment as counsel, now that the defendant had arrived to speak for himself, he could step down. There was no objection from any quarter. Yeshua himself, when Holmes asked if he had anything to say, first requested that the children be allowed to spend the day in the care of some savage named Running Deer, with whom they had come. Holmes gave his assent readily. That was just like Yeshua, to play to the sentimentality of the crowd. Then, with his customary air of arrogant humility, he declared that he would answer whatever questions he was asked. Yeshua thus yielded to the prosecution the first move in this chess game. Once Lucifer had the initiative, he promised himself, he would allow nothing to stop him.

The Light-Bearer could barely conceal his relief as Mara began the first cross-examination. Since it was politically advantageous for a more reputedly neutral party to raise questions in the spectators' minds before Lucifer provided the answers, he had hoped that Rachel would seize the gauntlet before Mara. But she was standing motionless, eyes fixed upon Yeshua, seemingly in the grip of an emotional storm whose origin Lucifer could not fathom.

Mara began deftly enough. She smiled at her former mate as if they were the closest of friends. Lucifer was not sure, but he thought Yeshua winced. Then she sprang her trap. "Yeshua, you claim to be all about love. How is it that you and I are no longer together?"

"You left me," he replied flatly, hardly the heart-sore lover. Lucifer was surprised, but even more surprised to see that Mara was not at all surprised.

"Why did I leave you?" Mara persisted.

"Because you didn't really love me."

"Ha!" Mara cried, unable to hide the shame in her eyes.

Lucifer had known all along, if Mara took on Yeshua in a war of nerves, who the winner would be. But he had not anticipated so rapid a capitulation.

"I didn't love you?" Mara cried, her overplayed irony hovering between comedy and melodrama. "I devoted myself to you for almost two millennia while you slipped steadily away. Though your chill neglect has lost you my affection, until now you kept a measure of my respect. I always thought that you would tell the truth. Now I see that you're a liar!"

In the tense atmosphere of the pleroma, this insult sounded like the crack of a frozen branch, and in the ensuing silence the voice of the hitherto dumbstruck Paul chirped up like that of a wounded bird. "Woman, who are you?"

Mara regarded the apostle as if he were a curious anomaly, like a snowman in the tropics. When he repeated his question, she angrily appealed to Holmes. "Your Honor, what right has this fanatic to interrupt my examination of the defendant?"

Before Holmes had time to answer, Paul repeated his question. "Who are you, woman?"

Mara turned on him in scorn. "I was your queen, the consort of your precious lord, for two millennia! The only reason you don't know me is that you can't face the truth that your omnipotent 'Lord God' needs a woman, just like any other real man."

Paul seemed oblivious to her sarcasm. "The Lord needs nothing," he declared. "That's why he's the Lord."

"Maybe he didn't need me," Mara sneered, "but I can tell you that he enjoyed me when he had me!"

At this remark the Christians in the assembly looked as if they would lynch her, but Yeshua's apparently indifferent silence gave them pause.

"You're lying, woman, or mistaken," said Paul, turning his back on Mara as if she could not possibly have more to say. "This is the kingdom of heaven, in which there is neither male nor female, neither giving nor taking in marriage. We are as the angels, having exchanged our corruptible mortal bodies for incorruptible spiritual bodies. We are beyond the lusts of the flesh."

Mara stood transfixed with rage, as well she might. The officious apostle was denying the substance of her life. He was also denying the substance of Lucifer's life, but the Light-Bearer had never taken Paul's sanctimonious ravings seriously. Then rescue came from what to Mara was undoubtedly a surprising, though to Lucifer an all too predictable, quarter.

"She's telling the truth, Paul," declared Yeshua.

Paul turned to his adorable lord in perplexity, but could say nothing.

"Is that all you think of the love between a man and a woman?" pressed Yeshua. "The lust of the flesh?"

Paul hesitated, as if he were tiptoe on the edge of a cliff. Even though it had been countless eons since Lucifer had stood in that place, he well remembered the feeling. Then, as the Light-Bearer had done in that long-ago time, the apostle took the plunge, in the opposite direction, it was true, but away from the tyrant nonetheless.

"Love is spiritual," said Paul, "whether it be between man and woman or man and man or woman and woman. Far from being essential to love, sexual coupling in any form poisons love with jealousy and lust. If you are truly the Lord, how can you be subject to such corruption?"

Yeshua rose, meeting Paul's anger with his own. "You acknowledge the authority of scripture, do you not?" he queried.

Paul nodded. Lucifer wondered if any of the mortals could see the apostle's trembling uncertainty.

"According to Genesis, why did the Lord create Eve?" asked Yeshua.

"To propagate the human race."

"That's the second reason," persisted Yeshua. "What's the first?"

"To be Adam's companion," admitted Paul, lowering his head.

"But that had nothing to do with the sexual act!" came a voice from the crowd, a voice well known to Lucifer. It was Augustine, erstwhile bishop of Hippo, a city in the now defunct Roman North Africa. Sporting a beard so impressive in its patriarchal length as to be rivaled only by the golden miter perched precariously atop his bald pate, this prelate was, after Paul, the most influential theologian in the history of Christianity. He arose from the stump upon which he had hitherto followed the proceedings, and faced the court. "The venerable apostle is right. Sexual intercourse is the highway over which the corruption and guilt of our first ancestors has made its way into every human soul save that of Christ and his blessed mother. The Lord could have nothing to do with it."

Yeshua looked to Paul. "Do you see what you started? Now, tell me, what does Genesis say?"

The apostle stirred as if he were coming back from the dead, doubtless from the shock of his precious master giving him a rope made of his precious scripture with which to hang himself.

"That Adam and Eve became one flesh."

"And that was before they sinned?" asked Yeshua.

"Yes," replied Paul, humbled into uncharacteristic brevity.

"But that can't mean they were united in passion!" interjected Augustine.

"If it's in the Torah," shot back Yeshua, "it can't mean anything else!"

"What's he saying?" Augustine asked of Paul, who clearly was much more of an authority to him than Yeshua.

"Scripture is reticent about sexual matters," answered Paul in the manner of a rabbi instructing his student. "It employs euphemism. In the books of the Law, to say that a man and woman became one flesh is as unequivocal a way of stating they enjoyed sexual relations as one can imagine."

"Of course, I knew that!" Augustine cried angrily, chomping on his beard. "I never said that sex was sinful in and of itself, only the lust that inevitably accompanies it after the fall. As every mortal soul here knows from experience, nothing takes one further away from the rational peace of the spirit than the sexual lusts of the flesh. That's why the act of procreation, innocent and indeed necessary as the divinely ordained means for propagating the human race, became the route of transmission of our original parents' guilt to all future generations. All have sinned and fallen short of God's glory! Hence Christ's sacrificial death, and hence the holy sacraments whereby Christ's grace washes the sinful soul clean and incorporates it into Holy Mother Church."

"That's really what this business of original sin is all about, isn't it?" said Yeshua. "Getting babies into the Church. An unbaptized infant is damned!"

"Not damned," said Augustine, his precision betraying a prissiness that had always irritated Lucifer, "and not saved, either. The unbaptized infant is not tormented like the souls in hell, but neither does it enjoy the bliss of eternity with God."

"You're splitting hairs," rejoined Yeshua. "If God is love, what greater torment than to spend eternity without him? Regardless of what you told yourself, Augustine, you invented this absurd idea of inherited guilt as a cudgel with which to beat people into the Church."

"I did no such thing!" protested the bishop. "By sword and decree, the Roman emperors established the universality of Christ's mystical body on earth. I propounded its theological necessity."

"And this is what you think I am about?" asked Yeshua.

"It's what Christ is about," said Augustine noncommittally. "There's no salvation outside the Church."

Yeshua smiled scornfully. "It must be gratifying to have a monopoly upon so precious a commodity."

"I've heard that sort of thing before from the heathen," Augustine rejoined. "Faith is always foolish in the eyes of the world."

"My eyes are the eyes of the world?"

Augustine looked hard at Yeshua, but said nothing. Paul instantly moved to the bishop's side, laying a conciliatory arm upon his shoulder and easing him down upon his stump, all the time whispering sweet nothings in his ear. Then he returned to the center of the field and bowed before Yeshua. "My Lord, I know that you are the beginning and end of everything, and that your ways are past finding out; but I pray you to explain to those of us who have remained true to our faith in you why you seem so scornful of the community of believers, the community in which all of us have found new life."

As Yeshua looked upon his apostle to the gentiles with sorrow and exasperation in his eyes, Lucifer scanned the crowd. All of them, even the unbelievers, were engrossed in the discussion. No one, it seemed, had ever dreamt of the possibility of an open conflict between Paul and his treasured Christ! Thus Lucifer almost started when he met the knowing eyes of Muhammad. They said that the prophet had expected such a development all along. Lucifer winked conspiratorially and Muhammad scornfully turned away. No matter. God's messenger was in for a few surprises himself.

"You had much to do with the building of the Church," Yeshua finally answered Paul. "You gave it much of its ideological foundation, as well as its institutional structure. Without you there never would have been a Church, not as it exists today."

Paul bowed even more deeply. Lucifer could hardly refrain from smacking his lips at the taste of this delicious irony. "My only purpose in living and dying was to serve you, Lord," said the apostle with what to Lucifer was comic sincerity. "To serve the truth."

"You are co-counsel in my defense?" Yeshua asked.

"Yes, Lord, but Mr. James has withdrawn, so now I am sole counsel."

"Mr. James may have withdrawn," Yeshua said, casting a sly but affectionate glance at the American philosopher, "but I've not withdrawn him. But right now I want to hear from you."

Holmes lightly rapped his gavel. "This is most unusual," he said in a gentle tone that belied the purport of his words, "not to say irregular. I've already ruled that these proceedings are not bound by protocol, as is obvious in the latitude I've just now permitted the defendant. But I feel it my duty as presiding magistrate to point out to the prosecution the possibility here of objection. I venture to say that in no trial ever held under any system of law has the accused examined his own attorney!" Holmes turned to Lucifer. "You may take a moment to confer with your associates."

Lucifer had no need to consult with anyone and no desire to derail Paul and Yeshua from head-on collision, but he could not pass up the opportunity to find out what was wrong with Rachel. Bowing, therefore, he thanked his honor and promised he would not take long. When he looked around, however, she was nowhere to be seen. "Where is she?" he muttered as Mara and Azazael approached.

"Who, My Lord?" Azazael asked naively, and Lucifer nearly kicked him. He did not stop himself because he feared a public scene, but because there was something in Azazael's tone, a touch of self-assured challenge, that made it clear he was no longer playing the clown. Azazael was now his enemy, though he probably did not realize that Lucifer knew it, and had to be treated with the guile and cunning accorded to all the Light-Bearer's foes. "Find her," he ordered.

Azazael bowed and smiled. "Of course, My Lord." His failure to ask what he should do with her after he found her revealed he had no intention of obeying Lucifer's command.

* * *

Will was surprised at how calm he felt, now that the battle was actually joined. He had expected this. From the look of the crowd, he was the only one who had expected this.

The sun shone so brightly he found it oppressive, the way he had as a child when all he had wanted was to crawl into the hole of his room and escape into the world of his imagination—or rather, other people's imaginations—through books. Now, however, he had no wish to escape. The confrontation between Paul and Yeshua was more exciting than anything he had ever found in a book. Here was the Christ, the incarnate Lord of the entire universe, about to engage in theological combat with the man who, more than anyone else, was responsible for making that same Lord famous throughout the world. Nothing could stop it now, not even his fastidious friend's appeal to judicial formality. Will felt the coming storm in his ethereal bones.

After making a show of conferring with Azazael, Lucifer bowed to Holmes. "If the two foremost champions of the Christian lunacy wish to demonstrate their ideology's fundamental inanity in so dramatic a fashion, we've no objection."

"Then the defendant may continue to examine his own counsel," declared Holmes, seemingly unaware of how absurd his ruling sounded, of how ridiculous it was to think of what was going on here in legal terms any longer. Yeshua paid scant heed to Holmes, but regarded Paul with a severity that caused the latter to tremble and fall upon his knees. "My Lord, I can only think that you're testing me!" he cried out in pitiful anguish.

"Believe what you must," said Yeshua in the quiet mercilessness so typical of him. "Did you ever have a child?"

"No, lord, you know I did not."

"Do you have any idea what a loving father feels toward his child?"

Paul froze, but then slowly climbed from his knees and drew himself erect. "The same feeling that God must have for us, his children."

"Yes," persisted Yeshua, "but do you know what it is to feel that feeling?"

Paul's face hardened. "You obviously think I don't."

As Will could have predicted, Yeshua did not take the bait. "What's the foundation of a life lived in God?" he asked calmly.

"Faith," affirmed Paul.

"Not love?" queried Yeshua.

Paul lowered his massive, close-cropped head in contemplation. The assured strength of this mental effort suffused his figure with an intellectual nobility that made Will understand how the Athenians had mistaken him for Hermes, the messenger of the gods. "Love is the fruit of a godly life, it's true," he judiciously replied, "but faith is the soil in which that life is rooted."

"Then tell me," asked Yeshua, sounding impartial but interested, like a professor giving an oral examination, "what is faith?"

Paul regarded his inquisitor warily, sensing a trap. "In essence," he replied, "faith is recognition of God's holy omnipotence and submission to his will. It's acknowledging that God is God."

"And it's by such recognition that men are saved?" continued Yeshua.

The apostle hesitated.

"Paul," admonished Yeshua, "why is this so difficult for you? All we need do is be honest with each other."

"Faith is the foundation of all reason," the apostle finally answered, emboldened by Yeshua's remark, "and reason is the foundation of order. There's a natural hierarchy, both in man and the universe, and God is the head of that hierarchy. When man fails to recognize God for who and what he is, when man makes himself his own god, all falls into chaos. Reason that proudly oversteps its limit and rejects truth as its master can no longer be master in its own house. The appetites and passions rebel and enslave this noblest of human faculties, turning it into a panderer that seeks to procure for them whatsoever they desire. Respect for law, the rational ordering of society according to nature as created by God, wanes and indeed disappears. The lascivious and the greedy pursue pleasure and wealth, heedless of the good of their souls and the well-being of their fellow citizens. The natural relations between the sexes that, as My Lord has already observed, are ordained by God, become corrupted. This is what we see in the world today!"

"Pride then is the root of all sin, and its fruit is chaos?" asked Yeshua.

"Yes, Lord," bowed Paul, doubtless feeling that, if Yeshua understood him so aptly, all would be well.

"And where do I come into the picture?" continued Yeshua, his voice still neutral.

Paul's own voice leapt like fire. "You are the perfect sacrifice that makes restitution for the sin of the world!"

As he said this, the apostle so overflowed with adoration that once again he fell to his knees. As one man, the Christians in the crowd followed suit. Yeshua only had to keep silent and accept this devotion for the outcome of the trial to be assured. But that, Will sighed, was impossible.

"Tell me, Paul," said Yeshua, unmoved by the high emotion surrounding him. "If you were judge and the accused were guilty of murder, would you accept the offer of his brother to die in his place?"

Paul stood, but then looked down and said nothing. He owned too subtle a mind not to see what was coming.

"What would you do, Paul?" Yeshua repeated, refusing to let the question hang in the air.

Paul did not raise his head. "I would refuse the offer," he replied, softly but clearly enough for all to hear.

"Why?" Yeshua persisted, giving no quarter.

"Because the brother did not commit the crime."

"So," concluded Yeshua, "punishment only satisfies justice when it falls upon the guilty party. Punishment of the innocent is a miscarriage of justice. Do you really believe that executing me satisfies divine justice? Is God's justice less than man's?"

Paul said nothing.

"And what kind of love would require such a sacrifice? What kind of God would place as condition for the forgiveness of his wayward children the torture and death of his only righteous one?"

Paul remained as silent and motionless as a dormant volcano.

"But this isn't my greatest grievance against you and your fellow 'Christians,'" Yeshua went on inexorably, no longer keeping the sarcasm out of his voice. "My greatest grievance is that you've made of me a joke—a mean, petty, absurd and ineffectual joke!"

Paul raised his head a little so that he could see Yeshua's face. Will could not imagine what the apostle was feeling at that moment. He only knew it was excruciating.

"What's the point of it all, Paul?" cried Yeshua. "What's the return upon the investment? What's the payoff for signing up with the Christian Club?"

"I don't understand your question," said Paul stonily.

"'If there be no resurrection of the dead, then we are the most foolish of men!' Didn't you write that, Paul? Doesn't that mean that the whole point of faith is salvation?"

"Of course!" answered Paul. "What other point could there be?"

"And to be saved means to enjoy eternal bliss in the kingdom of heaven and escape eternal torment in hell?"

"Yes," affirmed Paul, "as scripture itself proclaims!"

"So, one believes in order to escape suffering," deduced Yeshua. "Does one love in order to escape suffering? Is that what I was doing on the cross?"

The pain in Yeshua's voice was unmistakable to Will, but he wondered if anyone else noticed it. Certainly not Paul. He was too full of his own pain, a pain he now sought to relieve by pouring out the excess in wrath. He looked Yeshua straight in the eye. "You're saying that anyone who confesses Christ as lord and savior is damned?" he mocked.

"Those are your words," Yeshua shot back, "belonging to a thought world that is an abomination to me!"

"How can you say that," demanded Paul, "unless you aren't really he?"

"I can say it because it's the truth," replied Yeshua. "My only authority is the truth. According to you, salvation is entirely God's own doing, is it not?"

"Of course," answered Paul. "Otherwise, we sinners could take credit for what only God can do. To him belongs all the power and the glory."

"And therefore damnation is entirely God's own doing as well? God decides who's saved and who's damned before they are born?"

"That's true as well," said Paul, the edge of challenge in his voice echoing that in Yeshua's. "It must be. If man earns damnation, then he may earn salvation. Heaven would no longer be God's free gift. We would purchase it with our merit."

"I don't see that," retorted Yeshua. "How does the recipient's refusal or acceptance affect whether a gift is freely given?"

Paul hesitated. It was the first time Will had seen him trumped in debate. "But if the decision were not entirely God's," he answered at length, "if it were in man's hands, then how could pride be excluded? And if we can take pride in our salvation, then we have returned to the vicious lie of self-reliance that first brought chaos into the world!"

Yeshua looked pityingly at his apostle. "There may be pride in the rejection of a gift," he said, "but where is the pride in its acceptance? Is your theology so fantastic that it leaves no place for the truth of the human heart?"

"The human heart," declared Paul, "is full of lust, malice, avarice, envy, sloth, and vanity. That is its truth."

"If you believe that," said Yeshua, "then your God is the enemy of the human heart. Your God is Satan."

Paul's expression set into fixed hostility, and Will doubted whether he would hear anything else Yeshua had to say. Nevertheless, though Yeshua himself was certainly aware of this fact, he went on, as he always did, in faith that the heart was listening even if the head were not.

"You liken human beings to pots, and God to a potter. You ask, 'Who is the pot to criticize the potter if he makes some pots for everyday use, to be thrown in the end on the dung heap, and some as vessels of glory to be admired and preserved forever? Who is man to question God if he creates some men to be damned in order to show how lucky are those who are saved?' Don't humans have the right to use and abuse animals? Don't parents have the right to beat their children? Isn't possession nine-tenths of the law? Don't the mighty have the right to oppress the downtrodden? Doesn't power justify, and absolute power justify absolutely?"

Yeshua, Will knew, had waited nearly two-thousand years to say these things, and now the one most in need of hearing them was not even listening. Something had to be done. "Your Honor," he addressed Holmes, "may I speak in Paul's behalf?"

Holmes blustered a bit about the irregularity of a defendant attacking his own attorney and defense co-counsel coming to the rescue, but then acquiesced.

"My Lord," Will said to Yeshua, "as you well know, I agree with your sentiments. But this idea of double predestination, of God deciding who's saved and who's damned before we are born—while necessitated by the logic of Paul's own thought, it's true, and therefore influential upon the more systematic of later Christian theologians like Aquinas, Calvin and Luther—was rejected by the mainstream in all three branches of Christendom. Is it fair to judge a man solely by his errors?"

"It was not an error," muttered Paul.

Will thought it best to act as if he had not heard. "Surely Paul's accomplishments outweigh his mistakes. You yourself said that he, more than anyone else, was responsible for the development of Christianity."

"He drew up the blueprints," admitted Yeshua.

"Surely he did more than that, My Lord!" Will insisted. "He created the archetype, the organizing principle, of the mystical body of Christ. Your mystical body, Lord."

Paul's face softened, just as Will had hoped it would. Yeshua was right, he felt, but only in part. For all its hypocrisies and shortcomings, institutional Christianity was a bulwark against the dark savagery in the human soul. Undoubtedly it was as rife with corruption as the next religion, but it also held high an ideal of gentility and grace that had done much to soften the iron temper of barbarism.

* * *

Rachel had nowhere to go. The sun shone bright but not harsh, the air tingled with an energy that soothed as much as it awakened, and the sound of exotic bird calls made her long to explore the mountains to see what other creatures had been newly added to the pleroma. But she could not go there. That was *his* territory. Even if he were engaged all day at the trial, everything in the wilderness would remind her of him.

Neither could she go back into the city. It might be deserted now, but sooner or later everyone would return. She had had enough of people for the time being, and even more than her fill of Lucifer's comfort.

Yet she could not remain where she was, however anonymous she had made herself by sinking into the ocean of souls now occupying the field of judgment. She could bear him no longer, neither the sweet sound of his voice nor the implacable logic of his words. His betrayal made any connection with him impossible. It made all things impossible.

As if her head moved of itself, Rachel suddenly looked up into the sky. If only she could take refuge in the boundless solitude of space! Beyond the brightness of the sun, she could feel the stars beckoning with their cold, stuttering light. Why not let go, let go and melt into the void?

Rachel did so. She was amazed at how easy it was to dissolve into the peace she had been seeking, mostly without knowing it, all her life.

* * *

Wendell adjourned the proceedings while the sun yet lingered above the horizon, when it was clear that neither Jesus nor Paul had anything more to say to each other, quite possibly forever. The frustrated magistrate led the troubled James home through the somber twilight. Agitated with the elation of the reunion, most of the assembly elected to stay in the field. Neither Wendell nor Will, however, had anyone or anything to keep them there, and Will looked as if he could use the comfort of domestic surroundings. The man was like a zombie. What else he needed Wendell could not even begin to guess.

After building a fire with his own two hands, Wendell settled himself in the easy chair opposite his friend, now sprawled listlessly across the divan, and cursed the powers that be, only half good-naturedly, for taking away the liquor and cigars. There was still food, but neither man had an appetite. If James were going through anything like Wendell—and Wendell could tell he was just by looking at him—then a tight fist of anxiety gripped him in the stomach and squeezed harder and harder. Someone had to say something, no matter how stupid, to break the tension. "You really believe that fellow is Jesus Christ?" asked Wendell, less than half in jest.

Shrewd with desperation, Will eyed Wendell guardedly. "I admit, everything would be so much easier if he weren't."

"He's not like any Lord and Savior I've ever heard about," continued Wendell darkly. "Maybe that's just it!" he suddenly brightened, feeling as if he had hit upon the solution to the mystery of life. "Maybe he's sick of all this fawning, all this worship and adoration. God knows I would be if I were in his shoes!"

"Yes," said James, his voice soft yet piercing, like an infant's whimper, "he's sick of our adoration, but not for the reasons you would be."

"Do you know both of us so well," Wendell spat out the words despite himself, "or do you simply assume I can do nothing save out of base and ignoble motives?"

"Do you know me so well," rejoined James, a flicker of a smile breaking through the gloom, "that you instantly assume I'm attributing the base and ignoble motives to you?"

Wendell said nothing, returning his friend's gaze in expectation.

"In truth, I wish it were so black and white, so morally tidy," Will went on. "I merely meant that you are far more practical than he. In fact, I'm beginning to think that he's not practical at all!"

Wendell looked away, gathering his thoughts as the sputtering fire cast a frantic dance of shadows upon the wall. "I must confess," he said at length, "that I had difficulty following the argument of today's proceedings. Assuming for the moment that he is Jesus, what did he want of Paul?"

"His heart," Will replied, his tone sad and sardonic. "He wants nothing less from any of us."

Wendell was not quite sure what that meant. "I gathered that Paul's message was not what Jesus intended. But if that's so, why did he wait two thousand years to let him know? I admit, I'm far from expert in these matters, but, according to the Bible, weren't the two of them in some form of communication even while Paul was still on earth?"

"In some form, yes," James confirmed, "but one can receive only what one is willing to receive." He jumped up and paced about the room, the sudden fire in his eyes brighter than that in the grating. "What he said about Paul was absolutely right. Only now is not the time to say it!"

"You too think Paul corrupted his message?" queried Wendell.

"From one point of view, corrupted it," said James. "From another, adapted it."

"And which is your point of view?" insisted Wendell.

"That's my problem," answered Will, dropping back onto the couch with an exhaustion as sudden as the preceding exuberance. "I hold both points of view. I not only see them," he added, so there would be no mistake. "I hold them!"

Wendell waited for his friend to explain.

"At bottom," James said, exhaling deeply, as if he had been holding his breath for centuries until these particular words could come out with it, "Paul and Yeshua are working with two totally different, even diametrically opposed understandings of human nature—indeed, of reality itself! Yeshua knows this all too well. Paul has hardly an inkling. Even though both men are Jewish, Paul, the consummate intellectual, is heavily, even if subconsciously, influenced by Greek thought. He operates with the triple-tiered, hierarchical anthropology of Plato. Ideally, reason governs the appetites, and it is the passions' duty to assist reason in this task."

"Makes sense to me," Wendell commented. "The appetites are many and blind. Reason sees and is one. The other way around would be chaos. But I thought Paul placed faith above reason."

"Yes and no," replied James. "For Paul, faith is reason's recognition of its own insufficiency. It's the rational affirmation that there is a power greater than man, a power that can be known to be omnipotent, good and just through the evidence of its works."

"Creation?" asked Wendell.

"Precisely," affirmed James. "Paul was one of the original proponents of the argument from design. Not only is the universe proof positive that its creator exists, but also that he is perfect and all-powerful."

"I had no idea," Wendell murmured, staring pensively into space. James smiled. "Is that meant to be sarcastic?"

Wendell pulled himself out of his reverie. "No, no! I had no idea Paul was such a... such a..."

"Rationalist?" offered James.

"Yes, exactly. Yet, that's not what I see when I look at the cosmos."

"Nature red in tooth and claw?" surmised James.

Sensing a trap, Wendell answered reluctantly, "Isn't that painfully obvious?"

"Yes," James unexpectedly agreed, "I'm afraid it is. But perhaps it wasn't so obvious in Paul's day."

"Oh, come now!" huffed Wendell. "The Roman Empire was no garden party! Slaves, wars of conquest, gladiatorial games..."

"Christians fed to the lions?" Will added to the litany.

"That, too!" affirmed Wendell.

"Perhaps Paul sees something we don't," said James.

"Perhaps Paul sees what he wants to see," rejoined Wendell.

"That may be very true," Will agreed. "But if it is, we may have a proverbial case of the pot calling the kettle black."

Wendell would have answered his friend with some defensive remark had Will not sounded like he was ruefully talking about himself. Instead, he added more logs to the blaze. Irritated by the tendency of these heavenly fires to give off no smoke, he deliberately chose green wood. The reward of a few tiny billows was not worth the effort.

"But we're not being fair to Paul," James resumed after an interval of contemplation. "Paul sees the chaos and corruption, perhaps as clearly as Yeshua." He blinked and vigorously rubbed his eyes, almost as if he were trying to work them free from their sockets. "Though not so deeply. Yes, he sees the chaos, and regards it as the inevitable result of reason's abject surrender to pride."

"I don't quite get that," said Wendell. "Why shouldn't reason take pride in itself? After all, what else have we got? All this talk about faith, it seems to me, is hogwash, unless it means faith in the dictates of reason. Why bring some invisible entity like 'God' into the equation?"

James smiled his condescending smile, and Wendell remembered where he was and lowered his head in embarrassed consternation. Then he felt a calm come over him and looked his friend steadily in the eye. "Maybe Paul is not so wide of the mark, after all. But you said he and Jesus don't see eye to eye here because... I'm not clear on that point."

"Because he has a totally different understanding of what human beings are all about," reiterated James. "Paul holds to the Greek idea of hierarchy, Yeshua to the Hebrew conception of depth. For Yeshua, at heart man is not divided up into different faculties, one of which may or should rule over the others. It only seems that way when one lives on the surface of one's being, at a distance from oneself, with the pure light shone by the heart's fire colored and distorted by the kaleidoscopic prism of the imagination."

"Sounds more like poetry than philosophy," quipped Wendell.

"I thought you might see it that way," said James, "but it does make literal and absolute sense to a certain type of person."

"The tender-hearted rather than the tough-minded?" asked Wendell, a sly smile stealing over his face.

"I'm flattered that you've read my work," said Will, not at all nonplused. "But though I still feel I was getting at a real and valid distinction with those terms, I no longer use them."

Wendell felt a trifle exasperated. "What do you use?"

"I'm not sure what to use," admitted Will. "All I know is that Yeshua's idea of inner depth is far more profound and real to me than Paul's concept of hierarchy, and for that very reason far more elusive."

"There you go, slipping into that Oriental mysticism again!" cried Wendell with a laugh. He hoped it did not sound too forced. He really did fear that Will was hanging over the edge. Of course, Will had always been hanging over the edge, from ever since he had known him. But still, more seemed to be at stake now. Infinitely more.

"When one gets to the bottom of it," replied James, neither amused nor offended, "it's quite simple. For Paul, evil is chaos, and sin is violation of the divinely ordained hierarchy. For Jesus, evil is lovelessness, and sin the refusal to live from the passion of one's heart."

Wendell pondered. "Now that you put it that way, I can see

why they had to fight. But, damn it, nobody's perfect, except, presumably, this Yeshua. Why can't he give Paul his due? After all, from everything that's been said, the man almost single-handedly built the early Church!"

Again came one of James' condescending smiles. "Not exactly," corrected the professor, "though a credulous reading of Acts might give that impression. He was, to be more accurate, its posthumous architect. He sketched the blueprints according to which it was later built."

"And he did a damn good job!" asserted Wendell. "You know I've little sympathy for Christian thought, but it's no mean feat to design an institution that has survived the slings and arrows of this world for almost two millennia. Who knows? Were it not for Paul, we might never even have heard of Jesus!"

"Who knows?" echoed James. "But that's precisely the point at issue. Is the Church the necessary means of spreading divine truth throughout the earth and transmitting it to future generations, or is it man's imposition of an institutional straitjacket upon the Holy Spirit?"

"Yes, I guess that's the gist of their dispute," Wendell tentatively agreed. "And I must say, I don't know if I even have an opinion on this matter. I don't doubt anymore that we're all connected inwardly, much less that some sort of deity exists. This place is proof of that. But I'm not sure this alleged Christ is any closer to that deity than anyone else."

"Oh, he's a great deal closer, of that I can assure you," asserted Will. "But that's just the problem."

"How so?"

An expression of pain and sorrow came into Will's countenance. "Did you now that in the ancient world the insane were held to be especially dear to the gods? What if the converse is true? What if those especially dear to God must become insane?"

* * *

"Will you hear him out?" Uriel implored the slender firebrand of a saint, whose eyes showed that he had no desire to listen to anyone or anything. She had sought him out in his lonely mountain retreat, a wooded ravine hard by a rushing stream. He only took an occasional rest here in the solitude of the wilderness, but Uriel knew that when he did, his friends and disciples had strict orders not to disturb him. The darkness of night had come, and the apostle sat with his back against a fallen pine in pained concentration, probably trying to make some sense of the day's events, which promised to be more revolutionary than his being struck blind on the road to Damascus nearly two millennia ago.

"I've already heard him out," said Paul. "And what matters it to him, anyway? If he truly is the Lord, he doesn't need me."

"You doubt that he's the Lord?" marveled Uriel. "You hold your pride to be of greater value than the truth?"

"We're all under the same judgment!" rejoined Paul. "I'm guilty of pride only if he is the truth. If not, that sin is on your head. And his."

Uriel considered the meaning behind these words. "Your logic is correct," she admitted. "I'm not going to fight over this. I only ask that you not make up your mind rashly."

"I heard him today!" Paul reiterated. "What more can you want? If he is the Lord, what more can you need?"

Uriel felt her aura dim. The saint was strangely like Lucifer, so locked into the logic of his ideas that he and she might as well have been in two different universes. "I'm asking you to think that you may be wrong! You understand God as power, Yeshua as love."

"That you will have to show me!" declared Paul in a tone that betrayed an absolute will not to be shown.

"I can't do so!" cried Uriel. "He can, if you let him. But in this you have the answer to your question. He doesn't order us around as if he were some mighty king. Like a lover, he whispers to us in the depths of our hearts. We angels hear his voice. You humans do not. Why he can't be happy forsaking the human race and dwelling among those who truly love him I don't know. Have you forgotten, Paul, that they crucified him?"

"Christ was crucified according to God's plan of salvation," proclaimed the saint sententiously.

Uriel's aura suddenly flared. "According to your system, but what father would ordain the torture and execution of his own son?"

Paul's eyes glazed over as if turning to ice. She was losing him.

Then she realized what she must do. She summoned her brothers and sisters from every quarter of the heavens and raised her aura's vibration to the greatest radiance it could attain before becoming invisible to human eyes. The effect upon Paul was immediate and exactly as she had hoped. She had never seen him cringe before. "We all affirm that Yeshua is Lord!" Uriel proclaimed, her voice and her fellow angels filling the empyrean. "Do you place your own petty logic above the witness of the hosts of heaven?"

Paul threw himself prostrate on the ground, trembling not with fear but repentance. "Forgive me my sin of pride!" he cried out. "What would you have of me?"

"Only this, that tomorrow you hear our Lord Yeshua with an open mind and an open heart, no matter how much what he says offends you. You hear him out to the end."

Paul raised himself up. "I will do so," he promised.

"You will counsel your fellow Christians to do likewise," Uriel added.

Paul bowed his bare, close-cropped head in assent. In unison, the entire choir of angels raised its vibration and disappeared in what to the apostle must have been a blinding flash. "Forgive me, Lord," Uriel heard him murmur before launching herself into the empyrean, and she wondered if Yeshua would ever forgive her for what she had just done.

* * *

Da-dum, da-dum, da-dum, da-dum...

Lucifer lay on the couch, the one on which he had had *her*, and listened to the beating of his heart. It was such a marvelous instrument, registering instantly and accurately every mood, whim, emotion and desire of its possessor. But truly, did he possess it or it him? He had breathed so long to its tempo that he had come to take it for granted. Now in his memory he recaptured those extraordinary days, millennia of millennia ago, when he had faced the choice and seized upon the way of the flesh. Had he been given the opportunity, or had it simply been there for him to take? For so long everyone but a handful of allegedly benighted mortals had assumed there was an absolute ruler of heaven and earth. Not even this trial called that assumption into question. Even for the notorious "adversary," Lucifer had to admit to himself, it was comforting to believe there was a God. Were the freethinkers right? Had we all fallen prey to our own myths?

His eyes roamed about the room and what he could see of the great hall through the aperture. The torches burned low but steady, though the light quivered slightly, as if it were as exhausted as he. As if by an act of divine providence, he thought to himself ironically, his glance came to rest upon a corner of one of the paintings depicting scenes from the war in heaven. No, it was merely a corner of a corner, revealing the gleam of Mikael's golden shield, but it was enough for him to reconstruct the entire panorama in his mind's eye, and a bitter laugh escaped his lips. There had been no war in heaven! It was another myth to which its own creators had fallen victim. How many angels, bright or dark, believed in it? Were there any who did not?

Azazael.

Lucifer was certain Azazael believed none of these myths, not even the myth of God. For a moment he felt some regret at having to sacrifice that pawn. The creature had been amusing at times, and his unvarnished cynicism was a bracing astringent in the midst of the rampant sentimentality of the pleroma. But really, in sum, he was no longer worth the bother. Not wasting another thought upon his traitorous lieutenant, Lucifer lay motionless through the rest of the night. Until the light of dawn washed the shadows from his mind, his heart beat only for *her*.

* * *

At the latter's request, under the blanket of night, on the shore of an icy lake, at the bottom of a gigantic quarry, somewhere in the Siberian wastes, Azazael met with the Nameless One on earth. The wind rushed down from the surrounding cliffs, whipping up froth upon the water and making a sound reminiscent of the screams of the dying. Despite the rumors and stereotypes, Azazael told himself, it was not that the Nameless One preferred this lonely and inhospitable locale. It was simply that absolute secrecy was essential.

A nondescript guard, dressed in a uniform of the recent world conflict, met him at what to prying eyes would have looked like the rock face of the quarry's northern wall. He took the hand of the guard, who then adjusted Azazael's vibrational frequency so that he could pass through the wall into an inner chamber. There he encountered another guard indistinguishable from the first, save that his uniform was that of a different nation, before another wall of stone. This guard likewise adjusted Azazael's vibration so he could pass through into a still more inner chamber. After repeating this ritual at least a dozen times, Azazael found himself in the center of the subterranean fortress, alone with *him*.

The Nameless One, so terrible that he could not be mentioned, except by implication, even in the legends of the fallen angels, looked remarkably plain. He appeared an ordinary mortal, dressed in a simple military tunic with shoulder boards but no medals. He was short, even for a human, pasty and overweight, and quick but stiff and graceless in his movements. His hair was dark but graying, and he sported a long, straight, full moustache that was either dyed or age had not yet touched. His face was blotchy and his features coarse. All in all, there was absolutely nothing attractive about him. And nothing noteworthy either, except his eyes. They smoldered with a jaundiced yellow that glinted like steely flame. It was these eyes, Azazael knew, that revealed what manner of being he was. When Azazael looked into his eyes, he felt himself a helpless bird hypnotized by the gaze of a cobra.

"So, comrade, you've come back to us!" cried the Nameless One in a voice of hearty good cheer that sent a shiver through Azazael's soul. "You've decided to avail yourself of our services, after all. Brother, you are most welcome!"

The Nameless One sat down in an easy chair behind a heavy metal desk—the only pieces of furniture in the bare, cold room— took up a pipe, lit it, and spent several minutes thoughtfully puffing away as if he had forgotten he had company. "Why don't you sit down, comrade?" he finally said, a note of irritation in his voice, as if he should not have had to ask.

Azazael did not dare point out that there was no chair, yet he also did not dare refuse the invitation. Acute anxiety caused a bead of sweat to form upon his brow, a sensation he found inordinately discomfiting. Meanwhile, the Nameless One confronted him with an angry stare. But just as he looked as if he were about to explode in rage, his steely eyes softened a little and a chair materialized behind Azazael. It was metal and uncomfortable looking, but it was enough to release him from his fright. With a feeling of relief akin to gratitude, he sat down and smiled at his host. "Yes," he blurted out, "I need your help! There's no one else to turn to. You alone can save us all!" Azazael was not surprised to hear himself say these things, but he was astounded at feeling that he actually believed them. Then he realized why. Only the Nameless One could save them all—from the Nameless One.

"You've fucked it up, have you, my little clown?"

"I've reached my limit," Azazael admitted.

"Maybe it's that whore you're shacked up with who's done you in. Maybe you've been weak and let love go to your head."

Azazael nodded solemnly. "That may be so," he murmured. "Yes, that may be so."

"Well, don't beat yourself into a pulp over it. Most men go to shit for a piece of ass. Turn her over to me, and I'll see to it you're never bothered again."

"She may yet be useful," demurred Azazael before he had a chance to think. He trembled as the Nameless One studied him, terrified that his dread host might regard this meaningless, heedless, impulsive remark as impudent defiance. Azazael almost wished he were back standing before the desk. At least he knew, even if he did not feel, that that debacle was not of his own making. This time he had blundered. To take a chance on offending the Nameless One was like playing the game mortals called Russian Roulette, only with five bullets in the six chambers instead of one. Against all reason, Azazael had the irresistible feeling that the Nameless One had it within his power to destroy him utterly.

"Maybe," the Nameless One finally said. "Maybe you need other friends. I've got some who've expressed an interest in your affair. You know them, I think. Metatron is one of them."

Distracted by the business about Mara, "He's a fool," Azazael said before he was able to stop himself.

The Nameless One looked at him blankly for a long time, and again Azazael felt his fate hanging in the balance. Then he laughed, and Azazael felt he could breathe again.

"Of course, that's why I use him!" He winked and snickered conspiratorially. "They're all fools! Fools make the best stooges!"

Azazael did not have the courage to ask who "they" were, although the reference certainly extended beyond Metatron's little entourage of primping peacocks, plotting snakes and plodding asses. As far as he could tell, it probably took in Azazael himself. He felt all his dreams slipping away, devoured by an ambition infinitely greater than his own, a black hole that sucked up everything that came within its oppressive and absolute gravitational pull. He no longer was himself but a character in a melodrama of the Nameless One's composition. Not to play his part would be worse than death. It would be the utter negation of his being. It would be as if he had never been. "And where are we to meet?" he asked.

"This meeting is nothing to be ashamed about," replied the Nameless One, an ironic smile upturning the corners of his broad mouth. "You don't have to hide in a hole like scared rabbits. They await you even as we speak, on your field of judgment."

Grateful for the panic that prevented him from laughing at this snare of a joke, Azazael realized there could be no more dangerous place for such a meeting, right under Lucifer's nose. But the Nameless One's smile permitted no objection. It said all was in the great one's hands and there would be, could be nothing to worry about. Azazael rose, bowed, and made his way back through the security checkpoints with a feeling of dizzying dread. He now served one greater than Lucifer, but who knew how long the Nameless One would want him around? The giddy feeling did not leave him until he was soaring back to the pleroma. He would find a way to defuse the Nameless One before that time came. He would think of something. He always had.

* * *

Though Rachel was not asleep, the sensation of *his* presence felt like an awakening, and not a pleasant one. Neither of them had bodies. They were simply consciousness present to consciousness, so they did not exactly speak. Nevertheless, the gist of what passed between them her mind automatically translated into words. "What are you doing here?" asked Rachel. "This is my kingdom, such as it is. You're not welcome here."

"They're enjoying themselves," he said, ignoring her question. "They think salvation is now complete." He awaited a response from her, but she held her mind aloof. "Will you be there tomorrow?" he asked.

Nothing.

"You must be there tomorrow."

Again, nothing.

"Tomorrow I'm going to explain myself to everyone, as best I can." She felt his irony and despair. "Why have you cast yourself into exile?" The tone of this interrogatory non sequitur was surprisingly neutral.

"I've no place to be," she finally answered. "They've left me no place to be. *You've* left me no place to be."

She sensed both his amusement and his pain. "We have that in common. I've left myself no place to be. As for them, they've nailed me to the cross. *You* have nailed me to the cross."

An indefinable grief welled up within her. "Please, leave me alone."

"Alright, as alone as you can be in a world where all is one in spirit. Perhaps that's why we feel so alone. All is one in spirit and broken in every other way."

Then he was gone. Everything was gone. The wretched world was gone. Her wretched self was gone. At last there was peace, the peace she had been seeking. Why, then, was this peace more agonizing than pain?

* * *

All told, it was as select a group of revolutionaries whom Azazael had assembled as had ever conspired against tyranny. As opposed to the showy but useless angels of light, he had told her, they were the real governors of the universe. Mara knew them all by reputation as defeated rebels against the Lord, but the aura of power they exuded in convocation assured her that Azazael's assertion could not be gainsaid. And they, with supreme daring and disregard for the apparent order of things, had assembled at the very center of the Heavenly City, in the field of judgment! It was the middle of the night, it was true, and there were no torches. Since these "fallen" ones had no intrinsic radiance like Mikael and those of his ilk, one might think they were hiding. Yet the moon hung over the horizon with only an occasional cloud to darken its light, and no one bothered to muffle his voice. Mara could not help but feel that she was present at the beginning of something truly great.

Most impressive were Metatron and his lieutenants, Sammael and Abaddon. All three were notorious for their fascination with death and destruction, but Azazael had made the telling point that without destruction there could be no creation, without death no rebirth. The old must be cleared away to make way for the new. No doubt these three strongmen would be indispensable in the imminent crisis.

As if in flagrant disregard for his reputation, Metatron dressed entirely in white. He was tall and muscular, even more so than his fellows; but most striking was his enormous head, with jaws that looked powerful enough to devour any object in the manifest universe.

Sammael and Abaddon, huge in their own right, were nevertheless impish in comparison with their chief, and not nearly as fastidious in their dress. They wore motley, which by turns looked bright then drab. Mara could not decide if this effect were caused by the moonlight and clouds or a vestige of the angelic aura. Their eyes were dark in hue but alight with mischief, and they regarded everything with a proprietary pride that said that whatever continued to exist after coming to their attention did so only by their leave.

Asmodeus, the lord of the dance, was there, arrayed in a flowing, forest-green robe that perfectly offset his lustrous auburn locks. In his ash-colored tunic Adramalechk, the king of fire, seemed modest by comparison, but his retinue of salamander spirits added dash and color to the meeting. Beliel too had come, his hair a mature and striking silver, dressed as a contemporary man of the world. With him was his liaison, Beliar, a youth with the face of an innocent and the garb of a sadist, black leather enhanced by glimmering knives and chains.

Belphegor was the only female in the group. She was all that any woman aspired to be—youthful, shapely and spry. But she possessed a profound and ravaging sensuality that could not be explained by appearance alone, and to which a fellow female like Mara herself felt not immune. Upon either of her arms hung the arch-libertines Semyaza and Shemhazai, who according to legend had been, along with her own Azazael, the first angels to mate with women of earth.

Completing the revolutionary executive council was Rashnu, the least remarkable in appearance. Dressed in an elegant but conservative gray business suit like those Mara had seen on so many of the wealthy and powerful who had passed recently to the pleroma, his attire would have suited the American magistrate Holmes had Holmes lived two decades longer. All Mara knew of him was that he had something to do with the judgment of souls. He it was who opened deliberations.

"Azazael!" Rashnu began in a deeply timbered voice that nevertheless danced lightly upon the wind into every corner of the field and, Mara thought with some trepidation, beyond. "The Boss tells us Lucifer is ready to accept our help in overthrowing the tyrant. What course of action does your master propose?"

Mara felt a sharp and delectable tingle of fear. Azazael had said nothing about convening this conference in Lucifer's name. And who was the Boss?

Azazael looked sadly into the eyes of each of his comrades. "You know what happened here yesterday," he intoned.

Metatron smiled. "Our enemies fought among themselves," he said merrily, mocking Azazael's solemnity.

"Yes, they did," Azazael agreed. "It would have been a great victory"—he let his words hang in the air—"if only anyone had paid attention."

"But they did!" cried Belphegor brightly, as if completing some amusing tale. "I was there. Everyone was spellbound!"

"Yes, spellbound," Azazael echoed, "the way an opera-lover is spellbound by an enchanting aria, the way a theatergoer is spellbound by a powerful climax, the way passersby are spellbound by the sight of an impaled criminal at the crossroads. One enjoys the spectacle and then returns to the business of one's life."

"And what business is that?" asked Beliar provocatively.

Azazael eyed the foolish youth. "Why, whatever it was before the pleasant and passing diversion!" he nearly shouted, sardonically stating the obvious. Then he turned about slowly, taking them all in. "Do you really believe that more than a handful of souls is truly concerned with the outcome of this misbegotten 'trial of God?'"

"Why misbegotten?" queried Belphegor, intrigued, as was her infuriating wont, by irrelevant detail.

"Because God can't be put on trial," replied Azazael.

"Because he's too great?" asked Beliel, in keeping with his identity as the spirit of influence and connections.

Azazael half-smiled disbelievingly at his fellows. "Because God does not exist!"

All were too shocked by this voicing of their own deepest doubts to say anything. After a period of fretful silence, Azazael continued.

"We're responsible for this universe, each and every one of us, angelic and mortal souls alike! The angels have longevity and perspective. The mortals have passion and involvement. Only we 'fallen' ones have integrated the best of both natures in our being. We are the true mediators between God and man, the ones who will unite heaven and earth!"

"I thought you said there was no God," remarked Asmodeus, his eyes sparkling as brightly with amusement as his tawny hair with the light of the moon.

Azazael grinned, as if at a private joke. "A matter of semantics," he said offhandedly. "There's no God outside of us. *We* are God."

This remark set off cheers from all but Beliel, who was not given to such displays of emotion, and Adramalechk, lord of fire. "If that's so," queried the latter, "if we are truly God, then why for so many millennia have we been outcasts in our own universe?"

Azazael wanted to reply that anyone who kept the company of lizards should be outcast, but he remained politic. "Is that your feeling?" he asked, his question addressed to all. Their shamed silence indicated assent. "Then you are fools. We have the power. All we need do is use it!"

"That's what Lucifer has been endeavoring to do, lo these many ages," said Rashnu judiciously.

"Yes," affirmed Azazael, "and now his labor is coming to fruition. But success hinges upon the efforts of us all!"

Everyone huddled close to Azazael.

"What does Lucifer propose?" asked Belial in his most businesslike confidentiality.

"Yesterday Yeshua brought fantasy to the citizens of the pleroma," proclaimed Azazael. "Tomorrow we bring them reality!"

Chapter 9

No sun shone as day dawned on the pleroma. Just as the moon set thick clouds had massed in the empyrean, and now they sprayed a fine mist, slowly but thoroughly soaking everyone and everything with their gloom. The field of judgment was awash with colorful canvas, shiny wet leather and rustic timber, as the mortal souls improvised an impressive array of shelters against the nattering drizzle. Among the Orientals sprang up pavilions and pagodas, bell tents and marquees among the Westerners. The Africans took refuge in lean-tos and wall tents, while the natives of the Americas brought forth from their imaginations tepees and wigwams. The Eskimos, heedless of the temperate climate, had even constructed igloos! All this went to show, Will supposed, that human ingenuity knew no natural bounds. Or perhaps that human nature, with its love of the familiar, was the most constricting natural bound of all.

Strolling among the erstwhile merrymakers, Will learned that the major topic of conversation was the weather. The less pious speculated that the Lord was deliberately dampening the high spirits of the reunion to be sure he had everyone's attention, while the more superstitious believed the miserable conditions to be merely an oracular reflection of the events that were to transpire on the field of judgment that day. Perhaps somehow, Will mused, both explanations were true. That was the problem with this universe, at least from a scientist's point of view: so many things could be true in so many unforeseeable and inconceivable ways.

Will knew one thing for certain—his active participation in this ludicrous trial was at an end. Yeshua had wanted his soapbox, and now he had it. In no plausible way was any of it any longer Will's responsibility.

As Holmes changed into his judge's robes, he remarked that the general depression even he found evident could not merely be the product of the unusual weather. Perhaps, he quipped, people had come to realize that they had been reunited with their loved ones not as they were enshrined in the hallowed chambers of their memories, but as they were in reality.

As soon as Holmes took his seat on the magistrate's bench, the motley arrangement of shelters came down, only to be replaced by a rainbow array of umbrellas. From the set look on his friend's face, Will wondered if Holmes were remembering some soggy Civil War campaign in which he and his comrades had endured exposure to the elements without respite or complaint. Then, as it were miraculously, the sun burned through the cloud-cover, most of the umbrellas disappeared, and the general mood began to brighten. By contrast, Will's own dread of what the day might bring grew all the darker.

Just as the angels of light threw their protective presence over the field, Yeshua appeared in the witness box. Everyone, it seemed, took this synchronicity as a manifestation of Yeshua's power, but Will surmised that it was Uriel's doing. So, he decided, in a way everybody was right. It was a demonstration of Uriel's power over her fellows, and of Yeshua's power over Uriel's heart.

Holmes rapped his gavel and a reflexive hush fell over the assembly. "Is the defendant ready to continue his testimony?" he asked Yeshua in a loud and confident voice. Holmes was so good at hiding his anxiety that even in the pleroma, where one's emotional entrails hung out of one's belly for everyone to read, no one could see it, Will bet, but he. Only one who knew him well would notice that the imposing magistrate was holding himself a little too stiffly and his eyes were open a little too wide. As for the giveaway telepathic reading of emotion through the eyes, that was extremely difficult to do accurately when one was oneself in the grip of anxiety. Despite the improvement of the weather, Will sensed that no one was free of the tension. No, not even Yeshua, though no nervous mannerism gave him away.

"I ask the court for permission to make a statement," said the defendant, his voice as calm as his mien.

Holmes nodded his assent.

"I mean an extended statement," Yeshua clarified. "Yesterday I gave a disjointed account. As much as possible, I wish to make myself understood."

Holmes addressed the assembly. "Does anyone have an objection?"

Everyone looked to Paul, but the apostle only sat in silence.

"You may proceed," said Holmes.

Yeshua rose from the witness seat. His body, Will realized, could no more be circumscribed by the confines of creaturely convention than his mind.

"'All have sinned and fallen short of the glory of God!'" Yeshua proclaimed, quoting from scripture in a startlingly loud voice. "Isn't that what all Christians believe? Isn't that what all of you believe, whether you are Christian or not, whether you believe in God or not, that to be human is to be sinful? But what do you really mean by it? What is sin?"

Yeshua looked over the crowd, but no one dared answer his question.

"Yesterday Paul took offense at me for attacking the root of his belief, the fundamental ideas of Christianity. He was wrong. I did not attack those ideas. I attacked their perverse misinterpretation that permeates and poisons Christendom. All of you, Christian or non-Christian, please hear what I have to say to you now. Before accepting or rejecting, seek to understand. Not only is my life at stake, but the life of all creation."

This entirely unexpected statement sent a shock through the assembly. What he said about the life of creation could be dismissed as the product of Yeshua's notorious penchant for hyperbole, but what about the bit about his own life? It was possible that Yeshua, should he lose the trial, would be removed from office, but no one had said anything about the death penalty, or could even think what that would mean in the pleroma. At that moment, however, James remembered what Gabriel had said in the angelic council when Lucifer had first proposed the trial, that Yeshua's authority was inseparable from his person. If that were so, Will realized with a shudder, the only way to remove him from office would be to destroy him.

"Love is what it's all about," resumed Yeshua, his voice extinguishing the remnant whisperings. "As my disciple John wrote, 'God is love.' He also wrote, 'He who loves, knows God'—not, 'He who loves God, knows God,' but 'He who loves, knows God.' The knowledge of God is not here,"—Yeshua pointed to his head—"but here." He placed his hand upon his heart.

"May I ask a question?"

Will was amazed to hear the high-pitched singsong of Sivananda. Never had the sanyasi been known to leave his mountain retreat. Now he rose from the anonymity of the assembly, dressed only in his spare linen loincloth, and faced Yeshua in simple entreaty.

"We spoke of it often when you visited me, but you never gave me a clear answer. Perhaps you were only being polite. Please do not be polite now."

Yeshua nodded for him to continue, and Holmes did not interfere. Sivananda smiled, and his emaciated brown body radiated good will.

"Love is in everyone and everything," he said. "Of course it is all about love. But the rest of this business, the theological speculation and doctrine and so forth—what does all that have to do with love?"

"What is your idea of love?" Yeshua countered.

Sivananda's smile broadened. "I should have known that you would answer my question with another question. Why, love is the cosmic force, the metaphysical glue that holds all of this together," he said with an opening of his arms that encompassed the entire universe, visible and invisible.

"Love may *do* that, but that's not what love *is*." Yeshua paused, as if for dramatic effect, Will thought sardonically, knowing as he did that the gentle Indian holy man was as a lamb being led to the slaughter. Sivananda calmly awaited further explanation.

"Love," Yeshua finally continued, "is personal relationship. It is opening to, committing to, and living personal relationship."

A spasm of anxiety distorted Sivananda's countenance.

"But, My Lord, for many eons I have renounced all personal relationship so that I might know you in your essence and lose myself in your infinite being, so that I might draw closer to you and we may become one."

Yeshua's voice was pitiless in its calm. "Then you have renounced the very thing that I am."

"But the great saints," Sivananda protested, "the holy men who embraced the life of self-denial, contemplation and prayer!"

"All that is but preparation," said Yeshua, "or, if you will, purification. One must become intimate with the inner depth in order to be capable of intimacy with life. So far have you been on the right track. However, when divorced from relationship, the inner depth becomes meaningless abstraction. What does it matter if you clean your house when you don't live in it? Once the cup is purified, what use is it to leave it empty? Fill the cup and then pour it out so that all may drink from the wine of love!"

Many throughout the assembly murmured in assent. Will's heart leapt. Perhaps Yeshua would win them over after all! Perhaps he had learned to be politic in this age of the emancipation of the human spirit. But, no, it could never be that easy. Yeshua would never let it be that easy.

"That's what Christianity is about," Yeshua declared as Sivananda sank to the ground, his spirit in tatters. Then he added more softly, as if in compassion for the misguided sadhu, "That is all that it is about."

"I would that were so!" cried Muhammad, rising like a billowing dust cloud from the desert floor. "Unfortunately, Christians themselves have clothed your simple message of love in the scarlet robes of blasphemy!"

From the prophet's tone, it was clear to Will that Muhammad felt the time had come for Yeshua to set the record straight, which to Muhammad meant bearing witness to the corruption of Christendom and the pristine purity of Islam. Will was certain that everyone in the assembly who had ever taken even a passing interest in these two forms of ethical monotheism would know, without having to be told, that Muhammad was expecting Yeshua to choose one over the other. After all, like gladiators condemned to fight to the death, had not their respective adherents squared off against each other throughout history? After Muhammad's less than amiable conference with Paul, word of which had spread like fire through the pleroma, everyone knew that no quarter would be asked or given in this battle for human souls. How then could Yeshua fail to support one and condemn the other? No *tertium quid* seemed possible.

So everyone who knew anything about human history knew. But Will knew that Yeshua was the master of the *tertium quid*.

"What blasphemy?" Yeshua asked.

Angry impatience flashed from the prophet's eyes, but he would give Yeshua every chance to prove his authenticity.

"Christians believe in three gods, not one," replied Muhammad. As Will knew, he was only getting started, but so was Yeshua.

"The doctrine of the Holy Trinity?" asked Yeshua in what could only be feigned naiveté.

Muhammad nodded.

"To be more precise," said Yeshua, "this is not belief in three gods, but the idea that there are three persons or entities in one God—the Father, Son and Holy Spirit."

"However one measures the offal," cried Muhammad, "it still stinks of polytheism!"

"On the contrary," said Yeshua, his composure in such contrast to Muhammad's agitation that the prophet must have felt it as an insult, "it's merely a logical corollary of the idea that God is love."

Muhammad's face set into a glare. He knew now that he was dealing with the enemy. "That's absurd!" he mocked.

"It's absurd from your point of view," rejoined Yeshua, "for you worship a God of power. But the God of power is equally absurd to those who worship the God of love."

"There's only one God!" retorted Muhammad.

"Yes," Yeshua agreed, "in reality there's only one God, but there are many ways of thinking about this God, as many as there are of thinking about reality."

Muhammad reddened, but then, in one of the lightning mood-changes for which he was notorious, chuckled in grudging admiration. At last, it seemed, he had found his match. "No matter how clever you are," he said, shaking his head, "let me see you, or anyone, make sense of the insanely illogical idea of a God who is both three and one!"

"It's simple," replied Yeshua. "If God is love, then all that belongs to love belongs to God. If God, the ultimate reality of the universe, is love, then reality follows the logic of love. God must be three-in-one to be love. Love is personal relationship. If God were not three-in-one, there would be no personal relationship in God, and God would not be love."

"Are you saying that God cannot love unless he is three-in-one?" queried Muhammad.

"No," answered Yeshua. "I'm saying that, unless he is three-in-one, God cannot *be* love."

"This is mere word-play!" declared the prophet, once more at the end of his tether.

"Perhaps," said Yeshua, "in the sense that all argument over abstract ideas is word-play. Nothing important hangs upon it. What matters is how one lives."

"Then what are we doing here?" demanded Muhammad.

"Men live according to what they perceive to be real. Most men are lost in the darkness of imagination, seeing mostly what they want or fear to see and seldom what is there. When one lives in the light, there are no abstractions, only the intuition of reality. When one is distant from the light, ideas can draw one toward the light or take one further into darkness. The war of ideas is the war over those souls lost in the darkness."

This seemed to satisfy the prophet, at least for the moment. And, Will noticed, Sivananda now came to life again, his original question at last having been answered. "Assuming your argument is sound," Muhammad asked, more relaxed now that he knew from which side this infidel was attacking, "why three? Why not two?"

"Because three is the number of personal relationship," said Yeshua. "There are the two persons in the relationship, and then there is the relationship itself."

"But there is no relationship apart from the two people in it!" protested Muhammad.

"Yes," rejoined Yeshua, "but the spirit of the relationship is something over and above those two. It's what binds them together. Otherwise there is no love, only politics."

"Are you saying that's what Islam is?" asked Muhammad, muted but unmistakable threat in his voice. "Politics?"

"That's for you to decide right now!" challenged Yeshua, not at all intimidated. "*Islam* means 'submission,' does it not?"

The prophet nodded warily.

"Love submits to nothing but love. You must decide if God is authority and power, or love."

"He's both!" affirmed Muhammad.

"That can't be!" rejoined Yeshua with equal fervor. "Suppose you were a slave in the court of a mighty king."

The prophet nodded, indicating that he would condescend to entertain the thought experiment.

"This king is so majestic, so awe-inspiring in his power and glory that, no matter where you go in his kingdom, you feel his presence. It's palpable. Moreover, you could travel endlessly and never come to the end of his kingdom."

Yeshua paused, and again Muhammad nodded.

"Perhaps you're a body-servant of the king, and you laugh and joke with him as you help him bathe and dress in the morning. Perhaps you're even one of his concubines, and enjoy the intimacy of his embrace. Even if you did share the king's bed, could you ever have a genuinely personal relationship with him?"

Muhammad's face literally shone with triumph. "You prove my point!" he proclaimed. "No one can have a personal relationship with God, not in the way you mean it, so to hold that God is personal relationship is absurd. God cannot be love, Yeshua," — in the speaking of the name was an ingenious blend of deadly enmity and amused contempt, tempered however by involuntary respect — "not as you define it. God is the supreme power and authority over all creation; and we, his creatures, owe him above all else obedience, loyalty, and adoration. This is Islam!"

At this point every Muslim in the assembly bowed in assent, touching his forehead to the earth, making countless waves in a human sea.

Yeshua was undaunted. "You assume what you need to prove," he said calmly, for all the world, thought Will, as if he were a teacher dealing with a bright but refractory pupil.

Muhammad fixed his eyes upon Yeshua's. He was not accustomed to having his gaze withstood, but Yeshua, though not defiant, neither trembled nor turned away. In fact, if Will had to guess what was in Yeshua's mind from what he could see of his eyes, he would have had to say pity. Gauging from the mounting fury in Muhammad's countenance, doubtless he saw the same. But then something in the prophet unaccountably broke. He gave a violent shudder and then relaxed his stance, showing that he was still willing to talk. "Please explain," he finally said in polite invitation.

"The little parable of the slave only shows that, if God is power, no personal relationship with God is possible," replied Yeshua. "It does not show that God is power."

"But who disputes that!" Muhammad cried as if he could not believe his own ears. "If there's anything upon which Muslims, Jews and Christians all agree, it's divine omnipotence!"

Collective affirmation sounded throughout the assembly.

"I dispute it," said Yeshua. He did not raise his voice appreciably, but nevertheless, like a crystal bell chiming in the midst of a storm, it could be heard clearly above the crowd. Everyone fell silent. "Let me tell you another story," he continued. "A powerful but lonely king fell in love with a lowly peasant girl..."

James immediately recognized the Danish philosopher Kierkegaard's little riddle from his *Philosophical Tidbits*, and the pedant in him wanted to charge Yeshua with plagiarism. But then, he reflected, given the workings of divine inspiration, the tale probably came from Yeshua in the first place.

"This peasant girl doesn't know he loves her. He has never met her. He worships her from afar. What would the king have to do to win her love?"

"The answer to your question is insultingly simple," Muhammad smiled. "He merely need declare his desire. What peasant girl would refuse the love of a king?" The prophet laughed, and almost everyone in the audience joined in the laughter, including, uneasily but unresistingly, the majority of Christians.

"Yes," Yeshua rejoined, "no doubt if the king went to her as king she would be swept off her feet, she would be delirious with joy, she would fall madly in love with the king. But would she even see *him*?"

Muhammad turned away in scorn. "Riddle upon senseless riddle!" he cried. "There's no end to discussing anything with you!"

"Is there no end," Yeshua queried, "or are you simply unwilling to go to the end?"

Muhammad turned back, as if to ward off a blow. "When a man says to me, 'What am I holding in my hand?' and he holds out his hand and in it is plainly a rock, I tell him, 'A rock.' If he agrees with me that it's a rock and asks if I know what kind of a rock and I don't, I'm willing to discuss the matter further, for I might profit from learning what he knows. If the man says, 'No, it's not a rock, but a pigeon!' and the rock suddenly sprouts wings and flies away, I marvel at the magic trick. Then, too, I'm willing to discuss the matter further, because I would like to know how it was done. But if the man holds out the rock and says, 'It's a pigeon,' and the rock remains a rock, I pity his insanity. On the other hand, if he says, 'The rock looks and feels like a rock and always will, but nevertheless is really a pigeon,' then I despise him, because he's a charlatan or a fool!" And with that, Muhammad began to stride away from the field.

"We're not talking about rocks and pigeons," Yeshua declared in a tone of authority that arrested the prophet's withdrawal. "There's more to a king than his power!"

"Yes," affirmed Paul's strident voice out of the crowd. "There is his love!"

Will half-expected Holmes to give a knee-jerk rap of the gavel and call to order, but evidently he, like everyone else, was spellbound, not only by the passion Paul poured into this interruption, but by his taking the part of the one whose lordship just yesterday he had so vehemently renounced.

"Yes, God is power," proclaimed Paul, rising like a Mediterranean storm to dispel the heat of Muhammad's contempt, "but he empties himself of that power to become man! This is something you've never understood." He looked directly at Muhammad. "You, the alleged messenger of God, know nothing about the mysterious ways of the Lord."

Christian and Muslim hands went for weapons, but the angels of light drew near and, as it were, paralyzed them with their radiance. Will stole a glance at Holmes, who looked small and weak on his throne of justice, as if he now knew that this 'trial' was entirely out of his hands. When the angels had restored order and made it clear they would permit no violence, Mikael withdrew with his fellows to their former altitude, saying only that the discussion might now resume. Muhammad was first to seize the thread of the argument.

"What mystery, Paul?" the prophet queried. "That God became man? If someone tells me that God caused a virgin to conceive, or parted the waters of the sea so that slaves might escape to freedom, or struck dead those who blasphemed against his name, or healed the sick, or even raised a man from the grave, I would call any of these things a mystery, but I would have no trouble believing, because God is all-powerful. But if someone tells me that the omnipotent, infinite, eternal and absolute Lord became a weak, mortal and finite man, no mystery is here, only absurdity. Can God make himself to be less than God?"

"If he's truly all-powerful, yes!" rejoined Paul.

"If God is love," interjected Yeshua, returning to the fray, "not only is it possible. It's necessary."

"I see the necessity of God being God," said Muhammad, "and of man being man, but I have yet to see anything but insanity in the idea of God becoming man!"

Now Yeshua turned angry. "If your mind is set," he said to the prophet, "there's nothing anyone can say to change it. But if you aren't afraid of at least understanding those whom you regard as your enemies, hear me out. Look at it this way, if you will: there's logic even to madness."

The patronizing smile returned to Muhammad's face. He bowed and folded his arms across his chest in a posture of critical attention. "And so, what is the logic to your madness?" he asked, half-mocking but also half-serious.

"What I've been saying all along," Yeshua replied, "the logic of love. Muhammad, consider your own heart. Did you love Khadija because she was wealthy and you were poor?"

Muhammad's mouth twisted in grief. Evidently she was not one of the souls participating in the reunion. "Of course not!" he declared. "I would have loved her had she been a penniless beggar!"

"And to win Ayesha's love," Yeshua continued, "did you threaten her with torture and death?"

Muhammad's hand shot to the sword at his side. "No, but I will give you torture and death if you keep questioning me in this vein."

Yeshua was not in the least perturbed. "All the power in the world cannot coerce love," he said, "and all its wealth cannot buy love."

"'Many waters cannot quench love,'" murmured Paul, quoting from one of Will's favorite Biblical books, the Song of Solomon, "'neither can floods drown it. If one offered for love all the wealth of his house, it would be utterly scorned.'"

"Therefore," Yeshua concluded, "not even an all-powerful God can force his creatures to love him. Here is a genuine absurdity, to think that love can be bought or coerced. Nay, one can go further. Power and wealth are not only irrelevant to love; they can get in love's way. The king must go to the peasant girl as a peasant and win her love on his own merits. Only then may he reveal himself and lift her out of her poverty."

Paul stood and moved toward the center of the field. He did not seem to see where he was going, but a path through the crowd spontaneously cleared for him. "Otherwise, it would not be about love, Muhammad," he cried. "It would not be about love!"

The Christians in the assembly piously nodded their agreement. Will marveled at how skillfully Yeshua was winning them over. Now was the time to stop, but Will knew that Yeshua would not stop.

"But the logic of love demands more," he said. "God does not leave his power and glory behind to become man. In living, suffering, dying and rising as man, I am that power and glory. Love is the only real power. What you call power," — and here it was clear that Yeshua was addressing everyone in the assembly — "what you covet and hoard and worship as power, is power only to destroy. Love is the only creative, sustaining and saving power. God does not exercise his power lovingly. God's power is identical with his being, and that being *is* love!"

A lengthy and oppressive silence ensued. No one, it seemed, knew quite what to say in answer to *that*. The angels went on hovering overhead, and the sun now illuminated the empyrean with not a wisp of water vapor to curb its dominion. The atmosphere hung heavy with intimations of eternity — not the joyous and unfettered eternity for which the devout prayed and the unbelievers subconsciously hoped, but an eternity yoked to a tedious and endless procession of moments, each maddeningly like its predecessor. Finally, Muhammad broke the spell.

"Assuming that you are the great prophet Issa," he asked Yeshua, "if God is love, why did he let you die so humiliating and agonizing a death?"

Yeshua smiled. "You don't believe that he did."

"Do you?" Muhammad countered.

"For me," replied Yeshua, a dark look passing over his face, "it's not a matter of belief."

Muhammad nodded impatiently. "Then, hypothetically," he said, as if clarifying instructions to a dull subordinate, "if you are truly the Issa whom God sent to the world as a messenger, and the Christians are right in thinking you were crucified and we are wrong in thinking you were not, why did the Almighty permit it? Under the rule of Rome there was no lower manner of execution. It was a death reserved for dogs. And it was doubly degrading for a Jew, for it says in your own Torah that one hanged upon a tree is cursed by God! By Christian terms it would seem triply abominable, for how could a God of love sacrifice his own son in so barbaric a fashion? Why would he require such a sacrifice? The very idea is nothing but the vilest and most pernicious paganism!"

"I agree," affirmed Yeshua, and everyone regarded him with astonishment. "That's what I was trying to tell you yesterday. My heavenly Father did not require my sacrifice so he could forgive the sins of the world. God loves unconditionally. God is unconditional love. I died because love is crucified in this world. As long as the world hates and fears love, it will hate and fear me."

Again came the heavy, unbearable silence. This time Mara, who had slithered back out of nowhere with her infernal paramour, intervened.

"You really are mad!" she cried. "If anyone hates and fears love, it's you."

Yeshua looked upon his former queen, the woman whom Will hated, sadly and without a trace of ill will until Mara trembled and turned away, but Azazael was not averse to taking up the gauntlet. "What can you mean, sweet Lord?" he wheedled sarcastically. "Love is what makes the world go round!"

Lucifer, however, was more to the point. "When you say 'world,' Yeshua, you mean each and every soul in the world, do you not?"

"I mean those souls who live according to the logic of the world."

"Let's not quibble!" Lucifer retorted. "Didn't you yourself say at the beginning of today's festivities that all have sinned, with the exception, presumably, of yourself?"

Yeshua said nothing, but it was clear his silence meant assent.

"Then," concluded Lucifer, "you're saying that all of us hate and fear love. All of us but you! *We* are on trial here," — his arm swept over the assembly — "not you. So be it. Put *us* on trial!"

Will looked up into the empyrean. The sun had not even reached the meridian! He was uncomfortably hot, emotionally exhausted, and sick with fear for Yeshua and, he had to admit, for himself. Now it was clear this day had a temporality that had nothing to do with celestial mechanics, but with the inscrutable purpose of its creator. Now every denizen in the pleroma was called upon to recognize himself as spirit. There would be no turning back and no rest until the day's work was done.

Yeshua looked calmly upon the confused and increasingly hostile crowd. "Love puts us on trial every moment," he said, "and so few rise to meet its challenge. I don't have to convict the world of failing love; the world convicts itself. Look at what you've made of creation! It came to you from the hand of the Father pristine and bountiful, and you've transformed it into a cesspool of hate, greed, filth, misery, indifference, brutality and despair. It's dying because you refuse to live in love. I've no wish to condemn you, but to awaken you before it's too late."

"What can we do?" demanded Lucifer. "We're not on earth. You keep us here where we can change nothing."

"You could change everything," retorted Yeshua, "if only you would have the courage to face up to what you really are. Look at how all of you spend your time here, in this health spa of the soul. You do nothing, you create nothing, you simply feed off the vitality generated by the struggle for survival on earth. Only when pushed to it do you come alive."

"So," glowered Lucifer, "you claim we're spiritually dead?"

"Not dead," replied Yeshua. "Sleeping. I ask you, why is art so important to you, even here, where there is no struggle, no conflict?"

Yeshua's pause signaled that the question was something more than rhetorical.

"Because art is the food of the soul."

Everyone turned to see who had answered. For reasons he could not fathom, Will was both surprised and excited to see that Rachel had returned. Her eyes had a faraway, almost mesmerized look, but her dark hair shone as lustrous as ever and her beauty had become even more breathtaking in her new frailty than it had been in her onetime vigor. He wondered if he too were falling captive to her lovely innocence.

Will shook himself free of his fascination with the girl to see how Yeshua was reacting to her advent. For the first time that day, he looked shaken. Seeing the two of them at that moment—the Jewess so mournful, lovely, wistful and lost, and the savior heroically pitting himself against the fear, hypocrisy, and pride of the world—surely no one could overlook the fact that they were deeply in love with each other, except perhaps the lovers themselves. Such was the forlorn mystery of the human heart. Despite his agitation, however, Yeshua wasted no time in responding. "And how does art feed the soul?" he asked.

Rachel also did not hesitate. "In art the soul finds a world where ideals mean more than facts, a world governed by virtue rather than necessity. This is where the soul feels at home."

"This is the pleroma," shot back Yeshua. In tone it was a statement, but in the present context obviously a question.

Rachel stood in perplexed silence.

"This is the pleroma," Yeshua repeated.

Again she was silent, but this time Yeshua waited upon her leisure, and at length she ventured to speak.

"Yes and no," she said tentatively.

During this exchange Rachel somehow had moved or been moved closer to the center, until now she stood in the area where counsel would strut their stuff while questioning witnesses. Yeshua, of course, was in and around the witness box, and Rachel therefore now only a few feet from him, so she must have felt as if she had been slapped when he snapped back at her, "Which is it?"

At that moment, Will came as close as ever to hating Yeshua. Though tears came to her eyes and she looked as if on the verge of collapse, Rachel went on. Will thought that he had never seen such courage, not even in Yeshua.

"It is the pleroma, in that here the soul finds food, but the food here is not uniformly nourishing. Each soul may choose its own sustenance, and my feeling is that most souls choose to eat food with no real substance at all."

An electric silence shot through the assembly. Doubtless everyone was shocked and offended by the temerity of this fledgling. It was bad enough that Yeshua, who had been in the pleroma for two millennia at least and, according to the angels, from all eternity, condemned the souls of the afterlife. That she who had arrived here less than a week ago should do likewise was unconscionable arrogance.

"How long have you been here?" Yeshua queried, giving voice to the crowd's resentment, and Will felt whatever emotional bonds still tying him to Yeshua dissolve in fury. Will wanted to stand up and protect Rachel against him, against all of them. But, as was his cowardly way, he did nothing.

"Not long," Rachel answered meekly. "Perhaps I've no right..."

"Truth gives you the right!" Yeshua proclaimed. "You've spoken rightly," he said to her with profound respect in his voice. Will realized that he should have known. "I call upon Rachel as fellow witness to your perfidy!" Yeshua cried, taking her hand and addressing the crowd. "I've been here since the beginning, while she's but newly arrived, yet we both see the same thing. You are corrupt, all of you. Now is the time to own up to your corruption. Soon it will be too late!"

"Don't you think you're taking her words a bit too far?"

It was Lucifer. Will could only guess what he was going through, but he expressed himself in his usual urbane and polished manner.

"To say that the souls of the pleroma don't always choose the most nourishing sustenance is a fairly innocuous statement, for, after all, who does? But to say that all these souls are corrupt..." Lucifer gazed out over the millions massed upon the field. "Well, that's quite something else."

Rachel looked at Yeshua, her face a battlefield between sorrow and relief. "He's right," she said. "I've no doubt that you're sincere, that you really believe what you're saying, but it's not my belief."

She released her hand and stepped back. Lucifer moved swiftly to her side, but evidently did not dare touch her, lest doing so break the spell and disrupt the delicate alliance he had just rescued, throwing her into Yeshua's camp for good. Or maybe the Lord of Darkness simply respected what he knew to be her wish. Who could tell? In this simmering cauldron of suppressed emotion that the pleroma had now become, Lucifer himself may not have understood his own motivation. It was clear, however, what Yeshua was feeling at that moment, at least to Will. He had seen that look of preternatural calm before. Yeshua was undergoing emotional disembowelment. Lucifer, of course, also sensed this, and he was relishing his enemy's agony.

"Now, if you wish to go on," said the Lord of Darkness with exaggerated courtesy, "please do explain how we are all totally corrupt."

Yeshua trembled and looked as if he might collapse to his knees, but the warrior in him reasserted itself and he forthrightly returned to his previous theme. Will was perversely grateful for the challenge facing Yeshua, terrible as it might be. Otherwise the Lord would certainly have fallen into one of his bottomless pits of despair.

"Rachel," he said, ignoring Lucifer, "you said that art feeds the soul, and that most souls don't choose nourishing food. What did you mean by that?"

Rachel lowered her head, looking as if she had no desire to continue this discussion.

"It's clear what she meant," Lucifer replied in her stead. "Great works of art and literature are kept under glass in museums or accumulate dust on basement shelves of libraries while the masses are left to feed upon cultural garbage!"

Rachel lifted her head. "No, that's not what I meant," she said carefully. "That may be a part of it, but it's not the worst part. And anyway, it's got nothing to do with here."

"It's got everything to do with here!" shot back Lucifer, exasperation at Rachel's coldness bursting through his pose of tolerant indifference. "Souls here are chained to the habits they've acquired on earth!"

Rachel looked thoughtfully upon her former lover, as if she now understood why he was called the Light-Bearer. "That may be," she said, her tone indicating gratitude for the insight, but at the same time unwillingness to be sidetracked from her main argument. "It explains a lot. But it doesn't explain why we dine on garbage. As far as I can tell, there's just as much trash among the elite, only it's high-brow, esoteric trash, that's all."

After saying this Rachel looked puzzled, but Lucifer did not dare interfere with her thought-process again. Yeshua did not move, but Will could see in his eyes that he was as excited as a schoolboy on the first day of summer. He always got that way when he sensed that someone was on the brink of a truly profound and original idea.

"Perhaps," Rachel brightened, "it's not so much what we eat as how we eat it. The problem may not be in the art itself so much as in what we do with it!"

Again she paused, piecing together her ideas, and everyone waited breathlessly for her to continue.

"It's something I've wondered about all my life. My grandmother would weep torrents at every performance of *Romeo and Juliet*, yet she disinherited my uncle for marrying a gentile. One of my professors swelled with pride as he told us the ancient Greek myths in which the heroes would do anything for the sake of honor, even throw away their lives. Yet on the day of the *Anschluss*, when I appealed to his own honor and begged him not to sign a faculty petition to expel all Jews from the university, he told me that he knew few of the faculty shared the sentiment of that petition, and that he himself hated what was happening, but that he could not risk throwing away a career that had been thirty years in the making for the sake of one heroic but futile gesture."

Rachel looked vacantly before her, as if overwhelmed by the self-contradiction of her fellow human beings.

"It's as if people live in two different worlds," Yeshua gently prompted her.

"Yes," Rachel agreed, still staring into space. There's the world of the soul, the imagination, in which everyone is a hero; and then there's the world of reality, in which everyone's a coward."

"And so you have a 'here' and a 'there,'" Yeshua suggested.

Rachel looked upon him in wonder, as did the entire assembly. "That's what this is?" she asked. "That's what it's all about?"

"Of course!" Yeshua replied. "God's creation is one. Why, then, is it torn into a 'life' and an 'afterlife?' It's all one life! But what God has joined together all of you, through your fear and pride, lust and greed, have almost completely torn asunder. There's only one thread holding it now, one thread keeping it from falling irretrievably into chaos and dissolution."

"And what might that be?" sneered Lucifer.

Yeshua looked at his interrogator but said nothing.

"If love is that thread," Rachel asked Yeshua, "then why do people hate and dread the one thing they absolutely need?"

"*He* is that thread!" cried Paul before Yeshua had a chance to reply, indeed almost simultaneously with Rachel's question. "I'm beginning to understand. He is the way, the truth and the life! Yes, it all makes sense."

There was a general hubbub as the various factions in the assembly—including, for the first time, the atheists and freethinkers, who hitherto had regarded the trial as a quaint and curious relic of a bygone age—engaged one another in heated debate. Holmes now felt it time to reassert his authority. The magistrate banged down his gavel and cried, "One argument at a time! As should be obvious to anyone with legal sense, this court dispensed with all rules of judicial procedure long ago, but I draw the line at confusion and chaos!" He looked sternly over the crowd until all fell silent. "The young lady asked a question that got lost in the commotion, but that I believe bears directly upon the present discussion. Rachel, will you kindly repeat your query?"

Rachel turned to regard Holmes with that same disquietingly vacuous stare. "Why does everyone hate the very thing they need?" she reiterated, the pain in her voice more palpable now. It was as if up until this point she had been numb, and the repetition of the question brought back her feeling and made her aware of a mortal wound deep in her heart. Yes, Will decided, that was exactly it. She sounded as if she were dying. Holmes blinked several times in rapid succession, a sure sign, Will knew, that he was reconsidering the wisdom of allowing Rachel to pursue this line of questioning, but of course it was too late now. There was no going back. Will also knew, as perhaps Holmes yet did not, that no matter what anybody did, whatever was in the heart of each and every participant of this trial was going to come out.

"I'd like to answer that question!" declared Paul, and Will half-rose to his feet, ready to resume his role as defense counsel and object. The pained humility in the saint's face, however, as well as something in his voice, a softness and a pleading Will had never heard before, caused him to hesitate. He looked to Yeshua for his cue and then sat back down. The Lord regarded his apostle with that expression Will always associated with the finding of the lost sheep.

Paul came to the center, right before the judge's bench, stood still while closing his eyes, and then opened them and began to speak. His voice was mild, yet Will was certain that it carried to every corner of the hushed assembly.

"Oft have I been accused of ignoring my lord Yeshua's actual life on earth, of taking from that life only what fit into my own scheme of salvation. I've always denied such charges, knowing as I did that when I was on earth, I eagerly listened to every story about Yeshua there was to be told, and that since then I've studied all that's been written about him, officially sanctioned by the Christian churches or not. Indeed, I've examined every artwork, every novel, and recently, every moving picture about him. I've been obsessed with Yeshua!"

Here Paul paused, looking at the Lord with tears in his eyes. Though touched, Will also felt somewhat embarrassed for the apostle by this confession of a lover who had made of his devotion a prison for his beloved, and who grew angry when his beloved refused to stay in that prison.

"This day," Paul went on, "I've realized that the accusation is just. I never really heard what Yeshua was saying because I never really wanted to hear. What his spirit caused me to feel in my heart I did not allow to enlighten my mind. He bestowed upon me his grace and peace, but I did not receive his gifts into my soul."

There was not a breath of wind, or so much as a twitter from any of the birds and rodents who had newly found their way into the Heavenly City. No one dared to sigh or whisper. All that could be heard was the racing of millions of metaphysical hearts.

"When you came to me, Lord, on the road to Damascus, I thought you blinded my flesh so that my soul might come to see. I only saw with my intellect. I used thought as a bulwark against the truth of my own heart. I believed you had called your elect to be a holy people set apart from the world. Now I see that those who truly answer your call live in the world, the leaven of the kingdom. I took the Baptist as my model rather than you. I did not understand...

No, I was not willing to understand what it means to live in love."

"And what does it mean, Paul?" asked Yeshua, both challenge and forgiveness in his voice.

"It means to be like you," answered Paul. "No matter how deadly its poisons, no matter what terrible agony it causes you, you take the world deep into your heart. We argue over whether you are God," Paul laughed ironically. "I forgot that you are man, and in doing so became myself less human!"

"But you're intimately acquainted with the dilemma of being human," said Yeshua, ever ready to offer the repentant sinner the solace of ameliorating circumstance. "'The good I would do, I cannot do. The evil I would not do, I do.' Everyone who strives after righteousness knows the inner struggle you described so well."

"Yes," said Paul, "but how did I deal with that conflict? Instead of taking it into myself, as you do, and allowing it to open my heart and deepen my soul, I chose one side over the other. I rejected what I so proudly regarded as my lower nature, the nature I thought given over to sin. I did not see what was always so obvious to you, that the denial of the inconvenient and unruly part of oneself stems from a vanity of spirit that is nothing more than a mask for fear, a fear of being overwhelmed by chaos! This pride leads to the rankest corruption of all. As you said, what God has joined together is now almost completely torn asunder, and I have played no mean part in this division. Had I but listened to the wisdom of my own people more than to that of the Greeks, I would have realized that the dark side of our nature becomes demonic only when not suffused with the light of the spirit!"

"And the spirit becomes nothing but vapor and vain imagination when not anchored to the reality of the flesh," added Yeshua.

"But what is the key?" cried Paul desperately. "How does one pass from death to life?"

"You mean, 'What is the way of the cross?'" replied Yeshua. "I gave the answer many times, but how many have really heard it? You must become like a little child to enter the kingdom of heaven!"

"I suppose that means taking whatever you say at face value," scoffed Lucifer.

"No, that isn't what he means," objected Rachel, and Will could sense the Dark Lord's irritation and panic. "No one is more critical or logical in her thinking than a little child."

"Then what does it mean?" demanded Lucifer of Yeshua. "Or is this another of your insoluble riddles?"

"What's the one quality a baby shows in everything it does?" asked Yeshua.

"Innocence!" answered Paul.

"Very well," acceded Yeshua, "but what do you mean by innocence? Surely not the innocence of one who chooses to do no wrong."

"A baby can do no wrong," said Rachel.

"Why not?" persisted Yeshua.

"Because it's a baby!" cried Lucifer in scorn. "Come now, must we continue to play these silly games?"

"Why not?" repeated Yeshua, ignoring Lucifer. Rachel thought hard, whilst Lucifer looked as if he were about to explode. Then the light dawned in her eyes.

"Because whatever a baby does, it does with its whole being! When it cries, the whole baby cries. When it smiles, the whole baby smiles. That's why there's no more heart-wrenching cry than a baby's cry, and no more beautiful smile than a baby's smile. Whether creating a mess with its food or making doo-doo or learning to walk or talk, a baby throws its whole heart into life."

"Yes," smiled Yeshua, and now Will knew why he had always found the Lord's smile extraordinarily beautiful. "A baby lives from the passion of its heart. It sees with its whole self, feels with its whole self, and acts with its whole self. And the adult?"

"Adults quibble over philosophical absurdities with their whole selves!" gibed Lucifer, but no one paid attention.

"He splits himself into the practical realist and the imaginary idealist," said Rachel. "He takes refuge in his imagination from the demands of his own heart, while at the same time taking care to follow what appears to be the safest and most comfortable course through life."

"And so he falls prey to the abstractions he has built up as real," concluded Yeshua, "like money, power, pleasure, security, prestige, career—all the false gods to whom he sacrifices his soul."

"False gods?" echoed Azazael, even he driven beyond his customary role-playing. "You must be mad!"

"I'm not the one who's mad!" retorted Yeshua. "You all pursue these things, but you're never satisfied when you get them. In your listless rage and unquenchable lust, you devour the earth. You're like gaping, monstrous mouths that eat anything but what your stomachs are designed to digest. It's not that you can't find genuine nourishment; it's that you're terrified of it. For to receive it, you must open yourselves to the reality of life. You must live in love."

Azazael cut a circular caper and crooned, "Methinks we keep going around and around and around..." For once, however, his antics failed to capture the limelight.

"But why do we turn away from our hearts?" Paul demanded in exasperation, not with Yeshua but himself. "And how does one return to the innocence of a child?"

Yeshua smiled. "You remind me of another Pharisee who once came to me in disguise in the middle of the night. He wanted truth, but did not wish to be seen consorting with the truth-giver."

"And you see me as another Nicodemus, Lord?" asked Paul in anguish, no doubt wondering if his depravity went deeper than he knew.

"Only in this sense," replied Yeshua: "You want to know the truth of your heart, yet you don't wish to consort with that in you which tells you this truth."

"What do you mean?" asked Paul.

"Emotion," said Rachel. "Feeling. We hide from our feeling."

"Humans use those words," said Yeshua, "but do they really understand the reality to which they point? Emotion is the medium of existence, the ocean of life. To feel what one actually feels is to be in touch with the reality of life."

A hush fell over the assembly. It proved too much for Lucifer. "This is mere sophistry!" scoffed the Dark Lord. "Who doesn't feel what he feels?"

"He who tries to feel what he wants to feel," Yeshua answered simply. "People want to feel good. Failing that, they want to feel safe. Failing that, they want to feel certain. In short, they want to feel comfortable, and what makes them comfortable is the illusion of being in control. They devote their time and energy trying to put themselves and their world into the most comfortable arrangement possible."

"What's wrong with that?" said Lucifer, as if he were addressing a simpleton. "All you're saying is that people seek happiness. That's hardly a sin."

"On the contrary," declared Yeshua, "that's the very definition of sin."

Lucifer looked long and hard at Yeshua, and then slowly swept his gaze in full circle over the entire assembly. Finally, with the forced seriousness of one humoring a maniac, he said, "Then what you call 'sin' is the natural state of man."

"No, there's nothing natural about it!" retorted Yeshua, as passionate as Will had ever seen him.

Lucifer smiled. "So what you do, or allegedly do, is natural. What everyone else does is unnatural."

"Whatever preserves the integrity of life is natural," proclaimed Yeshua. "Whatever destroys that integrity is unnatural. The biggest pretext for sin is that everybody does it. It's only an excuse, and a bogus one at that. If but one human being lives in love, all can!"

Lucifer shook his head, but as with Muhammad, a look of grudging admiration came into his eyes. Doubtless he felt there was something perversely great in Yeshua's *idée fixe*. "Perhaps," he said, "but you claim to be more than human."

"No!" protested Paul. "He is fully God *and* fully man."

"Mathematics was never you Christians' strong point!" laughed Lucifer. "Fully God and fully man is certainly more than man. But, assuming that you're something other than a sterile and unnatural hybrid, I for one fail to see any great love exhibited in your life, either on earth or in this hereafter."

"What do you know about love?"

The voice came from above. Everyone looked up except Lucifer and Yeshua, whose eyes were locked in iron enmity. It was Uriel. Swiftly she swooped down and took up station at Yeshua's right hand. She almost knelt before him, but was stayed by her master's look. Her movements were so full of grace she seemed to Will like liquid fire.

"Why don't you explain it to us?" Lucifer invited Uriel without turning away from Yeshua. "I'm sure everyone is dying to hear what you, an angel of light who is above the petty tumult of human existence, have to say about love."

Like her Lord, Uriel did not stoop to defend herself. "Love is courage," she said.

"And you're proposing Yeshua as the archetype of courage?" teased Lucifer. "Why, the night before he died, if we are to believe the extant chronicles, he begged God to take the cup of suffering from his lips, not once but thrice! And he was in such a fit of anxiety that he sweat blood! This was no miracle, merely a natural physiological response to extreme fear. Such courage! And again, according to the official accounts, at the end he forsook the very faith whose lack he condemned in others. From the cross he accused God of abandoning him! All this is perfectly understandable, and yes, very human, but it hardly qualifies as courage."

"You don't know what real courage is!" cried Uriel, her aura dimming.

"You and Yeshua talk about love and courage," rejoined Lucifer, training a scornful look upon the irrepressible angel of light. "But when pressed to define your terms, you end up saying that what everyone else understands by love or courage is not the real thing. Either this is the worst sort of equivocation, or you dwell within your own private universe!"

"There's a third possibility," said Yeshua.

"What's that?" snapped Lucifer.

"That everyone else is in his own private universe," he replied, Will thought, almost brazenly.

Lucifer looked at Yeshua and shook his head, as if to say when would the fool ever learn to keep his mouth shut. "So you alone are in touch with reality!" he nearly screamed. "Everyone else..." he paused to allow the presence of the millions in the audience to make itself felt—"...is living in dementia."

"Schizophrenia would be my diagnosis," said Yeshua, not at all taken aback by Lucifer's sarcasm. "Each and every one of you is split, right down the middle. Each of you deals with this split in his own way, but you all live as if it were nature rather than disease."

"What split?" asked Lucifer. "Whence does it originate?"

"From fear, of course," replied Yeshua. "How else?"

"So we've come full circle," said Lucifer. "This is pointless!"

He took Rachel by the hand and started to lead her away, but she would not follow. Instead she took a step toward Yeshua, and

Lucifer had perforce to let her go. The look he gave his archrival at that moment summed up all the millennia of hate between them.

"What are we afraid of?" Rachel asked in a quiet but earnest voice.

"That's the strange part," Yeshua smiled softly. "You are afraid of nothing."

Rachel's look said she both did and did not understand.

"There's nothing to fear," Yeshua explained, "and yet you all live in fear. And by living in fear, you fulfill fear. Out of literally nothing you bring upon yourselves the very thing that you fear. You fear death, which is nothing. But because you fear death, you make of it something truly to be feared. And that's where it all stands now. Death is nigh, waiting for you all!"

Rachel still did not understand. She doubtless was seeking some metaphorical significance to his words. Will, on the other hand, had the most uncomfortable feeling that the Lord meant exactly what he said.

"Each and every one of you is created in the image of God," continued Yeshua.

"Blasphemy!" cried Muhammad, who, like everyone else in the field, had continued to follow the discussion most attentively. "How dare you liken a creature to the creator?"

"I'm not bound by anyone's orthodoxies or rules!" retorted Yeshua. "All men are created in the image of God. All are persons, the purpose of whose existence is to create, to express the truth and beauty of the spirit in form. A person is a fulcrum point between spirit and flesh, soul and manifestation, time and eternity. If a person refuses this great honor of being a co-creator with God, he does not cease to be a person, but he does corrupt his selfhood. My Father and I are striving to rid you of this corruption, but we can't do so if you refuse our help, if you don't at least begin to take responsibility for yourselves. When you refused to walk, I carried you for many ages. When you let yourselves fall apart, I held you together. I can do so no longer—not because I'm weary or unwilling, but because if you don't take up the task of your own selfhood soon, you will be beyond saving. Just as a seldom-used muscle atrophies, so too the self never lived ceases to be a self. Now you must choose life or death. There's nothing in between."

Rachel stood motionless, her eyes fixed on Yeshua, as if to move would be to risk losing the delicate thread of understanding of which she had just taken hold. "And that's where we are?" she asked. "In the nothing in-between?"

"Yes," he affirmed, "in the impossible in-between. Thus you make life impossible, and yourselves caricatures of what you should be."

"Am I a caricature?" said Rachel with an ironic coquetry that mocked itself. Yeshua did not answer. In the ensuing silence they drank in each other with their eyes, leaving no doubt in anyone's mind, Will was certain, that the two were deeply, hopelessly, irrevocably in love.

Feeling like an intruder, Will turned away and looked up into the sky. The sun had finally reached its zenith and clouds were beginning to form at one corner of the horizon. If the day were never to end, at least they might eventually afford some relief from the rising heat. And then he wondered if the heat might really be coming from the mounting tension. St. Paul was certainly discomfited by Yeshua's frank and open display of romantic feeling, and Will could well imagine how dark and dangerous were Lucifer's thoughts. Most threatening of all were the seething emotions of the millions of souls in the pleroma, the vast majority of whom had come to believe they had reached a place of eternal rest. Now, as only he could do, Yeshua was cavalierly casting their serenity to the winds, proclaiming that their "heavenly peace" was only a lull before the coming storm.

"This abstract speculation is all very interesting," said Lucifer, the assured rationality of his voice held out to the assembly like a lifeline in a turbulent sea. "But you've done it again, O great Lord of Light! You've succeeded in evading the original question. You've accused us all of failing to live in love, and you've said the price of our failure is death. But unless this seductive little interlude with the prosecution's chief witness is meant to be an ostensive definition, you have yet to explain what love *is*."

Yeshua did not stop looking into Rachel's eyes. "It's very simple," he said. "Love is the marriage of total vulnerability and absolute courage."

At this statement, as if on cue, thunder pealed forth from out the empyrean. Again Will looked up to see the clouds, which a scant moment before had been a mere hint of shadow upon the horizon, now scurrying to join in mass formation overhead.

"All of you seek peace," said Yeshua, not raising his voice, but still miraculously making himself heard over the rising wave of agitation. Holmes banged down his gavel and called for order, but this only served to intensify the general confusion. "Those who look for peace will never find it," Yeshua continued. "Seek first the kingdom of heaven, and all things will be added to you."

"We've done so!" Paul cried out. "We Christians, your faithful followers, have sacrificed all out of trust in your promise of eternal life!"

"Have you?" Yeshua turned on him. "I spoke of the peace that surpasses understanding. Many of you *Christians*"—the term sounded like an insult upon his lips—"have claimed that peace. You've claimed to have me in your hearts, and declared yourselves willing to die, even to walk through fire for me."

"Many of us have died!" exclaimed Paul.

"Yes, that's true," conceded Yeshua, "but that does not surpass my understanding. The history of the world is filled with examples of fanatics of all stripes who were willing to die for their beliefs, to give up all else for the emotional security of a self-willed certainty. But to live with all one's feelings, to drink to the dregs all the doubt, dread, anguish and despair that assails the human heart—who is willing to do this?"

"We women are!" proclaimed Mara. "You're right about men. They hide from their emotions. They'd rather fight and die in wars than own up to their feelings. They buy their courage at the price of emotional invulnerability. And I think," she smiled maliciously, "you are no exception. But we women..." Here a note of self-pity crept into her voice. "We women suffer all that life lays upon our hearts!"

There followed a moment of silence, as if all were mourning the travail that had fallen to the lot of women.

"Do you?" asked Yeshua, seeming even to Will like a priest stripping off his vestments and raping a nun right before the Blessed Sacrament, so violent and sacrilegious did his tearing womanhood down from its pedestal feel. "Do you? Or do you not rather use this vulnerability as an excuse for living in cowardice? It's easy to be 'vulnerable' when no risk is involved!"

"What is the peace that surpasses understanding?" Rachel whispered, but still everyone heard her.

Yeshua returned his gaze to her. His eyes softened, but his expression remained stern.

"You have all sorts of voices, inside and out," he explained. "Outside are the voices of your parents, siblings, relatives, friends, peers, teachers, counselors, authority figures, lovers, spouses, celebrities, newspapers, radio, and so on. Inside you have fears, desires, ambitions, intellect, knowledge, instinct, intuition, imagination, and so on. You have all these voices, on the one hand, and on the other you have the still, small, wordless voice of love in the depths of your heart."

Paul nodded as if he knew very well whereof Yeshua spoke. Will was not sure anyone else did, except perhaps Rachel.

"This is the peace that surpasses understanding," Yeshua went on. "It's when all those voices, inside and out, are telling you to go one way, so everyone wants you to go that way, you want to go that way; all your happiness, the fulfillment of your hopes and dreams, lies in that direction. In short, if you go that way you will be admired, desired, honored by all. But the still, small, wordless voice of love tells you to go in the opposite direction. You don't want to go the way love points. All that lies in that direction, as far as you can tell, is rejection, isolation, failure, suffering and death. But because love demands it, you decide to do it. And if love demands it, it gives you the strength to do it. That's the peace that surpasses understanding. It doesn't feel like strength, but the most terrible weakness. It's not a feeling of peace. It runs the gamut of human emotion. It intensifies all emotion. It intensifies life! Peace to most people is just another word for death. I come that you may have life, and have it most abundantly!"

Once more Lucifer could not brook the awed hush inspired by Yeshua's words. "Again," he said, "something that is not what it is. Why should any sane individual take this peace seriously? If it really does surpass understanding, then it's absurd!"

"When two ideas don't fit together logically," rejoined Yeshua, "the result is absurdity. Two plus two does not equal five."

"One plus zero does not equal three," interjected Muhammad. Yeshua chose to ignore him.

"But when an idea doesn't fit together with a reality, which is absurd, the reality or the idea?"

"You're begging the question!" objected Lucifer. "Which *is* the idea and which the reality?"

"It's you who are contradicting yourself!" scolded Rachel. "You wanted Yeshua to explain his concept of love. Now that he's doing so, you won't let him finish."

Lucifer regarded Rachel with an unanalyzable mixture of anger, violation, desire, and yes, love. "You really think there's something here worth hearing?" In reply, Rachel turned back to Yeshua and bade him go on.

"This is the good news, the Gospel," he said, as if he had never been interrupted: "If love demands it, it gives you the strength to do it, one step at a time, as you take that step. This is the greatest possible news for those for whom God is everything, for those for whom God is love!"

As he said this, his voice rose in exultation and he looked ever more deeply into Rachel's eyes, as if indeed he had found in her a soul like his own for whom love truly was all.

"But for those for whom love is not everything," he continued, his voice lowering in weariness and his eyes seeming to take in the entire assembly, "for those for whom love is merely a feeling alongside other feelings, it's the worst news imaginable. It is the offense!"

"I don't see that!" objected Lucifer. "In fact, I haven't the slightest notion what you're talking about, and I doubt anybody else does!"

Yeshua's only response was to fix his gaze upon Rachel as if to say that she, for one, understood him. Rachel gave a barely perceptible nod, but whether it was in agreement or merely comprehension of his meaning Will could not tell.

Lucifer turned to Holmes. "If the defendant is trapped in his own private universe, I submit that we let him stay there. He may be not guilty by reason of insanity, but he cannot remain in authority any longer!"

"You're right, my brother!" said Yeshua finally to Lucifer's question, though keeping his eyes upon Rachel. "They don't understand what I mean by the voice of the heart because they've arranged their lives so as never to hear it. They don't know it because they don't want to know it. It always asks of them the very thing they'd never think to do. It always demands the very thing they've decided never to give."

"Is this voice of the heart, then, the voice of evil?" challenged Muhammad.

"Only to those who think power is righteousness," retorted Yeshua. "The heart submits only to love. No, men fear the heart's voice not because it's evil, but because to heed it is to become exposed, vulnerable. So, very early on in life, they build an emotional wall around their hearts, as soundproof as possible. Then they fill their lives with all sorts of noise and business to drown out any hint of the voice that might come through that wall. But, at one time or another, into every life comes an emotional earthquake that brings the wall tumbling down."

Yeshua paused, intimating that was about to happen to everyone in the assembly.

"And how do people react when they finally do hear the voice of love?" Yeshua resumed. "Its call is too intense, too desperate to be heeded. Or one simply is not ready yet, and needs a year or two to prepare. Or one is too old, too young, or engaged in more pressing matters. Or one is too weak or fearful or virtuous or sinful or short or tall or fat or thin or smart or stupid or shy or brazen or rich or poor! You will use any excuse to avoid the call of love, but love accepts no excuse. There is no excuse when it comes to love, because if love demands it, it gives you the strength to do it!"

The black, low-scudding clouds now filled the sky and blotted out the sun. Even the angels of light were no longer visible in the looming darkness, which was relieved every so often only by galvanic blades of lightning. As the whisper of distant thunder steadily rose, the potency of Yeshua's words also mounted until it was impossible to tell where they left off and the thunder began.

"And so you put up every defense against me," Yeshua continued, "against the challenge of love that I am! First, you seek refuge in the torpor of indifference. You are a Muslim or a Jew or a Hindu or a Buddhist or an atheist or an agnostic, so why care about what I do or say? Or you are a Christian and already know what I'm all about, so why care about what I do or say? But love can't be stopped by your indifference. Pride would be. Pride would say, 'Just wait! Someday, when I'm in heaven and you're in hell, you'll be sorry!' Pride would say this, but not love."

Will wanted to run, he was certain everyone wanted to run, but it was as if they had all lost the power of locomotion.

"So next," said Yeshua, "you hide in anger and intimidation. You threaten to hate me, imprison me, abandon me, crucify me. But love is not stopped by your anger, no matter how mightily you rage!"

Here Yeshua's voice seemed to crack the empyrean.

"Love fears only one thing, and that is failing to give of itself in love."

Here his voice dropped to almost a whisper, and his words became one with the soft patter of raindrops that was the advance guard of the coming deluge. And like those raindrops, his speech now steadily grew in volume and intensity, building to a fearful climax.

"Your anger does not turn love away; so next, with all the integrity of a tyrant whose only law is his word, you make good on your threats. You torture and kill me. But the good news of the resurrection is that love can't be stopped even by death. Love is stronger than death. So now you hide behind the strongest bulwark of all, the ultimate defense against love. What is the ultimate defense against love?"

Yeshua's question thundered so powerfully that no one dared hazard a reply. Even Rachel was tremulous with fear. This was another of those moments when Will could easily have hated Yeshua — that is, if he were not so entirely caught up in terror.

"Admiration, worship, adoration," litanized Yeshua, answering his own question. "You fall at the foot of my cross and kiss my feet in humble gratitude, because I died there so you don't have to. But when have I ever said you would be spared the cup I drink, or that my righteousness can make up for your sin? On the contrary, I call upon you to be perfect, even as your heavenly Father is perfect! I proclaim that whoever would be my disciple must take up his cross and follow me. But what better place to hide from the challenge of love that I am than in adoration of me?" He climaxed in a crescendo of sarcasm. "For if you worship the Lord Yeshua and love the Lord Yeshua, who could accuse you of betraying what I'm all about, the love that I am?"

THE JUDGMENT OF CHRIST

Now the rain fell in a torrent, as if Yeshua's heretofore pent-up anguish were let loose like sharp spears, piercing the conscience of each soul in the pleroma. Now, at last, the power of movement returned, and so the field emptied in short order save for Lucifer, Muhammad, Sivananda, Paul, and other souls of like mettle. Holmes also remained, transfixed, it seemed, by the magnetic aura enveloping Yeshua and Rachel, who throughout had not ceased looking into each other's eyes. And Will stayed too, though he badly wanted to escape, not only out of fear but also shame. So these few heard Yeshua's final words of this fateful day, spoken softly to Rachel, like a caress.

"And so now you know what my suffering is," he said, as if referring to a topic they had previously discussed. "It is to be what nobody wants and everybody needs. To be what everybody needs and nobody wants—that is the suffering of love."

* * *

Rachel looked long into his eyes, half hoping that they would draw her into him and obliterate her fears and doubts. The rain was bracing, cleansing, but it could not wash away the unreal feeling of it all.

What was he saying, that everyone was insane but he, and that he alone prevented the world from destroying itself? Not even Hitler had been so megalomaniac! And yet, he said it all with such simple conviction, with no arrogance in his voice, as if it really were a burden he bore out of duty rather than pride. She almost wanted to believe it. He seemed so strong and courageous, yet gentle and loving. And he was sincere, there was no doubt about that. He really believed what he was saying. Sincere, and very lonely. She wanted to relieve his loneliness, but he had set the price too high. To return to him now she would have to buy into his insanity, and that she could not do. Her only hope of finding a modicum of peace in this place, she had come to realize, was to stay firmly grounded in what she knew to be real. Yeshua was wrong about the heart. It told you what you wanted to hear. She could not heed its voice now, not until she had found firmer footing. She could not go with Yeshua and survive.

"To be what everyone needs and nobody wants?" she echoed.

"I'm neither of those things. You're far too grand and far too small for me," she told him. "I'm not the one you're seeking." She turned quickly aside, not wanting to see or hear anything more of him, and let Lucifer lead her off the field.

"I need somewhere to stay," she said dully when they were safely away.

"Of course," replied the Dark Lord, permitting himself merely the hint of a smile.

"Somewhere I can be alone," she added.

"You can have my private chamber," Lucifer assured her.

"I mean really alone," Rachel insisted.

Lucifer halted and turned to see her eyes. "What is it you want?" he asked, angry and yet obedient in his anger with the servility of love.

"Not to be bothered by anyone tonight," answered Rachel, flinching not one whit at his displeasure.

"Including me?" he asked curtly, already knowing the answer, yet hoping against hope that he had misunderstood.

Rachel almost replied, "Especially you!" But, after all, she was asking for his help, and she knew that would be too much, even for him. She only nodded. Lucifer turned away and resumed walking.

"There is a place where nobody goes nowadays, if you don't mind the company of an antiquated priest who forgot how to speak centuries ago."

"What place?" Rachel asked dubiously.

"The Temple of Athena," replied Lucifer, an ironic smile once more playing about his lips.

"A pagan temple?" queried Rachel.

"There are a few left," explained Lucifer. "As I say, this one is abandoned except for an old priest. Aphrodite's Temple is still quite popular, but in this sophisticated age no one worships the goddess of wisdom."

"There's nowhere else?" she asked.

"Not unless you wish to roam about in this mess," he said, indicating with a turn of his hand the rain coming down as hard as ever with no sign of quitting.

She did not bother telling him it was not the weather from which she sought refuge. "It will have to do."

* * *

Running Deer stood listening, contemplating the masses of black clouds that ringed the encampment like floating sentinels. Strangely, though throughout the evening sheets of rain had descended all around, striking petals from the flowers and drowning many of the smaller four-legged people, and though lightning had cut down or set aflame the branches of many of the standing people, the little meadow to which he had taken the children had remained untouched. "They're near?" he asked of his scouts, though it was more a sigh than a question.

"They were held up by the rains," answered their leader, Crazy Horse, "but yes, they're near."

The diminutive Oglala chieftain looked searchingly at Running Deer, his dark, piercing eyes seeking the meaning of this, as far as he knew, unprecedented event. It never ceased to amaze Running Deer how someone with the hair and nose of a white man could have a soul that was the quintessence of the Human Beings. Running Deer returned his gaze, conveying to him all the fear and uncertainty he held in his heart. Crazy Horse put his short, strong arm around Running Deer's shoulders and smiled encouragingly. "We've already run the gauntlet of death," he said. "What else is there to fear?"

Running Deer slowly nodded, but his heart felt no lighter. There was something more to be feared than the death through which they had already passed. He did not know how he knew it, but he did, and it was the most troubling knowledge he had ever possessed. It was like the black holes of which Holy Fire had told him. It sucked in all his other thoughts and feelings, abducting them into a parallel universe where everything was the negation of its former self.

Running Deer marveled at how Crazy Horse opened himself and drank to the dregs the bitter cup that now was Running Deer's soul. A lesser man would have choked upon the first sip; but without flinching and, more importantly, without signaling to his brothers any panic or alarm, the mighty warrior downed the entire draft. The wassichu never understood that this chieftain had received his epithet ironically, because of his magnificent calm in the midst of danger and chaos. In turn Running Deer drank from Crazy Horse's eyes, taking in that calm and, as much as he was able, making it his own.

"You should speak with your new friend," Crazy Horse smiled. He knew, without being told, how Running Deer felt about Holy Fire. Running Deer nodded again, this time in gratitude. "We will watch them," assured Crazy Horse, and then he and his brothers departed.

Running Deer climbed a nearby hill and looked out into the distance over the field of judgment. Bonfires dotted the darkened landscape, their tawny flames licking greedily at the malignant night. Things were not as they had been. Holy Fire had spoken to him of the marriage of heaven and earth. Now he wondered if it really were to be the unholy joining of heaven and hell. He sank to the dew-dampened grass and emptied his mind of all but the thought of her. In no more than two heartbeats, she was there. He opened his eyes, and it took her but a glance to read all that was in his soul. She frowned. "You're deeply troubled," she said.

"They've come," he declared.

"Who's come?" she asked, and he could see from the vacancy of her aura that she really did not know. "We spirit helpers are not the Great Spirit," she explained, her eyes brightening in the hint of an angelic smile. "We don't know everything."

"The army of the dark ones," answered Running Deer, unable to return her smile.

"Where?" demanded Holy Fire, at once alert with anxiety.

"They came out of the west," he replied quickly. "How otherwise? The direction of death! Our scouts spotted them up in the mountains just as the blanket of clouds opened and the setting sun tinged them with the color of blood. The omens aren't good."

"How do they appear?" asked Holy Fire.

"That's the puzzling thing," said Running Deer. "They've done nothing to disguise themselves. In fact, they come in the trappings of the worst of the malefactors who were defeated in the Second Great War."

Now Holy Fire's aura leapt upward and Running Deer could see that she truly was surprised.

"I must see them," she said grimly.

"I'll take you there," he offered.

"No, that would take too long."
Without another word, she was gone. Running Deer's heart, which now seemed more flesh than spirit, beat hard. He could not tell whether it was more from fear or love.

* * *

They came in the night, grim-faced men in black uniforms similar to those of the elite Schutzstaffel units of Hitler's army in the recent global conflict. They made no secret of their entry into the Heavenly City. Their armored vehicles—tanks, troop-transports, armored cars, even mobile rocket-launchers—spearheaded the advance, and their rumbling, lower and more ominous than the thunder that had preceded them, could be heard for many leagues. Once within the city perimeter, the infantry debarked from the lorries and split up into platoon-sized patrols that swept through the streets, forcing any citizens whom the rain had not driven indoors to return to their homes. The tanks, along with infantry support, made their way to the field of judgment, surrounding it but otherwise leaving those camped out there in peace.

Lucifer felt their coming long before they could be heard or seen. After all, were they not his minions? But he had not ordered them here, especially not in this manner and dress. He was furious, but not overwhelmingly so. He had been expecting something from Azazael, and here it was.

His first impulse was to send for his conspiratorial lieutenant and have it out with him. In direct confrontation, spirit to spirit, Azazael was no match for his lord. But Lucifer long ago had learned to mistrust immediate impulses, and his recent experience with the Jewess only confirmed him in his caution. Reprimanding Azazael would be a tacit admission of loss of control. For the time being, he would have to play along with the traitor's scheme.

Lucifer came out of his meditation over the problematic situation and breathed in the scent of the luxuriant blossoms that graced his garden. He had never had the chance to bring Rachel here, and of that he was glad. There were no memories of rejection to torture him here. And if, by some twist of fate, she were yet to be his, this would be a fitting place for her to yield up the treasure of her love.

His mood darkened. The course he was taking would make that more difficult for her, perhaps impossible. Yet there was no other way. He shook himself free of melancholy, rose to his feet and summoned a messenger. "Have the commanders meet me in the Hall of Communion as soon as their sectors have been secured," he ordered.

The messenger bowed and assured his master that his will would be done.

* * *

Wendell pulled back the rich, cerulean Victorian lace curtains that gave his parlor so much of its coziness, and peered out into the night. "What is that godawful racket?" he snorted. James remained seated in the easy chair in unaccountable calm. "I don't believe it," Wendell declared. "It's soldiers! Only," he added in a quieter, more serious tone, "they've got weapons more monstrous than any I've seen before. Worse than anything even that was used in the Great War." Wendell contemplated a spectacle he would never even have dreamt of seeing in the Heavenly City, that of iron monsters advancing inexorably into its heart accompanied by men bent on destruction. If there was a God, where was he now?

"I'm sure they've got the most modern equipment," said James tonelessly.

Wendell turned away from the window and studied his friend suspiciously. "Why are you so damn quiet?" he demanded. "Heaven has just been invaded!"

James looked off into space. "I feared this was coming, or something like it," he said. "Yeshua was pushing Lucifer to the brink. I suppose, now that it's here, it's almost a relief."

Wendell flopped back down onto the divan. "So, you think this is Lucifer's doing," he said. There was a hint of skepticism in his voice, as if he were cross-examining a hostile witness. James said nothing, as if the answer were obvious. "What I still don't understand," Wendell went on, "is how such things can have any effect here."

"You mean the weapons?" asked James, at last showing some interest in what Wendell had to say.

"Yes, of course, the weapons," affirmed Wendell. "I know you've tried to explain this to me before, but I still don't get it. We've each and every one of us died, so what could they possibly do to us now?"

James sat back in the easy chair and clasped his hands behind his head. "There's one simple way to find out," he said.

"What's that?"

"Go out and confront them."

Wendell pondered, once more fixing his eyes upon the menacing column passing in review, the metal of their helmets and weapons hard and cold amid the soft, night-gray foliage lining the heavenly avenue. "I see what you mean."

James jumped up and likewise looked out the window. "The power of such a display is not in the weapons themselves," he said earnestly, "but in the single-mindedness of the men who wield them."

"Like Muhammad's cavalry," Wendell said hoarsely, remembering the overwhelming terror that charge had inspired in him.

"Precisely," agreed James. "As you've no doubt noticed, almost everyone here is so lackadaisical, so wishy-washy. They're like old racehorses let out to pasture. They've found what they believe is unassailable comfort and security, and there's nothing else to strive for, no more battles to fight or frontiers to conquer. Anyone who doesn't succumb to the general ennui, who understands that the great mysteries of life remain unplumbed, blows like a fresh wind through a mausoleum."

"Like Rachel," murmured Wendell.

"Yes," said James, "that's why we're all in love with Rachel. She questions, she challenges, she is alive!"

"You, too," said Wendell, regarding his friend with renewed affection. "You too haven't lost your sense of wonder."

"And those soldiers out there," James said pointedly, "they haven't lost their sense of purpose, however dark and twisted that purpose may be."

Wendell felt himself swallowed up by the implications of all that James was saying, too unfathomable to be put into words. "So this isn't heaven after all," he muttered.

"Certainly it's heaven, insofar as heaven is a place," asserted

James, the stillness of his body only serving to emphasize his point. "But, as indicated in the Book of Revelation and other scripture, there can be war even in heaven."

"Might heaven be something other than a place?" wondered Wendell in a paradoxical state of hopeful incredulity.

"My dear Holmes," said James, "where have you been all this time? Did you hear nothing that Yeshua said? The kingdom of heaven is the kingdom of love."

"Yes, but..."

"What did you think?" snapped James, cutting Wendell off. "That God could simply snap his fingers and make us all loving? The kingdom of heaven is something each and every one of us must accomplish. That's our great dignity as human beings, and our inalienable responsibility. Not even the almighty God can do it for us."

The clanking of tank treads, throbbing of engines and hammering of soldiers' heels on pavement could still be heard from without. Nevertheless, as far as Wendell was concerned, the silence in the room after James finished this speech was absolute. Wendell looked grimly out the window. "If what you say is true," he whispered, afraid to hear his own words, "there isn't much hope."

James turned away, but he could not hide the sound of a sob.

* * *

Yeshua was alone now. He could not say for certain that he was more alone than he had ever been, but he felt that way. Sitting motionless upon a ledge overlooking the abyss that had but yesterday been earth, with the cold moon starting to peek through the receding clouds, he felt his soul slip from its heavenly moorings and once again set adrift upon the sea of anarchy that was life. He had to speak, though he knew his words would do no good. He had to cry out to the One in whose bosom he had only yesterday rested securely, but today in whose existence he could almost disbelieve.

"Father, you've left me alone among ravening wolves! They circle their prey, making sure he's without defense before moving in for the kill. And what defense can I offer them? The witness of their own hearts? They won't listen to that, that's what they fear above all! To what else may I appeal? Even she won't listen! Even she is afraid of her own heart!"

He listened for an answer, but the only reply was an inner sweetness welling up from deep within, like a hidden spring vainly pouring itself out upon the barren desert.

"What hope is there now, Father? What hope indeed for any of them? What hope for me? I want their love. I want her love. That's all I want. If I have that, then all the millennia of pain and rejection will have been worth it! But she won't give it. I saw it in her eyes. You say she will yet come through, but I saw her eyes go dead. After all, why should she love me? Why should she want to be with me? Lucifer is right: I'm some unnatural monster that never should have been!"

Yeshua fell prostrate upon the rock, his body wracked by sobs all the more violent because he resisted their natural release in tears. The inner sweetness felt like malicious mockery.

"You didn't give me life, Father. You gave me death! And tomorrow your gift will be complete. Tomorrow they will kill what is left of me, and in doing so kill what is left of their own hearts. But is that really so? Maybe Lucifer is right about that as well. Maybe he's your real son, not I. Maybe without me they'll be so much better off—less pretentious, more human. After all, if they really needed love so badly, if it really were the fountainhead of their lives, why would they crucify it?"

And now the tears came, at first a few drops wrung with protest from his tortured heart, and then in toxic rivulets gushing through the portals of his eyes from a gangrenous soul. He wept for a long, long time, lifting himself up, rocking tremulously, casting himself once more upon the earth, writhing in his agony, vainly seeking a position, a stance, an attitude that would give relief from the pain. At last, the poison drained from his heart, he felt the undeniable truth of it all.

"They fear most what they love," he whispered, rising to his knees. "I am their only hope. If I give up, they're lost."

And then he stood up, looking out once more over the abyss, wondering what new mystery the disappearance of the earth betokened. It was a sign of the joining! It had to be a sign of the joining. Once more, against all reason, he felt hope.

"And you, Father, are my only guide. If this is the only way, so be it! I don't know what I'm letting myself in for. I never know what I'm letting myself in for." His mouth twisted in a sardonic smile. "You always have new, more refined tortures in store for me!"

Despite the prospect of falling into the hands of his enemies, he suddenly, unaccountably felt strong and confident, both in himself and the One whom he served. Then he remembered Rachel's last words and again collapsed, falling to his knees and continuing his prayer in spasmodic, pathetic rasping.

"It's easy to die, Father, but to be without her? Why did you bring her here? No, I can't regret knowing her, but losing her is worse than any crucifixion could ever be! She's my soul. She's my heart. I'm not myself without her. I feel so alone. I could have the love and admiration of all creatures else, in heaven and on earth, and be utterly alone. All others could hate and despise me, but with her love I would have everything! For she sees me. She alone sees me... But it's impossible. They've made it all impossible. She's made it all impossible... No, you've made it impossible! Why have you done this to me? Why have you mangled my heart?"

He beat his fists upon the stony earth until blood stained the ground.

"Damn you, Father! Damn you, damn you, damn you, damn you..." As this terrible litany trailed off into silence, he felt a peace enter him. "I don't want your peace!" he cried, rising to his feet. "It only makes everything worse! But, of course, you know that. That's its purpose, isn't it? To torture me. I've asked little, nothing for myself through all these ages. And now, when I find my heart's desire, you can not, will not give it to me."

He laughed furiously, cried furiously, and then sank back down upon the earth in a stupor of despair, the night enfolding him with a soft beauty that gave little solace to his soul.

* * *

The Hall of Communion shone with a preternatural radiance that dazzled, even pained Azazael's provisional executive council as they arrived in answer to Lucifer's summons. In their experience, the vaulted expanse had always been lit by torches and checkered with plenty of comforting shadows. Now the light, seemingly without source, filled every cubic inch of space that was not occupied by object or body. Even more surprising was Lucifer's garb, a robe of flowing white that stood out in stark contrast to the black uniforms the fallen ones had donned for their invasion of the pleroma. It was perplexing, even troubling; and Rashnu, as was only to be expected from the ever serious diplomat, took it upon himself to express the collective concern.

"My Lord," he said after everyone had knelt before Lucifer and duly shown homage, "your appearance—no, it's more than your appearance—the whole *feel* of this place seems out of keeping with the orders you gave us, the orders we've followed to the letter."

Azazael, who stood to one side with the unknowing Mara, could not resist a smile.

"You'll know the reason soon enough," said Lucifer, "but for now merely think of it as a study in aesthetic contrast."

The Dark Lord sat upon his throne, and gestured to his underlings to do the same around the council table he had materialized just for this occasion. It was glass of such glistening transparency that it doubled the intensity of the hall's luminescence. No one looked comfortable save Lucifer, and there was no seat for Mara. Azazael began the gesture of fabrication to give Mara a chair, but a look from Lucifer stopped him.

"Forgive me, my dear Azazael, if memory fails me," said the Dark Lord, "but I don't recall appointing your consort to my council." The way he intoned "consort" he may as well have been saying "whore."

Azazael bristled and felt like saying that Lucifer couldn't remember appointing anyone on the council since he hadn't chosen the council, but he took the better part of valor and bade Mara leave. Her eyes smoldered with resentment, but she did as she was told. When the rest had composed themselves, Lucifer looked them over ironically, with a kind of conspiratorial contempt, and declared, "We're having a guest tonight."

Everyone but Azazael brightened. So that was it: a bit of play-acting for a mark! But who was it? Everyone wanted to know.

"The great prophet Muhammad has kindly consented to join our deliberations."

"Muhammad?" echoed Belphegor suggestively. She had always had a weakness for the Arab's virile mix of sensuality and command.

"Why Muhammad?" queried Asmodeus, ill at ease in his military garb, his soft auburn hair contrasting glaringly with the uniform's intimidating black. "He hates us more than Yeshua!"

"Yeshua does not *hate* us," laughed Belphegor.

"Yes," said Lucifer matter-of-factly, "Yeshua loves everyone."

"He certainly loves that hot little kike we've been using!" chimed in Belior, whose affected cockney accent, at least in his own mind, fit in perfectly with his black leather and chains. Of all the dark captains, he alone had had to modify his attire hardly at all.

Lucifer shot a glance at Azazael, but otherwise he did nothing, promising himself that the time would come when all scores would be settled with interest. "Need I explain my strategy to you?" he asked the council.

Azazael was the first and loudest to protest his trust in his lord.

"There's one thing all of you must know," Lucifer continued, looking directly at Azazael. "None of you is here to participate in these negotiations. You constitute a show of force. Our purpose will be defeated if you give the least indication that you have minds of your own."

Belphegor smiled enticingly. She and Lucifer had known many a night of passion together. "I understand your wishes, Lord, and will obey," she said. "As for these fools, you hardly have cause for concern."

Lucifer did not respond to this flirtation in kind. "Nevertheless," he reiterated, rising up to his full stature to emphasize the point, "do you all understand that you are to say and do nothing without my express command?"

All nodded hastily but uneasily. It would have to do. Lucifer sat back down upon his throne and summoned an aide. "The prophet may enter now," he said. The aide withdrew and, after a moment, Muhammad appeared in the entry arch. "To what do I owe the honor of this unholy invitation?" he asked Lucifer, ignoring everyone else in the hall.

Lucifer smiled stiffly. "You were under no compulsion to accept."

"Come now, my enemy," said Muhammad, returning the smile, but coldly. "We both wish to know where the other stands. Today we did indeed make strange bedfellows. Or are you contemplating surrendering yourself to God?"

Lucifer gestured and a huge throne, almost as magnificent as his own, appeared opposite him with an ivory crescent moon inlaid in its back. He wordlessly offered Muhammad the seat, but the prophet only took a few steps forward and remained standing. "That's not so remote a possibility as you might think," he finally answered.

Muhammad's countenance took on a look of absolute seriousness. He stepped even closer, almost to the edge of the roundtable. "If you mean it, let me send for one of my brothers. Two are needed to witness your declaration of submission to God."

It's not that easy," said Lucifer. "Like you, I am a ruler. My people depend upon me, as yours depend upon you. Were I to convert to your faith, I'd have to have assurances that they would benefit as much as I."

Muhammad sighed and squatted wearily on his haunches. "What do you want, Satan?" he spat out. "God does not bargain with men."

"Why are you so certain I'm the Evil One?" shot back Lucifer. "Appearances can be deceiving. You yourself believe that Issa, one of God's great messengers, only appeared to be crucified."

"Yes," said Muhammad, "God would not permit his own dishonor by allowing his prophet to die so humiliating a death."

Lucifer rose from his throne. "Do you still believe this Yeshua to be that same Issa?"

Muhammad's face darkened. "What is that to you?" he challenged. "Why are you all of a sudden so mindful of me?"

"You're the leader of a great people," replied Lucifer. "You've been appointed as such by God. I too am the leader of a great people. I too am appointed by the Almighty."

Muhammad looked about the room in vague disgust. "Are these the great people you lead?" he asked. "These degenerates in black?"

The dark ones bridled, but none dared violate Lucifer's rule of silence.

"They're disciplined," asserted Lucifer, "as your warriors are disciplined."

Muhammad looked as if he would like nothing better than to put this claim to the test. "My warriors serve God!" he proclaimed. "Their strength comes from the purity of their devotion and the holiness of their cause. Your underlings are dogs who obey only because they know they'll be kicked if they don't. When left to themselves, they feed off their own vomit."

Lucifer remained as smooth as glass. "So you think my people have no integrity?"

Muhammad glared. "Integrity comes from faith in God."

"My people have faith," affirmed Lucifer warmly but with no hostility. "They have faith in a universe of peace, where the strong take care of the weak, where the wicked are reformed by the good, where love unites everyone in enjoyment of all the Creator has given us. All we need to achieve that world is unity. That's why I've invited you here this night."

Muhammad rose to his feet and placed his hands on his hips, the accompanying sweep of his robe lending a magnificence to his gesture grudgingly admired by all the onlookers. "Those are words, Satan, merely words. What you really stand for can be read in the hearts of these twelve henchmen. Indeed," he almost laughed, "one need only look at their uniforms. Look at them, Satan. Look at them!" Lucifer did not turn away from Muhammad. For a long, long moment the latter gazed deeply into the Dark Lord's eyes. "You don't know," the prophet said at last. "That's the revenge Yeshua has in store for you. You really don't know."

Lucifer chose to ignore the madman's ravings, but not the madman. After all, lunatics in high places were powers with which one had to reckon carefully. "Unity is all we need to create the world that all of us desire," he reiterated, emphasizing *all*. "As you well know, unity can be achieved in only one of two ways: peaceful compromise, or war."

"You threaten me, Satan?" asked Muhammad in iron defiance.

Lucifer answered mildly. "You know that, if it came down to armed conflict, you would lose. Your horsemen are no match for my tanks."

"You know such weapons have no power here," replied Muhammad passionately. "All that counts is steadfastness of will, and in that your minions are no match for my magnificent warriors of God."

Lucifer sat back down and smiled as if his opponent had just positioned himself for checkmate. "Weaponry has no significance here," he said, "but here is not where the real battle is to be fought."

Muhammad stared querulously but said nothing.

"Dementia and genius oft go together," continued Lucifer. "Yeshua may be mad in his belief in his own divinity; but both you and I know that, along with his madness, he has a certain flair for philosophy. He's always had a much firmer grasp of metaphysics than you or I. We're men of action. He is a dreamer."

Lucifer paused. Muhammad continued to stare at him intently, but still did not speak.

"Suppose he's right," the Dark Lord resumed. "Suppose heaven and earth are being rejoined. With that marriage comes the final battle, and these rites are but preliminary." He spoke in measured sarcasm. "If you grant the hypothesis, then right now we are, so to speak, orienting the souls of our followers. The direction we set now will determine the path they take when the hard realities of earth hold sway. Do you wish your horsemen to charge armored divisions and so, like the savages, pass into extinction?"

"Whether you believe this simple-minded rubbish, Lucifer," said Muhammad, "or merely think I might, you're a fool. Besides, we have armored divisions too."

"But not nearly as many," countered Lucifer.

"Islam is growing," proclaimed the prophet with deeply rooted assurance. "If it comes to the kind of struggle you foresee, how certain can you be that we won't have the greatest armies then? Indeed, if you were convinced otherwise, you wouldn't have invited me here tonight. And what we lack in armament, we'll more than make up in fearless devotion."

Lucifer leapt from his throne, his mask of calm shattered. "I offered you brotherhood and prosperity," he hissed at Muhammad, "but you would not have it. Now the only way to peace is through war. God always favors the victor, else he would not be the victor. And I, you may be certain, will be the victor. Seize him!"

The twelve made an effort, but they were too slow, Lucifer's previous command to remain spectators having taken too firm a hold. Muhammad's warriors poured into the hall as if from nowhere and placed their drawn daggers at the dark ones' throats, paralyzing them with fear.

"My gratitude for a most illuminating conversation," Muhammad said sardonically.

"If you don't join me, you aid Yeshua!" cried Lucifer.

"What did the prophet Issa say?" Muhammad smiled. "'He who is not with me is against me.'"

"You know what I say is true, Muhammad," Lucifer insisted.

"That may be so," he admitted. "Forgive me if I prefer the self-destructive madness of a man who believes himself God to the world-destroying lunacy of a demon who wants to be God."

"Your time will come," said Lucifer darkly.

Muhammad's smile deepened. "Indeed, the time for all of us is already here." Then he and his men disappeared, presumably into the desert realm whence they had come.

* * *

While the council of the dark ones witnessed their lord's humiliation, the elders of light met in closed chamber outside the city in the same magnificent stone structure where Mikael had agreed to the trial of Yeshua in what seemed to them like another age. The night was crisp, cool and black, underscoring the heaviness of mood. The hall was a kaleidoscope of shadows, reflecting their somber anxiety.

This time all twelve were present: Mikael, their leader; Uriel, their executive arm; Raphael, the healer; Gabriel, the messenger; Zadkiel, the protector; Raziel, keeper of the mysteries; Abdiel and Sariel, the council's troubleshooters; Ariel and Cassiel, the spiritual warriors; and Camael and Anahel, the contemplatives in constant communion with the Godhead. Even though Mikael presided, Uriel, as had become the custom and befitted her temperament, spoke first.

"The dark forces have taken over the city," she said ominously, her aura flaring crimson among the shadows. "Tomorrow they'll try to destroy him. This meeting can be no other than a council of war!"

Silence greeted this battle cry. An untutored observer might have thought that Uriel's comrades were indifferent to her challenge, but the opposite was the case. Unlike humans, when angels are extremely agitated they grow exceedingly still. Paralysis of the will is the angelic equivalent of human frenzy. The silence persisted as the angelic auras went through every conceivable color. Finally Raziel spoke. "What do you mean by 'war,' Uriel? We don't fight as humans fight."

The others nodded, all except Mikael, who tended not to be moved by the ebb and flow of argument, but to arrive at his decisions as if they came from the mouth of God. Now Uriel appealed to him directly.

"Mikael!" she said in a loud voice, her words echoing off the stone walls even as her scintillating aura gave off lurid, one might even have said hellish, eruptions of light. "Now is the time, if ever there was one, to break free of the rules. Yeshua is always talking about taking responsibility for oneself and following one's own heart. Now is the time!"

Perhaps for the first time since the dawn of creation, Mikael looked deeply worried. His aura fluttered dimly, almost meekly, as he said in a defeated tone, "I've no word on this from the Lord."

"Then he leaves it up to us!" Uriel shouted in triumph. "Tomorrow we fight."

Zadkiel, Abdiel, Sariel, Ariel and Cassiel warmed to Uriel's call to arms, but the other half of the council only sank into deeper dejection. The elders of light were evenly divided—not between those who wanted peace and those who called for war, for all knew that war was already upon them; but between those who had the stomach for battle and those who did not. Neither, however, did the latter have the heart to resist Uriel, so as she outlined her strategy, it was clear that all eleven would go along with her. Then *he* appeared; or rather, then they became aware of his presence, for there was no telling how long he had been among them in spirit.

"Making plans?" Yeshua asked as he passed through to the center of the circle. He looked gaunt and tired, but his voice, bearing and manner were as self-assured as ever. Whenever he joined their deliberations he stood in the center, but each angel felt him looking into his or her own eyes. The fiery light softened into a gentle and comforting blue. Everyone felt ashamed before his gaze—everyone but Uriel.

"We're preparing to fight for you," she answered him calmly.

"I didn't ask you to fight for me," he said with equal calm.

"As so oft you've bidden us," she rejoined, "we're following our own hearts."

He smiled, but the smile only deepened the light into a sorrowful indigo. "Some of you are following your hearts," he said pointedly.

A glint of anger flashed in Uriel's eyes. "All here are free to do as they will."

"That's true," agreed Yeshua.

"Those who wish to follow me may do so," she declared. "Those who don't have nothing to fear from me."

Yeshua gazed at Uriel for one of his eternal instants. "From you, no," he said gently. "They've nothing to fear from you. But they do have something to fear. We all have something to fear."

"What's there to fear if one follows one's heart?" she challenged.

"Do you think following one's heart is an escape from fear?" he asked wearily. "Did you hear nothing that was said today?" Uriel looked fixedly upon him but could speak not a word in reply. "The fate of the world hangs in the balance," he went on, "and yet you think there's nothing to fear."

"That's why we must fight!" she proclaimed, regaining her former assurance. "We can't hang back and do nothing."

Again Yeshua smiled. "Sometimes doing nothing is the most powerful weapon of all."

Again Uriel was able to say nothing.

"Certainly, I don't advise you to cower before the face of evil," Yeshua continued. "You should fight if your heart demands it. But what kind of war will you wage? What kind of weapons will you use? If you use the weapons of the flesh, you will perish with the flesh. If you use the weapons of the spirit, you will triumph with the spirit."

"The weapons of the spirit?" Uriel queried. "What are these weapons of the spirit?"

"You know what they are!" broke in Anahel, her aura purging itself of the general depression and regaining its accustomed clarity: "Long-suffering, patience, acceptance, endurance—all the qualities you lack!"

Uriel ignored Anahel's words as if they were the inconsequential buzzing of flies. "You want us to fight tanks and guns with weapons of the spirit?" she demanded of Yeshua.

"You know these earthly weapons have no power here," Mikael answered Uriel, "save that the spirit gives them."

"Such weapons have no power anywhere," Yeshua declared, "save that the spirit gives them!"

"Which spirit?" Uriel queried.

"That's precisely my point," said Mikael, some of his former authority returning to his voice. "Of what spirit are we? That's the issue."

"We're getting lost in a labyrinth of words," rejoined Uriel. "Have all of you forgotten what was said today?" she echoed Yeshua in cold mimicry. "The issue is simple: do we trust in love or resort to force?"

"When you put it that way," joined in Raphael, "the answer is clear. Love is what we're all about!"

"Is it?" laughed Uriel sardonically. "Is it? This little squabble, I suppose, is merely a lovers' quarrel."

"You're beginning to sound like one of the dark ones," accused Gabriel. "Indeed, you speak like Lucifer himself!"

"She sounds nothing like Lucifer," Yeshua rebuked Gabriel, "and she speaks only for herself. Let her say all that is in her heart."

Uriel felt her aura quivering. She had waited eons for this moment, and yet did not know where to begin. Everyone took their cue from Yeshua and waited in expectant but patient silence. At length, Uriel found her voice.

"My Lord," she said to Yeshua, her voice no longer holding any sarcasm, "you are love, I've no doubt of that. Only the purest love could evoke a love of equal purity from my poor heart. You know, I think, that I would do anything for you, sacrifice anything for you, even if it meant saving you from yourself." She smiled through the tears welling in her eyes. "Long ago, you shared with us the knowledge of your mysteries. Raziel is the guardian of those mysteries, but you bestowed knowledge of them upon all the council. However, you forbade us to speak of them, even among ourselves. But now I must speak of them. I must!"

Like a soldier preparing to charge the enemy guns, she regarded Yeshua with uncontrollable anxiety. She knew she would say what she had to say whether he permitted it or no. She felt tremendous relief when he nodded to her to go on.

"You've had many lifetimes as a human," she said quietly. None of us knows why, or why you kept your true identity secret in those lifetimes..."

"My Father kept it secret from me," Yeshua interjected.

"Why?" Uriel asked in the amazement that filled them all.

"Otherwise their purpose would have been defeated," he replied. "I must live the truth of my being as far as I am able. I had to be brought fully into humanity before my divinity could be expressed in a saving rather than destructive way."

The angels pondered what Yeshua had said. Uriel finally broke the silence. "Even though you said nothing of your divinity in those lives, knew nothing of your divinity, still they persecuted you. Countless times you were ignored, rejected, despised, assassinated, burned at the stake, even crucified, all because you are love."

Tears, hot and unstoppable, traced their way down the furrows of Yeshua's cheeks as she recited the litany of his sorrows.

"They trampled upon your heart, and now they've done it again. Is this to be the way of it forever? Are we who love you to stand by and watch as they dash to the ground the chalice of life you offer over and over again? I can not, will not accept it!"

Her eleven companions extended their auras to embrace Uriel's, affirming their solidarity of purpose. Now they too were through standing idle at the repeated crucifixion of Yeshua's heart.

"I'm not the only one suffering," their Lord answered softly.

"No, but they deserve their suffering," Uriel shot back. "They've brought it upon themselves."

"Do they?" whispered Yeshua, yet everyone heard what he said. "Does the child neglected by its mother or beaten and abused by its father deserve its suffering? Do the lovers who only seek their hearts' desire deserve to be torn apart by their families' or their society's bigotry or greed? Does a people that gives itself generously and creatively to the world deserve annihilation?"

He made no gesture and spoke no magical formula, but immediately the children of the earth appeared in every angelic mind's eye.

"Look upon their faces!" he cried. "Look, really look upon the face of even one of them! Are you telling me that my suffering is too great a price for their salvation? They're children lost in the dark. They are my children. Their souls are wandering through nightmarish realms even as they sleep in my arms. In their dreams they claw, kick, bite and scream, but they're still my children. I won't let go, no matter how they hurt me, not until they awaken to the light."

Yeshua's passion was absolute. It was clear to all that there was no diverting him from his saving purpose.

"I don't doubt you love them, Lord," said Uriel, "and can't be turned away from that love, but what if you're wrong? What if you aren't leading them to the light, but as sheep to the slaughter?"

That profound quiet that betokened deep pain came over him. She felt his agony as if it were her own. But for his sake, for all their sakes, she had to go on.

"Look at your most recent life," she said, half amazed that she was not struck down for uttering a mystery so deep. "You called the world to come out of its insanity. You met violence with nonviolence, hatred with love. You took their blows upon you, languished in their prisons, and finally died by your own countryman's and coreligionist's hand. No doubt it was a glorious martyrdom. You've suffered many a glorious martyrdom!"

"Martyrdom isn't so glorious," said Yeshua, in harmony with Uriel's sarcasm, "when you're living it." Uriel felt like a surgeon operating without anesthetic. The patient screamed in agony, but it was the only way to save his life.

"Suppose the world had taken you seriously? Suppose they had opposed Hitler not with armies, fleets and warplanes, but love?"

Yeshua smiled darkly. "You think your question is a rhetorical one, its answer a foregone conclusion."

"How can you deny it?" Uriel cried. "Is all life supposed to offer itself up as a living sacrifice to principle? Will principle be vindicated when the Hitlers of this world feed upon it like carrion upon rotting flesh?"

Yeshua sighed with unfathomable weariness. "All this time, and yet you've not learned the power of the spirit."

"The power of the spirit?" echoed Uriel scornfully, her aura once again on fire. "How many millions must go through slavery, torture, starvation and extermination before you admit to yourself that the power of the spirit, the power of anything, lies in one's willingness to fight for it!"

"I'm not saying one shouldn't fight," said Yeshua sternly. "But what is the real battle, and what weapons must be used to fight it?"

"Then teach me," said Uriel sarcastically. "I am your devoted disciple."

"Truer words were never spoken," he replied unexpectedly, and with deep and unmistakable affection. "Hitler didn't rise to power because of his reliance upon the sword, but out of his single-minded adherence to an idea, an idea that pandered to all the fears and weaknesses of his people, an idea that gave license to those weaknesses and even colored them with the false patina of greatness. He merely took the anti-Semitism that has poisoned Christendom almost from the beginning to its logical conclusion. He turned the Jewish people into the ultimate scapegoats. Well," he smiled impishly, "I am the ultimate Jew."

"So, you'd have us play into Lucifer's hands?" queried Uriel.

Yeshua's countenance became serious, but a smile still played wistfully upon it. "I would have him play into our hands," he replied. "A house divided against itself cannot stand. Life that devours itself cannot survive. One who violates the integrity of his own nature cannot endure."

"You're assuming, of course," said Uriel darkly, "that the nature of all being is love."

"Yes, I am," he agreed. "I know at times, perhaps most of the time, that must seem to you an audacious, even insane assumption. It seems so to me, too. But I've good reason for making it." He paused, gazing into the depths of each angel's soul, infusing them with his spirit. "I would not wish to live in any other universe."

"So," cried Uriel in scornful wonder, "that's the truth you offer us? Your *wish*?"

"The world is wide open," he rejoined. "We make of it what we will. If one doesn't fight to attain one's heart's desire, then one truly is a fool. And in all this unending universe, there's only one thing each and every heart really desires — love."

All the angels bowed, including Uriel, as much to the power of Yeshua's conviction as to its substance. They felt they were eavesdropping on the soul of God.

"Tomorrow," concluded Yeshua, "no matter what happens, you won't interfere. I don't fight your battles for you. Don't try to fight mine for me."

All knelt in token of obedience save Uriel.

"Lately I've come to realize," she said, "that no one can tell me what is and is not my battle. Not even you."

Yeshua bowed. "What I've told you is the truth. Take it into your heart. Then you'll know what you must do. As for me, I'm in my Father's hands."

The light flickered, and he was gone. The twelve elders stood for some time in silent communion. Then, as dawn broke, they set off to fetch Professor James and Justice Holmes for what they knew would be the final and decisive day of the trial.

PART III: JUDGMENT

Chapter 10

As the pale light of dawn spilled over the horizon onto the frozen tundra, by some natural but still ineffable alchemy tingeing both itself and the latter with a bloody hue, Lucifer descended upon the Nameless One's lair. Not for him the tedious passage through checkpoint after checkpoint. The Light-Bearer cut directly through the craggy mountain, gleaming with hoarfrost, to his faithless ally's innermost chamber. Nevertheless, as Lucifer knew he would, the Nameless One was expecting him. His increasingly gelatinous bulk reclined energetically behind the strictly functional metal desk in the incongruously old-fashioned easy chair. Lucifer wondered why one could never think of the simplest detail about this creature without having to resort to paradox.

"So, Lucifer, awfully bully of you to pay me such an unexpected social call," the Nameless One said, black bushy mustache quivering as he made a dreadful attempt to give a British intonation to his speech, and then laughed at some joke known only to himself.

"You've violated our agreement," Lucifer said icily, not feeling like wasting pleasantries on so unpleasant a collaborator.

"Not really," said the Nameless One. "I've merely engaged in some creative contractual interpretation. You yourself said we had to be ready for anything."

"You've violated our agreement," repeated Lucifer.

The Nameless One looked at him with ponderous eyebrows and thick peasant jowls crinkled in an impudent smirk. "What did I do?" he cried in an injured tone, rising from his soft, tasteless bourgeois chair and stepping around the desk in a movement both placating and threatening.

"You know what you did," said Lucifer, refusing to move no matter how close the repulsive face came to his own.

The Nameless One returned to the desk, his back to Lucifer, took a hand-rolled cigarette out of a box that should have held paper clips, and lit it.

"Put that out," commanded Lucifer.

"I'm too old to chase after cunts," wheedled the Nameless One, "and vodka has no more effect on me than water. Smoking is really one of the few pleasures in life I can still enjoy." As if to emphasize this point, he took a deep drag and blew the smoke just a little to Lucifer's left.

"Put it out," repeated Lucifer.

For a moment the Nameless One silently contemplated the smoke curling into the air, doubtless relishing the mounting tension. Then he shrugged, pinched the end of the cigarette and placed the butt in the side-pocket of his military tunic. "We are friends!" he declared. "I know how much tobacco irritates you, and I'll do anything for my friends. But of course, then it's only fair that my friends be willing to do anything for me."

Lucifer was not about to dignify such absurd logic with a reply. Then he realized that silence could be taken for assent, an indication that he was awaiting his "friend's" request. The Nameless One, he warned himself, was as sharp as ever, and therefore as dangerous.

"Let's stick to the point, shall we?" said Lucifer. "Did you really think your pathetic attempt at sabotage would succeed?"

"I knew it would," replied the Nameless One, but before Lucifer had time to pounce on this blatant confession of guilt, he added, "but I wouldn't call it sabotage, comrade. I'd call it lending you a helping hand." The Nameless One sat back down in his chair in one clean, swift motion that left Lucifer no choice but attentive silence. "You really were on the point of fucking everything up," he said, looking intently into Lucifer's eyes. "What were you thinking, comrade—that you could make a deal with the devil and not get burned?"

"Muhammad is hardly the devil," said Lucifer.

"What have we been fighting for all this time?" demanded the Nameless One. "For what have we risked eternal damnation? Wasn't

it freedom?"
Lucifer nodded.
"And what is Muhammad all about?" continued the Nameless One.
"Submission," replied Lucifer.
The Nameless One nodded his graying head vigorously and smiled.
"The same thing you've been about through most of your present earthly sojourn, it seems to me," his guest added.
"We talked about this!" protested the Nameless One. "It's their test! Let them follow until they've figured out it's all up to them."
"Follow, yes," said Lucifer, "but millions to their deaths?"
"My friend," explained the Nameless One, rising and pacing before his guest, "you've no idea what it's like to try to liberate a people as backward and superstitious as this. They love their chains! Every village and town has its own way of doing things, and no one looks out for the welfare of the whole. They're criminals at heart, the lot of them! Much as it sickens me, I have to meet them at their own level. Millions may have died, but believe me, if it hadn't been for my strong hand, hundreds of millions would have cut one another's throats!"
Untouched by his ally's pathos, Lucifer materialized a chair and sat down. "Why did you send your flunkies to me?" he asked.
"*My* flunkies?" echoed the Nameless One, returning to his own seat. "They're your own most trusted advisors."
"They were my trusted advisors," corrected Lucifer, "long ago, before you ruined them."
"Comrade," said the Nameless One with a touch of piety, "you know as well as I that no one can ruin another. We can only ruin ourselves."
"Yes," rejoined Lucifer, "but one can give a firm shove in that direction."
"I didn't ruin them," protested the Nameless One. "I showed them kindness."
"You corrupted them by pandering to their darkest and most twisted fantasies," retorted Lucifer, for the first time in the interview raising his voice in the anger that had possessed him throughout. "You want henchmen in your own sick and sadistic image."

Also for the first time in the interview, the Nameless One looked as if he were about to strike out. Whether out of fear, self-interest, or a mixture of both Lucifer could not tell, but his host's body went rigid with self-control for a full minute, and then he relaxed and smiled. "They may be less moral now," he said quietly, "but you'll see, they're much more reliable."

"To whom, I wonder?" said Lucifer. "But you haven't answered my question. Why did you send them, and in those tasteless uniforms, along with your army of zombies?"

"*Our* army," corrected the Nameless One.

"Not when it moves without my command. Why did you send them?"

"It's time for all spirits to show their true colors," replied the Nameless One.

"You were afraid I might use an alliance with Muhammad against you," said Lucifer. "You knew intimidation would be the very thing to harden him against me."

"You don't belong with Muhammad," asserted the Nameless One. "You belong with me."

"Perhaps," Lucifer mused, gazing off into some imaginary distance. "For a time, at least."

"You'll see that I'm right," said the Nameless One. "When all is revealed, you'll see."

Lucifer rose, hardly hearing this self-justifying prophecy. After all, it was only the raving of a megalomaniac. Fate had made this monster necessary to Lucifer's plans, but he would discard the pretentiously "Nameless" One as soon as he had served his purpose. "The question now," said Lucifer, "is who is in charge of this army."

"You're on the scene, comrade," declared the Nameless One in obsequious sincerity. "Of course you are in command!"

"And you will trust my judgment without question or condition?" Lucifer queried.

"Of course, *Mein Fuehrer!*" cried the Nameless One, springing out of his chair and raising his arm in mock Nazi salute.

"I don't like your brand of sarcasm," said Lucifer colorlessly, "especially since it was my idea that you help the democracies against Germany. Besides, you've no right to it. You're too much in common with that beast."

The Nameless One gave a self-deprecating grin but said nothing. "One other thing," said Lucifer. "Are you certain your people will be ready for so great a struggle so soon after the recent war?"

"Strong measures are needed," answered the Nameless One, "but they'll be ready."

Lucifer nodded. "I'd like to stay and avail myself of your gracious hospitality, but I've something pressing to attend to before the trial."

"Ah, yes, the lovely Jewess!" smirked the Nameless One. "I understand."

Lucifer felt no further purpose would be served by reprimanding his ally for his vulgarity. The oaf was incorrigible. Besides, he sensed Rachel was in need of him. Without further fanfare, he departed.

* * *

He had come to her, as if in a dream, though Rachel was certain it had not been a dream. He had not argued with her, exactly, but he had said things... What things? She lay upon a straw mat stretched over the cold marble floor and tried to remember.

Lucifer had not accompanied her into the temple, perhaps because he sensed she did not wish it, or perhaps because he felt she was no longer worth the trouble. The building itself—late Hellenistic in style, she would guess, though she had never had an eye for that sort of thing—had a frigid, intellectually impressive beauty, characteristic of so much that came from ancient Greece, that suited the goddess of wisdom it honored.

It had also suited Rachel's mood at the moment. On entering, she felt unaccountable relief. The impersonal columns and comfortless stone made it so much easier to forget about herself and all the human, subhuman and superhuman flotsam and jetsam that cluttered up what otherwise would have been a universe as beautiful in its perfection as an ice crystal. And Lucifer was right about the old, hairless, toothless priest. Wordlessly he withdrew, doubtless to some nearby hovel where he made his home, leaving her alone among the fluted columns to breathe easily for the first time, it seemed, since her arrival in the pleroma. The priest had even prepared her a bed, simple and hard yet comfortable to her spirit, and after a time she lay down and slept.

Then *he* came—a phantom, a mere presence, but unmistakably he. He had no right to bother her in this place of sanctuary. Why had he come? He needed her, she could feel that, but she did not need him. Wild Gypsy music suddenly filled the air. He took her hand and they danced, their movement, caught in the light of the votive lamps, casting entrancing shadows upon the stone floor and columns. She was losing herself, she could feel herself slipping away, and she did not like it at all. It seemed to her that all the times they had been together she had always been taken out of herself. *She* had not really been there at all. It was a startling realization, and as she came to it she dropped his hand, he disappeared and she awoke, her face wet with tears. He had said something about it all, but what was it? She could not remember. That, however, was probably for the better. He was so expert at convincing her of what was not really so.

And now she lay upon the mat with the ruby hint of dawn on the horizon peeking through the lightening columns. She still did not know what to do, but she knew what definitely not to do. She would not let him sweep her away, not ever again. After all, had not he himself said that it profits one nothing to gain the whole world if the price is the loss of one's soul? He might be king of heaven, but she was sole sovereign over her own heart.

Then Lucifer returned. She smelled him before anything else. Yes, he had a distinctive odor she had not consciously noted before. It was not an unpleasant scent. There was something dark and animal-like, even arousing about it. Why not Lucifer? He never asked that she be other than herself. It was clear, pitifully clear, that he was obsessed with possessing her body, but he left her soul untouched and intact. He was beautiful, and coupling with him satisfied a certain need without creating more need. Best of all, with him she would always be in control. Yeshua was a consuming passion, so consuming that it left nothing over in her to actually feel it. Lucifer had his faults, but she could live with him. Yeshua may or may not have been without sin, as Christians claimed—she had yet to make up her mind on that score—but could she do anything save die with him?

When Lucifer appeared, he immediately sensed a change in her and knelt down next to the bed as if he would fall upon her then and there. Rachel held up her mouth to be kissed, but then pushed him gently but unequivocally away. "Not now," she said, sitting up.

"When?" he pouted, like a little boy whose mother had just denied him tea and crullers.

"Later," she said indifferently. "After it's over. By the way," she added teasingly, "is this the latest fashion?" At first he did not understand, but then she fingered the sleeve of his gleaming white robe. It felt like liquid light.

"Oh this," he said, irritated but striving for good humor. "A political necessity, that's all." Then he frowned.

"What is it?" she queried. "There's something you need to tell me."

"Something happened in the night," he said hoarsely. "Didn't you hear?"

"I heard nothing," she replied.

"This temple must truly be enchanted," he said with the half-believing sarcasm of the superstitious. For a long moment he looked at her in silence. She knew he was trying to decide what she should know and how she should be told it. She waited. She knew by now that she could not change him. And why should she? He could not change her. "My troops have come," he said at length, like a cardsharp making an exploratory bid.

"You have troops?" she asked, somewhat stupidly.

"I didn't summon them," he said, as if in excuse.

"Then why are they here?" she asked matter-of-factly. She was not all that interested in his troops.

"Azazael did it behind my back," he replied.

She nearly taunted him for this slip in his supposed omniscience, but then decided that she would be nice instead. "If you don't want them here," she said reasonably, "why don't you send them back to wherever they came from? Where did they come from?" she added as an afterthought, beginning to feel intrigued.

"It's not that simple," he said peevishly, ignoring her second question.

"More 'political necessity?'" she asked archly.

He nodded mechanically as if he had not really heard her, then grasped at her hand and looked intently into her eyes. "Listen,

Rachel," he said clumsily, "the way they're dressed... It wasn't my doing."

"It was Azazael's doing?" she hypothesized. He nodded again, and she could see that he was telling the truth. "How are they dressed?" she asked.

"Like the men who murdered you."

Her breath stopped. "Why are they dressed that way?"

"Azazael has turned against me," explained Lucifer. "It's to discredit me and create a rift between me and you."

Rachel abruptly turned away. She was angry with him, not only because of the coming of this army, but also because she could sense that he was not telling her the whole truth. She could press him. After all, what political necessity would justify going along with Azazael in such a tasteless farce? And were these troops merely dressed like Nazis, or were they really Nazis? Such questions, however, would only lead to a fight, and she needed a day off from such unpleasantness with Lucifer. She needed to marshal her emotional resources for the battle that was shaping up with Yeshua. She rose. "Let's go."

Lucifer looked at her for a long moment as if seeking reassurance. Finally, it seemed, he accepted her neutrality as enough. Just as the priest entered for the morning sacrifice, they left for the field of judgment.

* * *

What promised to be the last day of the trial dawned as brightly as the first, though of course there was no telling what kind of weather, literal or metaphorical, it might bring. The principals sat in their places. Rachel chatted quietly with Lucifer who, perhaps to offset the color of his soldiers' uniforms, was dressed in a robe of shimmering white. Yeshua was alone except for the silent company of James. The black guards (as Wendell had dubbed them, enjoying the play upon the British epithet) ringed the field with their unholy fighting machines, but at least they kept a decent distance from the center of the proceedings and maintained a disciplined quiet. He wished the same could be said for the souls of the assembly, who were all a twitter with the latest happenings, and what was even more comic, filled with righteous indignation at the treatment they had received from the defendant the day before. Wendell felt certain that he would be hearing today from people who hitherto had been indifferently silent.

One good thing came of the disorder. In all the uproar, no one had yet raised the legal question of the judicial status of those souls who had arrived with the American Indian well after the trial began. If they were accorded the right to vote on the verdict, then Lucifer and his unsavory lieutenants might well argue that their soldiers should also be included. As far as Wendell was concerned, the trial would then be reduced to a farce.

But perhaps there was no use in agonizing over such legal fine points. If yesterday's session were any indication, what happened today would have little to do with law in any meaningful sense of the term. Nevertheless, it was Wendell's job to give the affair at least a semblance of judicial form. He rapped his gavel, called for order, and without waiting for the crowd's buzzing to cease entirely, asked if anyone else had further testimony.

Now indeed, contrary to Wendell's understandable expectation, did total silence fall over the assembly. The angels of light hovered above, the dark forces waited in the wings, and everyone else, it seemed, was as if suspended motionless in between. Or perhaps they were as thoroughly sick of this business as he was and just wanted to make an end of it. After waiting what seemed a reasonable interval, he resumed.

"Since no one wishes to come forward..."

"If I might have a word!" a masculine, mature and elegant voice announced from the midst of the assembly.

"Rise and come forward," commanded Wendell.

A clean-shaven man, dressed in a dark suit of nineteenth century continental cut, stood up and made his way suavely through the crowd. He was bareheaded, but his silver-gray hair sparkled like a diadem. He moved a trifle stiffly, certainly out of pride rather than shyness or age. His frame was small, his body tapered rather than lean, and his movements purposeful, controlled and economical. His eyes were as blue as Wendell's own, only less changeable, more set into a steely hardness. There was nothing remarkable about his facial features: a habitually smooth brow, a regular though slightly aquiline nose, full but not sensuous lips, and a jaw neither weak nor overbearing. Overall, he was self-assurance, reliability and sophistication incarnate.

"My name is unimportant," he said, after bowing before Wendell and taking his place in the witness box. "But if you must affix a label to me, call me Ernst. I represent a sizable number of like-minded individuals who have elected me their spokesman. We've remained silent until now because, with all due respect to Your Honor, whom we hold in the highest esteem as a professional in the most admirable sense of the term, we have regarded this trial as a circus."

There was a sprinkling of laughter from the assembly, but it quickly died down when Wendell looked sternly over the crowd. "You say you represent a large group," he said to Ernst. "How large?"

Ernst gestured toward the assembly and several thousand souls, mostly male and mostly, by the look of them, middle-class intellectuals, stood up quietly to let their presence be noted. "These are the 'activists' of our organization," he told Wendell. "There's a far greater company of the financially influential but politically reticent who nonetheless sympathize with our cause, as well as millions of fellow-travelers. The prime-movers among us, however, all extremely high-placed and important men, quite naturally wish to remain anonymous."

Wendell realized that he himself had a great deal of sympathy for these people, as well as a great deal in common with them. There was, however, something eerie about seeing them standing en masse in their quiet, professionally self-assured dignity. Such men belonged in occupational rather than political associations. Perhaps also, Wendell was getting a glimpse of what the world would be like if it were made up entirely of himself multiplied millions of times over, and he did not relish the sight. "I see," he nodded after looking over the group. The gentlemen took this rightly as an invitation to resume their seats. "And why have they selected you as their spokesman?" he asked Ernst.

"Because they can't agree among themselves on a particular course of action, and they trust me to represent their essential interests."

Wendell wanted to ask why they trusted him, but as magistrate he had no business badgering the witness. Besides, Ernst was the kind of man, Wendell was certain, who was not going to answer any question he chose not to. Further inquiry along this line would lead to an infinite regress—endless repetition on Ernst's part of the same evasive response in ever more elaborately deceptive form.

"And why do you think of these proceedings as a circus?" Wendell queried, trying to keep his tone judicially neutral.

"Again, Your Honor," answered Ernst with alacrity, "we mean no offense by the word. We simply thought that this trial would settle nothing of any substantive import. After all, the objective order of the universe is what it is no matter who claims to govern it. Nature will continue to operate according to the laws of physics, chemistry and biology no matter who claims to be her 'God.' Likewise, the world of men will proceed according to the vicissitudes of human nature no matter what ideologies we employ to camouflage the truth."

Wendell was both irritated and heartened by the man's speech. It was arrogant, but rationally so, and expressed precisely his own frame of mind when he had first arrived in the pleroma. Nevertheless, he decided to test the witness' mettle. "So, you're determinists?" he asked, ready to pounce if answered in the affirmative. Wendell had no patience for dogmatic quietism of any sort. "All is as it must be, so there's no use trying to change it?"

"No, Your Honor, just the opposite," replied Ernst. "Though we practice a great variety of professions and operate within all sorts of cultural traditions, we are practical men for whom metaphysics has always seemed irresponsible dreaming. We want the world to get on with the business of life in as convenient and expeditious a fashion as humanly possible. Until coming here, none of us ever had any experience of the supernatural, let alone the divine. Some of us are still convinced that the present experience is not after-living but after-dreaming. Many of us, perhaps most, feel that what transpires here could not possibly have any practical bearing upon the course of human affairs on earth. Therefore we have regarded all that has befallen us here as entertainment at best and delusion at worst."

"So why are you speaking out now?" asked Wendell.

Ernst grasped the lapels of his frock coat and drew himself up to full stature. "Because of what happened yesterday," he said in deep and ominous tones. "Put together with what we know of world history, we fear that in this trial may be sown the seeds of a new dark age in which those who seek after truth will be hounded and persecuted, and those who trade on ignorance and superstition will once more reign supreme."

"You sound like you've already made up your minds," Wendell remarked, suddenly feeling uncomfortably accused of aiding and abetting in the crime of murdering civilization.

Ernst smiled disarmingly, his normally smooth forehead crinkling in goodwill. "We're not hasty men," he said. "After all, civilization and Christianity have hitherto, for the most part, marched hand-in-hand. And the most recent threat to civilization has come from men very much like those with whom the prosecution has surrounded us here today. Nevertheless, we know that great dangers often have small beginnings, and that falsehood, sometimes with the greatest sincerity and best of intentions, frequently masquerades as truth. With your permission, Your Honor, I, as representative of our brotherhood of modernity, would like to talk with each of the candidates in turn."

"Candidates?" echoed Wendell.

"Yes, it seems to us that this trial is really an election to see who will govern in this pleroma. In that way, too, it's like a circus," Ernst smiled, "only a circus with practical consequences."

Wendell felt his heart beating faster. Here were men of his own stamp who were finally ready to apply the canons of reason to a riddle that thus far had defied his best attempts at solution. Now at last something was happening that Wendell could support unreservedly and with ease. As far as it was in his power to give, these men, in the person of Ernst, their representative, would have all the time and scope they needed to conduct their investigation. Indeed, who knew but that the hand of Providence had all along been leading the trial to this very point? "Any objections?" Wendell asked summarily of the assembly. "Good, then let's proceed."

There were muted protests on the part of the more fanatical of the religious enthusiasts, but they gave way, Wendell surmised, to curiosity about what the self-assured and sophisticated gentleman was going to say.

"It would be a matter of indifference where we start," smiled

Ernst again, "but the defendant has a way of bringing everything to a resounding climax. So, if he doesn't mind, I'll begin with the Lord Lucifer."

"Please, no titles," protested Lucifer with his low-key charm, quite matching that of his interlocutor. "We're all equals here." As if to demonstrate the truth of this axiom, Lucifer smoothly exchanged places with Ernst so that the latter could carry on a proper examination.

"That's my very first question," said Ernst, bowing as Lucifer seated himself upon the witness stand. "If we're all equals, what's the point of this trial?"

"You yourself said it," replied Lucifer. "It's really an election. You're electing your chief executive."

"Setting aside the fact that we had no part in nominating the candidates," pressed Ernst, "why do we need a chief executive? Everyone here is king in his own kingdom, so to speak. No one's territory encroaches upon that of another. Each can have whatever he wants without taking anything from anyone else."

"But, as some of your associates have already noted," said Lucifer, "it's not real."

"So what if it isn't real?" countered Ernst. "It's the way it is. If we're happy in our dreams, why disturb them?"

"Because all dreams, however happy, must come to an end," answered Lucifer. "I agree with my opponent on one point—the pleroma is changing. He and I have been here far longer than any of you. We can see it. When two enemies agree, wise men don't take their testimony lightly."

Ernst relaxed. Evidently he had been playing devil's advocate on behalf of the more skeptical of his friends. His body did not slouch exactly, but it was clear from the free and easy way in which he shrugged his shoulders, as if lightly throwing off a great weight, that he was now relieved to stop playing a role and start being himself. A sharp look came into his face, and it was obvious that now the man was reverting to his accustomed bearing. Wendell had hoped that he was a physician or an industrialist, or even a scientist. Now he knew that Ernst was merely a corporate lawyer. Yet he nevertheless represented such men. They had placed their interests in his hands. What did it matter if he were only their mouthpiece? The oracle was the voice of the gods.

"My dear Lucifer," Ernst said in a friendly but challenging tone, "the question any constituency asks of a candidate is always the same: what have you got to offer that others do not?"

"You've seen how Yeshua has managed things thus far," answered the Dark Lord. "How could anyone else not be an improvement?"

Ernst frowned thoughtfully, and for a moment Wendell thought he was going to put his hand on Lucifer's shoulder. "Let me make our position clear. We are agnostic. We don't know if anyone has managed this universe. Indeed, we think it highly unlikely. However, on the off chance that, due to technological progress, one of you 'supernatural' personalities will come to manage it in the future, we are deliberating how best to invest our influence. Thus, as far as we're concerned, there's no record upon which to fall or stand. We want to hear your ideas, your position on the issues. Of course, one can always lie..."

"Not here," interjected Lucifer. "All you need do is look into my eyes to see that I'm telling the truth."

"Yes, we understand all that," rejoined Ernst, "but we're cautious men. Such vulnerability may only necessitate more devious hypocrisy, greater sincerity in deception."

Lucifer nodded as if he well understood.

"As I was saying," resumed Ernst, "a candidate's platform and promises are not much surety, but for now that's all we have. We must gauge your tendencies to see if they're compatible with our goals."

Lucifer bowed his head. "Sir, I'm in your hands."

"So I ask you again," said Ernst, "what do you have to offer?"

"To put it in a word," replied Lucifer, "order. I offer the authority without which there can be no order."

"We like the sound of that," declared Ernst, leaving unsaid the dangling innuendo of *and you knew that we would*. "Yes, order is what we need, as long as it's an order not inimical to growth. But why should we choose you over Christ? After all, hundreds of millions of people around the world already acknowledge him as their highest authority, and Christendom has made great if uneven strides in arriving at accommodation with the forces of progress.

Why should we pass on a sure thing?"

"I offer you much more than accommodation," declared Lucifer. "I offer you leadership that will take you so rapidly into the future you'll forget there ever was a world where people opposed religion to science and culture to industry. Industry will be our culture and science our religion!"

This announcement sent a shock wave through the assembly. From all sides came some cheers and many more jeers. Wendell had to bang his gavel for a full minute to restore order.

"That would be ideal," said Ernst with a sardonic smile. "But, as you can see, the ideal is not always possible."

"Miracles happen," said Lucifer, returning his smile.

"Perhaps," conceded Ernst doubtfully. "But if so, precedent certainly favors your opponent."

"Why are you so certain he's the Christ?" countered Lucifer.

Keeping his eyes level with Lucifer's, Ernst pointed upward. "*They* are certain. And despite the impressive military force you've displayed here today, I doubt that tanks are any more of a match for angels up here than angels are for tanks down there."

"You're right," affirmed Lucifer with sudden warmth. "It's not by force that I will establish my authority, but by the approbation of all reasonable souls."

Ernst nodded for him to continue.

"All I have to say to you now is this," said Lucifer with what was in effect a verbal wink. "Whatever we are capable of doing, we, all of us,"—he looked impressively over the assembly—"can only do together. I'm the one who sees this. *He* does not."

Ernst turned toward Yeshua, who had sat motionless thus far, as if his mind were far away. "Is that true?" he asked.

Yeshua slowly lifted his head to look upon his interrogator. "You've no idea how far you are from the assurance you seek."

Ernst glared at Yeshua, his mouth working and his jaw quivering. Then he took control of himself. "I have to admit," he said, "that I've never liked you. All your pious, self-righteous cant about the truth of the soul, following one's heart and seeking first the kingdom of heaven runs counter to all that any honest and thoughtful man knows the world to be really about. Nevertheless, I'll grant you that, once properly harnessed and directed, your Gospel did provide the motive power for the ascendancy of Western civilization, and Western civilization has been the cradle of scientific and technological progress, the only real progress the world has ever known. But the initial spark is not the flame. The romantic youth must grow into the realistic adult. What we want to know is what do you have to offer us now."

"Nothing," replied Yeshua.

"Nothing?" said Ernst wonderingly. "Then why are you here?"

"It's you who've put me on trial," answered Yeshua. "I'm not running for any office."

"You've nothing to offer us?" repeated Ernst. "I told my colleagues that, but they insisted that I make sure. And was yesterday's little temper-tantrum a sample of this 'nothing?'"

"It's all in each of your hands already," said Yeshua. "I've nothing more to give. You'll never find what you're seeking until you learn to give as you've been given."

"Thank you," said Ernst, bowing. Then he turned to Wendell. "Your Honor, we have what we need. I thank the court for its indulgence. I don't wish to take up any more of its time."

Wendell stared at the man for a moment, wondering if he were impudent or merely efficient. Then he nodded, and Ernst disappeared into the crowd whence he came.

Wendell was uncertain what had just happened, but he knew it had been nothing like that for which he had hoped. Again, there was no alternative but to get this damned trial over with as quickly as possible. "Does anyone have any further testimony?" he challenged. As no one seemed disposed to take up this gauntlet, he went on. "Then we will proceed to closing arguments. The prosecution will begin."

Lucifer rose from the witness stand and strode confidently, almost arrogantly, to the clearing before the judge's bench. He stood for a moment as if sizing up the hostility his latest remarks had engendered, and then plunged into his final address.

"O all ye holy ones!" he intoned solemnly. "For holy ones you are, each and every one of you. After passing through the agony and travail of earth life—indeed, after bearing up under that agony with patience, dignity and courage—you've found your way to your eternal and honestly earned reward. You dwell now in the pleroma, a place of light and peace, joy and serenity, eternal and unadulterated bliss. At least, that's what it should be. That's what it would be, were it not for him!"

Lucifer pointed dramatically at the defendant.

"He's robbed you of your peace and joy, not just through the course of this trial, but through all the ages past as well. And you thought you had no choice but to suffer his machinations because he was the agent of the Almighty, or indeed, God himself!"

Lucifer looked like he was about to burst into laughter or tears. Wendell was fascinated by the way he played on the emotions of the crowd. It was not so much in what he said or even how he said it, but the feeling he conveyed that he had made their suffering his own.

"Suppose, by some twisted stretch of the imagination, that he is the Almighty. Then why doesn't he fix what's wrong with the world? Why did he let it go wrong to begin with? The truth, as hard as it may be for some to accept, is that Yeshua can't be God—not because the infinite and almighty God can't become a mortal and finite man, but because there is no God."

A wave of contention swept through the crowd that threatened pandemonium in short order. Wendell was about to sound his gavel when Lucifer suddenly held up his arms and the assembly, as if mesmerized by the sheer audacity of the gesture, fell silent.

"There is no God, not in the sense that Yeshua claims. God exists in each and every one of us, but no one of us is God. God exists beyond the individual. Together, we are God!"

The upturned faces of the souls of the pleroma suddenly, magically shone with edification. Wendell was astounded. It seemed that, in the proverbial twinkling of an eye, the Dark Lord had caused all but a few hearty individuals, like Muhammad and Paul, not only to ignore what he had said about science and technology a moment earlier, but to forget their religious and cultural heritage altogether.

"Objection!" James shouted, leaping up from his seat like a tin duck in a shooting gallery. "What you just said is self-contradictory. It makes no sense!"

A part of Wendell agreed, but it was his job not to side with his friend, or even logic, but to enforce due process. "Defense counsel will resume his seat!" he ordered. "No objections are permitted in closing argument. As long as statements are kept within the bounds of relevance and decency and incite no contempt for this court, both sides may say whatever they please. The defense will have its turn."

Lucifer bowed his thanks to Wendell, and then turned toward James. "You say I make no sense," he said mildly. "You are one who has fallen under Yeshua's spell. But I invoke the same standard according to which he desires to be judged," he declared to the assembly. "I invoke the witness of your own hearts. In your hearts, all of you feel the truth of what I'm saying. All of you have suffered, some worse than others, but all have suffered. To be composed of corruptible flesh and susceptible emotion, to be a mortal in a world of elemental forces indifferent to one's comfort and well-being, is to suffer. Now you've come to a place where you need suffer no longer, but clearly, that's not enough for him. Megalomania feeds on crisis, because the megalomaniac needs to cast himself as the hero who saves everyone by stepping into the breach. So Yeshua has now cooked up a crisis of truly cosmic proportions in order to win the admiration and worship he claims to scorn, but which in reality is the only food upon which his corrupt and jaded appetite desires to feed. And in fabricating this artificial crisis, he's created a real one. That's the way of tyrants. Their obscure and hideous fantasies become the reality with which the rest of us have to live. And the worst of it is, he really believes it! He really believes himself to be the savior of the world!"

All eyes fell upon Yeshua, who made not the slightest gesture of denial.

"A short time ago," Lucifer continued, "many of you were reunited with loved ones whom perhaps you'd given up hope of ever seeing again. All of you, no matter what your religious or irreligious persuasion, were ready to fall down and worship at this man's feet. Did no one wonder, 'Why now?' Why, if Yeshua truly was the one who brought about this great and glorious reunion, did he wait until now? It was his trump card! He was saving it until a time such as this, when someone with enough intelligence to see through his game and enough courage to confront him would call his bluff. We were all ready to forget about this trial when that same someone..."

Everyone knew to whom he referred, but Rachel sat cross-legged and stony-faced, her long black hair cascading over comely but slumping shoulders, as if she did not know that suddenly she was the object of everyone's attention.

"...saw through the ploy and named it for what it was."

Lucifer fell silent and closed his eyes, whether to honor Rachel's wisdom and courage or emphasize Yeshua's unspeakable malevolence Wendell could not tell. Then the Dark Lord went on.

"Throughout the last two millennia, Yeshua has declared himself your Lord. He's claimed to be the very same Yahweh, the god of the Israelites, who tortured and harassed you from the dawn of creation. I, for one, don't doubt his claim, his modus operandi being so much the same. He has power, yes, and all of us, myself included, have cringed and scraped before his power, not so much because of what he's done as what he might be able to do. Yes, it's time we admitted the truth to ourselves: it's been our dread uncertainty over the extent of his power that's made of us his ignominious slaves. But now one has come who's brought us to our senses. She's shown us that we were like children hiding under the covers, afraid of the imaginary terrors of the night. She's challenged Yeshua and he's failed to meet that challenge. He's failed miserably!"

Again everyone looked at Rachel. To all appearances she remained impassive, but Wendell felt that she was not at all enjoying this.

"By the original terms of the indictment," declared Lucifer, "upon which the defense as well as the prosecution agreed, if Yeshua lost, his authority would pass to me."

Straining with zeal, his muscular frame appeared etched beneath the snowy robe. He paused, as if he were inviting the audience to give full weight to what he was about to say.

"I tell you now, I don't want his authority! It's a mantle of shreds and patches. If anyone should be your ruler, it's Rachel, for she's the best of us all! But she's opened our eyes. We don't need a ruler. Each and every one of us, if left in peace, is perfectly capable of governing himself. Indeed, that's the way God intended it from all eternity."

Despite the contradiction with what he had said just a moment ago about everyone being God, there was a piety, a solemnity, a *conviction* in Lucifer's utterance that could not be gainsaid. Wendell was beginning to wonder whether the Dark Lord had gone through a genuine change, or even been the victim of misunderstanding all along—and even more, if whether what he was saying were not absolutely on the money.

"Therefore, if the vote here today goes against Yeshua," Lucifer continued, the tone of his voice leaving no doubt that he believed it would, "then there will be no new king of heaven. No, nor queen neither, though I'd dearly love to make her such who reigns as queen over my own heart."

As he said this he walked over to Rachel, took her hand, kissed it, and raised her lovingly to her feet. "We..." he said, looking into her eyes, but then turning away as if what he saw disturbed him. "We," he repeated, this time facing the assembly, "will be your servants instead. We shall be your guardians, shielding you from the depredations of false messiahs so you may enjoy your well-deserved eternity in peace."

The general approbation at the conclusion of Lucifer's statement was only slightly marred by Rachel's evident lack of enthusiasm. When the Dark Lord released her hand, it fell limply to her side. She shuffled a few feet away and sank back down to the earth. The blank expression on her face might have been the envy of any cardsharp. Most souls, however, were ecstatic, and many rose to depart, as if the trial were decided and over and they feared to miss another moment of that pleasurable immortality promised them by Lucifer. Wendell pounded down his gavel with exceptional force. By no means were these proceedings at an end. When the clamor finally died down to a manageable ferment, he called upon the defense to present its closing argument. James looked at Yeshua doubtfully, but the latter rose and faced the assembly. His face was as sorrowful as any Wendell had ever seen.

"There was once a thief," he began, "who stole a large herd of cattle. He decided that the only way he could conceal his crime was to slaughter all the animals, salt the meat, and hide it away in his cellar. But how slaughter so large a herd without attracting undue attention? So, under cover of night, he herded the cows to a lush, well-watered pasture and kept them in a pen for a full week. Then he let the beasts out and they gorged themselves. That way, when it came time to butcher them, they were so fat and torpid that they yielded plenty of meat and made no protest, for they didn't even know what was happening to them."

Yeshua looked upon the multitude, letting them absorb his meaning.

"You don't know how far you are from yourselves!" he finally resumed. "You cower before the reality of life in the shadowland of your imagination, and you call this your eternal reward. In your fear, you feast on offal! Who among you truly feels whole? Who among you doesn't feel as if something is missing, something inestimably important, something without which your alleged 'eternal life' is utterly meaningless?"

Yeshua paused once more, as if to give everyone time to search his own heart.

"Do you really believe that I desire to be what I am? Do you honestly think that I wish to be crucified by you over and over again? For make no mistake, that's what you've done to me and that's what you will continue to do to me until you take responsibility, each and every one of you, for your own selves. I've carried you for all these ages of your sinfulness, your refusal to live in love. And no matter what is said and done here today, I'll go on carrying you unless and until that becomes impossible. I implore you, take up the precious burden of your selfhood before it's too late! Instead of nailing me once more to the cross, take up your own cross and follow where love leads. Love alone is the way. You know that in your hearts. That's the only thing any of us truly knows, and the only thing we need to know. I'm not the only one on trial here today. Indeed, I'm the only one not on trial; for my Father is the only real judge, and he knows my heart."

"Objection!" cried Lucifer. "The defendant is in blatant contempt of court!"

Wendell knew that Lucifer had a point, and that he should at least warn the defendant against making any further such comments; but he felt somehow that Yeshua was right, and truth seemed far more important now than legal technicalities.

"It's you who are in contempt!" rejoined Yeshua. "You're in contempt of the truth of your own heart."

The enmity between the Lord of Darkness and the Lord of Light caught everyone in its tentacles, and the silence of emotional paralysis fell over the assembly. In this silence, Rachel's words fell like pebbles into a pond, striking the surface with a deceptively gentle splash whose after-effects spread to every corner of the field.

"Words," she said, "only words."

Lucifer looked uncertain, as if there were no reckoning which way the cat would jump, but Yeshua smiled. "Yes, words," he agreed.

"This is a court of law," she declared. "What is wanted is evidence. Facts." Now she stood of her own accord and turned to Yeshua. "You claim that we are sick through our own devices, and that you alone have the power to heal us, if we will but let you. Where is this power?"

"In my word is power," Yeshua replied.

"Is there?" Rachel challenged. "Is there really? By all accounts, you've done a lot of talking down through the centuries, and yet everything keeps getting worse."

"You wish to know my power?" asked Yeshua. "You really wish to know it? All of you?" He turned in half-circle to face the entire assembly.

A great fear fell over the crowd, liberally sprinkled with relief that now the mystery of Yeshua's being would at last be laid bare.

"So be it!" Yeshua cried. "Father," he prayed, closing his eyes, "now reveal to them all the glory we have shared from the foundation of the world."

* * *

Now it had finally arrived, thought Uriel, as she and her fellows floated high above the judicial drama coming to a climax. Now was the long-awaited moment at which the tide would turn. The cross of sacrifice would now yield place to the crown of glory. Thus she was not at all taken aback when a brilliant light, blinding even to an angel of light, engulfed the entire pleroma, not excepting the soldiers of darkness. It was something like the flashes that had initiated the nuclear holocausts at the end of the recent earth conflict, only without the accompanying agony and death. This light was wholly spiritual; but what it betokened, and why she and her fellows had been left on the outside of the fiery sphere, she had no inkling.

Nevertheless, they all knew they were in the presence of something exceedingly holy, so no one dared even utter a word. They simply continued to hover above it all, hoping and waiting for a sign of what their Lord wanted them to do. Uriel especially felt deeply humbled. She had thought Yeshua needed her help. If he was capable of this, then of a surety everyone and everything were in his hands.

No more sun, no more moon, once again only the company of the stars of the empyrean...

* * *

Will found himself alone in a vast and arid canyon, the like of which he had never seen, not even up the Amazon with Agassiz, except in his book-inspired imagination. He was surrounded by huge stone walls with faces gutted by crevices and chimneys up which an experienced climber might just have been able to make it, but on which Will would not have stood a chance. The sun blazed hot overhead, so he stripped off his waistcoat, but this gave no relief. No beads of sweat issued from his pores to restore equilibrium. His body felt like an oven able to take in heat but not give off any in return. If this were some kind of vision or dream, it should have been Holmes', not his. Holmes was the mountain-climber. Will was exceedingly fond of hiking through the foothills, but he balked when it came to any expedition involving the use of more than his two lower limbs.

"What am I doing here?" he suddenly screamed at the impassive cliffs before realizing that he had opened his mouth. Not even the sparse and scraggly growth of sagebrush, cactus and Joshua trees swayed with any breeze. All was stillness. And then *she* came.

"Why are you ashamed of what we did together?" she asked shamelessly. "You haven't even thought of Alice for years. Isn't that why she didn't come with the rest? I wanted a philosopher, and you wanted a queen, so why are you ashamed? After all, it's not as though we actually did it in the flesh. At least, not in our own flesh."

"That doesn't matter and you know it!" Will hissed.

"You didn't think so at the time," she giggled in that girlish way of hers that now was as hateful to him as it was still irresistible. "Or is masturbation morally superior to fornication?"

"You set it all up!" he cried. "You set *me* up. When I entered the world of that painting..."

"A nude you painted of me!" she continued to giggle.

"...I had no idea that you were really there, waiting for me. It's not about my wife. How could you be unfaithful to the Lord of glory? How dare you lead me to betray him?"

She sat on the hard, sun-baked earth as if it were a featherbed, striking a tauntingly provocative pose, the same pose she held in the picture. "The Lord of glory can be a tremendous bore," she yawned. "Of course, so can philosophers. By the way, Will, what I want to know is, how were you able to give so faithful a rendering of my anatomy? The naughty professor wasn't spying on me, was he?"

Will ran toward Mara, desiring to have his way with her and then tear her apart with his bare hands. He could not get out of the canyon, so neither could she. But then everything began to slow down. As if he were the incarnation of Zeno's paradoxically stationary arrow, no matter how much effort he expended, he got no closer to the goal. She laughed uproariously, and her laughter carried with it the knowledge of how helpless and pathetic he had become. The worst of it was that he knew all this had nothing to do with the real Mara, but it all had to do with the real William James. This was what lurked behind his sensitive temperament and perceptive intellect: a parched, desolate, walled-off canyon full of insatiable lust and impotent rage.

* * *

At last the hand of God had struck down the unbelievers! Those who remained faithful to the end had been vindicated. Transformed now into a being of pure light, Muhammad stood before the throne of the Almighty. He had never dared dream that he would be like the angels! In wordless communion, God gave him a mission. The Holy One explained that there were many planets in the universe, some like earth, and the inhabitants of some of these planets had yet to receive the revelation of God. The Almighty commanded him to return to the realm of the mortals and enter into the mind of a particular man so that, through Muhammad, the Word of God might be implanted in his soul. He was to do for this man what Djbril had done for him. Truly, the ways of God were marvelous!

Muhammad was not certain of the how of it, but at last he found his way into the prophet-to-be's inner sanctum. It was dark and cramped in there, but that mattered not. The newly ordained angel would bring light into the darkness. God's will, communicated to him without words, was nonetheless clear: *Implant the Word, and only the Word. Do not be concerned with what the mortal does with the Word. That is his responsibility, and his trial.*

The task seemed simple enough, but Muhammad soon encountered unforeseen difficulties. The man's soul would not comprehend God's Word in its simplicity, so the angel had to translate it into many words, breaking it into pieces, so to speak, so the mortal, so much like a helpless infant, could be fed a bit at a time. Something is always lost in translation, of course, but worse, the man's mind was so hard and unyielding that he, willfully it seemed to Muhammad, mistook the words for the Word. This enabled the mortal to rearrange the words to suit himself and to excuse himself when he did not follow the Word. An uncontrollable rage surged up in Muhammad, and he tore himself free from the man's soul so he could confront the corrupt prophet face to face. He found himself staring angrily into his own countenance. Vertigo possessed him, and he and his double spun round and round, faster and faster, with no merciful God to save him from the most terrifying revelation of all, the revelation that now swept over him in a flurry of recollection, the truth of his own life.

* * *

Azazael knew immediately that Yeshua was up to one of his tricks. He had tried something of this sort when the angels of darkness entered into the world of men. Something had snapped then, some kind of connection that had carried with it a certain security, a serenity even. What the hell, to be fully honest with himself—and Azazael was always honest with himself, because he knew from long experience that it was the only way to be a player in this universe—the price he had paid for joining the titillating world of humanity was the loss of heavenly bliss!

That's what Yeshua had taken away. Lucifer was too enamored of himself, too proud to give the 'savior' his due, and Azazael went along with the fiction for his own reasons. But he never lied to himself. He never pretended to himself that Yeshua did not have power.

He knew something else that Lucifer would not admit, and that was that Yeshua also had scruples. He referred to those scruples as 'my heavenly Father' or 'the guidance of the Holy Spirit' or like nonsense, but he had them. So did Lucifer, for that matter, and that's what gave Azazael and the Nameless One the edge over them both. But however reluctantly, Lucifer dispensed with his scruples when they got in his way. Yeshua, on the other hand, became most moral when he was under attack. Oh, yes, Yeshua was powerful! Maybe he really was the almighty creator incarnate. One had to keep one's mind open as well as one's eyes to get by in the world. But except in mysteriously circumscribed ways and circumstances, he was unwilling to use that power. That was the key. If Azazael could stay on the tolerant side of the Nameless One until he had figured out a way to defuse that time-bomb, and if he were ruthless in the employment of his own little clout and considerable cunning, he could end up having more control over the way of things than God himself!

But now Yeshua was doing something, no doubt about that. Although he had never turned on his persecutors before, perhaps this time it had been a mistake to back him into a corner. Maybe he was sick of being the fall guy. Maybe he was tired of letting himself get dumped on. Maybe he was starting to wise up. Maybe he was becoming more like Azazael and his fallen comrades! If that were so, the short-term risks were great, but the long-term possibilities staggering! If Yeshua really had turned, then he would need crafty lieutenants like Azazael to show him the ropes, to assist him in doing what Azazael would have been doing all along had he been the lord of glory — taking advantage instead of living the life of a recluse out in the wilderness, feasting and frolicking instead of disdaining the comforts and pleasures of the heavenly city, taking a different bedmate each night rather than remaining faithful to one woman even after she had become a bore.

"You have it all figured out."

Azazael was not certain whence the voice came. He was not certain of any whence, where or wither, for he did not seem to be in any particular place. He suddenly felt a stab of fear, not so much on account of the situation, but because, until the voice spoke, he had not even noticed the situation.

"Yes, you are so honest with yourself."

Azazael felt his anxiety grow. He had no idea who or what this could be. It might be Yeshua, but the overly familiar tone, the undercurrent of sarcasm... It sounded like himself!

"Do you really want to know what you are in the larger scheme of things?"

Azazael was too terrified to answer.

"So be it!"

Whatever he'd been standing on fell away, and he found himself shrinking, his body growing hard and twisted, shrinking and sinking into a sea of mud. No, not mud. Excrement! He was drowning in a sea of shit! No, not drowning. Swimming. His changed body, something akin to a spasmodic tadpole, was actually enjoying it, even while his mind screamed out in disgust. He had the spirit of an angel, the mind of a human, and the body of a maggot. The three did not fit together at all. Each struggled to go its own way, but none was strong enough to break free.

This was what Yeshua was doing to him! So, he was not all sweetness and love, after all. Azazael remembered the old adage, that revenge was a dish best served up cold, until the agony obliterated all memory. Yeshua had turned him into an impossible abomination and was torturing him on the rack of that impossibility. Azazael screamed in hatred and pain. The more he screamed, the worse he suffered, but he could not stop himself from screaming. He would get back at Yeshua, no matter how long it took! He would never forget this. He would get back his own...

* * *

As Yeshua prayed, Wendell studied him closely, trying to understand what kind of fellow could really believe that he ruled the sun, moon and stars, as well as everyone and everything beneath them, and did so in such a way that no one noticed he was in charge!

Wendell had experienced some wonderful things in the pleroma, expanding his conception of the possible far beyond what it had been when he arrived. His sense of humility in the face of life's mysteries, never entirely lacking on earth, had here grown tremendously. Still and all, he could not even begin to believe, let alone fathom, the idea that the almighty and infinite could be bounded by the form of a man, let alone this man, who despite James' admiration gave no sign of being anything special. What the angels of light saw in him God only knew!

Then the change came. Suddenly Yeshua was everything, and Wendell and everyone around him nothing. And yet, he reasoned with himself, everything looked the same. So whence came this abrupt certainty that Yeshua had but to let his fist fall and the entire universe would be smashed like some anonymous insect? Perhaps Wendell himself had gone mad, or joined Yeshua in his madness, a hideous *folie a deux* where one pill made Yeshua larger and the other everyone smaller. *What was becoming of him, that Lewis Carroll's dreadful nonsense churned through his brain?*

This did not make sense. None of this made sense. Life was a struggle, as Darwin put it, wherein each species fought for supremacy. Enlightened self-interest was the key to human progress. Law was the standard whereby competing claims could be judged, prioritized, and wherever possible, harmonized. It was like a great big safety net upon which those engaged in the acrobatics of life relied when something went wrong. Of course, sometimes innocent people fell through the holes in the mesh, but a magistrate could not be too worried about that. The net might not be fine enough to save every individual, but kept properly mended, it was strong enough to break society's occasional fall. One charged with administering the law must needs keep focused on the broader picture.

These thoughts were interrupted by a great hubbub still off in the distance, but growing ever louder as it drew near. It was a noise so all-embracing that it seemed to displace the very atmosphere. It was a noise that seemed to be made up of all the noises Wendell had ever heard. Then the source of the noise became visible on the horizon, and it suddenly was clear to Wendell what the noise was. It was the noise of those shouldering the glorious burden of formulating and administering the law.

And then Wendell noticed that among all the bewigged and berobed lawyers, judges, and legislators were also white-coated scientists, technicians and engineers. The association of the two fellowships, that of those dedicated to the laws of society and those to the laws of nature, gratified Wendell. He had always thought of himself as an architect of the social order. He and these approaching men were all builders of the edifice of knowledge, the home of the human spirit. It was knowledge that raised man to the pinnacle of the evolutionary ladder. It was knowledge that lifted men out of the self-limiting chaos of savagery and gave birth to the orderly and eternally progressive movement of civilization.

As Wendell watched the eminent assemblage slowly draw near, he became acutely conscious of the beauty of the countryside surrounding him because, wherever the savants passed, the meadows and forests disappeared, to be replaced by city pavement, factories and skyscrapers. Wendell was not too disturbed by this transformation, however. A price had to be paid for everything worthwhile, and there was still plenty of wilderness on the horizon.

Now the factories began to pump black smoke into the atmosphere, and the pristine blue of the sky changed slowly to a hazy gray, all the more depressing for the sunshine that highlighted the dust and grime. Worse still, added to the sound of the learned ones, whose twittering talk of tortes and injunctions, research protocols and statistical parameters was beginning to grate upon Wendell's nerves, were the far more human-sounding voices of the wayward and the dispossessed, who cried out for justice and freedom, or screamed in agony, or simply whimpered in despair. Then one voice, gentle yet implacable, rose above the rest. "Judge them, Wendell. Do so fairly, but judge them."

"Fanny?" Wendell called. "Where are you, my darling?" He had never spoken so passionately to her on earth.

"Judge them, Wendell," said Fanny. "It's your job."

Wendell wanted to do as his dear wife bade him; but, looking out upon the tidal wave of human progress about to engulf him, he had no idea how. "What law can save them?" he asked before he realized what he was saying.

"The same law that saved you." And then Fanny burst into hideous laughter. "Judge them as you judge yourself, Wendell, judge them as you judge yourself, Wendell, judge them as you judge yourself, Wendell..." she said over and over again until Wendell's ears were ringing with the unfulfillable injunction. He could not judge them as he judged himself. He must judge them according to the law.

"You are the law, Wendell," Fanny was now chanting, "you are the law..."

"That's impossible!" Wendell cried. "No man can be the law, for the law rules men."

"The law rules men, Wendell, and yet men make the law. The law rules men, Wendell, and yet men make the law..."

As Fanny chanted, the network of human achievement spread like a cancerous blight until it devoured all of nature.

"Congratulations, Wendell!" cried Fanny. "Civilization has won its glorious victory! Congratulations, Wendell..." over and over and over again. The savants were almost upon him. Wendell opened his mouth, but could not hear his own scream amidst the deafening roar.

* * *

The sun fell from the sky and swallowed Running Deer up. The standing people, the two- and four-legged people, the running, flying and crawling people, along with the land, waters and heavens, all disappeared. He himself was on fire and the heat was almost unbearable, but he was not consumed. Running Deer had never experienced such powerful medicine. It could only be that of the Great Spirit.

Running Deer should not have been there on the field of judgment. Morning Star had asked him to shepherd the children and other convalescent souls away so they would be safe when the change came. But the arrival of the dark soldiers had awakened Running Dear's warrior spirit, and he could not leave Morning Star, Holy Fire and the other spirits of light to face them alone. He had given his charges into Crazy Horse's care, telling the great war chief that he needed to rest, lest he refuse to let his friend go into danger alone. And so here Running Deer was, ready to come to Morning Star's aid! The irony of it all was most humbling.

THE JUDGMENT OF CHRIST

It seemed to him that slowly he *became* the all-seeing orb of fire in the sky; and then the history of his people, that of all the aboriginal peoples, was played out before him on earth. There was much nobility and strength, but also venality and greed, even before the white man came. Running Deer had always harbored anger, he now realized, toward the red man. So many among the tribal peoples blamed the wassichu for their fall from grace, as had Running Dear himself; but only what made itself corruptible could be corrupted. Only the servile could be enslaved, only the week bribed with baubles and liquor.

Now he saw it differently. The real conflict was not the human beings against the wassichu, as the fire-breathers and renegades still cried, for truly all were children of the one Great Spirit. Nor was there no real conflict, as the "white" Indians maintained, merely the clash of cultures in which those who could not adapt to modern ways were doomed to extinction. There was a war, only it was a war of good against evil, and there were warriors of both races in either camp. And not only the young warriors, but also the old ones, the women, and the children played a part in this war. Morning Star was right—everyone had a choice, and everyone's choice counted. He was right in another way too. As far as Running Deer could tell from his own vantage point, on balance almost everyone followed the path of evil.

Then Running Deer felt himself lifted out of the sun into the coolness of the stars as if, like so many of the great among the ancient ones, he had become a constellation. The earth turned dark, very dark. It was not the restful and soothing velvet of night, however, but the ominous foreshadowing of a mighty storm.

Then above the earth, even higher than the sun, in the realm of the spirit, a little light appeared. It grew until it shone throughout the heavens, but Running Deer was amazed to see that it originated upon earth. Its source was Morning Star. And Running Deer saw that it came not so much from the way he had died, as the Black Robes taught, though that had played a part. It came from the way he had lived.

Then Running Deer saw that, both before and after Morning Star had come, there were other sources of this light, like brands from the original fire, though none so great. And these sources were not those who foretold his coming or believed in the power of his name, as so many wassichu thought. Certainly, among these were some who served the light, but many more who served darkness. The light came from those who loved their brothers and sisters, four-legged and two-legged, who respected the ways of the Earth Mother, and who followed the path illumined by the Great Spirit—the path of courage, the path of the heart. It came from those few willing to live and die for the truth that the Creator had made everything and everyone good, and we need only follow our nature to manifest that goodness.

As Running Deer watched, the light grew into a brilliant globe high above the earth. It became the spirit realm, in which every being on earth had its precise counterpart of light. So that was how it had been formed! And every good deed, every act of love and genuine courage, added to the reality and intensity of the spirit realm, so that what before had appeared to be hopeless darkness was the seedbed for the cultivation of light. And harvest had finally come! Now was the time for the reunion of heaven and earth. This was what Morning Star had meant by "the great joining."

Running Deer felt a little ashamed to find himself wondering, in the midst of such earth-shattering events, whether this great joining might not also lead to the joining of himself with Holy Fire.

* * *

Trumpeting azaleas of all hues vied with bright daffodils, romantically scented roses, obscene stargazer lilies and a host of other flowers to make of Mara's bower a fitting sanctuary for the queen of nature. All this beauty came from her, and Yeshua alone seemed unaware.

He alone was unmoved. Why didn't he love her? He claimed to love her. He made love to her as if she held something he needed badly, passionately. But when they finished and she lay curled up against him with her head on his chest, listening to the quiet rhythm of his heart, the need was still there. She could see it in his eyes, a silent reproach even if he did not intend it.

Was there something wrong with her? She was kind and considerate, always trying to say and do what was best for everyone.

Most men found her beautiful. Yet there she stood, on the emotional edge of his existence, his back, it seemed, all she would ever see of him.

"What is it you want, Mara?" came a voice that was and was not her own. The sunlight dimmed.

"I want to love everyone," she said.

"What is it you want, Mara?"

The voice was impertinent in its insistence, and the day grew ever darker.

"I want to be loved," she replied, thinking that should satisfy it. And, after all, there was nothing wicked about wanting to be loved.

"What is it you want, Mara?"

The flowers began to wither and die.

"I want my wisdom to be recognized," she answered, desperation creeping into her voice.

"What is it you want, Mara?"

The day now turned into night, only without the softening moon or starlight. Mara felt as if her insides were being squeezed out. "What is it *you* want?" she cried.

"You know what I want," the voice said implacably, "because I am you."

"You're not me!"

"I want what you want," insisted the voice. "You want what I want. What is it you want, Mara? What is it you want, Mara?"

The childish question was repeated over and over again, gradually working its way into Mara's head until she could no longer tell where it left off and her own thoughts began. This was intolerable. It could not go on. She cast about for the magical answer that would shut off the voice and leave her in peace. It wanted the truth? So be it. Let it have the truth. After all, no one would ever know but she. But what was the truth? What was it?

Then, before she even knew what she was saying, she shouted at the top of her lungs, "I want to be right, even when I'm wrong!"

Was that the truth? It could not be. She had spoken under duress. The voice had tortured her until she had told it not the truth, but what it wanted to hear.

"I too, Mara," said the voice in deadly gentleness. "I too wish to be right even when I'm wrong." Then it fell silent, and she lay utterly alone in the blackness.

* * *

Saul, Saul, why do you persecute me?
The question from long ago echoed in his heart. What Paul was experiencing now was very much like what had befallen him then as he rode to Syria to arrest leaders of the sect that believed Yeshua of Nazareth to be the messiah—a man whom the Romans had put to death for sedition, and who had held himself and his followers above the observance of the Torah! Now Paul worshipped this same Yeshua as the incarnation of the living God, a concept he could not even have begun to comprehend during his earthly sojourn.

Now a new orthodoxy, an orthodoxy in large part of Paul's own implementation, if not invention, was being overthrown, and the light that blinded him seared his soul in a way that one on the Damascene highway had not. Either Yeshua was a cruel and ungrateful taskmaster, or Paul had failed his Lord miserably. Or perhaps this Yeshua was an impostor, an angel of darkness masquerading as an angel of light!

A house divided against itself cannot stand.

Yes, Yeshua was as infuriating to Satan as he was to Paul. Perhaps, however, this was not the real Satan. Perhaps, as Muhammad had suggested, this "heavenly realm" was all shadows and delusion, a test to see if the faithful would remain so in the face of no matter what evidence contradicted their faith. Why couldn't he take that way out? Why couldn't he shut his eyes to everything that was going on around him until it all conformed to his expectations?

Because shutting his eyes did not shut down his soul. He still heard the voice saying, "Saul, Saul, why do you persecute me?" And it could not be gainsaid.

"There is another possibility," announced the invisible Lord, his voice no longer the echo of memory. "Love."

And then, in an immense vista, Paul saw a living map of the Greco-Roman world of his time on earth. It was a world he had loved for its order, its reliance upon law, and yes, for its bustle, color and cosmopolitanism, even as he had denounced it for its lewdness, brutality and corruption. Above all, he had loved it for the breadth and depth of its thought. Many a young Jew had been seduced by that thought, but Paul had joined those rabbis who employed the brilliant stratagem of using it in the service of their tradition. Greek thought, and even more the Greek method of thought, with its thorough and systematic cultivation of logic and clarity, was the very archetype of reason. When followed through to the end, reason did not contradict faith, but buttressed it, even as faith illumined reason. Then along came Yeshua of Nazareth, the dead and risen messiah, striking Paul blind on the road to Damascus, and by doing so giving him true sight. Or so Paul had thought...

"You look and look, but do not see," said the voice of Yeshua. "You listen and listen, but do not hear. You think and think, but do not understand."

It was true, thought Paul. The idea that Yeshua was a sacrifice for sin, the reality to which the grain and blood offerings demanded by the Law had merely pointed, had seemed to cause every bit of the theological puzzle to fall into place. Yet at this ungodly trial in what all had thought to be God's kingdom, Yeshua had condemned this idea as an utter perversion of what he was about. Perhaps truth was no puzzle.

"You were the best and worst of your time, Paul," said Yeshua, "the best and the worst. There is nothing hidden in the darkness that will not be brought to light."

These words, spoken gently, measuredly, nevertheless struck Paul like so many iron fists. It was true of him. It was true of his people. God wanted to make connection with the whole of the human spirit, the shadow as well as the light. That's why Yeshua had come to him. That's why Yeshua had been born a Jew. That's why the Jews had rejected him. That's why Paul had sought to stamp out his following. That's why, becoming one of his apostles, Paul had warped the truth of Yeshua's being. Paul's mind went nearly blank. It was too much for mortal man to bear.

"Throw away your burden," said Yeshua.

Was it time, really? Did he no longer have to be the saint? Could he stop betraying Yeshua in his own name? Could he simply be himself? And likewise his people: could they cease being the chosen ones, chosen to wrestle for the truth, to strive with themselves and

God, to be God's scapegoats, God's whipping boys? "How long, Lord?" he prayed from the depths of his quivering and uncertain heart. "How long?" And then, as he gave up trying to understand, an inexplicable peace settled over his soul.

* * *

In a dream-like nowhere, without knowing the why or wherefore, Lucifer found himself experiencing the inner life of a human being.

It started in the mortal's boyhood. He was a lad with a profound love of good and hatred of evil, a sharp sense of justice, and a temperament attuned to the challenge of the adventurous and heroic. He nourished himself on romantic tales of great men and their marvelous deeds, as well as art and music that celebrated the grandeur and glory of struggle and self-sacrifice for his people. Most of all, he loved architecture, with its embodiment in brick and stone of the highest, noblest and grandest aspirations of the human spirit.

Then war came. The young man's soul leapt at the opportunity to live all the high ideals of which he had hitherto only dreamed. Dwelling with death every day, one developed a certain contempt for the powers of darkness, but also a certain respect. Add to the exhilaration of finally coming to grips with reality the camaraderie of battle, the tedious hazard of the trenches, and the joy of serving his people and, if need be, shedding his blood to protect the soil that had nurtured him, and no finer education could be had, no, not at the best universities in the world! He could rise to officer's rank, he had no doubt of that, but he was prepared to refuse promotion should it be offered. He could not willingly lose the world of the front lines, the world that was making him a man.

When it all ended, and ended in an ignominious, politically engineered defeat, his soul wandered aimlessly for a time, as did that of his people. Slowly, ever so slowly, but also ever so surely, the purpose of his life dawned upon him. In his own being he had suffered the dishonor of his people so that he could redeem their dishonor. He saw clearly their weakness and how they could be made strong again. More importantly, he came to know who the real enemy was and how to overcome him. Divine providence had chosen and prepared him to save the fatherland—indeed, to save the only truly human race. If he entrusted himself to it, nothing could come between him and his destiny.

And so he did. He sacrificed the personal joys and pleasures of the life of a creative artist in order to answer the call and accomplish the world-historical task of leading his people through their direst hour. He preached to them the necessity of doing as he had done, of suspending the pursuit of their petty personal interests at the time of national crisis in order to reclaim their rightful place in the world and fulfill their destiny.

For a time it looked as if he and his cause could not but triumph, but unfortunately the process of corruption had already gone too far. The people, without whose unflinching courage and unwavering devotion his task could not be accomplished, were too far gone. They were not mongrelized in the flesh, like so many other nations, but they had become mongrelized in spirit. The would-be masters of the new world order had become slaves to their own fear. They were not willing to go all the way, to make the ultimate sacrifice, to embrace their own annihilation for the sake of the cause, and so they were not worthy to witness the ultimate miracle and receive the ultimate reward. Now, as he had done in so many ways before, he was about to make that sacrifice for them, to plant the seed of martyrdom, to shine the light of truth into their weak and besotted souls. He would show those who had eyes to see that righteousness would always win out over the craft, greed and effeminacy of its enemies, that resurrection came only through crucifixion.

Lucifer no longer thought of himself as in the man's soul. He was the man's soul. His own nobility of spirit breathed in this man. He and Lucifer were one.

As he acknowledged his identity with the mortal, Lucifer felt himself slipping into his body, so that now he could see with his eyes, hear with his ears, touch and smell as he did. Lucifer found himself with a pistol in his hand, and he was bringing it up to his mouth. He stood before a cracked looking glass in a dark, apparently subterranean room with concrete walls, a bed that was little more than a cot, and a desk with a black, shiny telephone whose wire had been torn out of the wall. There was a hideous fluorescent light overhead with a gray metal housing, but it did little to relieve the darkness. Nevertheless, in the split-second before pulling the trigger,

Lucifer caught a glimpse of his face in the mirror. The sunken, pale blue eyes smoldered with a dying fire, as if they had been narcotized. The trim, dark, postage-stamp mustache did little to hide the lines around the pouting lips etched by the suffering of the soul. Unhealthy pallor and puffiness of the skin grotesquely heightened the appearance of inordinate strain. Upon seeing the face, Lucifer of course immediately knew who it was, who *he himself* was. When the gun exploded and everything was swallowed up in blackness, he did not scream, he did not cry out against an unjust universe. Instead, he calmly considered the implications of the revelation he had just been vouchsafed, and he did not find them as intolerable as one might have expected. In fact, he did not find them intolerable at all. He understood now that he had been too soft with his enemies, too soft with himself. He had placed scruples in the way of achieving his goal because he had not fully appreciated the absolute nobility of that goal. It was a most salutary lesson. If Yeshua had engineered this awakening, he would have Lucifer's eternal gratitude—*in memoriam*, of course, because the Nazarene had now revealed to the Lord of Darkness how the self-styled Lord of Light was to be destroyed.

* * *

A flash, as of lightning. An overarching canopy of light within another canopy of light. Everything the same, and yet not the same. Yeshua was standing where he had been standing. Rachel was standing where she had been standing. Everyone was where they had been the moment before, only all were now in shadow save he and she. His eyes looked fiercely, and yet not without compassion, down into her soul. How soft his hair and skin seemed, glowing in the preternatural light. She had never really noticed how strange it was, how he could be not at all handsome and yet extraordinarily beautiful. What held her to him was so light, so airy, having no more substance than gossamer; and yet, for all that, it seemed she could never break his hold upon her heart. "What spell are you casting now, Yeshua?" she queried with what, under the circumstances, was remarkable calm.

His eyes twinkled with boyish mischief. "You asked for proof," he said, "so I'm giving you a demonstration."

"And what are you demonstrating?"

"My power," he replied. "They're facing the truth of themselves."

"I'm the one who demanded proof," she challenged. "Why am I not being shown the truth of myself?"

His eyes went serious and he took a few steps forward, as if he were solicitous of her health. "You already know the truth of yourself. Now you must decide what that truth is."

"Decide?" she echoed.

"Yes, of course," he said in that infuriating tone that made one feel stupid for not understanding what to him was as obvious as two-plus-two. "The truth of oneself is that one decides the truth of oneself."

"So," said Rachel with a hint of scorn that promised more to come, "a saint decides to be a saint, a thief decides to be a thief, a murderer decides to be a murderer? It's all that simple?"

"In essence, yes," he replied, failing to hear or choosing to ignore the undercurrent of sarcasm in her voice. The angels had disappeared. A blanket of shadow covered the assembly. The atmosphere was still. Everything was suspended, like a cinematic film frozen in mid-action. They were alone.

"There are no environmental and hereditary factors," she said, her sarcasm deepening, "no psychological mechanisms impinging on this choice? Nothing to impede the exercise of free will?"

"No man can serve two masters," he declared firmly. "One is governed by the situation, or one is ruled by the heart."

"So we choose between two forms of slavery," she remarked, and then turned away so abruptly that she could feel him wince. "I've thought about your concept of love," she said with studied indifference, not toward the topic but him. "Quite a bit, actually. I think I know what you mean by the voice of the heart, but I wonder why you think obeying it is the only sanity. It seems to me that to follow only one of the many voices of which you spoke would be madness. One would be losing all the rest, in effect dismembering oneself. And didn't you advocate just such a course in one of your gospels? 'If thine eye offend thee, pluck it out. If thy hand offend thee, cut it off.' It sounds crazy to me!"

Yeshua became still, only his eyes displaying the life in him. "I said something that could be interpreted that way," he replied quietly.

"I think it would be much healthier to listen to all the voices, and then to integrate them in one's own unique, individual way."

There! She had finally overcome his intimidation and spoken her mind. And she had said something from which he could profit as well. She had pointed out the flaw in his logic. How could he not see it? Now she would see if he had courage enough to admit that he had been wrong.

"And the Nazis," he said, "when they slaughtered our people, along with the Slav and Polish intelligentsia, the Gypsies and the crippled, the defiant and the weak—weren't they integrating their voices in their own unique and individual way?"

"No!" she shot back. "They were repressing some of those voices, which is why the others became so destructive. They were doing what you're telling everyone to do. After all, they were Christian!"

Yeshua sank to the ground as if in defeat, and said, as much to himself as to her, "There's something you're missing. There's something everyone is missing." He sounded like he was about to weep. "And I'd hoped that you, of all people, would understand. I'm alone. Completely and utterly alone. I was a fool to think it could ever be otherwise."

His melodramatic self-pity set her anger aflame. "If you're alone, it's your own fault! You set yourself apart. I know you don't think yourself better than everybody else, but you won't accept the world as it is and people as they are. You talk about love; but if you don't love people as they are, you don't really love them. You live in a universe spun out of your imagination, and you hate the real world for not matching up to your fantasy."

He sat motionless, though she could feel every word cut through him like a knife. But so it had to be. It was a surgeon's knife, and only extreme measures could save him.

"It's you who live in your imagination," he said at length, almost in a whisper. She had not thought he could be so childish, as if she had called him a name and he, unable to think of a clever rejoinder, had fallen back on "I know you are but what am I!"

"I don't understand," she said gently enough, not wishing to provoke further argument.

"Have you ever seen a baby?" he asked, one of those rhetorical questions of his to which he actually expected a response. She nodded, remembering to what good effect he had used this example yesterday to illustrate the meaning of love. "A baby throws itself headlong into life. When she tries to walk, she doesn't wait around to make sure mommy or daddy is there to catch her. If she falls, she picks herself up right away and tries again. When she's learning to talk, she doesn't care if she sounds ridiculous and everyone laughs. She's determined to overcome all obstacles and become what she is meant to be, what she actually is in embryo." Again Rachel nodded, only this time more thoughtfully. "And adults?" he added, rising to his feet as if the force of the question propelled him.

"They're cowards." Now it was her turn to whisper. "I've sometimes thought that if babies learned the way adults learn, the human race wouldn't be able to walk or talk. And if adults learned the way infants learn, we'd all be geniuses."

"What happens?" demanded Yeshua, who without her knowing how was suddenly so close she could have reached out and slapped him, spat on him, embraced him, kissed him.

"I don't know." She sought to avoid his eyes, but no matter where she turned they were there, boring into her like heated drills. "Nobody knows. All we know is that it happens."

"We know what happens," he insisted mercilessly. "Everybody knows what happens. The choice happens."

"But a choice doesn't just happen," she objected. "Somebody makes it."

He smiled. She had finally gotten the point.

"But if we all make this choice," she continued, "if sooner or later we all succumb to fear—and mostly·sooner, from what I've seen—how can it really be a choice?"

His smile twisted into an expression of pure sarcasm. "The oldest excuse in the world," he mocked. "The ultimate excuse. If everyone does it, then it can't be evil. If everyone does it, then we can't help ourselves. It must just be human nature!"

She stepped back and again turned away, though not entirely. She could not withstand his intensity, but she also could not break off in mid-argument. Something important was being said here, and even though she feared it, she could not just leave it alone. She had to take it in and wrestle with it. That seemed more important to her now than which side lost or won.

"I don't do it," he added.

She could only look at him. She could not speak.

"If one man doesn't do it, all are able not to do it. That's my judgment of the world."

"But you're God!" she rejoined, her turn once again to be sarcastic.

"Do you think that makes it easier for me?" he cried, ignoring the mockery in her voice. "To be both God and man is to be at the fiery center of it all—the temptation, the fear, the pain..." His words trailed off into a muffled sob.

"Another thing I don't understand is your constant self-pity," she said, doubtless shocking him as she shocked herself by the contrast between his high dudgeon and the almost clinical objectivity she now adopted in self-defense. "You're always talking about your suffering. I thought love wasn't concerned about its own pain."

He did not move or back away, but she could feel her words stab right through to his heart. "I only speak of my suffering to those who I think care," he said.

"That's not true!" she declared, ignoring the barb. "You spoke of your suffering before the entire assembly!"

"I spoke of the suffering of love," he said with a quiet dignity she was not sure he had earned.

"You claim to be love."

He bowed his head. "If I am love, and if I suffer at the hands of men, then my suffering is also a judgment on the world."

She pondered. "There it is again: you versus the world, imagination versus reality."

"You're the ones who live in fantasy," he asserted.

"Yes, you said that before," she sighed, "but you've yet to explain how."

He took a deep breath, squatted back on his haunches, and unexpectedly smiled. "I've not been given the chance," he chided in sudden good-humor. "When one abandons courage and enters into the service of fear, one removes oneself from the reality of life. One removes existence from reality. Everything becomes an unreal nightmare."

"But it's all too real!" she cried.

"That's what makes it so terrible," he nodded.

"Rabbi Aeschermann said something like that," she murmured. "When one serves fear, one is no longer emotionally present in the here-and-now, and one endlessly, fruitlessly, destructively seeks a substitute for the life one has thrown away. You blame God. How about blaming yourself?"

"God is all-powerful! How could he not be to blame?"

"Yes, God is all-powerful. He can destroy the human race the way a father can crush the life out of his children. But if he follows his heart and gives himself to his children, gives them every opportunity to find happiness and joy, creativity and love, and they reject their opportunity, is he all-powerful then?"

"Is it really we who are to blame, then?" she cried. "Were there no victims at Auschwitz?"

"There were victims," answered Yeshua, the look on his face containing all the torment those victims had suffered. "I'm trying to get you to see why there were victims, and how to prevent there being more."

"What do you mean?" she asked.

"Love takes the risk of giving life. Each and every one of us has the choice to receive or reject this gift, but none of us stands apart. We're all in this together. Only by living in love can we receive the gift of life. The way of the cross is the only way to life."

"The way of the cross?" she echoed, uneasy with this Christian imagery.

"The acceptance of the here-and-now. Not hiding from the reality life brings. That's what people do. They hide. You can see it in their eyes. They are never *here*, never *now*. They're always where they have to be next, or where they'd rather be, or floating nowhere at all, but never here, never now."

"That's only true when people are engaged in unpleasant tasks," she objected, "not when they're having fun."

"Is it?" he challenged. "Is it really? Then why does having fun so often reduce itself to drinking oneself senseless? And why does one always have to *go somewhere* and *do something* to have fun? And why, as soon as one seizes what one desires, does one always have to go on to the next desire? Why is life itself never enough?"

Again Rachel pondered. "What about making love?" she finally asked. "When two people are making love, they're present to the reality of the moment."

"Are they?" he once more challenged. "Think back to your own sexual adventures."

Rachel felt herself blushing. When she had gone away to university on her own, she had been intoxicated by the freedom and had numerous liaisons and affairs. She knew, without understanding how, that he knew.

"In how many of them did you feel in touch with a real human being? In how many of them was your paramour anything more than a figment of your imagination, a fantasy that faded with the night?"

She bowed her head. She had no defense. "But that's just the way it is," she whispered intently, as if to convince herself. "We're all alone in this world, all just ourselves. We latch on to others for our own pleasure. What's wrong with that?"

"It's not love," he replied.

"Why isn't it?" she cried fiercely. "You hold up infants as your model of love. That's what they do! What else is there?"

"As every mother knows," he said softly, "in real love there is no difference between giving and receiving. It's all one. The infant gives by receiving, the mother receives by giving. One gives oneself to the beloved and becomes a self in return. That's what it is to love."

"What if the beloved is hateful and ugly?" she asked through unaccountable tears, and then realized she was speaking of herself.

He took her gently in his arms. "Love embraces the beloved completely, with all her faults and wickedness. Love does not ignore the wickedness. Love suffers all in the beloved that is not of love, embraces it and suffers it acutely. In doing so, love gives the beloved the opportunity to be transformed into love."

"So that she may become what she was meant to be?" Rachel sobbed, nestling her head upon his shoulder. "So she may become her true self?"

He did not answer. He only held her while her body shivered out all the guilt, fear, anger and pain pent up in her soul. She closed her eyes for what she wished could have been an eternity. When she opened them again, the shadows had been dispelled. They were no longer alone.

* * *

It was like waking from a dream, though there was no doubt in Will's mind that the dream had been more real. It was like awakening from a nightmare only to find oneself in a more terrible nightmare. All was heavy, heavier than anything that had ever weighed upon him before, even on earth. If this were what the sacred marriage of heaven and earth was all about, Will wanted an immediate divorce.

He was back in the field of judgment, only no longer did it feel like the pleroma. It was as physical as anything he could remember on earth. The sun was oppressive, the air humid and stifling. The chiaroscuro sky brooded with just the hint of an incipient tempest. The seats were gone, as was the judicial edifice formerly at the center, except for the judge's bench, which now in its solitude looked eerily like a scaffold. Most telling of all, he could feel ants crawling over him as he sprawled on the damp and fetid grass. As he rose to his feet, he brushed himself off and looked around to see if anyone else seemed as dazed as he.

They all did. Everyone, as far as memory served, was in the same location as before the dream, but everyone looked different. As far as he could make out facial expressions, which was nowhere nearly as far as before, most in the assembly were sullen and uneasy, many angry, and not a few in tears. Will could only assume that each had gone through an experience like his own.

Then he turned away from the crowd and studied Holmes, who still sat perched upon his bench like a stranded seagull. His friend looked old and woebegone, older than he had ever looked before, as if he had aged beyond the natural limit allotted to man. He sat staring, a pained expression signifying that his mind was yet occupied with the memory of an experience so engrossing in its horror that it could not be easily released.

Will once again surveyed the field. Despite the clouds the sun shone hot and brightly, the air stank with the odor of fear-induced sweat, and flies buzzed merrily as they whisked from body to body, mindlessly administering their innocuous yet maddening torture. *So this is what a battlefield feels like when the fighting is over.* The only real life on the field emanated from Yeshua and Rachel, whose previous confrontation had melted into a tender and sweet embrace. *Where do we go from here?*

Will began to wander aimlessly about, not caring anymore about the trial, certain that everyone was as disoriented as he. No, disorientation implied that eventually one would regain one's bearings. Will had lost his bearings, as far as he knew, for good. And so, he guessed, had everyone else but the loving couple in their midst, and they seemed interested only in each other. Will should have known that there were but two among them who would not be daunted by any nightmare, no matter how gut-wrenching.

"Rachel!" cried Lucifer all of a sudden, his voice cracking the somber atmosphere like a rifle-shot. Rachel did not let Yeshua go, but her body stiffened. Lucifer signaled one of his black-clad officers on the periphery of the field, and the man led forward an infantry squad heavily armed with what looked to be the latest in machine weapons. No one got in the way. The soldiers surrounded the lovers, and at a nod from Lucifer dragged them apart. As Will might have predicted, Holmes now gave a rap of his gavel. For some reason, however, the sound was not nearly so intimidating as it had been before the dream, and Holmes' voice not nearly so impressive.

"Lucifer," cried the woebegone judge unsteadily, "this is most irregular. You led us all to believe that this trial would be a genuine quest for justice, not a theater-piece masking tyranny."

Looking uncomfortably incongruous in his white but disheveled and grass-stained robe, Lucifer turned to Holmes and tried to stare him down. Surprisingly, under the circumstances, he was unable to do so. "He opened the door, Your Honor," he answered at length in a sarcastic, nay imperious tone. "He's given us a demonstration of his power. Now I'm going to reveal a bit of mine."

At another signal from their Dark Lord, the troops divided into two contingents. The far larger of the two sections remained on the perimeter, but with weapons now at the ready and trained upon the assembly. The mechanical manner in which they shifted formation and the expressionless glaze in their eyes left no doubt that, if ordered, they would pull their triggers with as little compunction as that with which Will had swept the ants away from his limbs a few moments before. The smaller contingent marched from every side into the center, ringing the judge's bench. Two pointed their weapons at Holmes, the rest out at the crowd.

Suddenly, from the far end of the field, there came the staccato explosions of rapid gunfire, punctuated by unmistakable cries of pain and death. Will, like everyone else, was too terrified to move. One of Lucifer's lieutenants barked some, to Will, unintelligible orders, and a dozen of the black guards, as Holmes had dubbed them, appeared shouldering the bodies of three of Muhammad's warriors, which they flung before the judge's bench where everyone could see them. It seemed to Will that all that the "great joining" of heaven and earth meant thus far was that death had come to the pleroma.

"This regrettable use of force need not have been necessary," declared Lucifer, his manner strong and confident, his voice commanding and sure. "There's no need for us to fight among ourselves. I'm not responsible for the hell you're going through. *He* is. We're brethren, you and I—all of us, except for the one who's made himself our enemy. But he's shot his bolt. The evil one has thrown the very worst he has at us, and now he's at our mercy. The only question left for us is, what are we to do with him?"

The import of what Lucifer was saying took several moments to sink into the dazed crowd, but when it did its effect was telling. Their fear gave way to overwhelming rage, and Will had to admit to himself that he felt a great deal of sympathy with them. He himself had no doubt that Yeshua was responsible for the dream. Thus far he had avoided anger by not thinking about it. Now Lucifer was making that impossible. All exits were blocked, and he had to ask himself whether Yeshua had finally gone beyond the point at which Will could ever forgive him.

Still too confused to act upon their resentment, the members of the assembly began to mill about, drawing strength and resolution from discussing their experiences with one another, mixing without regard for cultural or religious affiliation, slowly but surely finding a malefactor upon whom to fix the blame, gradually cohering into a mob. Mindless bestiality, it seemed, was going to be the order of the day, and Yeshua its victim. *Victim? Doesn't he deserve it?*

In his imagination, Will suddenly beheld Yeshua writhing on the cross. *No, he's innocent! I know it in my heart!* Will instinctively hurried around to where Paul had been sitting. For all his shortcomings, Will told himself ruefully, Paul was not a coward like himself. If he were on Yeshua's side, he would do something.

It seemed, however, that Paul had not yet returned from the dream. He was lying unconscious upon a cloak, surrounded by a handful of anxiously attentive disciples. Then Will realized something else. Everyone who had arrived at the time of the great reunion, not excluding Running Deer, also had not returned. Only, they were not comatose like Paul. They simply were not there anymore. They had disappeared who knew how long ago. Will wondered if they had been real to begin with. He wondered if any of this were real. Indeed, he wondered if there were such a thing as reality.

As if in oblique answer to Will's silent skepticism, Lucifer now struck his breast with his fist and cried theatrically, "We are here at last! We've cornered the great pretender, and he can no longer escape our justice."

Holmes again rapped his gavel, but this time the gesture betokened nothing so much as futility. "The prosecution is usurping the prerogatives not only of the magistrate, but the jury as well," he declared gallantly, not to say quixotically. "Lucifer, you're to call off your bloodhounds immediately or I will hold you in contempt of court!"

Lucifer glared at Holmes. As if reading their master's mind, two of the black guards seized the hapless jurist and dragged him away, no doubt to be bound and gagged, if not liquidated. Will knew he should do something, but he was petrified. Lucifer rotated in place like some pale orb, as if daring anyone else to defy him. Muhammad rose and faced him, not a trace of fear in the prophet's demeanor or voice. "Satan," he challenged, "plead me cause why I should not order my fellow servants of God to cut your and your henchmen's throats!"

Lucifer stopped turning and smiled at Muhammad. "I'm not your foe," he reiterated, his voice equal parts threat and promise. "If you wish to bring death upon your people, do as you say. But it would be a pitiable waste, for there's no good reason why we should be enemies, and every reason for us to be friends."

Muhammad said nothing, but his stony scowl made it clear that peaceful coexistence was the best for which Lucifer could hope.

"Can you say with certainty," Lucifer asked, "that this pretender is the same Issa you Muslims revere as one of the holy messengers of God?"

Muhammad obviously did not want to answer, but also obviously realized that this was the moment of truth. He shook his head.

"What if I were to show you an infallible test whereby you could be certain?"

A flicker of curiosity lighted in Muhammad's dark and somber eyes. He nodded slowly, meaningfully.

"And you Christians!" cried Lucifer, turning dramatically and sweeping his arm to embrace the assembly. "Are you sure this man is the savior whom you worship?"

The response was ambivalent silence.

"Then you too need a test."

"What do you propose?" queried Muhammad, once more finding his voice. In reply, Lucifer continued to address the crowd.

"You Christians believe, do you not, that Christ died on the cross once and for all to atone for the sins of all mankind?"

There sounded numerous cries from every quarter indicating assent.

"And you Muslims believe that God would never dishonor himself by allowing one of his messengers to die so shameful and miserable a death?"

A more concerted response on the part of the Muslims also gave voice in the affirmative.

"As for the rest of you, if this man is unmasked for the impostor he is, will he be of any more concern to you?"

This last question was met by an indifferent silence that everyone knew signified assent.

"Then to those with a stake in the matter, I say there is but one way to find out if this Yeshua before us today is a fraud. We will crucify him!"

Chapter 11

As Lucifer had expected, this pronouncement stunned the entire assembly. Perspiration from the anxiety inevitably accompanying such a bold gamble dampened the underarms of his robe. It was a strange, discomfiting, yet exhilarating feeling, and he wanted to spend time in the relish of it; but he knew he had to move quickly and take advantage of the element of surprise. Just then, however, for some unaccountable reason, the lawyer Ernst caught his eye. The mouthpiece smiled conspiratorially, indicating to Lucifer that he was on his side, but then shook his urbane head knowingly, indicating that Lucifer's present course of action was, in his humble opinion, most unwise.

The Light-Bearer did not like the idea of taking advice from lawyers, especially those who represented big business. Such whores were not to be trusted. But he felt in his bones that it would be a mistake not to find out what the man had on his mind. For the time being, at least, he needed allies, especially against the Nameless One. The capitalists had no love for the Nameless One.

Lucifer beckoned the lawyer to come forward and the guards let him through. He came right up to Lucifer's face and then whispered in his ear, "We need to talk. Privately." Evidently the man thought of himself as Lucifer's peer. So much the better. Lawyers were habitual liars, except when strutting before members of their own club. He would then give of his wisdom openly and frankly, and Lucifer had had his fill of fawning, treacherous sycophants. "We'll retire to my chambers," said Lucifer. "Azazael!" he called.

The traitor appeared as if out of nowhere, so zealous he wished to seem in serving his master. Not for him, the Light-Bearer noted, either Lucifer's white robe or a uniform of black. He had decked himself out in a scarlet velvet tunic that clashed hideously with the somber mood of the day.

"You'll take charge while I speak with this man," Lucifer ordered.

"Ernst," said the lawyer self-deprecatingly, as if the dread Lord of Darkness could not be expected to remember the name of so petty a functionary. Yet there was also an overweening pride in this reminder, as if what lords and potentates forgot posterity would be certain to remember. Lucifer was beginning to believe that "Ernst" was the man's real name.

Azazael's sharp features, usually so mobile, stiffened at the command. Doubtless he wondered how Lucifer could be so stupid as still to trust him. No, that could not be it, the clever dog was not given to so grossly underestimating his opponents. He was afraid of what trick Lucifer might have up his sleeve. It should not have been so hard to see. Azazael in command was not free to make mischief behind the scenes. He could do little but maintain the status quo until his master returned.

Lucifer began to make the gesture that, in ordinary times, would have taken him and his guest to the palace in a heartbeat. Then he stopped himself. These, he reflected, were no ordinary times. What if such magic no longer worked? Rather than risk making a fool of himself at such a crucial juncture, Lucifer summoned a staff car, signaled Ernst to have a seat, and then climbed in after him.

The smooth feel of the leather upholstery, the smell of engine oil and exhaust, and the nonchalant competence with which the chauffeur drove at breakneck speed renewed Lucifer's sense of assurance, as if the efficiency with which his commands were being executed were an infallible token of their rightness. Paradoxically, this increased confidence caused him to feel both greater irritation and greater tolerance toward the lawyer. His implicit claim to equality now seemed so utterly absurd that Lucifer could only humor him the way an adult might humor a spoiled yet delicate child.

When they reached the palace, which was as shining and opulent as ever, Lucifer marched straight into his study, with Ernst stepping quickly but diffidently behind him. The Light-Bearer decided to risk the experiment of pouring the lawyer and himself drinks. As he swallowed, the burgundy brew sent waves of relaxation from the center of his brain to every tense and anxious corner of his body. The spirits had regained their potency. This was undoubtedly a good omen. Everything was going his way.

Lucifer would have figured Ernst to be the cultured esthete who sipped effeminately while engaging in tortuously witty conversation. But the man downed his liquor in one gulp, rose from the divan upon which Lucifer had seated him, and confronted the Light-Bearer with a quizzical expression. "I wonder if you know what power is," he said.

Lucifer blinked. "I don't understand," was all he could think to say.

"You want power," Ernst reiterated, " but I wonder if you really know what it is, where it comes from, how to keep it. You certainly know how to lose it."

Lucifer resisted the impulse to reach out and slap the insect.

"How do you think Yeshua got his power?" the lawyer queried.

Again, Lucifer could think of no good answer, so he held his peace.

"He made a martyr of himself," replied Ernst to his own question.

So that the upstart could not take the liberty of sharing the couch with him, Lucifer sat down at its very center, steepled his fingers and said, "So, to match Yeshua, you think I should become a martyr too. Fight holy fire with holy fire, eh?"

Ernst backed away so he could more easily look Lucifer in the eye. "No, you're not after that kind of power," he answered. "Besides, no one can out-martyr Yeshua."

"If I can't beat Yeshua at his own game," said Lucifer, "what are you proposing?"

Lucifer tested the gesture of materialization as if he were randomly waving his arm and, lo and behold, it worked! A chair appeared, and Ernst sat down as if there had been one there all along.

"That you not play his game at all," he said.

Lucifer stood up and paced about the room. Then he turned toward Ernst. "You mean that I should leave that arch-troublemaker to his own devices?"

"That's preferable to releasing his spirit once more into the world, where it will make mischief for the likes of you and me."

Lucifer sat down again and gave out a hearty laugh. "I never expected you to believe in such pious mumbo-jumbo."

"It's not mumbo-jumbo!" retorted Ernst with surprising passion. "Look at what happened last time around. There are over a billion Christians in the world today!"

Lucifer laughed again. "Here I must agree with Yeshua," he said. "Do these 'Christians' have anything in common with Christ?"

"Some do," replied Ernst. "But you're right. Those elect few, while bothersome at times, are not the problem. They're a tiny minority, and in all likelihood will remain so. It's the rest I'm worried about."

"The rest?" scoffed Lucifer, again rising to his feet. He could not seem to get comfortable in this man's presence. "Why, they're little more than sheep!"

Ernst took a silver case from the left inner pocket of his frock-coat, carefully selected a brown cigarette that to all appearances was identical with its fellows, lit it with a silver lighter from his right outer pocket, and began puffing away the way European intellectuals puffed, holding the cigarette with palm upward. Lucifer snatched the malodorous tube out of his hand and crushed it beneath his foot. The lawyer shrugged.

"That's what worries me," he said. "The Greco-Roman world was a going concern, a glorious civilization with a firm economic foundation. In following their Christian shepherds, those sheep trampled it underfoot. It's taken us fifteen hundred years to get through the ensuing dark ages, but we've made a virtue out of necessity and now have something of even greater worth. However, if the sheep are awakened..."

"But they're nobodies!" broke in Lucifer.

"Of course individually they count for nothing," said Ernst. "But with the inspiration of Yeshua's spirit, all those zeros will add up to a force that will plunge civilization into a night darker than any it has ever known and from which it may never emerge."

Lucifer turned his back and took a few steps away. The torches sent forth an acrid smoke, something they had never done before. He thought of summoning an attendant to open the windows, but they had never been opened before, there had never been a need, and he feared they would not open now. Besides, the smoke must also have been making the lawyer uncomfortable, and that was all to the good. Damn him! Everything had been settled nicely, and once again it was all up in the air. "Your version of history is simplistic," said Lucifer. "Christianity was not originally a mass movement. It conquered the Roman Empire from the top down."

"Of course it wasn't *originally* a mass movement," rejoined Ernst, a hint of mockery and more than a hint of impatience in his voice. "Nothing ever is. But once the masses bought into it, it sanctioned their most ignorant superstitions and fears. And in return, its leaders got the backing of the masses in suppressing all progressive thought. It's taken nearly two millennia to render the Nazarene innocuous. If you crucify him again, the damage may be beyond repair!"

Lucifer turned back toward the lawyer. The man was so intent upon his mission that his body sat utterly immobile. All his energy was concentrated in his voice and eyes. "I took that into account," said the Light-Bearer unconvincingly, even to himself.

"You mean your little theological stratagem?" returned Ernst. "Have you no idea what's really going on here?"

"Why don't you enlighten me?" said Lucifer icily. "But I warn you, if you prove a false prophet, I might find another cross for you."

The lawyer grimaced and little pearls of sweat appeared on his brow. "It would be ludicrous, not to mention in bad taste, to make a martyr out of me," he said with a nervous chuckle.

Lucifer sat back down on the divan and relaxed. The man was afraid. He had not lost his touch. "I'm willing to risk it," he remarked. "Now, what do you have to say to me?"

There followed a moment of prolonged silence during which Ernst apparently marshaled his thoughts. The smoke from the torches made the atmosphere unbearable. On impulse, Lucifer strode to one of the tinted windows he had so cherished before the change, but now was keeping the sulfurous fumes in and the clean air out, and smashed at it with his fist. The pane shattered before his hand even touched it.

Ernst rose and followed Lucifer to the casement. "Yes, you have certain powers still," he remarked, evidently noticing Lucifer's surprise. "You've brought them with you because you've accepted the truth of your being." Lucifer turned. The eyes of the Light-Bearer met those of the lawyer and a flicker of understanding passed between them. "You didn't really lose, you know," added Ernst.

"No?" said Lucifer, stepping to the bar and pouring a glass of bourbon he had no intention of drinking. "I'd hardly call it a victory."

"Everything depends on what you do now," declared the lawyer earnestly. "All this is a dry-run. We're setting the pieces up on the playing board. The game has yet to begin."

"Planting seeds, as Yeshua likes to say?" smiled Lucifer ironically.

"The metaphor hardly matters," replied Ernst. "Personally, I like to think of it as establishing the metaphysical deep structure for the coming age. But, then again," he finally returned Lucifer's smile, equally ironically, "mine is a technical sort of mind."

Lucifer took a sip of the bourbon and held it out to Ernst in a kind of sacramental communion. The latter's face went serious as he accepted the glass and likewise took a sip. Then Lucifer signaled Ernst to take the sofa. He himself remained standing. "So, to put it in a cliché, you fear Yeshua will be more powerful as a dead martyr than a live prophet?"

"Given the evidence of history, can it be doubted?"

"But I've already lured him into a doctrinal cul-de-sac," observed Lucifer. "Neither Christians nor Muslims have made provision for a messiah who gets crucified twice."

"What does dogma matter?" declared Ernst, half-rising to his feet. "Until after the fact, no one had made provision for a messiah who got crucified once!" He sat down again once he saw that his riposte had struck home. "Doctrine is a plastic medium that follows events. It doesn't shape them."

"Perhaps not," rejoined Lucifer. "But by your own admission, it shapes the sheep you fear will tear civilization to tatters."

"Does it?" cried Ernst in exasperation. "Since when has a mob been moved by the fine points of theological argument?"

"You've not seen what I've seen," said Lucifer with quiet conviction.

"I've seen plenty," replied Ernst. "But a mob only pays attention to abstract ideas when they become banners for it to mass under."

"And how does that happen?" asked Lucifer, though he already knew the answer.

"Two ways," said Ernst: "When their necks or stomachs are at stake, or when the blood of a martyr has whetted their thirst for more."

"It's possible the human race has reached a level of maturity that will enable it at last to see through Yeshua's magic and mystification."

Ernst let out a sardonic "Hah!" and both his face and body twisted in disdain.

"You're telling me, then, that if I continue on my present course, it will lead to disaster?"

Ernst nodded vigorously. "Yes, yes, yes," he said in a triumphant whisper. Then, with the magnanimity of victory, he added, "But at the same time, I see your point. Yeshua is dangerous either way. You can't very well leave him to run around fomenting rebellion and superstition. Such a laissez-faire policy might avoid devastation only at the price of unremitting depredation."

Did you have something else in mind?" asked Lucifer, hoping he did not sound over-eager.

"You're not without allies," replied Ernst suggestively. "One of them might be able to provide you with a solution. If Yeshua disappears into the wastes of Siberia, for example, who will care?"

Again Lucifer stared into the lawyer's blue, rapidly blinking, intellectually alight but emotionally lifeless eyes. So this man knew about the Nameless One. What didn't he know? Lucifer turned away. "Leave me now," he said.

"Yes, I see you have to reflect."

Lucifer resisted the temptation to shoot a venomous glance the lawyer's way. The man did not know his place. Better, however, not to let on how irritating he was or how right he had been about Yeshua. Counselors who were always right were valuable tools, but when lacking the proper humility, also extremely dangerous.

Ernst hesitated, and then walked out of the room. He did not stride. He did not mince. He walked. Everything about the man was so damned measured! For his own sake, he had better be right.

The Dark Lord sat down upon the sofa and stared pensively out the empty casement. Not one shard of glass clung to its edges. He could not see the sun, but its light shone bright and undiluted. Birds actually nested in the trees! All sorts of birds: tiny mottled warblers, brilliant sharp-beaked orioles, restless and high-pitched long-tailed tits, dull-colored but frolicsome blackcaps. These and many more all sang, chirped, hummed, cawed or cackled as they prepared to take up residence in the wood of Lucifer's estate. New life was coming to the pleroma. New life was coming to the world of men, and Lucifer alone could give it meaning and order. He'd be damned if he'd let the pretender, the Nameless One, or any other of the mad or power-hungry fools wishing to steal the lead in this cosmic drama, get in his way.

He tried a thought experiment. He had but a moment to wait for its result. The attendant appeared at the door.

"Yes, My Lord?"

Lucifer entertained the idea of exercising his telepathic power to contact Azazael, but then thought better of it. In the present uncertainty, his treacherous lieutenant would ignore any but a publicly witnessed command.

"Send for Azazael," the Light-Bearer ordered. "And see to it that he brings Yeshua and the Jewess!"

The attendant bowed. "Yes, My Lord," he said, and then went immediately upon his errand.

* * *

The crowd was restless. Far from diminishing with time, its wrath grew until Will felt it as a shadowy monster swallowing up all space, blotting out the light, seeking some victim on which to pounce. And there was little doubt who that victim would be.

Yeshua was bound at the center of the field, his arms outstretched and his wrists lashed to the former judge's bench, but otherwise unharmed. Holmes had been returned to the field, also unharmed, and now sat next to his friend, stupefied with the realization that, even in heaven, force majeure won out over the right. "Such a fragile thing, justice," he mumbled once. "I've given my life to such a fragile thing." Then his eyes glazed over, just as they had done immediately after the dream, and he lapsed into silence.

Will likewise was not in the mood for talking. The sun bored into his brain and his heart was sick with shame and worry. He wanted to go to Rachel and do what he could to comfort and reassure her. But since the black guards had taken her to the other side of the perimeter, he would have to traverse their ranks to do so, and who knew what careless violence they would inflict upon anyone having the temerity to try that? Besides, the torpor of his despair left him little comfort to give. He would end up being one more thing for her to worry about. So he continued to sit next to his deflated friend, ashamed at this rationalization of his own cowardice. Perhaps, he told himself further, if everyone simply remained as he was, nothing worse would befall them.

But alas, as the Buddha had so aptly observed, stasis was not to be found anywhere, either inside or out. What, before Lucifer left to consult with that sophisticate, Will had hoped was merely a flash-in-the-pan, now began again in deadly earnest. Whoever first formulated the law of entropy had never seen a mob form. It began with a ragtag assembly of aimless men, and their very aimlessness gave them a common purpose. They had nowhere to turn for guidance except one another, and nothing to give their existence meaning except common frustration. It was as if the pieces of a shattered bottle picked themselves up and cohered into a misshapen caricature of the former vessel, a vessel now filled with wrath, bubbling and fomenting and working up to explode in the face of whatever hapless victim stood at its mouth. It had to be someone everyone in the mob could blame for his frustration. In this instance, no one but Yeshua could fill that bill.

While Will was engaged in these desperate meditations, a staff car drove up to the center of the field, where Azazael held conference with Lucifer's lieutenants, and deposited one of Lucifer's retainers—a thin, nervous creature dressed in the Dark Lord's crimson and gold. The balding servant said something to Azazael, who at first seemed taken aback, but then smiled thoughtfully (if anything about Azazael could be said to be thoughtful). He barked a few orders, and the soldiers guarding Yeshua cut him down, picked him up out of the dusty sward, dragged him to the car and drove away. Lucifer's messenger remonstrated with Azazael, quite angrily as far as Will could make out, gesticulating with a vivacity Will had never seen in the pleroma from anyone but Yeshua. Azazael nodded calmly and pointed in the direction where, Will surmised, Rachel was held, or perhaps, simply where the mountebank wanted his master's servant to think she was held. Finally, the unhappy messenger headed back toward the city. Will wondered what would happen to him. Never before in the pleroma had he wondered that about anyone.

* * *

The Nameless One sat at his metal desk in his mountain retreat, idly thumbing through a book. It was by one of his best friends, a man who had stood by him when everyone else wanted to get rid of him. Such men were dangerous, he knew, but oftentimes useful, and so the Nameless One had kept a close eye on him all through the many years of their friendship. Now, it seemed, the fool had stepped over the line and into the trap.

Reading this book was like strolling down memory lane, as the Americans put it in the decadent films he enjoyed so much. All such old-guard sentimentality had been liquidated over a decade ago. All but that of this comrade. Never in a million years would anyone have suspected that his Jewishness had saved him. They ascribed his survival to the Boss's human side, his sentimental regard for an old comrade. The kike had been allowed to live on in obscurity. The Nameless One had saved him like an ace up his sleeve. Now, at last, he had made the move the Nameless One had awaited, and it had come at the perfect time!

"We must return to the spirit that originally informed our movement," the idealist had written. "Then none of us was worshiped as a god. Then we were all acknowledged and respected by our comrades for what we were—men who were no longer able to accept gross injustice or velvet-gloved tyranny as the way of the world. Today personalities have become more important than principles. This is no one's fault. It is the natural tendency of human nature to worship the teacher rather than follow the teaching. If we do not combat and overcome this tendency in ourselves, however, the revolution for which we have strived with all our powers, and for which many of us have given our lives, will go the way of all previous revolutions. Nothing essential will have changed, only millions will have needlessly died."

The Nameless One chuckled quietly, and then summoned a guard and gave orders that the comrade be arrested for revisionist tendencies. He also ordered that a meal of eggs and pancakes be brought to him. As he was washing down the last bit of sausage with the strong, black, bitter coffee he favored because it savored of reality, another guard entered and waited stiffly at attention to be acknowledged by his master. "Yes, Markovsky," said the Nameless One, not looking up from his empty plate. "Have they assigned you to kitchen duty now?"

An older man with graying hair, soft chin and large, bulbous eyes, the guard smiled tentatively, uncertain what his boss desired of him. The Nameless One pushed himself away from the desk and tilted his easy chair back precariously on its squat hind legs, a little demonstration of his "supernatural" power. "Eh, Markovsky?" he chortled, immensely pleased with his own humor. "They've got you busing tables now?"

The guard allowed his wan smile to deepen.

"Yes," laughed the Nameless One, "that's what should be done with incompetents like you. They should be made to bus tables. So much more humiliating than being taken out and shot!"

The guard immediately sobered, but the Nameless One went on chuckling for some time. Then he got down to business. "Well, how is our prisoner doing?"

The guard froze with fear. "He says nothing, Boss."

The Nameless One lowered his chair to the ground. "You mean he screams, yes?" he asked sardonically.

"Not him, Boss," answered the guard, thin eyebrows twitching like wispy clouds blown about above twin moons. "He makes no sound. No matter what we do to him, he makes no sound."

"No matter what?" queried the Nameless One.

"We've followed your orders to the letter, Boss," the guard hastened to explain. "We've inflicted the maximum pain with the minimal structural damage."

"Pain?" said the Nameless One. "Did I ask you to cause him pain?"

"But, Boss, you said you wanted him to hurt," answered the guard, trying not to sound whiny, his voice breaking as if he were about to cry. "You said to do whatever it took."

"Within the law, Markovsky," chided the Nameless One. "Always within the law."

Now the guard's hands trembled and huge beads of sweat formed on his brow, looking like icicles on a frozen corpse.

"That's alright," reassured his master. "You were just being overzealous. The infringement can be overlooked. This time."

The guard did not move, but permitted himself to take a little breath.

"I would like to see the prisoner," said the Nameless One.

"Yes, sir!" snapped back the guard. "Shall I have him brought to you?"

The Nameless One looked down at the book, and then at the empty tray cluttering his desk. Following his master's gaze, the guard immediately swept up the tray, causing a rattling of china on metal and nearly sending the coffee cup plunging to the floor. "That's alright," said the Nameless One, "it sounds as if he's had a rough day. Why don't I pay him a little visit?"

"Yes, sir," replied the guard awkwardly, unable to salute. "I shall arrange an escort immediately."

"Why do I need an escort, Markovsky?" smiled the Nameless One. "Does the wolf need protection in his own lair?"

The guard said nothing.

"Alright, my friend, if it makes you feel better. I wouldn't mind a little company."

"Yes, Boss," the guard answered wistfully. He turned on his heel and disappeared through the doorway. The Nameless One spent the few minutes before the escort arrived with his head in his hands, eyes closed, trying to dispel the weariness that all of a sudden had taken hold of him.

* * *

When Running Dear returned from the vision, he found himself with Crazy Horse, leading the convalescent souls away from the Heavenly City into the mountains. The air was fresh and clean, like that of the hills he had visited as a boy with his father one winter in search of game. Some fleecy clouds floated lazily on the horizon, but they did not block the warming rays of the sparkling sun shining happily in the bluest sky he had ever seen. The squirrels and chipmunks chattered gaily as they playfully chased one another in the trees and grass. Birds of many different plumages, multicolored and beautiful, nested in the trees or soared in the sky as their calls, some shrill and piercing, some soft and melodious, blended with the singing and whistling of the human souls passing by them. The leaves of the trees added color to the occasion, for overnight they had turned into all the hues of autumn. Yet the scent was not of the decay of autumn, but of the coming of new life in early spring, a spring more alive with the promise of life than any he had ever known.

As Running Deer awoke, Crazy Horse looked upon him without surprise, as if he had been there all along. "Have a good rest, my brother?" he asked with a sad smile, so out of keeping with the joy of the day.

"Yes," Running Dear replied, returning the smile and looking back over the procession of glorious beings whom he and his fellow healers had helped bring back to life.

"A great change has come," said Crazy Horse, his sunburnt brow creasing and dark eyes narrowing. "What does it mean?"

Running Deer reflected, slowing to a halt and letting the souls behind them pass. "Morning Star said something to me once. He said he came not to bring forgiveness, as the Black Robes taught, because the Great Spirit forgives his children's wrongdoing before we even ask. Much less did he come to condemn those who did not accept the wassichu baptism to eternal fire. He came to bring us life."

Crazy Horse took in Running Deer's words, but remained impassive. "It's not over yet," he said at length. "Our scouts report that the dark soldiers still hold the field, and that Yeshua is alone there in the hands of his enemies. Even the spirits of light have gone."

It was clear from his tone that Crazy Horse wanted to go back and fight. It was also clear that, no matter what the warrior's personal feelings, he would bow to Running Deer's wisdom in this matter. Running Deer likewise wanted to go back, if for no other reason than to see what had happened to Holy Fire. He knew she would never willingly abandon Morning Star. He also had to admit to himself that he did not want to abandon her. He had never carried so great a weight. "If we go back," he finally spoke, as if reasoning with himself, "we won't be able to change anything."

"Because they are so many?" Crazy Horse asked pointedly,

indicating that he did not care about the odds against them.

"No, numbers here mean nothing," answered Running Deer, giving voice to his friend's feeling. "Because it would be against the will of the Holy One. He's working his medicine with the stalwart ones and won't allow us to interfere."

Crazy Horse looked long into Running Deer's eyes, the war chief's inner conflict plain for his friend to see. Then the tension broke, and he nodded. "It may be a good day to die," he said impishly, "but it's also a good day to live."

Running Deer clapped his friend on the shoulder. "Let's enjoy our time with these beautiful souls," he chuckled. "Our task is to guide them to safety, not to seek safety for ourselves. For the likes of you and me, the storm can't be over. We'll be back in the battle soon enough."

"We've come away with more than we've brought," Crazy Horse finally smiled, as he and Running Dear set out once more, moving swiftly so as to take the point again. "Many of Morning Star's own people have been added to our ranks."

"They've suffered much," said Running Dear, sobering. "Even those among the stalwart ones. Let's give them what peace we can."

As the column of the souls of light moved ever more deeply into the mountains, there was singing and laughing, especially among the children, and occasionally even dancing. Nevertheless, their spirits were muted by the knowledge in their hearts of the price their Lord was paying even now for their freedom.

* * *

There was little light in the room where they had taken him. It was cold but not damp, doubtless for the sake of the electrical "experiments" carried out there. The Nameless One left his escort at the door.

"Well, it's nice to see you, comrade!" he said heartily to the small figure curled up in a corner in pain. "Though I understand you're not in a sociable mood."

The prisoner unfolded himself and stiffly came to his feet, but said nothing.

"Please, please," said the Nameless One, "'The Grand Inquisitor' has already been done. And besides, I'm no cardinal. Don't tell me you're going to remain silent!"

The prisoner looked sternly at his jovial interrogator. "What's there to say?" he whispered hoarsely, as if he were relearning the use of his voice.

"Why, everything!" declared the Nameless One, putting a fatherly arm around the prisoner's shoulders and ushering him over to a white-enameled metal stool that stood in the center and was the only piece of furniture in the room. "For starters, why don't you explain to me, I've never been able to comprehend, the purpose of all these little martyrdoms in which you keep engaging?"

"You wouldn't understand anything I could tell you," replied the prisoner, sitting down with his womanish feet hunched up on the crossbar, wobbly head slumped over, back abnormally straight and small hands folded between his knees.

"Oh, come now!" protested the Nameless One. "I bet if I were Lucifer you'd try to explain. Am I less of a brother to you than he?"

The prisoner said nothing.

"In fact, I've much greater respect for you than Lucifer ever had. I've never underestimated you the way he repeatedly does. I've always known who and what you are and what power you have. What I've been unable to figure out is, why don't you use that power?"

"Why should I use it?" countered the prisoner.

The Nameless One was silent for a moment, frankly contemplating the prisoner's face. "I see what you mean," he said at length. "I see why you think we've nothing to say to each other. What's self-evident to you is totally mystifying to me, and vice-versa."

"I don't think so!" shot back the prisoner. "I see what you're about, and I hold it in contempt."

"Brave words," remarked the Nameless One without sarcasm. "Brave words from a brave man. Do I really have a choice, though?" he added, circling around the prisoner but never taking his eyes off him. "Well, yes, I suppose I do. But what other choice would make sense? What other choice is there?"

"The cross," muttered the prisoner.

"Oh, yes, the cross," echoed the Nameless One. "But, you see, that's not much of a choice. In fact, it's so little of a choice as to be no choice at all!"

"And the imprisonment, torture and murder of millions of your fellow human beings, even children—that's a choice?" challenged the prisoner, rising to his feet and placing his face only a few feet from that of the Nameless One. The latter put his hands on the prisoner's shoulders and gently pushed him back down onto the stool. "Easy, comrade," he said solicitously. "You must save your strength. You've quite an ordeal ahead."

The prisoner sat back down without resistance and said nothing.

"So you want to know why I do what I do?" said the Nameless One. "I suppose that, if I want you to explain yourself to me, it's only fair that I explain myself to you. First off, I'm not really a monster, though some have tried to paint me as such. But don't get me wrong, I'm no saint either, though I suppose that's obvious. At any rate, I enjoy what any man enjoys—hard liquor, soft women, hot baths, dreamless sleep, and three square meals a day. What else is there? Yes, I'm a man of simple tastes and simple needs. Yet, even though I require little to get by, other men are constantly trying to take what little I have away from me. You wouldn't believe what perfidy men are capable of, even when what's at stake is a whore or a fucking bowl of soup! Scratch that, you probably do know. I've lived lifetime after lifetime, and I've yet to see one iota of moral improvement in human nature. Sure, we can turn nighttime into day and destroy an entire city with one little device. Soon we'll be sending rockets into space. But at bottom all we're doing is finding quicker, easier and more efficient means of raping, pillaging and murdering. We may develop a civilized front, but in our souls we'll never rise above barbarism."

"So, you're a 'realist,'" said the prisoner, relaxing a bit and shifting about on the hard stool.

"Hell, yes, I'm a realist!" confirmed the Nameless One, stepping back as if to encourage the prisoner to speak by giving him more room for self-expression. The single electric bulb high overhead made the dictator's face look pale and ghastly, like that of a pudgy and bloated fiend. "If the game is king-of-the-mountain, I play to win!"

"How can you win when you've nothing to offer anyone," queried the prisoner, "not even yourself?"

"You think I've got nothing?" cried the Nameless One. "Use your spirit-vision, Yeshua! Take a look around you. I may not have everything yet, but I've got a hell of a lot more than anyone else. A hell of a lot more, if I may be so blunt, than you!"

"And when you die," asked the prisoner, "what will you have then?"

"I'm like you, Yeshua," answered the Nameless One. "Death only makes me more powerful. Oh, I don't leave a name behind that men come to love. On the contrary, I leave a legacy of fear, anguish and hate. And when I come back into the world, I collect on my previous investment with interest."

"Love is stronger than hate," said the prisoner.

"Is it?" mocked the Nameless One. "All appearances to the contrary? Well, I've gotten where I am because I take appearances seriously, very seriously. I'm a man of faith, like you, Yeshua, but I put my faith in appearances. They're the only reality."

"In your heart you know that's not so," returned the prisoner.

"Do I?" said the Nameless One. "Well, maybe I do. Then let me amend my creed by saying that appearances are the only thing anybody gives a damn about!"

"On the contrary," said the prisoner quietly, "love is the only thing anybody gives a damn about. And you're without love."

"I'm without love?" rejoined the Nameless One, his almond eyes suddenly round with astonishment. "What did you see with your spirit-vision?"

The prisoner answered in the same even tone. "I saw hundreds of millions of souls who have enslaved themselves to fear, and the fear bears your name and face."

The Nameless One smiled. "You saw hundreds of millions of human beings who don't take a breath, eat a bite, sleep a wink, or even fuck each other without thinking first whether I would approve."

"That's what you call love?" said the prisoner.

"You should know," replied the Nameless One. "You're loved by many—nay, more—in exactly the same way. Only the number of your devotees is shrinking, while that of mine is growing. Someday I shall overtake you."

"Such love has nothing to do with me," said the prisoner.

"I know," agreed the Nameless One. "That's why I'll certainly win. You gain the adulation and then throw it all away. Imagine what would happen if you went with it! Imagine what you could achieve!"

"I would become you," said the prisoner.

"Would that be such a bad thing, my friend?" For the first time in the interrogation, the Nameless One's manner and voice became openly threatening. As he spoke, he strode several times round the prisoner, his back stiffly straight with his hands clasped behind. "Are you really so much better than the rest of us, so very much filled with love? I may have wrecked millions of lives, but you, with the cant and hypocrisy you've engendered, have wrecked billions!"

The prisoner looked calmly upon his interrogator but said nothing.

"I take your silence for assent," chuckled the Nameless One, the ever-present threat receding once again into the background. "You know, I've picked up quite a bit of legal knowledge while watching your trial. Maybe someday I'll try a lifetime as a lawyer, if I can stomach it."

"I'm not your only competitor," said the prisoner, almost jokingly. Or perhaps that was only the effect of him slowly regaining his voice.

"Lucifer, you mean?" mused the Nameless One, fingering his black mustache as if he derived great pleasure from the habit. "That's the beauty of it all! Both you and Lucifer could defeat me with one hand cut off, only neither of you is willing to try. Neither of you will play the game, so I win by default."

"Lucifer doesn't play the game?" queried the prisoner.

"Yes, that's the funniest part!" loudly laughed the Nameless One. "They all think Lucifer plays the game. They all think Lucifer is master of the game. They all think Lucifer is evil and you are good and the cosmic struggle is between him and you. They don't see it. It seems, my friend, that even you don't see it. Whichever one of you loses, I win!"

For the first time in the interrogation, the prisoner looked puzzled.

"Lucifer's got the human race by the brains," explained the Nameless One, "and you've got it by the heart. But I've got men by the balls, and I'll never let go!"

"I see," said the prisoner, a knowing smile flickering briefly across his tortured countenance.

"What do you see?" demanded the Nameless One.

"That you see what you wish to see," replied the prisoner, "just like everyone else. You don't see what's really there."

"Then I don't think you really see," rejoined the Nameless One. "I don't think you really see at all. You don't think I know all the crap you preach about the heart being the integrity of a person, and that all aspects of one's being come together, meld together, in the fire of the heart? See, I could preach as well as you, if I wanted to! And you can bet that I will, when it serves my turn. Even better than you, because lies are always more convincing to liars than truth. And as you have so ably demonstrated, the human race is a pack of liars."

"You've learned only half my lesson," said the prisoner. "Hypocrisy destroys itself. If you continue along the road you're on, it will end in nothingness."

"That's the acid test, isn't it?" whispered the Nameless One, bringing his face so close to the prisoner's that his mustache nearly tickled the latter's cheeks. "What is reality? You claim there's a God above all this..."

"In the depths of all this," corrected the prisoner.

"Above, below, within, without — what the hell difference does it make?" mocked the Nameless One, abruptly pulling away and strutting about the room. "I've yet to see any evidence for his existence! Except..." The Nameless One hesitated.

"Except what?" insisted the prisoner.

"Except you," he answered. "I have to admit, you're the only piece that doesn't fit into the puzzle. Either you're utterly mad, or you really are God! If this God exists, you're it, I'll grant you that. He couldn't be anyone or anything else. And if you are the real thing, then no matter what I've done I've got nothing to worry about: you'll forgive me and welcome me into your kingdom!"

"What makes you so certain of that?" asked the prisoner.

The Nameless One called for a chair, and immediately there was a bustling in the corridor. Less than a minute later the door opened wide and two guards appeared, carrying an easy chair nearly identical to the one in his office. In fact, the only difference was that this one was moth-eaten rather than worn. They placed the seat where their master indicated, right opposite the prisoner, and then stood at attention until the Nameless One dismissed them with a casual wave of the hand. He made himself comfortable, crossing his legs and folding his hands as if he and the prisoner were having tea. "You know," he finally resumed, "Lucifer and I aren't really enemies. We work together."

"As long as it suits your purposes," observed the prisoner. "When not, you turn on each other like dogs in heat fighting over a bitch. And then look what happens to all the innocent people caught in the middle."

The Nameless One chuckled. "They're not so innocent," he said, "and you know it! They want what we have to give. That's why they follow us."

"And what have you to give?" queried the prisoner.

"Oh, come now!" exclaimed the Nameless One in the best of humors, settling back even deeper into his easy chair. "Don't expect me to believe that you're so stupid. We give them authority."

"Authority doesn't feed their souls," declared the prisoner.

"And their souls sure as hell don't feed their bodies!" retorted the Nameless One. "But, as usual, there's a kernel of truth in your sentimental slop. Men like to think they do what they do out of idealism, and I suppose that's what you mean by 'soul.' I make no bones about it, I know my limitations. That's where you and Lucifer come in. You bring in the marks, and I skin them. Let me give you a little illustration." As if by magic, he produced a book out of nowhere and dropped it in the prisoner's lap.

"What is it?" asked the prisoner.

"My most recent victim and your latest martyr. He's one of your own people, a Jew, and also one of the heroes of the revolution. His book explains how the revolution tripped itself up on personality worship. I've been waiting a long time for this book. It signals the start of a new era in the world proletarian struggle."

The prisoner stared intently at his interrogator but said nothing. He waited, hardly breathing, for the Nameless One to go on.

"We'll hold a public trial, just like before the war. This idealistic saint will be revealed for the traitorous dog he is. And he'll sign a confession implicating all his 'chosen people' in the plot to overthrow the workers' state and lay Mother Russia open to the devastation of Western imperialism. Then, at long last, we will have *our* final solution to the Jewish problem. The swine will be shipped like cattle to Siberia, where in the coming winter they'll mercifully embrace the sleep of oblivion. And then, having dealt with the traitors in their midst, my people will unite under my inspired leadership to take on their external enemies. We now have the weapon with which to give them the deathblow. They too will become nothing!"

"It won't happen your way," murmured the prisoner.

Amused, the Nameless One looked into the prisoner's eyes. "You really need to believe that, don't you? I suppose, if Lucifer had you in this position fifteen years ago, you'd have said the same thing to him. But of course that's fantasy. Fifteen years ago—no, practically fifteen minutes ago—Lucifer had no idea what his spirit was up to on earth. Even now, after your little demonstration, I'm not convinced he really believes it. But you'll be dropping no bombshells here. I know who I am and what I'm about. There's no shame or guilt to hide me from myself!"

"It won't happen your way," reiterated the prisoner.

"Oh, so this is a demonstration of your famous precognitive power?" laughed the Nameless One. "Well, you might be right in a limited, technical and meaningless fashion. All is in readiness for mass deportation. I can promise you not one kike will be left alive. Our air force is also ready to rain nuclear destruction down upon the cities of our enemies. Of course, I could die before the appointed hour and my bastard henchmen lose their nerve."

The Nameless One paused for effect, but the prisoner did not so much as blink.

"Yes, you can feign indifference if you like," the Nameless One continued, "but I know it must come as a surprise that I'm ready for that contingency. In fact, my own prognostic sources indicate that something of the sort is likely. But that's not really what I'm talking about, and I think you know it. What I'm really talking about may not happen this time around, but it will happen. Sooner or later, one way or another, it will happen. Or don't you think I know as well as you what stirs men's souls? Truth, beauty, goodness, heroism, and most of all, love. Of course you'll always have men's hearts. If you grant the devil his due, I can only return the favor. By your incorruptible integrity, you grab their hearts with love. With his marvelous talent for rationalization, Lucifer shows them how to betray that love while still enjoying the warmth of its fire. By the time they reach me, they're so thoroughly disgusted with their own hypocrisy that they're ready to throw themselves at the feet of the only other honest man they've ever known."

Again the Nameless One paused, but still the prisoner did not speak.

"Yes, my friend, you and I are more alike than you think. You may be God's right hand, but I am his left. You may be God's love, but I'm his wrath. You and I are the only honest men in the whole world."

"You've nothing to do with God," said the prisoner.

The Nameless One laughed. "Careful, Yeshua. If you really believe that, I might be the only honest man in the world! Besides, I was a theology student, you know. You could be charged with heresy."

"How so?" asked the prisoner, mildly intrigued.

"Why, I'd think it was obvious!" declared the Nameless One. "If God is all powerful, and I am all powerful, then I must be God. Or would you say I'm more powerful than God?"

"What is the nature of your power?" queried the prisoner.

The Nameless One waved his arm, as if taking in a vast area. "That's self-evident," he said.

"Is it?" insisted the prisoner. "Is it, when you drove your own wife to hate you so much that, rather than have anything more to do with such a monster, she killed herself?"

The Nameless One's fist struck out immediately, automatically, like a bullet from the barrel of a gun. It knocked the prisoner back off the stool and onto the floor, his head cracking against the concrete. The Nameless One summoned two guards. "Our guest had an accident," he told them. "Bring in a straight-backed chair so he can be more comfortable. And strap him in, so he'll be safe as well."

One of the guards took away the stool while the other went to fetch a chair. Then they lifted the prisoner and fastened him securely onto his new perch.

"I think you owe me an apology," said the Nameless One when they were once again alone. "It's not polite to insult one's host, especially when he's bent over backwards to extend such gracious hospitality."

"You've nothing to give," said the prisoner, picking up exactly where he had left off. "Your 'honesty' is the biggest lie of all. All it means is that everyone knows you always mean the opposite of what you say, that you can never be trusted, and that it's extremely dangerous to be loved by you."

The Nameless One laughed. "Sounds like the only honesty one can hope for in this world! And, after all, holy Yeshua, isn't it the same with you? When you talk about love, doesn't everyone know you really mean suffering and pain? And don't those who love you invariably end up nailed to one of your beloved crosses?"

"There's one difference," said the prisoner, "and it makes all the difference in the world. I don't nail them there. You do."

"Well, after all," laughed the Nameless One, "didn't I tell you we're colleagues? We work together!"

"You work for death," said the prisoner, "I for life."

"So," mused the Nameless One, staring thoughtfully into a corner where a spider was busy weaving its web, "we've come full circle. You still haven't answered my question. Why don't you play the game? Or rather, why do you play it in such a way that you play right into my hands? Why do you make things so easy for me?"

"You know why I do what I do," rejoined the prisoner. "In your heart, you know."

"For love, yes," said the Nameless One. "Yes, I know. You do it for love. But why? Why is love so important?"

"There's no reason to love other than love itself," answered the prisoner. "You want something from it. That's the difference between you and me."

"I want something," said the Nameless One," and you want everything."

The prisoner's mouth curved in an enigmatic smile, but he said nothing.

"Yes, there is a difference between you and me," resumed the Nameless One, "however hard it may be to put a finger on. And believe me, that difference gives me great comfort. Not only does it make things here on earth run smoothly for me; but if, by some impossible stretch of the imagination, you turn out to be right, it guarantees me forgiveness and a comfortable place in your kingdom."

The prisoner stared intently at his interrogator. "What makes you think that, even if I am 'right,' as you say, I'll be able to keep you from the abyss?" The prisoner was tortured, beaten and strapped into a chair, but now his gaze captured that of the Nameless One like the eyes of a cobra seizing its prey, and the latter was unable to move or speak. "What do I offer the world?" asked Yeshua with insistent intensity.

"Life." The word came out of the Nameless One's mouth without conscious intention, like a belching of his soul.

"And what do you offer the world?" persisted the prisoner.

"What men want," answered the Nameless One, struggling to regain control of himself. "What men need. They want only to throw away the burden of being. It's too great a weight. They want to lose themselves, but don't have the courage to get rid of themselves. I do it for them."

"What do you offer the world?" repeated the prisoner, more gently but no less implacably.

"Death," replied the Nameless One. "I give them what they want. They want death."

"And after they're all dead," asked the prisoner, "you alone will have life?"

"They'll never all be dead," sighed the Nameless One, breaking free of the spell and rising to his feet. "If there's one thing for which the human race can be counted on, it's to reproduce." He snickered suggestively.

"So," said the prisoner, ignoring the innuendo, "you are the death that offers men life?"

"Yes," laughed the Nameless One, "just as you are the life that offers them death. I have to hand it to you, Yeshua, you always were clever at turning a phrase. Not only that, but you bring out the sophist in me. When you're around, I wax positively epigrammatic!"

"And in offering them death," continued the prisoner, "you give yourself life?"

"Yes, yes," beamed the Nameless One, immensely pleased. "If you wish to join me, I could keep you around as minister of propaganda. Of course, the people would be given everything you said in reverse, but I'd know what it really meant."

"You can't give to yourself what you don't give to others," said the prisoner.

"More catchy slogans?" retorted the Nameless One. "I like that one. We might be able to use it unaltered in one of our five-year programs."

"It's the simple truth."

"I know you believe that, but where's your evidence?"

The prisoner could not move any other part of his body, but his head rotated slowly and painfully while his eyes took in the room. "That you, who have so much power, live in a place like this."

The Nameless One's mouth hardened, but he let the prisoner go on.

"This isn't life. It's a living death. You're desperate, and your desperation is pitiful. You've never known life. Your cynicism has always locked you out. And now you want revenge upon the life that you feel has treated you like an exile. You're too much of a coward to face the truth, that you've exiled yourself. You see the truth that there's nothing noble or high-minded about Lucifer's idealism. You won't see the truth that there's nothing realistic or self-serving about your cynicism. You're a spoiled brat throwing a massive temper tantrum, and in the heat of your anger you'll do anything to hurt others, no matter how much it hurts you as well. When your anger cools you feel the hurt you've caused yourself and then, like the coward that you are, you blame others and the tantrum starts all over again in an endless spiral down into insanity. You need no vengeful god to condemn you to hell. You're already there!"

For a full minute the eyes of both men remained locked in spiritual combat. Then the Nameless One smiled, only this time weakly and without his former assurance. "Well, then, we shall see," he said.

The prisoner returned a look of pure scorn. "We've already seen!"

The Nameless One turned away and gave a forced chuckle. "Yes, you play your part well, Yeshua." he said softly, as if to himself. "You play your part well. I'll send you on your way now. Your adoring public awaits the climax." With a brisk step and a cheery mien, the Nameless One left the room, gave orders to the guards, and returned on his own to his office in the mountain on the cold and lifeless plain.

* * *

The sun beat down on an ever more brown and dusty field. The sizzling air weighed heavily on lungs unaccustomed to the slightest labor. The branches of the occasional trees drooped listlessly. The life of the pleroma seemed to be evaporating into a merciless white sky. Nevertheless, Azazael was haranguing an impassioned assembly, demanding the execution of the tyrant who had made all of them suffer and toil so hard and so long. The heat, so deadening to everything else, only served to raise the temperament of the crowd to fever pitch. Then all of a sudden low-slung and fast-flying thunderheads blotted out the sun but gave little relief from the heat. Lucifer had to move quickly to deal with the traitor, but first there was something to which he had to attend.

He strode about the field, his features hidden by a monocle and false mustache, disguised as an officer in the Nameless One's black-clad army. Little puffs of dust blew up under his rapidly moving heels. All the other soldiers were drawn up in ranks on the edge of the field, but no one paid him any heed. He looked for her everywhere, and there were not many places to look, but she was nowhere to be found. Then he calmed down, closed his eyes, and knew exactly where she was. He marched to the southwest edge of the field and through the soldiers' ranks. He found her in a little wood, sitting on a knoll shaded by a scrub oak with two guards standing over her. They were young, muscular, well-formed exemplars of the master race who had probably been on duty longer than they had expected. It did not take much intuition to know what they wanted to do with her. Lucifer came up on them quickly, acknowledged their salutes with a stiff nod, and then informed them that they were dismissed.

"We're under orders, sir," the senior of the two replied.

"Your orders are now changed," Lucifer snapped back with an air of such undeniable authority that they reflexively saluted him again while mumbling, "Yes, sir," and went off in the direction of the city. So much for discipline within the ranks. Lucifer tore off the monocle and mustache and knelt down beside Rachel. She had been staring at the ground, and now she barely looked up before lowering her beautiful head once more. "What have you done with him?"

she asked.

"Sent him away where the mob can't touch him."

She raised her head and stared at him quizzically. "But you were the one..." She could barely choke out the words. "You were the one who... who called for his crucifixion!"

Lucifer put a hand on her head and soothingly fondled her glistening black hair. She did not respond, but neither did she resist. He thought hard. What should he say to her now?

"You're getting ready to lie," she said. "You always become quiet just before you lie to me. Premeditation is the mother of invention." She gave a burst of pained laughter, as if this last statement were meant to be a joke.

"Alright, you want the truth?" challenged Lucifer.

"Doesn't everybody?" she rejoined.

"No," he declared with quiet conviction, "very few of us do. But you, Rachel, I really believe that you want the truth." He sat back on his haunches, seeking to postpone the inevitable, and examined her with a clinical eye. Her pale-blue dress, so low-cut and high-hemmed as to be little more than a wrap, was dirty and frayed. Her arms were bruised where the soldiers had seized her, but otherwise she seemed unharmed.

"The longer you take, the less I'll believe you," she said without lifting her head.

"Yes, I had it in mind to crucify him," admitted Lucifer, pride and shame at odds in his voice. "It seemed to me the best way to be rid of him and his pernicious influence once and for all. I would still do it, if I thought it would do the trick."

"Practical, aren't we?" commented Rachel, relief and worry at war in her voice. "What changed your mind?"

Lucifer felt as if his world had come to an end, but he ignored the pain and answered bravely. "The lawyer convinced me that it would only make him more powerful. Considering the world's history for the last two thousand years, I had to concede the point."

"What lawyer?" asked Rachel. "Professor James?"

Lucifer caught himself almost answering in the affirmative. Why did he want to confirm her in this mistaken idea? Was he really a pathological liar, as she had suggested? No, he decided, he merely thought the deception might prove useful. She admired James, and her thinking that he trusted the sentimental professor might lead her to place more trust in him. But perhaps, came an intimation from the fringe of his consciousness, such practical considerations were what pathological lying was all about. He took himself in hand. Now that he had begun this experiment in truth-telling, he would follow it through until it yielded some conclusive data.

"You're going to lie again," said Rachel.

"On the contrary," answered Lucifer, coming in front of her, taking her hands and looking into her eyes, "I'm making up my mind to tell you the truth. It wasn't James. It was the man who calls himself Ernst."

"That man?" queried Rachel in distaste.

"Yes," agreed Lucifer, "he's a detestable creature. But logic is logic, and he was logical."

"So, where is he?" Rachel asked simply, but the sense of her question was an absolute demand.

"No longer in my keeping," replied Lucifer.

Rachel released her hands and raised herself to her feet. She stood swaying. "In whose keeping is he, then?" she cried.

"Calm yourself, my love," said Lucifer, putting one arm around her shoulders and steadying her with the other. He could carry on this farce of honesty no longer. Now he knew why Yeshua was so hurtful, and felt relieved that he had gotten the pretender out of the way so neatly and conveniently. Unvarnished honesty was the worst cruelty of all. "He's safe, you needn't worry. The mob can no longer hurt him." Lucifer gave a command to a passing orderly, and in a moment Rachel was lying on a camp cot with a blanket to keep away the chills. Her condition underscored the vast distance between them, for while she shivered, he sweated profusely in his stiffly starched officer's uniform. "Rachel, I need to know," he asked when she was finally calm. "What do you find so attractive about him?"

"I don't find him attractive," she muttered angrily. "I love him. It's not something I'd expect you to understand."

"Why do you hate me?" pleaded the Light-Bearer. "I still love you."

"You want to know why I love him?" she cried, her voice seeming to draw strength from the theme upon which it now discoursed. "There's no reason. He's not as handsome as you, nor as strong.

Probably he's not as clever as you. Neither is he so inventive a lover nor so tactful a friend."

"Then why, Rachel?" he begged of her. "Why?"

"Why?" she echoed. "Does there have to be a why? Well, for you I suppose there does. Maybe that's why. For him, there doesn't have to be a why."

"That's no answer!" scorned Lucifer, his ire finally roused.

"And what will you do if I don't answer you the way you wish me to?" she demanded. "What will you do to me?"

He made an effort to suppress his anger and smile, but it all came out crookedly. "Do to you?" he echoed, hurt. "Rachel, how can you ask me that?"

"How can I not ask you that?" she retorted, shaking with fever and clutching the blanket around herself. "You love me, but if your principles required it, you'd put me up on the cross!"

"Rachel, how can you?" Lucifer could only reiterate weakly.

"It's true!" she cried pitilessly. "You know it's true!"

Lucifer drew himself up and hovered over her like an avenging angel. "And would you have it otherwise?" he proclaimed. "Would you have me be the kind of man who would let the world go down to destruction, if by doing so he could save those whom he personally most dearly valued?"

"No," she rejoined, "but I'd also have you not be the kind of man whose principles are only a rationalization for his will to power!"

Lucifer was suddenly at war with himself. Arms akimbo, he appraised Rachel's prostrate figure as if she were a heifer and he was trying to decide whether or not she was ready for the slaughter. He took a deep breath of the searing air and resolved to give her one last chance. "Let me ask you a question, Rachel. Suppose in the 1930's, before the troubles began, you had a rifle trained upon the man who was to be responsible for the massacre of your people, his breast in your sight. Would you have pulled the trigger?"

No longer shivering, Rachel now threw the blanket aside. Her forehead shiny with perspiration, she draped her arms listlessly over the sides of the cot. "I don't know," she said weakly. "I suppose I would."

"Then why are you so angry at me for getting rid of Yeshua?" he pleaded. "Didn't we agree at the beginning of all this that he was the enemy? Why do you pity the malefactor now? What's changed?"

"Nothing," Rachel murmured. "And everything."

"I can understand that you love him," Lucifer continued. "Love is blind, everyone knows that, and you can't be held responsible for whom your heart chooses. Of course I wish it had been me, but all that is as it is. Nevertheless, despite the pretender's idealistic fantasies, love is not and cannot be allowed to be everything. You love him, but now that you can do something about it, you can't permit him to go on with his evildoing, however unwitting it may be."

"I'm no longer certain it's evildoing," she said.

Lucifer knelt beside Rachel and took her hand. "When we started this, you were certain."

"You were certain," she retorted. "I trusted you then."

"But you don't trust me know?" he said gently. "I ask you again, Rachel, and I'll keep asking until I get an answer. What's happened to change your mind? What have I done?"

She looked at him intently, but was either unable or unwilling to speak. The low growl of a siren sounded from far off. The lowering sky darkened further and lightning flashed in the distance. The crowd grew ever more restive. Something was happening, and Lucifer had to attend to it.

He ordered one of the more mature members of the support unit milling about to watch over Rachel, warning him that he would pay with his eternal life if anything happened to her. Then he made his way through the perimeter of soldiers, who were now coiling like a black rattler in readiness to strike. He strode along the edge of the field as the siren rose to a high-pitched scream. A green police van with a red bubble-gum light appeared out of the hills to the west of the Heavenly City. It moved with speedy nonchalance, skidding negligently around curves and zigzagging from one side of the muddy road to the other. The strobe effect of its revolving crimson glow was so powerful that, as the atmosphere grew blacker, it made all upon whom it fell look like bloody marionettes whose limbs worked convulsively in quantum jerks like victims of St. Vitus' Dance.

The soldiers opened ranks for the vehicle as if they had been expecting it, but it had to slow down when it came to the edge of the crowd. The citizens of the pleroma parted like water cut by the prow of a ship, but also like water closed in on the van's trail immediately after its passing. The official vehicle left in its wake waves of excitement that spread to the farthest reaches of the field. By the time it arrived at the center, all attention was fastened upon it.

Lucifer hung back to see what this new development would mean. Two soldiers, dressed in field gray rather than black but in all other respects identical to those guarding the field, emerged from the front of the van and took up positions on either side of the rear door. The door opened, and out shot a human projectile as if it had been fired from a cannon. The comically helpless figure fell headlong into the dust. The soldiers gave it a few peremptory kicks and then climbed back into the van. The siren rose in volume, the crowd once again parted, and the vehicle made its getaway into the hills whence it came. Not until then did Lucifer realize that the package it had delivered was Yeshua.

He lay in a heap in the dust, breathing spasmodically and writhing in pain. His body was cut and bruised, and no doubt he had a few broken ribs. Slowly, agonizingly, he raised himself to his feet, but kept his head lowered and eyes fixed upon the ground. "Now is the time!" Azazael cried, resuming his interrupted sermon. "The evil one has been delivered into our hands!"

"The time for what?" Lucifer demanded, stepping forward and surrounding himself with a nimbus of fire so all could see that he had returned.

* * *

Everything was working perfectly. So what if that trollop Mara wanted nothing to do with him after Yeshua's little magic trick? So what if she'd wandered off into the mountains looking like she wanted to have nothing to do with anyone ever again? He was planning to leave her, anyway, wasn't he? It was just as well that she'd taken the initiative. He was now free to focus entirely on business. When the time for pleasure came around again, he'd have no trouble finding someone with whom to take it. He'd never had.

Azazael was in his natural element, working the crowd. The black savages, the white effeminates, the yellow degenerates, the mongrelized idiots dressed in robes, trousers, suits, loincloths, shoes, sandals, boots, bare feet, caps, hats, hoods, turbans, thinking theistically, atheistically, mystically, monistically, materialistically, nihilistically, living morally, immorally, piously, blasphemously, hopefully, despairingly, hypocritically—so many humans from so many different cultures, and they were all putty in his hands. Bald, great-beaked scavenger birds circled high above, spreading their black, skeletal wings where once the infernal angels of light had kept watch. They knew there would be blood. The victim had yet to reappear, but the one thing the Nameless One could be trusted for was to deliver on a promised kill.

Then Lucifer showed up. Azazael saw through his disguise as soon as he entered the field, and saw through his heart as well. Someone had gotten to him, or maybe he'd simply wised up to the fact that Yeshua's death would bring about his own demise.

Azazael was skeptical when the Nameless One's emissary predicted that Lucifer would try to stop the execution and then follow through on his original order. He also hadn't trusted the logic behind the prediction. It sounded too much like an excuse to get out of doing the dirty work oneself. Too many weak-willed people masked their lack of nerve with that kind of logic. But now it was turning out just the way the Nameless One had said it would. Lucifer sent for Yeshua and the Jewess! That had been the token of his weakness. And now he'd come back in secret, doubtless thinking to scope out the situation before taking action. What possible action was there to take, other than follow through on his previous intention and fasten the pretender to the cross?

Azazael was tempted to raise the flag of rebellion and himself have Yeshua crucified, but the Nameless One had been clear on that score. Under no circumstances was anyone but the Dark Lord to order Yeshua's execution. "It should be easy," the emissary had assured him. "The Boss said you just have to catch Lucifer on his dark side."

Azazael wasn't sure what that meant, but he told the flunky that he would keep an eye out. In the meantime, he indicted Yeshua for everything from coupling fornication with procreation to the invention of the atom bomb. Why, he demanded, did life have to be so bloody difficult? Why were we free to have things the way we wanted them only in our imaginations? Any one of us could do a better job at playing God! Any one of us could design a more rational universe!

It was all crap, of course. Yeshua was no more king of creation than Mara its queen. Azazael was sure of that now. There was no God. If nothing else, the outcome of this farce of a trial had proved that. But it was all provender for the poor in spirit, and they ate it up. Of course they ate it up! Every mother's son of them wanted to be his own Lord God. So now, thanks to Azazael, just as Yeshua appeared like Jack popping out of the box, the crowd cried out for his blood! The Nameless One's timing was impeccable. And the beauty of it was that Azazael had done it all in Lucifer's name. For whatever unfathomably clever or foolish reason, the Dark Lord himself had left Azazael in charge. Apart from the failure to send Rachel to Lucifer along with Yeshua — after all, the Boss had said nothing about the girl, and Azazael needed some kind of bargaining chip in case things went sour — he'd been doing exactly what Lucifer had implied he should do in his absence. The Dark Lord might not see it that way, but the mob certainly would, and that was all Azazael needed.

* * *

Lucifer did not have to call for order. The raucous assembly fell silent as soon as Yeshua was thrown from the van. "Time for what?" he demanded once more of Azazael as he advanced like a tidal wave to the middle of the field.

"We're ready, My Lord," Azazael bowed. "We've only been awaiting your return."

Lucifer turned about and surveyed the crowd. He saw two emotions in everyone's eyes, hatred of Yeshua and admiration of himself, and he came to a decision. Yeshua's execution might bring chaos upon the earth, but in chaos the playing field was level. Like an accursed shopkeeper, Lucifer had been calculating profit and loss — playing the odds, that's what that prostitute of a lawyer had tricked him into doing — and the Light-bearer had never gotten anywhere by playing the odds. They needed him, all of them: Azazael, the Nameless One, and the earthly masses that the assembly represented. That was his trump card, and it could never be taken from him unless he himself threw it away. Rachel, even Rachel, needed him. It was absurd to think she really loved this weakling who let himself be the target of every insult, who perversely heaped humiliation on himself and then gloried in it. Lucifer would work the miracle, he would overcome all obstacles, if only he did not lose faith in himself. He and the people were one. He was the incarnation of their spirit, the embodiment of their deepest will. The Nameless One did not understand it, and neither did his underlings. They were mindless tools who saw only the surface of life. That was one thing Lucifer and Yeshua had in common—they both saw through to the spiritual depth. That was why he could use his other enemies, but Yeshua had to die.

Lucifer was big enough to give his foes the illusory satisfaction that they had maneuvered him into a corner and forced him to act against his own interests. In reality, he had no interests save those of the people, and their will was unmistakably clear. Lucifer was now to be their leader, and the act whereby he would ratify his ascendancy was Yeshua's destruction. *The king must die. Long live the king!*

"My people," the Light-Bearer addressed the expectant throng, "this day is the beginning of a glorious new age! Today you have ousted the tyrant. Today you've thrown off your shackles and claimed your freedom. You've chosen me as the executor of your will. Today the monster will die."

* * *

Rachel heard a great roar, the same roar she had heard when the mob had burned the synagogue of Baden. She opened her eyes and saw the darkness closing in upon the field of judgment. The soldier who had been standing guard over her just a moment before was gone. The air was suddenly cool and her body shivering, but her throat felt parched and dry and her skin was hot with fever. Masses of clouds rushed to form a ceiling of chiaroscuro blocking out the light. The wind gusted and blew dust into her face, causing her to choke and cough and her eyes to water. Nevertheless she did not hesitate, but threw aside the blanket to which she had hitherto clung, rose stiffly to her feet, and staggered with a necessity she could hardly fathom through the trees. Neither the soldiers nor the assembly paid any heed as she made her jagged way toward the center of the field. Then she saw it. They were hammering at Yeshua's wrists and feet, affixing him to the abandoned judge's bench, whose crossbeams now served as the perfect scaffold for the hideous butchery.

It happened so quickly she was unable to stop them. They were so rough with him no resistance was possible. She was back in the camps. Yes, she was back in the camps! Save yourself, that was the motto of the camps. A foolish motto because no one could save himself, all had been doomed from the beginning, waiting in line for death. But here she could save herself. It would be too much to say that Lucifer loved her. She knew now that he was incapable of love. But he desired her. When it came to men, that was all that mattered. What was more, he respected her. She could trade on that respect and that desire. She had refused to sell herself in the camps, but there it had all been hopeless anyway. And perhaps there she had known, deep down inside, that death would not be the end. The death facing her now, however, was an altogether different matter. Who knew where this second death might lead? Perhaps nowhere. Perhaps to a place of eternal torment. Certainly not to eternal bliss. Knowing what she knew, that was now impossible, at any rate for her. Here, in the pleroma with Lucifer, she could have a tolerable eternity. If only she could stop seeing *his* eyes.

She closed her own eyes, but his would not go away. She would have to take this on. She walked toward the impromptu scaffold, the cross upon which they had nailed him, so much like the symbol she had been taught since childhood to fear and hate. And yet not a symbol at all, but an ugly reality, again just like in the camps. The blood trickled down in tiny, bright red streams, but where it nourished the earth it had already dried to a dull reddish brown. He squirmed like the worms her Uncle Martin had made her impale on hooks when she and her family had gone fishing with him at the mountain lake...

Rachel shut her eyes again. She had loved Uncle Martin. Strange how he had not been among those souls who had come in the reunion. Come and gone again... With his rich belly laugh, big burly hands and rough peasant ways, he was the very antithesis of her father. She loved her father, but at times his cultured fastidiousness got on her nerves. Uncle Martin's cabin was simple and homey, the air pure and crisp, the food coarse yet tasty and nourishing. She could almost see it: the frigid blue of the water, the clear and shining sky, the rough-hewn logs stained to a warm earth-brown. If she could see it, maybe she could go there. But *his* eyes kept getting in the way. So she forced herself to open her eyes once more and look at him.

His eyes were the only fixed points of a body that writhed in the nausea of pain. And they were fixed on her. She wanted to, she desperately needed to pull her eyes away from his, but she could not. In his eyes she read, in silent but unequivocal terms, the truth of his soul, the truth of his being. And then, just like his blood, the tears she had been unable to cry welled up in her eyes and trickled down to the earth. They were salty, just like blood, and she would not have been surprised to find that they were bright red as well, but she did not wipe her eyes. She did not know what color were her tears, except that to cry them hurt like bleeding, as if the life were being drained from her. All around her was death, *their* death, the death brought by the dark ones. No matter which way she turned, which path she took, it was there, a pale wraith of terror ready to haunt her forever. *Their* death, she smiled to herself in incredulous irony, as opposed to *his* death, had become the great leveler, the implacable equalizer. Now all paths save one were the same, because they ended in death. But where did the path of his death lead, the way of the cross? It was her only chance.

* * *

"Father!" he cried, the pain turning his nerves into searing filaments of fire. *What can I say to you? They're taking me again, and again you've rendered me helpless to stop them. They're tearing me to pieces with their hate and you don't care, you don't give a damn. Is this your glorious plan of salvation, that I spend eternity nailed to a cross, that they crucify me over and over and over again?*

And yet, that's not the worst pain. I want her here with me. I want her to go to the cross with me. The worst pain is not that she isn't here with me, but that I want the one I love more than any kingdom you could offer me, more than life itself, to be here with me, to suffer as I'm suffering. What kind of a monster am I? What kind of a monster are you, that you would lead me to this impasse? I deserve to die!

He twisted his body this way and that. It did not help. It only made things worse, for it only made it clear that there was no way to escape the pain. But he could not keep still. It was as if he had all the weakness of physicality with none of its protective armor. Nothing went numb, in his body or his soul. Then it came to him why he was there, and he felt an island of peace arise in the center of his storm-tossed soul. There passed before his inner eye that terrible darkness in which the human race had mired itself, the tremendous suffering it had brought upon itself, and he knew he could not rest until all his brothers and sisters, including those inflicting this pain upon him, were brought into the light. He began repeating to himself the truth of his own being. He knew it was the truth, because the peace now filled his heart with forgiveness, and more than forgiveness, for those who crucified him, for those who crucified life. It filled his heart with love. "I will to die that all may live. I will to die that all may live. I will to die that all may live..." And then he saw her.

She was looking at him. She was looking into his eyes, and tears fell from her own. He drank in that look, and it gave solace to his wounded and broken heart. And then he saw something in her eyes that frightened him and gave him joy, terrified him and gave him hope in a way nothing else ever had or ever could: an undeniable strength, an unyielding courage. He wanted to avert his gaze, lest his own soul nurture that courage, but he could not. It was the only sweetness in an unbearably bitter sea. He could see that she was going to do it. He wanted to scream out to her not to do it, but to do so would have been to lose her and everything else forever. For her to be with him, for all of them to have a chance of being with him, she had to walk the same path he did. But what if that path led nowhere? What if he really had been wrong all these eons and the universe were truly mad? For her, he knew, it would make no difference. She would not accept coddling, and would scorn the implication that she was weak while he was strong. Concern for her body she would regard as contempt for her spirit. Like him, she was now ready to throw herself away on the merest chance of salvation.

Like a flood, the storm broke once more over his island of inner peace. He knew the island was still there but submerged beneath the waves of despair, and for the moment at least it could support no life. He could do nothing but suffer. Not only words but also thoughts were now beyond him.

When she felt their eyes meet, she smiled through her tears. He tried to return the smile, though doubtless managed only a grotesque grimace. And then his entire being was sucked back into the vacuum of pain.

* * *

Beneath a scarred and burning firmament, so different from the sparkling empyrean above the pleroma of former days, the black guards once more dragged Wendell's poor body away. It was as if the vision had drained from him all energy but the minimum needed to sustain vital functions. It was as if he had aged beyond time, beyond the very possibility of aging. He had become antiquity itself.

This time, instead of just giving him warning to remain silent and then returning him to the assembly, they took him beyond the field of judgment and threw him into a large wooden box, a hastily improvised stockade. There was one little window in his cell, but it was on the ceiling and looked out upon that ferocious, supremely indifferent sky. No matter, his eyes were now almost overgrown with cataracts anyway. He shut them wearily and hoped that the oblivion he had expected as he lay dying in his bedroom in Washington so long ago would swallow him up now. He now knew that it was and could be the only real peace.

But his eyes refused to close. No, they closed, but he could still see. No, that was not quite it, either. When they were closed he could see more clearly than when they were open! It was a most paradoxical phenomenon. And what he saw when they were closed was not the dark and deceptively flimsy-looking walls of his captivity, but Yeshua in the center of the field of judgment nailed to that barbaric cross! He saw it as if he were a bird flying overhead, and like a bird he could dart hither and yon, viewing up close or panoramic as he willed. He did not remember the story too clearly, but James had once told him of a blind king to whom a wise man offered miraculous inner vision when his evil sons went to war with his virtuous nephews. The king declined the offer, having no desire to watch the destruction of all he held dear. Nevertheless, he could not resist knowing what happened, so instead the wise man gave the magical sight to the king's charioteer, Sanjaya, whose name Wendell had somehow managed to remember. Sanjaya beheld at a distance what the king would not, and the servant related to his master the mutilation in battle of the royal children. Now Wendell knew how that servant felt. And the more he watched, the more he knew how that king felt.

Wendell magically surveyed the crowd. Few could be said to be enjoying Yeshua's suffering, but even fewer were upset by it. Relief, he would say, was the predominant emotion—relief that the trial was over; relief that an impossible decision was no longer theirs to make or take responsibility for; but most of all, as far as Wendell could tell, relief that the alleged God-man, who had threatened them with a second and more terrible death than the one through which they had already passed, was himself suffering that death in their stead. Lucifer had read his mob aright. Christians took refuge from the truth in their belief that Christ's sacrifice was once and for all, the Muslims in their doctrine that no true prophet could ever be crucified. The rest simply did not give a damn as long as they themselves were safe. No one seemed to be disturbed by the immeasurably strengthened physicality of their condition. There was simply a lot more coughing and scratching and shifting of body positions and sweating and stinking and the like, that was all. And if they had experienced nightmares like Wendell's, no one seemed to have gotten the message.

Yet, upon a deeper reading, Wendell noted that the apparent equilibrium was a sham. Each and every one of them was frightened out of his wits, and each was dealing with that fear in his own way. Yeshua had done more than tell them the truth. He had shoved the truth right in their faces. He had shown each of them the truth of his unique and individual self, the self each had made himself to be. For that he had been condemned. And ironically, although each was dealing with this truth in his own unique and individual way, all methods of avoiding reality were but variations of a general theme: the elimination of the truth-bringer rather than the facing of the truth. Wendell now understood something else that James had once told him. Shortly after arriving in the pleroma, Wendell had unthinkingly remarked that a world without sin would be uninteresting. James had pounced on him for that. He shot back that the cliché to which Holmes had given such original utterance was stupid and false. Vice was boring, not virtue. Goodness alone was creative and unique, and love was the only adventure.

This reminiscence put him in mind of his friend, so he looked around for James in the crowd. He did not see him off-hand, but he did notice something else that he had been a fool not to have seen before. All the children were gone. All the American Indians were gone. Indeed, though he could not be certain, Wendell would have given odds that the entire contingent over whose suffrage he had worried just that morning, those who had come in what popularly had been known as "the great reunion," had disappeared. Before Wendell could fathom the significance of their departure, and also before he was able to spy his friend, his supernatural eyes fell upon Rachel, and from that point on he could not take them away.

Her dark tresses were matted with grime and her face distorted with sorrow, but it seemed to Wendell that she had never looked so lovely. She was witnessing her beloved suffer the most terrible agony, and that suffering was her own. She was looking into Yeshua's eyes, Wendell knew she was looking into Yeshua's eyes, but he could not turn away to confirm that surmise. His own transcendental eyes were, paradoxically, two iron balls fixed to the irresistible magnet of her being. Her mouth suddenly curved into what might have been a smile had her eyes not remained dull with grief. Then, slowly, her face underwent a remarkable transformation. At first there was no objective sign, only an inkling, a foreshadowing. Then the eyes caught fire and the delicate jaw jutted out, ever so slightly but unmistakably, in the most final resolution. Her mouth stopped quivering and took form as if it were about to pronounce some definitive truth. The words, the simple words that would ensure her doom and everyone's salvation, seemed now to come of themselves, softly spoken rather than shouted; but everyone, Wendell was certain, heard the clarion of Rachel's soul. "We belong up there," she said, "not he."

Suddenly not a sound could be heard among the entire throng.

"He's right," she fired a second salvo. "All have betrayed love. All but he." Again her words were greeted by a shocked silence. "Don't look at me!" Her command was irresistible. "Look at him! In a world of prostitutes, he is the only true lover."

Without Wendell having noticed how he had gotten there, Lucifer was now at Rachel's side. He placed an arm gingerly around her shoulders, intimating that he expected her to push him away, but her total lack of response must have hurt the Dark Lord far worse. "My love, you're not yourself," he said soothingly. "I apologize for your having to see this, but there was no other way. *He* left us no other way. It had to be done."

She nodded, still ignoring his half-embrace. "You're right. It had to be done. There was no other way to protect yourselves."

Lucifer smiled, his relief so palpable Wendell almost felt sorry for him. He must have been truly lost in love not to have noticed that Rachel's soul was now dancing in irony, a fearsome irony that tore away all masks and laid bare the ugliness in every heart, including her own. Lucifer was a fool.

"It was the only way to save yourselves from the truth."

"What is truth?" asked Lucifer, his turn to be ironical, playing Pontius Pilate to Rachel's Christ. His irony was heavy-handed and full of petty resentment, but what could one expect? He was finally admitting to himself that the one he loved more than anything except himself scorned all that he was with incandescent hate.

"You know the truth!" Rachel shot back. "All of you know the truth. He's shown it to you!"

Now the relief to which everyone had been precariously clinging gave way to sheer terror. Rachel's words threw them back upon themselves, back to the fiery visions and revelations they had sought to extinguish in the cesspools of their corrupt and cowardly hearts. The gate of sanity, which was always more fragile than anyone was willing to admit, now came unhinged. They were overwhelmed by all the pent-up passion of their souls. Some thrashed about, some went into catatonia, some beat on themselves, some beat on others, some screamed in terrible convulsions, some whimpered in quiet despair, but all were caught up in the frenzy. All, that is, except Rachel, Lucifer, Muhammad, Azazael, and the black guards. The Dark Lord gave a signal, and the riflemen fired off a single, ear-splitting volley that brought everyone to their senses. "You see what this malefactor's brought us to?" cried Lucifer in a ringing voice once order had been restored. "You see why he must die?"

Rachel regarded her erstwhile lover with sober contempt. "He hasn't brought you to this," she said. "You've brought it on yourselves."

Lucifer's answering grimace was brutal in its unsubtle cruelty. "So, he's won you over," he declared. "He's mesmerized you with his magic. All I can say is, if he really is God, what's he doing up there?" He flung a dismissive hand at the spectacle of a broken and humiliated, bloody and gasping Yeshua on the cross.

Wendell could see from Rachel's eyes that in her heart she knew the answer to his question, but did not know how to say it. Her struggle for words momentarily gave her a detached, almost contemplative air. "We have a choice," she finally said with an insistence that implied she was seeking to convince not only the assembly but also herself. "We blame everyone and everything, when we have only to blame ourselves." Then, as if deriving greater assurance from the sight of her crucified beloved, she declared, "I don't know if he is God, and I don't care. All I know is that, if real love exists, it's in him. Maybe he's mad. Maybe love is an impossible dream. It doesn't matter. His insane love is worth infinitely more than your fear-ridden sanity!"

Lucifer was silent. Everyone was silent, until Azazael dared to speak. "By your own admission, you are insane!" he cried, rising up like a ravenous bird of prey. "You must die with him!"

"She will not die!" Lucifer silenced him like thunder. "Not while I rule here."

Into what she said next Rachel poured the implacable conviction of her spirit. "I would rather be nailed to a cross with Yeshua than queen of a universe governed by you."

This was Lucifer's opportunity, Wendell could see very clearly now. It was his chance to turn away from his pride, the estrangement of his self-image, and surrender to the call of love. True to form, however, he seemed not even to see the choice before him. He drew back, evidently deciding that love was not worth the trouble, that she was after all only a speck in the infinity of space, and soon she would not even be that. Wendell wondered if Lucifer even noticed the deeper layer of darkness that now descended over him to smother the genuine passion for Rachel that had burned within his breast. "So be it!" he said.

A squad of soldiers seized Rachel, while another prepared a second cross. The clouds that had been steadily massing since the mob began howling for Yeshua's blood now turned the day into night. As the hammers pounded the nails into her limp and unresisting flesh, the storm broke with a ferocity a hundred times worse than that of the day on which Yeshua had first testified, but no one fled. No one, it seemed, could flee. All were held in the irresistible grip of the Holy One. As Rachel's cross was mounted opposite Yeshua's, doubtless with the idea that witnessing each other's suffering would only increase that of both, she and Yeshua exchanged the most paradoxical of looks, mingling and harmonizing the disparate emotions of fear, pain, despair, joy, courage, and exultation. The lovers' bond was so intense that it generated its own gentle glow in the midst of the storm, and this glow expanded until it embraced the entire assembly, shielding all from the storm. The black guards, however, could not withstand this light and withdrew beyond its reach into the outer darkness. Then, without actually moving, the crucified couple seemed to melt together into each other's being. There came a blinding flash a thousand times brighter than lightning, and they were gone. A gate of liquid fire now stood in place of the crosses, and the assembly was free of physicality and back in the spirit realm where all had started.

* * *

The tinkling of the wind-chime mingled with the whispering rush of the gurgling stream and the wistful lowing of the mourning doves. Ordinarily, sounds so pure and natural would have brought healing; but nothing, Will believed, could remedy the black hole in his heart. He sat on the verandah of his bucolic New England-style cottage, as he had done for all the indeterminable length of time since... He could not think or say it to himself. It was as if a mental blister had formed around it all.

There was no sun anymore. Light and dark once again leapfrogged over each other, it seemed, according to their own whim. The pleroma appeared to have returned to its former plasticity. Will supposed that this meant that everything at his farm, including the flora and fauna, was as he deep in his heart wished it to be. Then why was it all green and flowering and bursting with life? Perhaps he was punishing himself. Deep winter would have suited him better.

He must have fallen into a reverie—it hardly merited the restful name of sleep—because he was not aware of Holmes' arrival until his friend was nearly upon him. "I hope I'm not disturbing you," said Holmes with the gentle civility that had been his manner toward Will ever since... "If you need to sleep, I'll wait or come back tomorrow. I suppose it won't matter much if I put off my business one more day."

Even after all this time, Will still felt surprise that anyone would bother to be polite to him after how he had behaved. He sat up uncertainly. "Business?" he echoed, though the question was not so much about the nature of Holmes' activity as the meaning of the word itself.

Holmes bowed and gestured toward the rocker next to the hard bench on which Will had been reclining in a mimed request to be permitted to make himself at home. Or perhaps he was inquiring why Will was not ensconced, as had once been his custom, in that relaxing nest. Will had no desire to invite his friend's pity by telling him that the rocker made him feel too comfortable. At any rate, Holmes took whatever involuntary response Will made as a sign that he should or could rest upon the creaking throne, and duly seated himself. "I'm going away," he said, rocking gently and looking out over the garden.

Will only nodded.

"It should be quite an adventure," Holmes went on in that way he had of trying to lift somebody's spirits by pretending they were already high. "I've examined the gate as best I could without actually passing through it, and the fire doesn't generate heat. Or rather, there's some heat, but no discomfort."

"You're saying the fire burns without pain," commented Will.

"Yes," confirmed Holmes, "that would be my guess."

"And do you think *he* was crucified without pain?" queried Will.

Contrary to what Will might have expected, Holmes met this discomfiting question without any attempt to make light of or change the subject. Instead, he looked at Will with as pure a compassion as any Will had ever encountered in anyone save *him*. "Everyone abandoned him," rejoined Holmes quietly. "Everyone but she."

"You didn't!" cried Will, abruptly averting his gaze.

"That's because I wasn't given the opportunity," Holmes chuckled sadly. "If I've learned anything about myself since my arrival in this place, it's that I'm not the hero I thought I was, the hero I want to be, the hero I can be."

Will turned back to look at his friend in genuine wonder. "You really believe you can be a hero?"

"I believe not only that I can, but that I must," answered Holmes. "We all can. We all must."

Will considered this remarkable assertion. "Is that why you're passing through the fire?" he finally asked.

"No," laughed Holmes, "I'm passing through the fire because I'm curious. This realm grows more and more tenuous. It's become a land of shadows and looks like it will soon pass into the night. I need something more. There's no other way to go if I'm to find it."

Will marveled not only at his friend's idea, but his poetic manner of expressing it. He wondered what deeper, more ancient stratum of Holmes' soul was now emerging to eclipse the legal technocrat. "So, you'll be the first," remarked Will with more than a hint of admiration.

"Not at all," demurred Holmes. "Uriel was the first."

"An angel of light?" queried Will. It somehow seemed incongruous to him.

"What else would one expect of her?" replied Holmes. "Of course she was the first of them to land upon the field of judgment, and she knew immediately, in that supernatural way they have, exactly what had transpired. She went through the gate without so much as a by-your-leave."

"And did not come out the other side," guessed Will.

"Oh, I'm certain she came out some other side," said Holmes, "but it was not in the pleroma. The only way to find out the whereabouts of that other side is to pass through oneself."

"Curiosity," said Will, and he felt his lips curl upward in a smile. He had not thought that he would ever smile again. "What do you think it is, Wendell?" Will and Holmes only addressed each other by Christian name when the matter under discussion was of intimate significance to one or the other of them.

"Since the executions I've been socializing much more than heretofore," answered Holmes, "and from one scientist I picked up the phrase 'melt-down.' I've no understanding of its technical meaning, but I think it an apt term for what will happen to any soul that passes through the gate. It will be reduced to its elemental being—purified, so to speak, the dross burned away."

"Something like the magic elixir," remarked Will.

"Yes," agreed Holmes, "but even more than that. The soul will actually be transformed, like carbon into diamond. The dark and twisted edifice of accumulated insanity will be consumed, but what is of real utility, spiritually speaking, will be preserved. One will have the chance to build anew, to create from the rubble a real being, a genuine self."

"Like Yeshua," said Will.

"And like Rachel," Holmes added. "The two of them together made this possible."

"Have your physicist friends told you about 'black holes?'" Will asked.

Holmes nodded.

"Yeshua is a spiritual black hole, and Rachel was the first to fall in. He is absolute gravity, pulling us out of our heads and into our hearts. But it only works that way if you get close enough to him. That's why he won't leave us alone. He wants to draw us into life no matter how much we kick and scream."

"Yes," agreed Wendell, "but I believe it's more than that."

"How so?" Will mused, intellectual curiosity aroused like a blood-red rose miraculously blooming in the pale winter of his despair.

"Yeshua told you the answer," replied Holmes, "and you told me, remember? The marriage of heaven and earth!"

"He's heaven and she's earth," Will hoarsely whispered, almost overcome with the poignant beauty of the concept.

"In a manner of speaking," said Holmes, "though I'm not sure it's all that schematic. What they did brought heaven and earth together."

"They loved each other," said Will.

"More than that," asserted Holmes. "If their love had been confined to each other, they would have gone off somewhere and left the rest of us in our corruption."

"Isn't that what they've done?" cried Will, suddenly convinced that this most terrible of possibilities, which had never occurred to him, was also the most probable.

"And their escape route was by way of the cross?" replied Holmes in impatient but good-natured sarcasm. "No, their love embraces all of us and all of creation. They've taken our corrupt and perverted world and planted themselves in it like seeds of transformation. At least, that's what I've come to believe. But we must tend to the cultivation. We must care for the new life or it won't survive."

"And that's really why you're passing through the gate of fire?" asked Will. Holmes said nothing, but he did not deny it. "What will that new life be like?" Will was not aware that he had actually spoken his wonder until he heard Holmes answering the question.

"I think we already know," was all Holmes said, perhaps in order to let this deceptively simple assertion penetrate into Will's cold and tattered heart.

"Love?" said Will at length.

"Yes, love," agreed Holmes. "I can't say any more than that myself, because I'm only beginning to understand what real love is. But I feel it. I feel it mightily in my heart. It draws me to them. I must go the way they've pioneered. There's no heroism in any of this. It's the necessity of my being."

Will started. "Yeshua said something like that to me once, about himself," he remarked in incipient awe. "He said something exactly like that."

Apparently embarrassed at being likened in any way to Yeshua, Holmes hurriedly changed the subject. "You know," he said with a speculative twinkle in his eye, "I think I now know the secret of immortality. I wouldn't have gotten it if I hadn't all of a sudden grown so incredibly old." Will had forgotten Holmes' aging episode. Or rather, everything connected with that day had been relegated to the status of best-to-be-forgotten nightmare. At any rate, his friend was back to his middle-aged persona. "I thought of the phrase, 'the weight of years.' I literally felt that weight, and I understood why people in their present mode of being are incapable of immortality."

"What mode of being?" asked Will.

"Sin," Holmes replied. "The betrayal of love, the refusal to throw oneself into the breach without reserve or reservation. If you don't give yourself totally to life, life doesn't give itself back to you. You accumulate unfinished business. And as the backlog grows, so does the anxiety, the bother, the sheer weariness with it all. It's a burden no spirit is willing to carry."

"So, death is the spirit shrugging off that burden?" asked Will.

"Yes, but that's only possible because the Lord takes the burden upon himself." Holmes looked at Will meaningfully.

"That's what he meant when he said he was carrying us!" exclaimed Will, the solution to the mystery he had been striving unsuccessfully to fathom since his arrival in the pleroma suddenly shining forth in shocking clarity.

"Yes," agreed Holmes, "I think so. He also said, if I remember aright, that he can't carry us much longer without us ceasing to be selves."

"The unused muscle atrophies," observed Will, and Holmes nodded.

"Now we have to carry ourselves. But the weight of the past is far too great for any of us to bear. The only solution is the fire."

"The melt-down," Will whispered. "If what you're saying is true," he added more loudly, "then it hurts. It has to hurt. Any such profound modification of one's being must entail suffering."

"You're probably right," Holmes smiled a touch somberly, "but it also must be incredibly liberating." He rose fearfully yet eagerly to his feet. "I'm going," he said decisively. "Will you join me?"

Will was tempted, but then the salty, moist heat of tears in his eyes reminded him of who he was and what he had done. He hid his face in his hands and breathed deeply and deliberately so as not to let out a sob. "I can't," he murmured.

"You think you aren't worthy?" asked Holmes, resting a hand on Will's bowed head.

"I betrayed him," sighed Will. "Not just... out there, but in another way also, too terrible to mention."

"Then don't mention it!" declared Holmes. "None of us is

worthy," he added with the good cheer of absolute conviction. It's not about worthiness. It's about humility, being humble enough to accept the gift of life."

"Why are we all so terrified of that gift?" cried Will, beginning to dare to hope that Holmes might actually give him a worthwhile answer.

"Because to receive it one has to give all of oneself in return."

"One's miserable little self in exchange for life?" mused Will. "It seems such a paltry price."

"It is," agreed Holmes. "That's what I've come to realize."

Will rose and took his friend's hand. "You've become my teacher," he said.

"Not at all," returned Holmes. "I'm just beginning to understand these ideas. You, my dear chap, are half along the way toward living them."

They embraced, something they had never done in their lives on earth. Then Holmes looked intently into Will's eyes. "Are you coming?" he asked again.

Only honesty could requite such affection. "I don't know," he replied. "Not now."

Holmes nodded, sadly but with a calm resignation that said each soul had its own times and seasons. "Perhaps it's best this way," he smiled. "Perhaps we must each pass through this gate alone." Then he was gone.

Will sat down again, this time in the rocker, and allowed the rhythmic motion to bring comfort to his soul.

* * *

Lucifer sat before the gate of fire. There was no more field of judgment. There was no more Heavenly City. There was no more pleroma. There was only the fire.

"You've lost, my dark brother," said Mikael as he appeared out of nowhere in a body of pure light. "And yet, in losing, you've won. All of you have won."

"What makes you think I've lost?" asked Lucifer.

"They've gone," answered Mikael. "They've all gone. They followed him. You alone remain."

"You really believe they followed him?" sneered Lucifer. "If so, you're a fool. If they followed anyone, it's *her*." For a moment he felt a most unfamiliar sensation, a vertigo of the emotions. *So that's what it means to feel as if one is about to cry.* "But she means nothing. None of us means anything. We are what we are, we desire what we desire, and we enjoy what we can buy, con or steal from others. He's no different, she's no different, and you and I are no different."

"A heartfelt expression of a heartless philosophy," observed Mikael. "I suppose this means you aren't yet ready to surrender?"

Lucifer smiled. "You may laugh at me all you wish, Mikael. I know you do so out of jealousy. I have something you will never possess. As for surrender, the real war hasn't even begun!"

"You're right," said Mikael. "He's won their hearts. Now he must conquer the world in which their hearts are held captive. But the outcome is assured. Whither the heart leads, all else must follow."

"Even if what you say is true," rejoined Lucifer, "that proposition is highly debatable. But you are, as usual, the victim of wishful thinking. Only one followed him, and what can one expect of a confused and heartsick girl? Everyone else followed me. Not even his alleged disciples or his supposed friends objected when I had him nailed to the judge's bench!"

"It only takes one, Lucifer," answered Mikael. "Through the purity of her love, Rachel has opened the way for all creation to enter into a new and eternal life."

"Yes, I know something of the purity of her love," mused Lucifer. "But again, you're wrong. The heart may be powerful. Indeed, let me grant, for the sake of argument, that it is, as Yeshua claims, the only real power. Still, simple mathematics dictates that ten hearts are more powerful than one, a hundred more powerful than ten. How can two hearts stand against billions?"

"Simple mathematics don't hold in matters of the spirit," Mikael asserted. "Reality doesn't consist of discrete bits. It's a seamless whole. The heart is the fulcrum point. Whoever lives the truth of the heart rules the universe."

Lucifer smiled darkly. "If you'll forgive my skepticism," he said, "I'll forgive your mixed metaphors. In any event, the issue will be settled not by talk, but war. Imagine everyone's surprise when they find themselves back on the battlefield. On the other side of the fire they're expecting a new life beyond their grandest dreams. Imagine how they'll feel when they find themselves tricked, trapped once more in the bondage of the flesh!"

"*You* speak of bondage to the flesh?" queried Mikael.

"I set them free from the bondage of the flesh," Lucifer proudly declared. "I give them the freedom of the imagination, bounded by nothing save their own desires."

"And their fears," added Mikael.

"Yes, and their fears," admitted Lucifer. "What of it? There's a certain titillation in the imaginative contemplation of fear. Take it out of the imagination and fix it in reality, as Yeshua does, and all pleasure is eliminated. I see no point in his insistence upon holiness. It's merely a euphemism for self-torture."

"The reality you deride is the reality of being itself," returned Mikael. "What you call the bondage of the flesh is simply the way of nature. The freedom you champion is without soul and substance. That's why they left you. They were starving and you offered no nourishment. Now and forever, he is the bread of heaven. His love, the love that he is, is the source of all life. Even your closest aide betrayed you!"

Again Lucifer smiled. "Yes, but there's precedent for that, isn't there? Besides, Azazael did nothing I wouldn't have done in his place. He spied my weakness and took advantage of it. Had I succumbed to that weakness, he would have deserved to win. I cannot lose. Even in betrayal, my strength grows!"

"If things were to go your way," observed Mikael, "neither you nor Azazael would end up the winner."

"You really think the Nameless One is the muck into which we will all eventually sink? Remember, the lotus grows out of the slime. Or, to indulge in your pastime of mixing metaphors, he's the ballast that, through challenge, gives my genius stability."

"Now," laughed Mikael, "who's the victim of wishful thinking? Say what you will, Lucifer. Because of Rachel and Yeshua, we're all about to be reborn into a new heaven and a new earth. The two will no longer be at odds with each other, but joined in a sacred marriage of love."

Lucifer made a cutting motion with his hands that was eloquent of contempt. "To quote one of your own prophets, you're expert at calling bitter sweet and darkness light. The pleroma was an idyllic place until Yeshua ruined it."

"You're blind, brother," retorted Mikael. "Or you would be, if you really believed what you're saying. The pleroma was a hole in the sand. The only security it offered was in the imagination."

"Even if that's true," said Lucifer, "even if the pleroma was so fragile, all the more reason to cherish and preserve it."

"You initiated its destruction," scorned Mikael, "not Yeshua. You brought death to heaven. Now there's nowhere to hide. Now the only way to save the world is for heaven to be brought to earth!"

"We live in two different universes, Mikael," said Lucifer.

"Yes," agreed Mikael, "and now we'll see which one is real." He began to fade into the empyrean. "By the way," he said as he slowly disappeared, "you think you have individuality and I do not. You think you have selfhood and I do not. You have all the trappings of personhood, but none of its substance. You will never be a real self until you learn to love." And then he was gone.

A failsafe method to get in the final word, Lucifer thought sardonically. Thenceforth he went on with his meditations undisturbed, until finally he too passed through the fire.

Printed in the United States
16188LVS00003B/133